Bat Blood

The Devil's Claw

By

Richard Myerscough

Other Works by Richard Myerscough

Bat Blood Part Two - Unshackled Demons

The Gilded Harvest

published by Richard Myerscough
www.richardmyerscough.com

I would like to thank my son Marquis for asking me "Could someone get AIDS from a Mosquito bite?" From that simple question, I discovered the foundation and science behind "The Devil's Claw" and the Bat Blood series.

I would also like to thank my daughter Claraicy who inspired me and to my lovely partner Laurie, who believed in my writing skills and stood by me.

Condensed Creaturese Dictionary

Like most languages, Creaturese doesn't follow English grammar. Words are combined for the sole purpose of relaying a message. This is a brief collection of the words emphasized in this novel.

Aaawww;	Claws
Eeeaaa;	Go
Mmmooo;	Dead or no longer all right
Mmarut Mmatat;	Respect and trust
Mmurr;	Injury
Nnaaarrr;	Stop
Rrahh;	Ear
Rrratatatat;	A cry of distress and warning
Sshuura;	Wing
Ssuurratatatat;	Circle around
Teeeesss;	Eyes
Uuratatatat;	A cry of disapproval
Wwaaaooowa;	A cry of battle
Wwoooaaa;	Home

Prelude

Terry's Legacy

Flying barely above the tree tops over the vast Northern Ontario boreal forest, a solitary, north-west bound, olive green and grey helicopter approached a crescent-shaped ridge. The huge ridge was nothing more than a gigantic mound of rocks, boulders and debris, created during the last ice age. Over time, the fine silt inside it had been washed away, leaving behind a labyrinth of tunnels, caves and caverns, along with the ridge's knuckle-like ravines. From the air, the mostly bare, pockmarked ridge was shaped like the decayed bones of a long, bent finger pointing to the east. From its long curled fingernail, to the hammer-like base at its southern end, the entire ridge had a diabolic look about it. Adding to the ridge's gloomy mystique was the muddy quagmire of swamps and fallen trees that encircled it.

The helicopter pilot felt the top of a tall tree scrape his landing gear as he tried to skim over it. "That was close."

A sweaty man in a dark blue suit and black tie sat beside him. Clinging tightly to his seatbelt, he choked out, "Get even closer if you have too. We can't afford to be picked up by their radar."

As the helicopter climbed upward, the pilot glanced over at his nervous passenger. "I'll try to stick to the large ravine that cuts across the ridge, but remember what I told you." On the top of the rocky ridge there was almost no vegetation to hide behind. The helicopter twirled the grass and short, weather beaten brush on both sides of the ravine as it skimmed over the ridge.

A red light came on in front of the sweaty man. "Damn it. They've picked us up."

While pushing his craft to its limits, the seasoned pilot responded, "I told you that they probably would. I also told you that we'll only be a couple quick bleeps on their screen before we vanish from sight again. It was to be expected."

On the far side of the ridge, the helicopter quickly sank into the forest and turned to the north. Hovering above the surface of large swamp, the sweaty man looked at his watch. "It's almost time. I just hope Doctor Brook wasn't caught."

Almost to the second, a loud explosion whipped the tree tops in front of them. The sweaty man watched the smoke and debris mushroom in the air. Carefully elevating the helicopter, the pilot smirked. "We don't have to worry about their radar anymore."

The sweaty man sat up straight and released a sigh of relief. Grinning at the pilot he commented, "Now all we have to do is find out if the doctor was successful or not."

A plume of smoke and flames rose out of what appeared to be a rocky knoll. As the plant-life covering the man-made mound burned away, they could see why the research facility was never spotted by their spy planes. The entire exterior surface of the domed facility had been hidden beneath a thick layer of soil and brush. The sweaty man peered through his binoculars as people ran out of the inferno. "This isn't right. I'm seeing too many white lab coats. Something must've gone wrong. There shouldn't be any research personnel escaping."

******

Duncan Stuart carried Terry MacIntosh out of the building's only remaining exit. Behind them, hand in hand, two chimps tried to sneak out. Dr. Stern spotted them and yelled, "Don't let them escape."

A guard quickly drew her pistol and shot the furthest one in the back of the head. As the chimp fell, the second chimp stopped and turned around. Laurie Irvine's second bullet landed in the centre of its forehead. Looking up, she saw the hovering helicopter turn around and fly away.

Patches of the fast paint job had flaked off the underside of the craft. A small section of the distinct Banting Pharmaceutical crest was clearly visible. Duncan's eyes followed the helicopter until it disappeared over the ridge.

With the clinic's star patient slung over his shoulder, Duncan forced his way through the thorn bushes that populated the swamp surrounding the facility. An hour later, he climbed out of the swamp next to one of the caves that littered Devil's Claw Ridge and dropped to his knees. He could feel the smoke-free air coming out of the small opening. A steady breeze was all it took to push air through the vast array of tunnels and cracks that wove throughout the ridge's porous structure. They were just lucky that the Devil's curled fingernail was able to deflect some warm southern wind, westward through the ridge. Duncan filled his lungs with long, swelling breaths. Every muscle of his body trembled from exhaustion. With Terry still perched on his shoulder, Duncan threw his head up and thought, *God, am I stupid?* He looked down at his hands. The scars covering his face and most of his body reminded him of why he had agreed to take the job. *How can they fulfill their part of the bargain now?*

The narrow entrance was far too small for Duncan's massive frame. Slightly leaning to one side, he slid Terry down his huge, blood-soaked arm and rolled him over into a sitting position. The thorns had ripped apart Duncan's clothes and skin. Every part of his body was either cut or stuck by them. In places, it was hard to tell whose blood was whose. As Duncan began pulling out as many thorns as he could, he told Terry, "Even if the fire spreads, the air flowing through the ridge should be able to protect you." Duncan stopped to hack some smoke out of his lungs. His head fell to his chest as he muttered, "I hope Doctor Scott didn't go back inside."

Terry looked up at him. "Me too." With a face that looked like a badly trowelled oil painting, Duncan's scars made him appear to be a terrifying, emotionless monster. The little kindness he had ever shown to Terry, had always been twisted by his grotesque appearance.

Terry was barely eighteen when the last of his family and friends had finally disowned him. All because of a single, stupid, drunken night and a self-centred, wretched girl with AIDS. He went from a promising young hockey star, to a helpless, bedridden skeleton. Now, as his health was finally starting to improve, all his hopes for a future were being engulfed by the distant flames. Terry looked past Duncan and watched the flames shoot up above the trees. Turning to Duncan, he asked, "Why did you bother saving me? There were plenty of others still in the building. You could've saved Tiffany. She was young and had her whole life ahead of her."

Duncan felt Terry's hollow-eyed stare gnawing at his wide chest as he stood up. "I didn't have a choice. I had my orders."

"You could've left me outside with the rest and gone back in for them. You didn't have to carry me all the way here. Tiffany and a lot of your co-workers were still trapped inside."

"That wasn't an option."

The scars on Duncan's face made it hard for Terry to read his emotions. "Why wasn't it?"

"Because she was just your nurse. She's easy to replace, but you, you're special. Your body is unique. For some reason it readily accepted the doctor's experimental treatments. Apparently, you have close to a billion dollars' worth of research floating around inside your veins. It took the doctor decades to get this far. The facility's investors can't afford to lose you. Especially now."

"Investors?"

Duncan looked at Terry's puzzled face. Dismissing his query, he continued, "You're the only patient I could save. Right now, you are one of a kind." Duncan looked over his shoulder at the flames, "Despite tripling the security, I just didn't count on a rogue insider."

Looking back at Terry, Duncan noticed him staring at the blood on the huge knife dangling from his waist.

Terry remembered seeing Doctor Brook's bloody body in the hallway. The clean cut that sliced through his throat had almost decapitated him. "You mean Doctor Brook, don't you?"

"Yeah. He ran up the stairs after I caught him trying to set a second bomb in the stairwell. I had to disarm it. If it had gone off, the upper floors would've been sealed off. All of the researchers, doctors and patients inside would've been killed. I guess Doctor Brook was given an offer that he was willing to kill for." Putting his hand on Terry's shoulder, Duncan smiled, "At least I got him before he got to you. He had already killed two patients before I caught up to him. Now that I've completed my orders, I have to get back to check on the doc. Don't worry, we'll be coming back for you as soon as possible. We won't be long. You should be all right until then."

Terry thought for a moment. *Why would a brilliant doctor want to destroy his own work? It doesn't make sense. Something isn't right. Unless?* Terry looked up and asked, "Who is really in charge? Who are these investors? Who are you really taking your orders from?"

Duncan looked at Terry and smiled. Without a word, he turned and began making his way back to the burning facility. Terry could only watch him go and question why Doctor Brook did it. Money and fame don't spur on a scientist like him. Their research is too deeply entwined with their own personal quest and religion. "Maybe the doctor had second thoughts on how his research was going to be used."

The cool evening air slowly crept into Terry's body. Dressed in only a flimsy hospital gown, he began to shiver. Gazing westward, he watched Duncan's head bob up and down in the dense, brush covered swamp. It seemed like the sun hovering above Duncan was being pulled out of the sky by the raging flames, and was being devoured by the fire's relentless appetite. As the two balls of fire slowly merged into one, Terry could hear a loud cracking sound coming from the facility. Shortly after that, the constant chorus of painful screams echoing from the burning building was suddenly drowned out by a loud explosion accompanied by a huge, black mushrooming cloud.

Terry clenched his tearing eyes in agony as his pain medication wore off. Seconds felt like minutes and minutes, hours.

The distant whisking sound of a helicopter woke him from his pain-induced comatose state. Its spotlight finally broke through both the thick cloud of smoke and the falling night's darkness. Terry quickly discovered that the extreme pain he was in had masked the thousands of harvesting needles that were extracting his blood. The mosquitoes' abdomens were swollen into small, crimson balloons. He didn't have the strength to scare them away. Looking upwards, he clenched his teeth and grinned. "And how many more plagues do you have for me? What did I do to deserve this?"

Terry suddenly gasped as pungent, burning fumes started to pour out of the cave, accompanied by a strange, high-pitched clicking. Curiously, he peered down the dark hole as a mass of fluttering, hungry bats engulfed him. Terry's body trembled, shaking off some of the mosquitoes. The fleeing, blood ripened insects stirred an even larger swarm of hungry bats exiting the cave into an instant feeding frenzy. Confined to the narrow opening, they started plucking and devouring the plump insects right off of Terry's petrified body. He tried to scream as he saw Duncan jump from the landing helicopter, followed by Dr. Scott. Terry's face was sprayed by minute droplets of his own blood as the creatures mashed the ripened mosquitoes between their sharp, crushing teeth. As a pair of black wings whipped his face, Terry's heart gave out and he gasped his last breath.

Duncan grabbed Terry and pulled him out of the confined shaft. Dr. Scott ran to Terry's side and valiantly attempted to revive him. Nothing he did seemed to help. As the doctor worked, Duncan picked up a large stick and fought off the anxious, darting bats. With lightning-quick reflexes, he wacked a few against the side of the ridge. Their mangled bodies slid to the ground. Several more simply fell out of the air and flopped about. Their broken wings made them easy targets for Duncan to crush under his heavy boots.

It was too late. In desperation, Dr. Scott started filling syringes with Terry's precious blood. He could feel his life's work slowly dying in front of him. He knew that the fragile cells he had helped engineer could only survive for a short period outside of a living, warm-blooded body. The doctor put the needle to his arm. His hands shook. He couldn't inject it. It would be like injecting a lethal dose of poison. The AIDS virus that still tainted Terry's blood, along with the cells' unique DNA profile, prevented him from ever transferring it into another human. Dr. Scott looked upwards with absolute hatred. The night's sky was full of tumbling bats gorging themselves on the fleeing, thieving insects.

A blood-drenched bat slowly crawled out from under Terry's body. The corpse was no longer offering it a safe haven. It twisted its battered head to face the angry pair. They paid no attention to it. Its head was covered with the blood dripping out of the incision where needles had once supplied Terry with hope. The enriched blood mingled with the creature's along a deep gash on the side of its head. As the two men looked upwards, several other injured bats slowly crawled to safety. Behind them, the cave's entrance was plastered in blood.

The doctor looked at the vials of blood. With every passing second, more of his precious cells were dying. As the doctor openly wept, within the shadows, all that remained of his research was slowly being infused into a primeval form of bat blood.

******

Slowly over the next three years, strange rumours began to spring up around the ridge. Most of them originated from the miners that harvested the gold there. It wasn't until Dr. Scott read the headline of the local weekly newspaper, 'Small Gremlins Terrorize Mine', that his foul mood started to change. "Maybe the rumours were true." Deep inside, he had always known that any form of life will fight to survive, even if it is manmade. He scrunched up the newspaper and threw it at the door. "Those damn bats. They were right there." He pounded his fist on his desk. "Why didn't I see it? They would've made ideal hosts. I could've injected a few of those creatures and saved everything."

Standing just inside Doctor Scott's office, Duncan questioned him. "How do you know they are the same creatures that attacked Terry?"

"There was blood everywhere. One or two of the creatures could have easily been infected. How else could a colony of bats evolve mentally to the point that they could terrorize a mine?"

Unique to the region, the Bear Den Mine started out as a bear's den on the side of Devil's Claw Ridge. Caught in a harsh winter storm, a trapper had sought refuge inside of the den in the mid-1900s. With freshly killed bear meat to live off of, he waited out the week-long storm. He explored the catacomb of natural caves, shelves and tunnels that riddled the ridge's interior. That was when he found the first few flakes of gold. The ridge's surrounding swampy marshes made it much too costly and dangerous to strip mine, not to mention all the environmental issues it would raise. Instead, the gold had to be carefully dug out of the unstable ridge's heart.

******

A month later, the headlines of the newspaper read, 'Gremlins Kill Two Miners.' The doctor read further into the article. 'The mine is presently shut down while the Ontario Ministry of Labour investigates the cause of the deaths. Reports suggest that the workers blame 'gremlins' for the deaths. Several miners had stated that they saw bat-like creatures with bodies the size of squirrels chewing on the electrical and hydraulic components of the excavating machine that caused the collapse.'

Looking over the results from his last batch of failed experiments, Doctor Scott slammed his fist down on his desktop. "I wish I knew exactly how Doctor Brook manipulated the stem cells he had used in his research." The doctor glanced over at the newspaper and summoned Duncan to his office.

Within a minute, Duncan entered. "What can I help you with?"

The doctor looked at him. "At least one of those creatures must still be carrying some of the doctor's original cells in it." In almost a growl, he added, "And I don't care if we have to kill every last one of them to find them."

Duncan wasted no time in contacting the mine's owners. They were grateful to sign over the troublesome mine, along with most of the mosquito-ridden swamp that surrounded Devil's Claw Ridge. Added to the property that the doctor already owned, the entire ridge was about to become his.

The day Doctor Scott took possession, the mine's entrance was blocked by Ontario Provincial Police officers wearing gas masks. Dismayed miners had illegally gained entry the previous night and laced it with a poisonous gas. The natural porous makeup of the ridge surrounding the mine had dispersed the toxic gas, and made it lethal to any living thing that came near it.

On the western side of the ridge, above where the hammer-like head swings north to form the handle, Doctor Scott placed both of his hands on the gate that denied him entrance. The team of men he had assembled quietly stood in front of the gateway. They all watched as tiny plumes of greenish-yellow smoke puffed out of the cracks and holes that riddled the long, wide ridge.

Doctor Scott turned away in total disbelief. Duncan placed his hand on the doctor's shoulder, "Remember, you built the cells to survive."

The doctor placed his hand over Duncan's. "They failed, Terry."

"Humans are fragile. Bats are tough and almost impossible to get rid of. Ask any exterminator. I wouldn't give up hope. Not yet."

Chapter One

The Gremlin Mine

It was several years before anyone would set foot near the abandoned mine. The locals had even renamed it the 'Gremlin Mine'. It started with a mere reckless teenage dare. Shortly afterwards, a young adventurous couple saw a lot of potential in its unique, eerie mystique.

******

Kristofer Poirier tenderly kissed Michaela Douglas outside the mine's entrance. "If we're going to put everything together on time, I've got to get busy setting up." He glanced over at her gaunt fragile sister and took a deep breath, "I'm sorry, I never thought you would actually bring Sarah along or I would have picked you up as soon as your father left for work. I know how you feel about your sister, but her wheelchair is going to really slow us down." Kristofer paused for a moment and looked into Michaela's sparkling blue eyes. "We better just get started."

The overgrown trees and bushes growing beside and along the middle of the mine's entrance road rendered the exit almost invisible from highway 599. Only the locals knew where to turn off the highway to get onto the long, twisted, double lane road. With swamp on both sides, a wrong swerve and you're buried in mud.

In front of the mine were posted 'No Trespassing' and other signs warning of dire hazards and danger. They were almost unreadable underneath the graffiti and bullet holes. As Kristofer opened the arched steel gates, he paid no attention to the old, rusted locks and thick chains that were cast aside with shiny chisel marks hacked into them. He looked back and waved to Michaela. Her long, curly red hair bounced around as she quickly placed a can of ginger ale into the beverage holder on Sarah's electric wheelchair and strapped her in.

Sarah insisted that she drive her chair down the ramps of the trailer without any help. Michaela clenched her teeth and fists as Sarah slowly made her way down. Beside the ramp, Kristofer stood with his hand stretched out in front of him, just in case anything happened. "You're lucky that there was enough room left on the trailer. We almost had to take your fold-up one."

Sarah smiled at him as she circled the bottom of the ramp. "I'm glad you made room. I would've felt lost without my wheels."

After re-adjusting the ramps, Kristofer jumped onto his ATV and drove it off of the trailer. After detaching the long, narrow trailer from the van, he re-attached it to the back of the ATV. On top of the pile of plywood already on the trailer, they loaded all the supplies and equipment that they had crammed into the van. "I'll see you inside in a bit. Just keep to the middle of the tunnel. You can't get lost."

Michaela bit her bottom lip as the light from his ATV illuminated the tunnel. Under her breath she squeezed out, "I hope that this isn't a big mistake."

The high-pitched whine from Kristofer's four wheel drive ATV rattled through every tunnel, shaft and cavern in the mine. He noticed small patches of fungus eating away at the old wooden support beams, along with the odd insect. To Kristofer they were some degree of reassurance that the poisonous gas was actually gone. Forcing down a lump in his throat, Kristofer wondered, *How did she talk me into this?* He knew that none of the other teenagers in the area were willing and capable of pulling off such a venture.

The ATV's headlight lit up 'ALL WELCOME TO ZEB'S MINE', sprayed in shiny, orange florescent paint on the tunnel's wall. Kristofer rolled to a stop. Even though Zeb had told everyone that he had been in the mine, Kristofer had thought that it was just idle boasting. Zeb had been trying to get even with him ever since Kristofer told his father, an O.P.P. constable, about Zeb's secret stash of illegal bear parts that he had helped poach for the oriental market. As a juvenile, Zeb got off with a fine and some community service. He didn't even have to rat out his accomplices. With all the money he had made, the fine was mere pocket change. It was the humiliating community service that ate away at Zeb's gut the most.

Grabbing a rock, Kristofer scraped and smashed off the words 'TO ZEB'S MINE', leaving only 'ALL WELCOME'. The stone wall was soft and dusty and the paint came off easily in large, shiny flakes.

Only a dozen steps away, a spider's web spanning the entire tunnel confirmed that no one, including Zeb, had travelled past that point for ages. In the mine's almost dead air it would take months for a spider's web to be laden with so much dust. It had only been a week since Zeb had boasted that he walked all though it.

Kristofer wasted no time getting to the mine's main cavern. It wasn't as high as he thought it would be, but much wider than he imagined. Working off his distaste for Zeb's boast, he quickly unloaded the bamboo garden torches off of the trailer. Methodically he placed them into his homemade stands made out of old tire rims and arranged them into a big circle. After filling each one with lamp oil, he lit them. The metallic specks on the cavern's wall sparkled in the flickering light. As the torches started to illuminate the monstrous cavern, Kristofer finally took a good look around. The cavern was once used for stockpiling ore before transporting it to an outside refinery. Now, except for a few pieces of broken machinery surrounding the elevator shaft leading to the lower levels, the cavern was empty. They were off to the side and shouldn't affect their plans.

Kristofer's spine trembled as a shiny, lightning shaped outcrop of golden ore glimmered off the top corner of the wall. All the miners knew about it. Where it was located, to dig it out could collapse the entire cavern, and maybe even that whole section of the ridge. It was too risky. The owners left it there to remind everyone what they were after. It was to be the last gold extracted from the mine.

All of the locals knew that the mine was poisoned, but with the high price of gold, none of Kristofer's friends believed that anyone would abandon it. Not when there was money to be made. There were plenty of ways to protect workers from the gas. Along with his peers, he had grown up with the scary jokes and seemingly tall tales about the mine's mischievous gremlins. Objects were moved or taken away, lunches stolen or eaten, equipment tampered with and even explosives removed from blasting holes within seconds of being detonated. The owners blamed the miners and the miners blamed the gremlins. Talking out loud, he muttered, "If the mine still contains gold, then why isn't anyone mining it? Those mythical gremlins really did a number on everyone."

Most of the region's population was terrified of the mine. Even years after the it was closed, the area seemed cursed with a rash of strange occurrences and bizarre accidents. The gremlins were the scapegoats for everything from misplaced items to mechanical breakdowns. But it was the eerie atmosphere the mine conjured up that made it the ideal place to stage a Halloween party. Costumes were optional; just showing up would be enough for everyone's hearts to race.

As Kristofer lit the wick of the last torch, the huge cavern became miraculously transformed by the flaming ring of radiant light. Yellow, green, blue and red flashes of colour adorned the cavern as the dancing flames bounced their playful light off of the irregular, chiselled rocks jutting out of the ceiling and walls.

The glassy emerald eyes of the two creatures crawling above Kristofer's head were lost in the glittering display. Clutching onto a support beam, the pair cautiously watched the strange intruder below them.

A loud 'thud' followed by a piercing, painful "AAAAAAAH" rang from the entrance tunnel into the cavern. The two creatures slunk back into a long, deep crevice between the beam and the roof. Only parts of their faces were left peering out.

Grabbing his flashlight, Kristofer ran to the tunnel. "Are you okay?"

A faint voice replied, "Yeah, Sarah's wheelchair ran up the side of a rock and tipped over, that's all."

"But are you all right?"

"We'll be fine. Just get back to work. Remember, we're on a deadline."

"All right. I'll see you in a bit." Returning to work, Kristofer kept an ear out for what was happening in the tunnel.

"Sarah, you gotta start being more careful." Michaela barked out while strapping Sarah back into her wheelchair. "Someday I won't be there for you." Picking up her lantern, she started to walk ahead to give Sarah as much light as possible.

All Sarah could think about was the mesmerizing glow that beamed from the end of the dark tunnel in front of her. As it taunted her, she felt jubilant for the first time in years. "Tell me this is really happening."

Michaela chuckled at her giddy sister. "Yes, and you're going to remember this day for the rest of your life. I promised you that, remember, and I keep my word. But right now, Kristofer needs our help to finish getting everything ready."

Following Kristofer's wide tire tracks, Sarah wiggled her way through the strewn debris that littered the tunnel. The mine's stale air slowly crept into her lungs and left the taste of chalky, overcooked liver eaten off of an old rusty fork. Stopping, she finished what was left of her ginger ale. As the bubbles tickled her throat, she thought out loud, "Michaela, if the doctors knew where I was, they would all flip. They can't prevent me from dying, but they sure don't want me to live, either."

The doctors had diagnosed Sarah's leukemia too late. With her body just rejecting a bone marrow transplant, her family knew that she would not be with them for much longer. Labelled a high risk, finding another donor fast enough was only a fairy-tale. Michaela smiled back. "They don't, but I do."

Sarah stopped at the cavern's opening, dazzled by the glimmering light show. The various flower-scented oils used in the lanterns created theillusion of an outdoor summer party. Their flickering flames produced a grand, multi coloured, ballroom effect as they bounced off the various mineral deposits embedded in the jagged rocks. "This is terrific." Her voice echoed throughout the mine. "Wow." She never thought Michaela and Kristofer's planning and hard work would ever muster up something this grand. "You guys did a great job."

As Kristofer finished setting up the audio equipment, Sarah helped Michaela with other chores. After setting up the fold-up tables for the food and drinks, the two girls stapled a blue skirt around them. Next, they stapled a red skirt to the several sheets of plywood that Kristofer had screwed on top of sawhorses to use as a stage. Sarah unravelled and held the skirt the best she could for Michaela to staple. "Thanks guys, this may be the only real party I'll ever get to."

Looking up, Michaela stretched her back into an arch. "You're welcome, but remember what you promised. Dad can't find out about today, so you better not get sick."

Smiling at Kristofer, Sarah bobbed her head. "You know, this is going to be the best Halloween dance anyone has ever pulled off. I'm just surprised that so many kids agreed to come."

"Hey, our parents get to go to their parties. Don't we deserve to have one too?"

Kristofer laughed without even looking up. "And this is going to be great. Think of it, nobody's place gets trashed and we don't even have to worry about the mess. At least not right away."

With the final twist of a wrench, Kristofer connected a string of car batteries to the inverter on his homemade control panel. Springing to his feet, he declared, "There, we're finished with time to spare. The others should be arriving any time now, it's almost nine."

With a flip of a switch, music rang throughout the mine with acoustics that surpassed Sarah's dreams. The sound improved even more as Kristofer fine-tuned his makeshift sound system. Echoing voices and beams of lights started to bounce around the tunnel. Despite all the excitement of the party, Sarah was slapped down from her emotional high as the first bunch of students arrived. Most of them had even taken the time to dress up. The arrival of the older teenagers made Sarah feel out of place. Biting her bottom lip, she slowly rolled her wheelchair backwards into the dark shadows behind the stage.

Michaela quickly glued on a long nose, wart and extended chin. She fluffed her hair into a wild mess and put on a ripped up shawl to finish converting herself into a witch. As the crowd flooded into the cavern, Michaela collected their contributions at the refreshment tables. A giant decorated punch bowl was transformed into her witch's cauldron. Sticks wrapped with wrinkled plastic embedded with pulsating battery-operated mini-lights had created the embers and flames. Floating objects, food colour, gummy worms and such had turned the sparkling punch into a witch's brew. Kristofer only had to put on an old, dirty leather work coat and hard hat with a light on it to quickly convert himself into a miner.

It wasn't long before Zeb Ferguson made his grand entrance with two bottles of vodka sticking out of his side pockets and a fake tommy-gun in his hand. He was accompanied by two of his hooligan cohorts dressed like mobsters, each carrying a case of beer. Dressing up as gangsters from the '30s seemed appropriate. Zeb pulled out the vodka bottles and set them on the table in front of Michaela. "These are for the punch. That'll get this party going."

Michaela flung her arms into the air in rage. "We told you, no alcohol! No one here can afford to go home smelling like booze. Are you trying to get everyone in trouble?"

"Hey, I'm Al Capone. I'm here to give these dry people what they really want."

Michaela grabbed a bottle and started pouring it on the ground. "No, you just want to cause trouble."

The commotion had alerted Kristofer. Before his feet left the stage, Zeb spotted him and started a wild chuckle. "So, the big squealer wants to stop everyone here from having some fun?"

Zeb's buddies quickly set the beer on the ground and flanked Kristofer as he advanced. Surrounded, Kristofer stopped short. They both weighed the same, but Kristofer was thicker in the shoulders and arms, where Zeb carried more of his weight around his waist and thighs. "If you want to drink, you'll have to leave and take it with you."

"You are your father's son." Zeb grinned as his cohorts seized Kristofer's arms. "Well, I'm going to have a beer and since this isn't even your property, there's no way I'm leaving." Adding in childish gibberish, "What's wrong? Your daddy's not here to run to. I wonder if he knows that you're throwing a party on private property? Ain't you afraid of getting in trouble? Your old man may even have to arrest you for unlawful trespassing and vandalism or something."

Kristofer lunged another step closer, dragging Zeb's goons with him. Zeb launched a hard upward knee to his groin. Kristofer dropped to his knees. The two cohorts let go of his arms and stood back chuckling. As Kristofer rolled around in agony, Zeb started to laugh, "What, you can't even stand up to me?"

Zeb bent over and clutched Kristofer's chin. "Who would want to come to your party anyhow? Everybody came today because I assured them it was going to be a real party. Not some lame goody goody get-together for geeks like you." Smiling at his partners, he added, "But I should thank you for setting everything up for us, it looks like you did a fairly decent job. I should be able to easily handle everything from here."

As Zeb stood up, he swatted Kristofer's face with an upwards wack of the back of his hand. The force of Zeb's strike sent Kristofer's hard hat flying. Climbing onto the stage, he grabbed the microphone and hoisted a beer into the air. "Did we come here to party or what? The punch is on me. Come and get it."

Michaela ran over to Kristofer. A few people, mostly from Zeb's crowd, started to line up as the vodka was poured into the punch. Most of the party goers stood back in amazement. It took time for the quiet crowd to digest what was happening. After only hearing mumbling from the crowd, Zeb violently shook his beer and sprayed it over them, yelling, "Come on, let's start this party!" He glimpsed at the foaming bottle and snickered before flinging it over his shoulder behind him.

The bottle smashed against the side of Sarah's wheelchair. The top of the bottle snapped off and flew up, knocking off her wig. "You're such a perve." Reaching down, Sarah picked up her beer-soaked wig and threw it as hard as she could. The wig missed him, hitting a stack of speakers instead. Two of them toppled off of the stage, stretching and pulling out wires as they fell.

"Look everyone, baldy's here." Looking down at the speakers, Zeb stood there with his hands on his hips, grinning. "And just look at what the stupid freak has done this time."

"It's all your fault." Sarah glared at him, yelling, "You always want to embarrass me! Look everyone, it's the sick freak with no hair!"

"How could I have known anyone was back there? Besides, I doubt very much that you're even supposed to be out of your bubble."

Kristofer hobbled over and stood in front of Sarah. "Drop it! Drop it now."

Michaela marched over to her sister, bellowing out, "She's thirteen going on nothing. If anything happens to her, you'll make your way to hell a lot sooner than you thought."

Feeling the crowd's sour mood, Zeb took a long deep breath and stomped over to the tangled speakers. "Sorry folks, the party's on hold while I fix the geek's lame sound system."

When Zeb tossed the speakers back onto the stage, they started to squeal. Zeb had left the system on while he reattached the wires. The high-pitched racket he created caused the crowd to slowly turn away from the stage with their hands clamped over their ears.

Kristofer helped Michaela pick pieces of broken glass out of Sarah's clothes and off her wheelchair. At the same time, Michaela looked her over for any cuts. Her ear and part of her cheek were the only parts that were bleeding. After releasing her seatbelt, the pair looked behind Sarah's back and for more shards. That was when Sarah looked up and saw strange giant shadows floating over them. The crowd was yakking to each other and nobody was paying attention to anything. The more Sarah watched the soaring shadows, the clearer they became. As the speakers continued to squeal, one of the creatures swooped downwards toward Zeb.

Sarah screamed out, "Get me out of here!"

Zeb quickly turned around and looked at the hysterical Sarah. The creature knocked the hat off of his head and spun in the air. As he fell head first onto the stage, the spinning creature headed straight for the trio behind him.

Kristofer and Michaela stopped talking, looked up and froze. The huge, winged creature managed to swerve around the pair and collided into Sarah. The impact flipped her chair backwards. As she tumbled out of it, the creature latched onto the back of Sarah's neck. It frantically clung to her side. Its teeth bit into her shoulder while its four sets of claws slashed into her back, face, neck and shoulder. In the shadows, Kristofer and Michaela couldn't see much. Sarah's screams and the two flailing bodies forced Michaela to cry out, "Do something!"

Kristofer picked up a heavy rock with both hands and waited for a clear shot. Seeing Sarah curl up into a ball, he saw his chance. Wasting no time, he hammered the creature with the rock. The side of the creature's head was crushed by the hard glancing blow. Still tightly clinging to Sarah, its blood gushed out. With the deep gashes it had sliced into Sarah's body, the creature's blood freely mingled with hers. By the time the entwined pair stopped thrashing, they were both plastered in blood-drenched mud.

Michaela looked around for any more creatures. Nothing. The second creature had vanished. It had retreated into a dark gap on top of a support beam. From there it cautiously watched its partner's demise. It hissed as loudly as it could in protest, but was easily drowned out by the curious, anxious crowd below.

Chapter Two

The Facility

With a short running punt, Kristofer kicked the creature off of Sarah like a football. After bouncing twice, its lifeless body hit the ground in a cloud of dust and rolled into the dark shadows next to the wall of the cavern. Michaela grabbed Sarah's arm and dragged her toward a nearby lantern, leaving behind a wide trail of blood.

Frightened by Sarah's motionless body, most of the crowd had drawn back. Some joked around thinking it was a Halloween prank. As Michaela frantically checked over Sarah's injuries, Zeb watched her from the stage. Even in the dim light, he realized the severity of Sarah's injuries. "It's not my fault. She shouldn't have been here in the first place. You can't blame this on me."

Kristofer looked up at him and snarled. "Nothing is ever your fault."

All of the crowd's suppressed anxiety about the mine started to surface. Their small talk had changed into morbid chatter. "Is she dead? Is it dead? What was it?" Panic struck as a lantern was knocked over by a hysterical girl, yelling, "It's the gremlins, they are attacking." The spilt lamp oil quickly ignited into a fast spreading fire. The bottom of a boy's homemade vampire cloak was lit on fire. He quickly tore it off and threw it to the ground. It acted like a giant wick and turned the spilt oil into a massive torch. Screams of terror rang through the panic ravished crowd. Another scared girl dressed as a rock singer walked backwards into another torch. Her red, gel-laced hair was set ablaze. Her boyfriend took off his pirate vest and smothered the flames. As he patted her singed hair to extinguish any embers, everyone started running to the exit.

"This party's over. We gotta get out of here." Kristofer picked up Sarah and ran to his ATV. As Michaela hopped onto the trailer, he gently placed Sarah on her lap. The tunnel had grown into a chaotic gauntlet of crazed teenagers. Kristofer drove as close to the wall as he could to avoid the crowd. As more and more people jumped onto the trailer, it flipped onto its side. Michaela and Sarah were tossed off. Michaela grabbed Sarah and placed herself between her and the mob.

Kristofer could feel the trailer roll onto its side. Before the ATV was even fully stopped, he leaped off and ran to the two girls. A crowd swarmed around the vehicle. As the mob righted the trailer and drove it off, the three of them were left stranded. Kristofer picked Sarah up and started running down the tunnel. Jostled about by the panic-stricken crowd, Kristofer stepped on a mound of loose rocks and fell. His arms and shoulder safely protected Sarah as they hit the ground. Michaela was following so close behind that she ran into them and rolled over the pair. Landing in front of them, she fell flat on her back. Kristofer cradled Sarah in one arm as he sat up. He tried to wipe the sweat from his forehead with his free blood-soaked arm. "Michaela, get to the van. We'll be right behind you."

Quickly bouncing up, she replied, "I'll see you there."

Michaela slid the side door open as Kristofer reached the van and gently helped him lay Sarah inside of it. With Sarah resting on her good side, Michaela climbed in beside her. Running around to the driver's seat, Kristofer called out. "Michaela, try to stop the bleeding. It'll take at least half an hour before we can get to the medical station in New Osnaburgh."

Behind the driver's seat, Michaela pulled out the bottom of the large bench built along the side. The padded bench slid down like a futon. Michaela carefully lifted her sister onto the bare cushion. She looked around the back of the van for anything that she could use. The van was set up for fishing and hunting trips. Most of Kristofer's stuff was taken out to make room for the party supplies. "She's bad. She needs to go to Sioux Lookout. She needs a real hospital."

As Kristofer swerved around the fleeing teenagers he argued, "She won't make it. New Osnaburgh is much closer."

Still looking around for something she could use, Michaela screamed out, "Where's your first aid kit?"

"It's back in the mine. I have some T-shirts in the drawer under the seat. You can tear them up and use them for bandages."

Michaela peered under the bed and decided that it was too much trouble. *Even if they were put in there clean, they probably aren't that way now.* Tearing away Sarah's top, Michaela saw the true extent of her injuries. Part of the creature's jaw was embedded into the back of Sarah's shoulder. When Kristofer hit it, he must've shattered its jaw. Wasting no time, she took off her shawl. Then she quickly removed her top and tore it into strips. She rolled some of the strips into thick, manageable pads that she could pack tightly next to the protruding jaw. Before bandaging it up with the remaining pieces of her top, Michaela overlapped the cups of her bra to shield the site and hold everything in place. As she finished tying everything in place, her makeshift bandages were already soaked in blood. "Kristofer, give me your jacket."

As Kristofer turned onto the highway he yelled back, "What? I missed what you said." Kristofer glimpsed in the rear-view mirror and saw Michaela's naked, scratched-up back. Even with her tattered witch's shawl back on, the bright red lines were clearly visible.

Michaela sharply repeated, "Your jacket."

Kristofer wiggled off his jacket and told her, "Take it."

Michaela stretched her blood drenched hand behind her and grabbed the jacket. After removing the shawl, she slipped on the jacket. She looked around the van for anything else she could use. Shivering from fear, she cried out, "Do you have any blankets in here I could cover her with?"

"I think I shoved one in the small cupboard across from the bed. The one above the counter." Looking in his rear-view mirror, he added, "My cell phone is back there, in the drawer below the stove. There's not always a doctor on duty. You better call ahead and tell them we're coming."

Dialling 911 was all she could think of, but that was good enough. Fumbling with the phone in one hand while applying pressure on the large gash in Sarah's neck, she finally got through. As Kristofer frantically drove, Michaela relayed Sarah's condition. Above the roaring engine she yelled out, "Kristofer, turn around and head south. They're going to have a helicopter meet us in the big lot where the logging trucks hold up and park for the night. From there, they will be flying Sarah to the hospital."

"Okay." Kristofer turned around in the middle of the road. Looking in the rear-view mirror, he watched Michaela tend to Sarah. A lump came to his throat as he saw the tears running down Michaela's quivering cheeks.

Sarah looked up at Michaela, feeling nothing. It was like a dream, no pain, no smells, not even the taste of the blood that had flowed from her cheek into her open mouth. Looking over at Michaela, Sarah worked up the strength to whisper, "Thanks Sis. Everything is okay," before passing out.

Michaela cried out, "You're not going to die on me."

Kristofer was barely stopped before spotting the helicopter. Refusing to leave Sarah, Michaela climbed in with her. She watched as the paramedics worked and jabbed an IV into Sarah's arm. Sarah flinched. A tall thin paramedic announced, "At least we know that she's still alive."

The paramedics slowly removed Michaela's crude bandages. They both froze and stared at the strange section of a jaw sticking out. A large canine tooth was embedded deep into an artery in Sarah's neck. Removing it would've caused a greater loss of blood than Sarah could afford. Turning to Michaela, the thin paramedic smiled, "I'm glad you didn't attempt to remove it. Using your bra to hold the jaw fragment in place was good thinking. You must love your sister, 'cause I never saw anyone willing to do that before." While packing the area with gauze, he took a closer look at the section of jaw. "What attacked her?"

"It resembled a giant ugly bat. It almost looked like the demons you see on fake Halloween tombstones."

Both paramedics worked quickly, bandaging Sarah back up. "That jaw is not from any bat. Did you actually see it? Was it a young wolf, a wolverine or some kind of big cat?"

Michaela didn't know what to say. Besides her, only Sarah and Kristofer saw it. Even Zeb barely got a glimpse. "It dropped down on her from the ceiling of the main cavern of the old abandoned Gremlin Mine. It had wings and its body was almost half my size."

In a half a chuckle, one paramedic jested, "That rules out the gremlins. Any stories I've heard about them, they are only a foot tall."

"You weren't there."

"Wolverines are good climbers and they love to jump on top of an easy kill. There have been a few sightings of them around here. They go straight for the throat. I bet that's what it was. Maybe even a racoon. They climb and can get really vicious. Maybe it just fell off of a support beam and landed on her. As far as the wings go, in a dark, poorly lit mine, you probably just saw shadows."

Michaela tried remembering what happened. Shadows were everywhere. Everything was so quick and the lighting wasn't the greatest. Trying to remember every detail was too much for her. Maybe her imagination had got the better of her. Was it flying, gliding in a long plunge or merely falling? It all happened so fast. Maybe it landed on Zeb's head and simply bounced back onto Sarah. Could it have been a wolverine? What looked like wings could have been shadows. It may have been hiding on one of the thick beams supporting the roof of the cavern.

In the hospital, the doctors checked Michaela over for any cuts or sores in case of rabies before she was allowed in to see Sarah. It was mid-afternoon before Sarah finally woke up and felt Michaela's hand. "I'm sorry I ruined your bash."

Squeezing Sarah's hand, Michaela blabbered out, "You're the only sister I have. I don't want you to die."

The two quietly enjoyed each other's company until their father stepped into the doorway. "If your mother was still alive, she would have a fit."

Sarah jerked as Michaela jumped up and wrapped her arms around her teary-eyed father. With her head buried in his chest, she told him, "I'm sorry. It was all my fault."

Still dressed in his dusty work clothes, Robert Douglas looked around the private room as he made his way to Sarah's bed. "I wasn't sure I got the right room. They first told me that she was in a ward in the children's wing." He reached over and took Sarah's hand. "I'm sorry, it took a while for the foreman to reach me and get me out of the mine." Dropping to his knees, he added. "You scared the shit out of me." Despite the extra chair in the room, he remained kneeling on the floor next to Sarah's bed as a group of doctors came in.

"Mr. Douglas, I'm Doctor Scott. I need to talk to you about your daughter."

Robert looked at him, "Where's her regular doctor? I've never seen you before. What's going on here?"

"I'm sorry for the confusion. I'm a specialist from a private medical research facility near Savant Lake. I was brought in on your daughter's case by the new owner of the Bear Den Mine. I'm the one that arranged for her to be moved into a private room. Under the circumstances, I thought that it might be best for her." The tall, well-groomed doctor studied Robert's confused reaction before continuing. "You know that she was trespassing on private property that was posted well beyond what the law required for liability."

"I know the mine."

"Despite this, the owner wants to make sure your daughter is properly cared for. They want to circumvent any additional bad publicity to the mine. They feel that it'll be hard enough to reopen it as is."

The words 'reopen the mine', brought Robert's eyebrows to attention. For a brief moment his back straightened and he forgot about Sarah. Then Michaela squeezed his hand and his tears started to flow again.

Robert's unexpected reaction made Doctor Scott wait a couple seconds before continuing. "The owner is also willing to issue a cash settlement under the condition that I personally oversee your daughter's recovery to the very end, with your full co-operation, plus your silence."

"What about her cancer?"

"I've been made aware of your daughter's cancer treatments. The facility that I manage has all the medical resources required to both continue the treatments and look after her recovery."

"I never heard of any cancer research facility in this area."

"We're a privately funded research facility with no need to draw attention to ourselves. Our research is cutting edge and very secretive in nature. A high level of security is very important to us until all our pending patents can be secured."

"So, are you or are you not doing cancer research?"

"I can't confirm or deny the nature of our research to anyone. However, I can assure you that we want your daughter to recover as quickly as possible. She will receive the best possible care. I've looked over her medical history and know that we can offer her a lot more than she has ever received before. We're offering her access to one of Canada's most advanced medical research facilities, one of the best in the world. She won't get another chance like this."

Robert Douglas looked at Sarah's bandaged face. "How long does she have?"

"Before this happened, her doctors gave her only a few months to live. I saw her records and I've done a few quick tests of my own. Her blood and tissue type are very good matches for the research that we are doing. If you agree to let us treat her, we could give her years instead of months. If we are completely successful in every aspect of our research, she may even be able to provide you with a grandchild."

Sarah's father put his hands on top of his head and took a couple deep breaths. *My kids were trespassing. They broke the law. Now Sarah has the chance to be rewarded with a future to prevent bad publicity? It's like winning the lottery without buying a ticket.* Looking up at the doctor, he asked, "How often could we see her?"

"Visits will have to be arranged." Doctor Scott looked at the bewildered father and handed him some papers. "Here is the paperwork that I need you to sign before we can get started. Any delay could cost your daughter her life. She was very fragile before this occurred. With all the blood she has lost, time is extremely critical."

Flipping through the pages, the tears in his eyes melted the letters and words together. Sitting on the bed next to Sarah's lifeless body, he simply found the last page and signed it. "There, but if anything happens to her, I'll become your worst nightmare."

Before leaving the room, Dr. Scott turned to Michaela, "Were you injured? I couldn't help but notice all the blood on your jacket."

"No, this is my boyfriend's jacket. He gave it to me after I tore my blouse into bandages. The blood is Sarah's. He was wearing it when he carried her out of the mine."

Doctor Scott briefly looked the jacket over. It was made of heavy leather. Nothing could have soaked through it and survived. He quickly glanced over at her father and Sarah. Anxious to get her to his facility, he decided he had to let it go. Smiling, he replied, "That was nice of him." After taking a step, he turned back and asked, "By the way, did anyone else get close to the creature that caused all this?"

"Yeah, Zeb Ferguson. The creature knocked his hat off before attacking Sarah."

After watching Sarah and her father fly off in a helicopter, Michaela sat on a bench outside of the hospital and waited for Kristofer for what seemed to be an eternity. Almost five hours had passed since they were airlifted to the hospital and her thoughts fled from Sarah to Kristofer. The way he drives, it should have only taken him an hour and a half to get to the hospital. Bracing her elbows to her knees, she cradled her chin in her hands. She tried to ignore all the chatter of patients and visitors discussing possible outcomes of various test results. All she wanted to hear was the distinctive hum of Kristofer's van. As a heavy weight gripped her shoulder, she jumped.

Michaela turned and sharply said, "Don't do that!"

"I'm sorry. You must have been somewhere else when I was talking to you."

It was the thin paramedic from the helicopter. "I was. First my sister and now my boyfriend, you know, the one that was driving the van. He's missing. I feel that I'm in the twilight zone or something."

"I wouldn't worry about him. A few minutes after we got your sister admitted, a hooded team of white suits wearing gas masks came out and hosed down the helicopter. They used some kind of plumbing solvent to scrub everything the blood could have come in contact with. The stuff was strong enough to strip off the wax and peel away some of the paint. Those guys took everything. Then they checked me over to make sure I wasn't infected. They probably stopped your boyfriend and did the same thing." Staring at Michaela's blank face, he added, "I haven't been through anything like that since that laboratory was destroyed a few years back. Tell me, what really happened back there?"

The paramedic looked down at the blood-stained jacket Michaela was wearing. Lifting his hand, he stepped back and checked to see if any blood had gotten onto him. Michaela watched him run to the hand sanitizer dispenser beside the door. As he looked back at her, the anguish on his face ran shivers up her spine.

Michaela's jaw fell. She didn't know what to tell him.

Chapter Three

Fort Scott

Robert glanced out of the side window of the helicopter as the bottom of the Devil's Claw came into sight. The mine's entrance was hidden behind the blunt western head of the ridge's claw hammer-like bottom. The helicopter flew along three-quarters of the hammer's curved eastern claw before heading due east to Doctor Scott's newly constructed research facility. As they got closer to the ground, Robert could see a narrow, one lane roadway wiggle its way through the swamp. "Why would anyone build a research facility in the middle of a marsh?"

Doctor Scott turned his head and calmly answered, "Privacy. Out here, we have no neighbours to worry about."

While the helicopter was landing on the roof, a semi-circle of a half dozen men and women in flapping, white lab jackets anxiously waited for Sarah's arrival. As she was wheeled from the helicopter to the elevator, Dr. Scott noticed Duncan waiting by the emergency door. The doctor lingered behind as the others piled into the crowded elevator. Turning to Duncan, he inquired, "Has the crew phoned in yet about the boy in the van?"

"Yes, sir. They had to remove the rug, the bed and several other objects from the van. There was a lot of blood. My men had to do quite a number on it. They are bringing all of the stuff back, along with the boy's clothes and bedding."

"Did anyone see it?"

"A few onlookers drove by," Duncan continued with a smirk. "With the men dressed in disposable coverall and masks, plus the magnetic 'Infectious Disease Control' signage we stuck onto the van, nobody stayed long enough to get a good look."

"What about the boy?"

"I think he's clean. I put Laurie Irvine in charge. I thought a female would create less resistance."

Doctor Scott twitched the side of his mouth. "Did it work?"

"Not this time. She still had to sedate him in order to confiscate his clothes and check him over. Apparently he had a few cuts and bruises. She took a bunch of blood and skin samples from him. As ordered, when he woke up he was given some coveralls, a generous amount of cash to cover the damages and was sent on his way. Nothing was left behind to suggest who we were and he never saw anyone's face or heard anyone's real voice."

"What about his cuts? Could any of the girl's blood have gotten into them?"

"Anything is possible, but from the video that I had seen it's not likely. The cuts on his hands were pumping out a lot of blood. His steering wheel was covered in it. I don't think anything could've gotten in at the rate it was flowing out. Any cells he would've came in contact with would've been immediately flushed away. The rest of the cuts were on his legs. They were protected by his heavy denim pants. The material alone would've filtered out the cells."

"I want to examine the video of the search for myself." Looking over the trees at the top of Devil's Claw Ridge, the doctor added, "Any news yet about the creature that attacked Sarah?"

"No. I personally led the squad of men that searched the cavern where the attack occurred. It wasn't there. All we found were two areas of the floor drenched in blood. We dug it all up and bagged it, just in case anyone got nosey. They used a flame thrower to destroy anything we missed. I left some men there with orders to keep on looking for the creature."

"Good. Now, I want you to personally look after doubling your present manpower. With the activity that is going on in the area, people may suspect that we have rebuilt the centre. I don't want any of my work destroyed or compromised ever again. No ex-cops, they are too nosey and hard to control. Stick to ex-military personnel. They know how to obey orders a lot better."

"Is that all?"

"No. I want you to enlist the best PR and legal representatives you can get. With all the kids at that party, the media is probably already aware of the attack. I don't want anyone to link us to the creature."

Without hesitation, Duncan answered, "I already thought of that. I found someone. She's expensive, but she comes with her own team."

"Very good." Tapping his index finger against his lips, the doctor added, "There are two more things that I want you to do. One, there was a Zeb Ferguson who may have had contact with the creature. I want you to pay him a visit."

Duncan calmly responded, "No problem. It's a small community. He shouldn't be hard to find."

"Second, I want one of your men to lift the jacket that Sarah's sister was wearing. It was drenched in blood. We can't take any chances. All our competitors need is one cell to publicly expose our research to the media. It doesn't matter if it is dead or alive. Tell your man to be very careful. I don't want to upset the Douglas family too much right now."

"I've got the perfect man for that. George even knows the place."

Doctor Scott got out of the elevator and walked to Sarah's new quarters. Looking down at her, he smiled. "How do you like the room we prepared for you?"

A groggy Sarah looked up. Still thinking that she was in the hospital, she answered, "Sure. At least it's not another noisy children's ward."

Under heavy medication, Sarah spent the next two days in a coma. On the third day, she started fading in and out of consciousness as her mind began to process the strange, muffled sounds of people scurrying about her room. By noon things had started to settle down. Slowly blinking her eyes, it took time for her to focus long enough to look around. She thought she was hallucinating. The wall across from the bed resembled a mini apartment. It had a huge TV, bookcases full of movies and books, and even a mini fridge. Along the side wall was a messy portable cot with a pillow scrunched under a couple blankets. Her response was barely a whisper. "Am I going to be just staying awhile or living here?"

"Just staying until you're well enough to go home." Her father's voice surprised her. Her excitement overwhelmed her and set the buzzers on several pieces of equipment blaring.

Mr. Douglas had heard too many hospital monitors to get alarmed. He glanced at the top graph on the monitor. After seeing Sarah's heartbeat calm down, he softly added, "Dr. Scott told me that I could stay until you woke up and showed signs that you were going to be all right. I needed to know that you were in good hands."

"Where am I?"

Robert grasped her hand. "You're in a very special hospital."

At Robert's last word the door flew open. Doctor Scott ran in with two guards, both with their hands on their unclipped, but still holstered pistols. A nurse quickly followed them in. With barely a glance at Sarah, he examined the monitors. "Stand down. The patient's all right."

After sitting down at the computer, the doctor faced the stunned Robert and added, "The equipment in this room can keep a dead man clinically alive indefinitely. I never thought that she would shake off the sedatives so fast or I would've had someone stationed in the room with her."

Seeing the doctor's wild glare as he studied the instrument readings, Robert believed him. His face beamed like a fisherman's after struggling an hour to haul in a ten-kilo salmon on a three-kilo line.

Minutes passed as the doctor silently studied the graphs and charts of compiled data that had flowed through the equipment. He finally took a good look at Sarah. "There's no way that I'd allow even death to take you away from me."

The doctor's words sent an icy tremor up Robert's back. *Beware, if something is too good to be true, there's always a catch.* His rosy, contented grin slowly drooped into a pale thoughtful worry.

Over the years, Sarah had learned how to read medical charts. As the doctor review them, she cried out, "Stop, back up." On the monitor, two straight lines appeared. "What happened there? Did you have problems with the equipment?"

Doctor Scott soberly looked at her. Bluntly, he replied, "If you were at a regular hospital they would have pulled the plug on you. You were clinically dead." Looking back at the monitor, he added, "Actually, you had died twice since you got here. Once during the first night and once early this morning as we tried to change your medication. That attack has taken a lot out of you. My toys brought you back to life both times, without your body accruing any additional damage." He turned to her father, "I told you this place was her only chance. Are you satisfied now?"

Tears flowed from Robert's eyes as he stood up and stared at his daughter. "You saved her life. She would be dead is it wasn't for you." Along with the racks of hanging bags being injected into her, she had dozens of wires coming out of her, feeding all the monitors and computers that covered almost an entire wall of the room. Several tubes attached to a series of pumps, injected medicine, fluids and even a liquid oxygen mixture directly into her lungs. Another half dozen set of tubes pumped blood in and out of various parts of her body, legs and neck. The blood was recycled through a series of dialysis and analytical equipment that filled another quarter of the room. She resembled a marionette waiting to be brought to life by a crazed puppeteer who called himself a doctor. Robert knew his daughter had no other option but to keep on living, and at that moment, that was all he wanted. Turning to the doctor, he finally answered, "Of course I'm satisfied. She's alive, isn't she?"

The guard standing beside him turned and broke the silence. "Mr. Douglas, now that you know she's all right, it's time for you to leave."

"I know, I promised I would." Robert stood up and kissed Sarah's forehead. "Everything is going to be all right. I'll be back as soon as I can."

Exiting the building involved two elevators, each only going down a single floor. Electronic locks were attached to every door and corridor entrance. There were three armed check points. At each, both the guard and Robert had to produce signed paperwork before being allowed to pass. After taking off the track suit they had provided him, he had to shower, walk through a corridor naked with nozzles spraying a smelly mist over him, and then take a second shower to wash the chemicals off of him. In the end, he had to put on the same filthy work clothes that he came in, and was escorted out of the building to a waiting helicopter. Along with the landing site on the roof, Robert noticed three more heliports surrounding the facility. All of them situated inside of a tall doubled layered security fence.

Shortly after lifting off, the pilot pointed out the long narrow dirt road winding its way through the forest and swamp that ended at highway 599. "That's the road you will have to take when you come for visits. I hope you have a good four wheel drive. You'll need it."

About half way back to his truck in Sioux Lookout, Robert mustered up the nerve to ask the pilot, "What's all the high tech security about? I work at a gold mine, and our security is next to nothing compared to that."

"That's research. Everyone wants to know what we are doing, the media, animal activists, both domestic and foreign governments, competitors, everyone. Curiosity and suspicion are rampant. With today's technology, data can be transferred into a pill and swallowed or inserted as a suppository. It can even be attached to a person's skin, hair extension, disguised as a tooth or even a toenail. No one is allowed to leave the facility without being completely scanned, inside and out."

Robert looked at him, "All they did to me is give me a shower."

"The chemicals in the shower make it easier for the hidden scanners to detect any irregularities in your body. For instance, the mesh they used in your hernia operation, the beans you ate yesterday or the small wooden splinter on the side of your right thumb." The pilot glanced quickly at Robert. "I read your printout before we boarded."

Robert rubbed his thumb. "I can't feel anything."

"It's probably too small for you to feel, but it is there." The pilot looked at Robert's blank face. "We were hired to prevent any leaks. We're talking mega bucks here. If someone was suspected of carrying useful data, there are people out there that would think nothing of draining every drop of blood out of them in order to get to it. It is an extremely vicious, ruthless and cutthroat industry."

"I never noticed any signs. Does the research facility even have a name?"

"Not really. However, we sometimes call it Fort Scott."

As soon as he returned to the facility, the pilot immediately went to Dr. Scott's office. Before he could knock on the door, the doctor yelled, "Come on in. Did Mr. Douglas question you?"

On the wall of the office, the guard noticed a large screen monitor displaying an array of camera images. "Yes, sir. He asked about the high security and I responded as per your orders, sir."

"Good work, now do me a favour and go to haematology and get me all the test results from Sarah, the kid in the van and Zeb Ferguson. Dismissed."

Upon the pilot's return, the doctor pulled the results out of the sealed courier pouch. His eyes started to bulge. He scrunched up the papers in his fist and marched out of his office. The guards saw him coming and doors were flung open with a single pointing finger. Dr. Roger Hamilton was too intensely glued to the scanner to notice him enter.

The doctor clamped his free hand down on Roger's shoulder. Roger's forehead started to sweat under his painful grip. Doctor Scott released his grip and swung Roger around in his chair. Shoving the report in his face, the doctor's wide eyes and huge grin made Roger sweat even more. "Are these the results of Sarah's blood samples?"

Roger's face went pale as he answered, "Yes, sir."

Doctor Scott grin spread from ear to ear. "That's absolutely terrific."

The bewildered Doctor Hamilton rattled on, "But did you notice those strange flat golden flecks in a few of the cells that the centrifuge had separated out? They look exactly like the chemically derived computer chips that I've been trying to create for you in laboratory three." Roger looked at Doctor Scott's strange smile, "Why am I finding them embedded in living cells? Are they a competitor's? I need to run another series of tests on them in order to conclude my results. I could run them right now if you want."

"Calm down, no one has copied our work. They are ours. I helped create those chips years ago. These cells are the combined result of over a decade of research. When Doctor Brook destroyed the old facility, we lost virtually all of our research. Right now, I've got Doctor Stern trying to recreate Doctor Brook's work in laboratory nine." Stepping back, Scott walked around the lab. "I wanted you to do the blood tests because I knew that if they were there, you would find them. Good work."

"Thanks."

"Next to me, I think that you are the smartest one in this place. That's why I am intrusting you with another project. Doctor Stern lacks the genius touch you possess. He is too human and not enough scientist. The rest of the doctors are mere drones."

Doctor Hamilton smiled, "Thanks again, it is nice to know that I wasn't just hired as eye candy for the nurses." After a short chuckle he added, "What do you want me to do?"

"Yeah, I want you to analyse any data you can from the chips extracted from Sarah Douglas' blood. I should warn you, they were crudely developed and extremely delicate. It was almost by accident that they were produced at all. Outside of a living body they die much quicker than normal cells. When they do die, all the data the chips contain is automatically deleted. They need a living body's electrical field to function. Also, they have no surge protection, so any change in electricity could fry them. Good luck. You'll need it. You may need something to compare your results to. I'll be sending you data to check against your findings."

"Sure, but first I want to know how you produced the chip cells that long ago. We're just refining the technique now."

"That's right. You're just refining it. People have been pouring chemicals on gold flakes to make organically manufactured computer chips since before you were born. It just wasn't public knowledge, that's all. That part of our research is ancient. Remember me telling you about Doctor Brook's work?"

"Yeah."

"Well, he was the one responsible for taking blank, undefined stem cells and engineering them to accept the chips as part of their own nucleus." Looking straight into Roger's eyes, he added, "He had also designed them to be able to self-replicate under the right conditions. Even the chips themselves were designed to split with the cells and self-duplicate. After all, they are only clusters of chemicals mixed together to form artificial, programmable DNA."

Doctor Hamilton paced the floor, "So the cells consider the chips a living part of themselves. Doctor Brook was truly a genius."

"He had some help." Doctor Scott stood there with his hands folded in front of him. "My humble contribution was limited to giving the cells the ability to produce the right viral agents. We had to ensure they had the correct controlling effect they needed to do their job. Remember me telling you about the hockey player?"

"Sure, Terry MacIntosh. What about him?"

"These particular cells were originally programmed for him, using his own DNA."

"I can remember you telling me that he started to recover before the fiasco." Roger thought for a moment. "But what are they doing in Sarah?"

"That's a long story."

Roger vented his confusion by slapping his thighs. "Then give me the short version."

"She had enriched blood injected directly into her veins during the attack. The chemotherapy that she was taking, had left her nothing to fight them off with. Over the last three days, the cells had free reign over her body. They are using her body like an incubator."

"How can they be multiplying so fast?"

Doctor Scott grinned, "With help. They are like parasites. They are absorbing the nutrients that we've been pumping into her and multiplying like crazy."

Roger looked deep into Doctor Scott's wild eyes. In a subdued voice, he asked, "So what's happening inside her body right now?"

"Forget about Sarah. You need to understand how the cells work. When they come in contact with a cell that doesn't match the DNA profile embedded in their memory chip, they treat it as a mutant. First, they release an enzyme that kills them. Then, they secrete another enzyme to stimulate the creation of stem cells that they can genetically manipulate in order to repair and replace the damaged tissue."

"You mean, they can reverse the growth of cancerous tumours?"

"Correct, plus, with the right numbers and given enough time, they have the ability to destroy any illness or infection that threatens their host." In a low serene voice he added, "Cancer, AIDS, and even cellular degeneration can soon be under our control. How much would you pay to get unlimited perfect health? Imagine never getting sick or even growing old. How much would someone be willing to pay for that?"

Roger's jaw slowly fell. "What? That's suicide. The entire pharmaceutical industry could collapse. They would lose trillions of dollars a year. If they find out about it before it hits the mass market, we are dead. Even after it hits the market, they'll be trying to find a way to either discredit or exterminate us."

"But think of it. We could make trillions of dollars at their expense." Putting on a face that would make a pit bull urinate in fear, he added, "So don't be stupid like your predecessors. Do your job, don't talk to anyone and survive until all patent rights are ironclad. Then you can live like a king anywhere you want. If you are worried about the drug companies, you'll have enough money to hire your own private army to protect you."

Roger bit the side of his lip. "These chip cells were surviving out there without any medical guidance. How do you expect to control them?"

"They were just the first prototypes. The next generation will be designed completely differently, and the next, even better yet. We need to have total control over their reproductive capability. We also need total control over the chemicals that they need to reproduce. They have to be unique and patentable so no one can copy our research and the maintenance procedures the cells need to survive. Without our supervised control, over time, they'll die out like any other cell."

Roger studied the doctor's face. "You weren't kidding about the billion-dollar completion fee, were you?"

"I never kid. It might even multiply if everyone does their job right." Turning his head away from Roger, Dr. Scott grinned at the female guard standing next to him. "Keep in mind, I'm willing to pay these insurance agents twenty-five million each, under the same conditions. Double that if they find any traces of treason, and it multiplies after that. I don't intend to be robbed again." Looking down at the guard's name-tag then up to study her face, he added, "What would the young Ms. L. Irvine be capable of doing to ensure her financial future before her thirtieth birthday?"

Striking a cold attention with a curled upper lip that revealed her teeth, the guard barked out, "Sir, anything required of me, sir."

Roger saw the guard's frozen glare. He remembered the chimps. Despite her size and striking appearance, he knew that she would cut his throat if he stood in her way. She was only one of the small army of mercenaries Duncan had recruited. He knew he was trapped. "I got the message. Do my job, no questions, stay alive and get rich." Shutting his eyes, Roger took a deep breath and mumbled, "I guess that half million-dollar signing bonus was only the bait."

"I had lost a lot of good scientists, and I needed to replace them with the best I could find. You qualified. Think about it, you could retire a very rich man before you're thirty-five." Looking over at the young guard, he added, "Maybe you can retire together. You've plenty of time to get acquainted. Maybe the guard that is looking over her shoulder, making sure that she does her job, could be the one that looks out for both of you."

The very intimidated Roger slowly asked Dr. Scott one last question. "If the cells are designed to slowly turn the bats into little Terrys, what's going wrong? It has been years now and all they have done is create larger and stranger creatures."

Doctor Scott slowly turned to the door. Looking up at the ceiling, he took a deep breath. "We still only know a small fraction of what is going on in the long coded DNA strands that make us who we are. Most of it is unused remnants that we have acquired since leaving the primeval ooze that all life forms derive from. The bats that stole the cells contain a vast amount of the same DNA." The doctor turned and faced Roger. "If the cells are not programmed properly, they could overlook some of the minute variations in different types of tissue. A few off-on switches can make the difference between a monkey and a squirrel. Man and bats are much closer than that."

"So in the next generation of cells we also have to tighten up on what the cells believe to be normal."

The Doctor started to walk towards the door. "That'll be part of my job."

On the way back to his office, Dr. Scott was somber. The cells were still out there. They were first implanted into Terry, then stolen by the mosquitoes, then over time infected the bats. How they survived until they were transmitted to Sarah was a mystery. He mulled over all the reported mutations the bats had gone through. His collection of newspapers and jotted down miners' tales were all he had to go by. He wondered if anything else had been infected or mutated by the cells. If they can be transmitted easily to lower life forms, he could lose all control over them.

Dr. Scott ran down the hallway to his office. After ordering Duncan to start constructing a barricade around the entire property, he checked the long, detailed, permission form Robert Douglas had signed. Giving out a sigh of relief, he said out loud, "By keeping her alive after she had flat-lined, all of our obligations are legally satisfied. Until she is of legal age, her body is mine."

******

Three guards shone their flashlights along the walls and ceiling of one of the many tunnels in the mine. Thompson looked back. A shadow shifted along an overhead beam. "Halt, I think we missed something."

A guard waved his flashlight around behind him. "Was it one of them?"

"I'm not sure." Thompson put his hand on the other guard's shoulder. "Cover our rear." Turning to the third guard, he told him, "You take the right side, and I'll take the left. Stay close to the wall so nothing can get behind you."

The two guards slowly crept down the tunnel, each taking one silent step and stopping before taking the next. It took a while before they reached the beam where Thompson had noticed the shadow. After a couple quick hand signals, they both ran four paces and turned around. There was nothing there. Thompson examined the beam more closely as the other guard looked around. A faint ray of light coming from the third guard's flashlight revealed a gap above the beam. Thompson was sure that the gap wasn't there before. After waving the third guard to join them, he examined both sides of the beam. "Something was hiding up there. Did either of you see anything?"

One guard just shook his head and the other said, "Nothing."

"I'm calling it in anyway." Thompson looked around while he pressed on his headset. "I think we may have found one of them. No visual at this time, but I'm sure it's here."

"I'll send in reinforcements." The guard stood up at the table set up in the main cavern and briefly examined the map in front of him. "Units two and four, proceed to unit one's location. Use caution; creature sighted but remains elusive. Unit three, proceed to tunnel intersection number six and seal off tunnel D4. Make sure the creature can't escape."

As the clamour of six pairs of boots echoed through the tunnels, Thompson noticed that a protruding rock on the wall was twisting. Suddenly a round form appeared on the side of it. Then its other ear unfolded outward. What looked like a rocky ledge was actually a clinging creature. The guards took aim as their comrades rounded the bend and came in the line of fire. Even a ricocheting bullet could be deadly. The creature looked back and forth at each group of men. With lightning fast reflexes it sprang away from the wall and bounced off of the adjacent wall, ceiling and then the floor as it made its way towards the trio. They held their fire as the other guards formed a human wall across the tunnel.

"No one shoot." Thompson yelled out, "We have to let it through." Noticing a large indent in the wall behind a post, he pointed to it and ordered, "Everyone, behind the post. Let's give them a clear line of fire."

As the creature lunged towards them, they ran and flattened themselves against the wall. The creature took flight as the third guard leaped towards the crowded depression. The creature glided along the wall. With bullets whisking by, the creature grabbed the back of the third guard and twisted him around. Two bullets caught the guard's arm and thigh. The firing stopped as the creature crawled along the wall using the crumpled up guard as a shield.

Thompson yelled, "We've got it from here." Jumping over the wounded guard, they opened fire. In the poor light and dust kicked up by the barrage of bullets, the creature was a mere shadow. Thompson could hear the others racing behind him as he ran after it.

The creature looked back. Weaving all over the place, the bullets whizzed by it and only added to the growing cloud of dust that the creature used to his advantage. It could see light ahead of it as it approached a pair of crossing tunnels. The gunfire stopped. The curious creature looked back. The clamour of boots had slowed to a fast walk. As it looked ahead, it flew into an almost invisible net that another group of guards had fastened across two support posts. Dazed, it took the creature a second before it could begin slicing apart the net with its claws. While it tried to get its wings untangled, three guards jumped out and opened fire.

By the time Thompson got to it, the creature's body was torn apart. Turning to the guards, he smiled. "I just hope you left enough for the doctor to examine." Poking at the creature with the barrel of his rifle, Thompson spread the creature's wings to take a better look. "Sarah's sister was right. They do look like the bat-winged demons on fake Halloween tombstones. Man, it's vicious looking." As one of its eyes peaked opened, the creature's hands grabbed the barrel. Thompson stepped back and pulled the trigger. The bullet blew off part of the creature's skull.

The guard standing beside him snickered, "The doc has even less to work on now."

The creature was spread out on the stainless steel examining table. Doctor Stern lifted up its head to examine how the wings worked. Two sets of shoulder blades were attached to an enlarged, modified collar and backbone. The wing tissue was attached to three-quarters of its upper legs and partly down its tail. Turning to Doctor Scott, he commented, "Everything works completely independent of each other. It's as if it's two creatures in the same body. It can both run and fly." After placing the creature back down, the doctor ran his hands up and down its entire skeleton. "If you cut the wings and tail off, it could almost pass for a dog-faced ape."

Doctor Scott carefully smeared some of its blood onto a slide. Holding it up to the light, the doctor smiled. Two shiny specks prevented the light from penetrating through the cell's nucleus. "I don't need a microscope to see them. Their wonderful glitter is everywhere."

"Too bad the information on the cells was deleted. The data on them would've been very interesting." Doctor Stern walked over to the doctor and peered at the specks of light bouncing off of the slide. "How they are getting the nutrients needed to reproduce them?"

"Like elephants and a lot of other creatures, their bodies tell them what it needs. Some creatures search and travel great distances to satisfy their strange cravings. The fact that they don't seem to be travelling much means that they are getting it locally. We must find out where they are getting it from and how they are exacting it."

Chapter Four

Miracle or Curse

A month later, Dr. Scott quietly entered Sarah's room with his hands behind his back. Using his foot to shut the door behind him, he looked at Sarah and inquired, "And how is our star patient doing this morning?"

Through a shallow, barred window, Sarah watched a moose and calf feeding in the marsh that surrounded the facility. Using their front hooves, they broke the thin layer of ice before burying their heads into the cold water. Sarah shook the bars. They didn't break like the ice. With her head resting on her crossed arms, she mumbled. "Bored. Why don't I have a phone jack in here? How can I chat to my friends or get on the Internet to catch up on my school work?"

"I'm sorry. This facility has a strict communication blackout policy in order to protect our research. You could consider this as a school vacation or, if you want to, we could arrange to have your work sent here. I understand that you were being home schooled anyway."

"So, I'm a prisoner here?"

"No, you're not. In prison, pets are not allowed."

Sarah turned to face him, "What do you mean?"

Revealing the white and orange cat he was hiding behind his back, the doctor smiled, "We use a lot of animals in our research and we don't have the time to pet and play with them all like we should. I thought you might like to help us out with that."

Sarah maneuvered her wheelchair over to take the cat from Dr. Scott's hands. "Does it have a name?"

"Not really, just a series of numbers. You can call it anything you want. It doesn't respond to C237 very well."

The large number behind the 'C' made her flinch. "So you want me to work for my room and board by playing with your lab animals do you?" Sarah held the cat to her face, touching its nose to hers. Sections of the cat's legs were shaved and she could see red dots where needles had been injected. She knew the huge cost of animal life in medical research. "I long as I don't get too attached to any of them, I think I might be able to handle that."

"Well, we do have more than just cats." Closely studying Sarah's face, he added, "We have dogs, monkeys, rats and we just started using bats. I was thinking, if you want to, I could move a few cages into your room and you could play with any one you want, at any time you want."

"No bats! Keep those things away from me! But monkeys may be fun."

After handing the cat over to a nurse, Dr. Scott knelt beside Sarah and started to pull back her bandages. "Boy, have you come a long way. You could barely move a muscle when you first arrived. Now you're full of energy." He looked up at Sarah's face, emitting its first truly healthy glow of her stay. "When you first came here, you were a thirteen-year-old stuck in a seven-year-old body. Now, look at you. You've even put on some weight."

"Are you sure?" Sarah started to chuckle. "I thought that would be impossible with all the blood and tissue samples you're constantly taking from me."

"And I have another surprise for you." The doctor smiled at her. "You're starting physiotherapy after lunch. Since the last group of tests came back negative, I'm going to give you plenty to do. You are about to become a very busy girl."

When the doctor left, Sarah rolled her wheelchair over to a full length mirror on the wall. For over a year, she avoided mirrors. Who was this person she saw? It wasn't her. Small dark hairs had started to sprout on her head, replacing the blonde ones that she had lost. Her old slack jaw was now strong. Her eyes were wider and darker. Her skin tone had turned from newspaper gray to a light tan. She slowly felt the smooth flesh on the side of her head that wasn't still bandaged. Gazing at her hands, they were no longer boney and weak. "What has happened to me? Do I have to change into someone else in order to be cured?"

She was glued to the mirror as Michaela and her father entered the room. "God, Sarah, is that you?"

"Michaela!" Sarah wheeled her chair around and smiled. "It's about time you came to see me. Dad kept telling me that you are always too busy with projects and homework when his visitation could be coordinated with the staff here."

"I'm sorry. I guess I felt that it was my fault that you are here in the first place. If I didn't convince you to go to the party, you wouldn't have been in the dark where that beast attacked you. I should've looked out for you better than that."

"Look at me. If it wasn't for you and that mine monster, I may never have found this place. Cancer could've even taken me by now." Her huge grin puffed her face into a ball. "I've never felt this good in my life." She wheeled her chair beside Michaela and gave her a hug.

Robert stood smiling as his two daughters embraced. "Dr. Scott said that you will be starting therapy today. We're going to stay and watch. Imagine what it would be like to walk after all this time?"

"Great. But Michaela, did you see my new hair? No more baldy."

"How could I miss it? But black. There's no black hair in our family."

"Weird, isn't it?"

Sarah was giddy for the entire visit. In therapy she had managed to kick her legs enough to splash everyone around the small pool. In the days following the visit, all she could think of was her new body. How many books could she lift? How long could she hold her arms out straight? Every aching muscle made her smile. Despite her daily, two hour sections as a human mannequin, her mind couldn't stop. Instead of dying, she was starting to feel alive again.

Two weeks later, her father and Michaela watched her briefly stand without assistance for the first time in almost three years. By Christmas, Sarah was able to walk around on crutches. A big, beautifully decorated Christmas tree adorned the far corner of the cafeteria. Along the same wall, lights encircled the narrow windows. Silver and white garland had turned their bars into icicles. Almost all of the guards and staff had squeezed into the cafeteria shortly after the sun started to shine. Even Robert and Michaela were invited. Using a lot of padding, Doctor Hamilton had put on the jolly suit and Laurie Irvine donned an elf's. Everyone there received at least two presents. One from their secret Santa, another from either Dr. Scott or Duncan. Any additional presents were from close friends and were usually some sort of gag gift to lighten the mood.

Being the only child in the facility, Sarah got a lot of more presents than anyone else. To most of them, a smiling child on Christmas morning is what made it Christmas. The guards had pitched in for a preloaded MP3 player and headphones, the technicians gave her a gold charm bracelet and the doctors got her a new laptop computer. In addition to the joint presents, several smaller ones were slipped under the tree for her as well. A set of beautiful hair brushes from Laurie Irvine made her almost jump up, but she caught herself and landed on her side. Other guards gave her sweaters and jogging pants, most of which had things written on them, like, 'Princess', 'Spoiled rotten' and the one she liked the best, 'Little Sister'. As the presents dwindled, Michaela walked over to Sarah. From behind her back she handed Sarah a box. Both her father and Michaela went to their knees and gave Sarah a big hug. "Merry Christmas."

Inside the box was a beautiful pair of hand-made moccasins. In addition to the usual beadwork around the edges, the tongue was custom designed just for her. On each one was sewn a small portrait of her mother using various colours and sizes of beads. She had died in a car crash two days before Sarah's first Christmas. Sarah instantly recognized her image from the photos. "This must of taken Mary ages to make." Sarah looked at Michaela and then over at her father. "Thanks, mom never did see me walk. Now she can."

In no time, Sarah had replaced the crutches with a pair of canes. As things got easier for her, Sarah wanted more. Her room suddenly became cramped and confined. Baldy was only a memory and so was her wheelchair. She felt that no one had any reason to poke fun at her anymore. She had become accustomed to the thick bandages on the side of her face, head, neck and shoulders. To her, they were no bother. All she wanted to do was show everyone her new beautiful, strong legs and thick hair. Sarah was only five when she was told that she had acute lymphoblastic leukemia. Since then, she could only fantasize being like everyone else. Now, she wanted to go for a hike in the woods, or maybe even learn how to dance.

She rushed over to her father when he came into her room and gave him a hug. "Dad, I want a dress to wear when I come home. Maybe a bright red one. Please."

"A dress?"

"Everyone gets new clothes for Easter, don't they?"

"But a dress?"

"I want everyone to see my new hair and legs. I'm getting so bored, I even miss Mary standing over me while I do my schoolwork."

"I'll have Michaela pick you out a dress, but you can't come home right away." Tears started to trickle down his cheek as he hugged her. "Sarah, you may have to stay here for a little while longer. Don't worry about your schooling. The doctors have had better luck with the cancer than they had with the damage caused by that creature. The bandages can't come off quite yet." Robert straightened up and looked at her. "Sarah, the doctors have been showing me pictures of the damaged area around the infection. The wounds don't want to heal properly. The doctors have to find out why. They told me that it may be the cancer treatment they were using. They can only fix one thing at a time. They need to keep you here until you're totally cured."

Releasing her father, Sarah stood back. "I've been here forever already. How long do they want to hold me prisoner for?"

"According to Dr. Scott, at your present rate, maybe only a couple more months. You should be home by summer." Robert followed Sarah and sat beside her on her bed. "You have grown the equivalent of two to three years since you've been here. The doctors suspect that you will maintain an accelerated growth rate until your body is where it should be. They need to closely monitor your growth and see how your body copes with it."

Sarah didn't want to hear about her continued sentence and looked away. Staring at the mirror across the room, she asked, "Dad, who is the girl in the mirror? My hair, jaw and nose have all changed. There is nothing about my body that is the same. Everything about me looks different."

Her father stood behind her and put his hands on her shoulders. "The treatments they are using may have some side effects on your development. They told me to expect some additional changes in your appearance because of your accelerated growth rate. After they are certain all the cancer is gone, they will need to flush out all of the anti-cancer agents that they had used, before they can start treating the infection."

"So how long will that take?"

"The entire process could take anywhere from another half a year to even several more years. After that, you should be able to grow up and live a long, full life."

Crossing her arms, she pouted, "So why can't I go home now and come back for checkups? I can't even get on a computer to chat with my friends." Her father couldn't answer, nor could anyone else at the facility to her satisfaction. She was to remain a bored, frustrated teenager with nothing to do but pet her favourite cat.

The guards, including Laurie, had become her playmates. They referred to her as Little Sister, mostly because she liked to wear that sweater most of the time. Out of boredom, Sarah made up her own favourite game. She would race ahead of the guards through the corridors and try to slip through the check point between her room and the examining room. Sarah knew they never worried about her escaping. The only way off of her floor was a locked elevator across from the examining room and constantly guarded emergency exits. Except for Doctor Scott and Duncan, nobody had total access through every exit. Even the guards were only given limited access on a rotating basis.

Sarah watched the guards as they punched a code to unlock each door. Every day they used a new set of numbers. When the guard unlocked the corridor doorway, she inquired, "What would happen if there was a fire or sometime like that?"

"Little sister, I've seen the blueprints to this place. It's built to withstand a raging forest fire. The Pentagon itself couldn't take half of what this place can." Rubbing Sarah's hair, Laurie added. "I wouldn't worry about anything. Not here."

After the guard unlocked her door, Sarah asked, "What happens if you punch in the wrong number?"

"Simple, I don't. The lock gives me two tries. If I goof on the third one, everything in this place will shut down. After that, the door would open and I would be treated like a terrorist. I'd end up back on the roof, doing turret duty with the rookies."

It was only two days later that Sarah saw a chance. At the same time that Laurie was escorting her past the elevator, two guards were getting out. Sarah had seen the code that morning. Falling behind, she snuck around the exiting guards and into the elevator. Squeezing into the nearest front corner, she waited for the door to finally close. "Now what?"

Standing back, she looked at the control panel. She quickly punched in the series of six numbers. Nothing happened. She tried again. Halfway through the sequence, the elevator door opened.

Dr. Scott was there waiting for her with six guards. Kneeling down, he talked softly. "You really want to get out of here, don't you?"

Looking down at her feet, she answered, "I guess."

"Well, you leave me no choice. I've been overlooking your childish games because of your age. Now, I'm going to have to talk to your father." Standing up and turning to face a puzzled Duncan, Dr. Scott said sharply, "This is a high security research facility. We cannot let anyone run around loose, can we? Not even our star patient. Am I clear?"

"Crystal, sir." Duncan grabbed Sarah's wrist and bound it with a cloth pad with two heavy plastic ties running through it. The nylon leash attached to the cloth pads was handed to Laurie. "Take her to her room. Then, and only then, can you remove her wrist restraint. After that, you are to lock her door and guard it."

Sarah laid on her bed for hours until she eventually dozed off. Stirring from the movement of her bed, she opened her eyes. Her throat seized at the site of her father sitting beside her, with his face buried in his cupped hands. "Dad, all I wanted to do was go home."

"We found that out." A still angry Dr. Scott spoke out from the other side of the bed. "That is why you're leaving. You were never our prisoner here. Everyone here did everything in their power to help you and make you feel comfortable, but you insisted on playing your childish games. Your father has agreed that you will come back here twice a week or maybe even more often if required for testing, replacing your bandages and any medical requirements you might need. Your father has a list of all the other conditions that you must obey in order for you to go home. Young lady, this is a very sensitive, high security research facility. I'm sorry, but we can't have you running around. We can't risk the chance of you contaminating our research."

Robert placed his finger across Sarah's mouth as she tried to speak. It was a long time since she saw him look that way. Her suitcase was already packed and waiting at the door, with a change of clothes laying on top of the dresser. "Get changed. I've gotta talk to the doctor about your medication, but I'll be right back."

As they got into the elevator, Sarah watched the guard at the panel. He placed his thumb on an identity scanner while entering the code. She had only been concentrating on the numbers. After the third corridor check point and entering the second elevator, she felt like a fool. There was no way that she could've made it out. The place was a maze of locked doors and multiple security checks. As the sunlight hit her, she walked to the truck and didn't look back. Sarah took in a deep breath of fresh air. Once in the truck, she closed her eyes and hugged her father, "I'm glad I'm going home, even if it means being grounded."

Duncan stood beside Doctor Scott as they drove away. "What now?"

"Now we can experiment on her some more. This time we'll have to be a little stealthier about it, that's all."

"What about her daily treatments?"

"We have pumped a lot of nutrients into her since she got here, and the cells have spread to every part of her body. Maybe it is time to see how they react without our help. That may give us a clue on what happened to the bats."

Duncan turned to Doctor Scott. "We could've taken her off of the medications here. What if we lose control over her?"

"If she becomes too much of a problem, we'll get rid of her." The doctor smiled at Duncan. "A tragic, unexplainable side effect from the cancer treatments. But it still would be nice to discover the cells' full potential. "

As they pulled into the driveway, the first thing Sarah noticed was her electric chair under the wood shelter beside the house. It looked like new. Sarah turned to her father, "You even waxed it."

Still clutching the steering wheel, her father looked at her. "That was how Duncan delivered it. I guess it was a bloody mess when they found it."

The next morning, after her father had left for work and Michaela went to school, Sarah felt out of place. Her school books were stacked on her desk. She knew that coming home meant that her home schooling could resume. Sitting at her computer, she started going through her emails. Her chair felt uncomfortable. She had to adjust it several times before she even opened her schoolwork. Everything she touched seemed awkward and strange.

Mary Powless, her next door neighbour, came over to make sure she did her work, like she had done before. Her late husband, a white man, had worked with Robert in the mines and, despite their age difference, had been best friends. After the mine accident, she had nowhere else to go. Her own family had shunned both her and her half-breed children. Now, with her children having families of their own, the spry sixty-three year old woman lived alone, supporting herself with her traditional native crafts and leatherwork.

Sarah heard the kitchen door squeak as Mary entered. She got up and walked into the kitchen. Mary saw her and jolted backward. Her coffee cup slipped from her hand and shattered on the floor. Sarah ran over to help pick up the broken pieces. Kneeling next to Sarah, a bewildered Mary asked, "Who are you?"

"It's me, Sarah Douglas. I've changed a lot since you saw me last. That's all."

"Your hair, your face, you're too big and dark skinned to be Sarah."

"Yeah, I've got legs again. Isn't it great?"

They sat quietly at the kitchen table until Mary was over the shock. "Why are you still wearing so many bandages? The accident was months and months ago."

"I don't know. At first the doctors kept replacing them every day, then only twice a week, usually after taking a whole lot of tissue samples. They say I'll have to wear them at least a few more months, maybe even longer."

"Have you ever seen your scars?"

"No, the doctor said it's best I don't. Something about mentally scarring. I guess they are still quite ugly. All I know for sure is that they are really itchy. Isn't that supposed to be a sign of healing?" Even as she said it, Sarah knew that she was trying to convince herself more than Mary that the wounds were healing.

Taking a deep breath, Mary stood up. "Well, how about you spend your time today figuring out where you are with your school work? Tomorrow, if you are good, we could go for a walk to The Depot for lunch. It would be my treat."

"You mean it?"

"Only if you are good and can get some serious work done between now and then."

Sarah's biggest problem was trying to recall all the steps and formulas in math and chemistry, along with figuring out where she was in her other subjects. The cancer had never affected her brain. Before the attack, she was able to do some of the same schoolwork that Michaela and Kristofer had been doing in high school. Being housebound with nothing else to do meant she could focus all her energy into her schooling.

Mary was always close by with her needle in hand. Her hand-made moccasins sold well at The Depot with the tourists. With tanned hides left at her doorstep every once and a while, all it cost her was time. Using porcupine quills and dyed bones, Mary proudly made her beadwork as traditionally as she could. Sarah knew the real reason Mary wanted to go to The Depot was to show off what she had made. Mary loved getting Sarah's opinion on her fancy beadwork and stitching.

By the time the following noon came, Sarah was depressed. Mary looked down at her, "Cheer up. You're getting out into the world for a while." her remarks received only a sigh.

"I don't have anything nice to wear. I've outgrown all my good clothes. All I have are the sweaters and jogging pants I got for Christmas."

Without replying, Mary went home and promptly returned with two grocery bags. "I wasn't sure about that, so I asked around and got some clothes for you. See if anything fits." Mary passed Sarah a bag stuffed full of clothes. Some still had their price tags on them.

Sarah looked at a few of the tags and smiled. "Thank you."

"They are just odd things nobody else wanted, so you can keep them if you want." Mary slapped her thighs. "What do you think? Do you like any of them?"

Pulling out a dark brown skirt and tan blouse, Sarah let the rest of the bag tumble to the floor. "These will look great on me."

Mary pulled a pair of moccasins out of the other bag she carried and handed them to Sarah. "Especially with these. I can't have you walking around outside wearing your mother, those are for indoors. I was going to save these for your birthday but, happy early birthday, Sarah. Your dad told me to make them a bit bigger. Now, I hope I made them big enough."

Mary's hand stitched rubber soles were hard to miss. "Mary, you did a beautiful job on them. Thank you."

Sarah barely heard, "You're welcome," behind her, as she dashed into her bedroom to change.

Sauntering out, Sarah held the top of her blouse together as she complained to Mary. "With these bandages on, I can't do up my top."

Mary smiled. "That's easy to cover up. You just need a couple pins and a well-placed scarf." When Mary was finished, Sarah couldn't believe the image in the mirror.

The Depot was a few kilometres down the road and they both wanted to walk. They called it The Depot because it stocked a little bit of everything, for anyone who entered the door. For better prices and selection, a lot of the locals drove to Sioux Lookout about once a month, but for convenience, there was The Depot. Before Mary opened the door, she told Sarah, "We will order what we want to eat, and then while we are waiting for the food, I'll show you some of the stuff I made since you were gone."

Sarah glimpsed at Mary's display beside the door. No tourist or anyone else could miss it. Running over to the counter in front of the grill, Sarah told Mrs. Ferguson that she wanted a cheeseburger, French fries and a chocolate milkshake.

As Mary slowly sat down beside Sarah, Mrs. Ferguson smiled, "So, which one of your granddaughters is this one?"

"None. This is Sarah Douglas. She's out of the hospital now."

"I thought she died." Mrs. Ferguson put her pad in her apron and stood back. Taking a sincere look at Sarah, she called to her son. "Zeb, come here."

Zeb had come home for lunch with two of his friends. From the far end of the counter he slowly got up and cantered over to his mother. "What do you want?"

"Zeb, you told me that you saw Sarah Douglas get torn apart by some wild animal in the old mine, didn't you?"

"Sure, mom. What about it?"

Pointing over at Sarah, Mrs. Ferguson added, "Is this Sarah Douglas? You knew her better than I did."

"No way. Sarah was a skinny bald runt that couldn't even walk. And she's no Douglas, look at her." Zeb shook his head and waved his arms in front of him. "Besides, that creature tore her apart. Some kids tried to see if she made it to the Osnaburgh House clinic and they told me that she didn't even get there. Even the hospital in Sioux Lookout never had her registered as a patient. Unless she was airlifted south, there is nowhere else she could have gone but to the grave."

"You went to school with her sister. Didn't you question her about Sarah?"

"Sure, but Michaela clams up at the mention of Sarah's name. She's dead. That's why none of the family has been around. They are all in mourning or something."

Sarah jumped up and looked straight at him. "If I died, how could I be standing here?"

"I can prove you're not Sarah."

Zeb's wide grim infuriated her. With her hands on her waist, Sarah sneered. "Well, I can prove I am."

Zeb rushed over and grabbed Sarah's scarf. Throwing up her arms, Sarah tried to repel his advance. Zeb tightened his grip. Sarah grabbed Zeb's arm. With his other arm, he pushed Sarah backwards. As she fought to regain her footing, he ripped off the scarf. Still pinned to the scarf, half of the bandage taped to her neck was torn off with it.

"See it's not..." Zeb froze as he glared at the side of Sarah's face and neck. The thin, fine wires that had been woven into her bandage only added to his hysteria. "It is. It can't be." He almost fell backwards as he ran out the door, yelling, "Keep that zombie away from me."

Chapter Five

The Taunting

Mary quickly wrapped her shawl around Sarah to cover her neck. "We're leaving." Mary almost carried Sarah out the door. Rushing her behind the store, the couple faded into the bush. Looking back between the branches, Mary saw Zeb and two other figures surveying the road. "They are not following us. They don't know where we are. You are safe in here."

"What's going on?" Sarah cried.

As Mary lead Sarah deeper into the woods, she told her, "The doctors told you the scars were ugly and that you were never to see them. Well, they are more than just ugly." Sarah had to stop. Resting on a fallen tree, Mary sat Sarah on her lap and gently rocked her until her legs started aching from the weight. "I better take you home."

Mary was envied by many people twenty years younger for her fortitude, stamina and agility. Sarah, on the other hand, wasn't use to crawling over rocks and fallen trees. She needed to take more time resting than she did travelling. A couple hours later, Sarah could see the back of her house. They quickly snuck in the back door and locked it. Sarah ran to her bedroom. Mary followed her. By the time she got to the door, Sarah was curled up under her blankets. Gently sitting at the foot of the bed, Mary softly began humming lullabies to her.

An hour passed before Sarah allowed Mary to pry back the covers and replace the bandages with some from the first aid kit. "Mary, are they really that awful?"

"For now, yes they are. You must remember that the doctors are still treating them. They told you that the bandages must stay on until the infection is under control." After giving her a hug, she added, "You are still Sarah Douglas. A few scars won't change that."

Michaela dashed off of the school bus and ran all the way to the house. "Sarah, are you okay?"

Mary called out, "She's in here."

As she entered Sarah's room, Michaela blurted out, "Zeb didn't hurt her, did he?"

In a calm voice, Mary answered, "Not physically. But he shook the soul right out of her. She hasn't stopped shivering since he tore part of her bandages off."

Michaela gripped Mary's arm and led her out into the living room. "What do the scars really look like? The word being spread around school is that she has giant, black, hairy leeches all over her, and she's been transformed into some kind of zombie or something. Her head was even supposed to have been tied on with wires."

"You should never listen to gossip. Everyone knows that everything gets blown up. Remember that Sarah's doctors are still treating the scars, and that is why she has to keep the bandages on. When they are through, she will be fine." Mary saw Michaela scrunch up her face and knew her words were falling short. "Zeb only saw what he wanted to see. He never even had time to get a good look at them. He was under the silly impression that Sarah had died. He was shocked by the fact that she was still alive, that's all."

"So the scars are not as bad as they say?"

"No, of course not." Mary grinned. "The way you described it, she should have great big footballs crawling around her neck. Look at her. She just has some bandages on, that's all."

"I guess you are right." Michaela plopped down on the couch, shaking her head. "That Zeb, he went back to school just to cause trouble."

Mary stayed until Robert came home from work. When he arrived, she turned and saw Michaela standing in the kitchen doorway, "Go and check on Sarah, your father and I have to talk."

Putting his lunch bucket on the counter, Robert slowly sat down with Mary at the table. "Did something happen to Sarah?"

"I'm afraid so, and it's all my fault. I took her to The Depot for lunch and Zeb Ferguson was there. The idiot ripped off some of Sarah's bandages. Robert, there are much more than just scars hidden under them. I think she'll be needing a lot of cosmetic surgery before it is all over."

"Did Sarah see them?"

"No, I made sure of that."

"Good. The doctors had shown me pictures of them, and they are really nasty. They had already told me that some surgery might be needed, but they can't do it until they get rid of the infection." Peering down at his fists, he added, "Sarah should never see the scars. That could emotionally destroy her for life. The doctor assured me that when it was all over, she would be normal."

"Robert, Zeb saw them. He is exaggerating them into something even worse and is making up horror stories about them. Even Michaela heard some of his stories this afternoon at school." Mary took a deep breath. "Zeb really flipped out in front of Sarah and called to her a zombie. She hasn't left her bed since we got home."

Mary watched Robert go to the cupboard and pull out a bottle of whiskey. After a couple of big swallows, he stood there looking out the kitchen window over the sink. "I can't go on like this. My wife had lain in the hospital for two weeks and I could do nothing. Sarah had been suffering from cancer for almost a decade, and all I did was stand around feeling helpless. At first I thought Sarah being attacked was some divine blessing in disguise. Just because it got her to the research facility for treatments. Those creatures killed your husband. They can't be killed. That poison we set off killed everything except them. If she is infected with whatever they got, what chance do the doctors really have of curing her?"

Mary put a hand on his shoulder. "I don't know, but right now, the doctors are all Sarah has."

"And I pray they can help her. Unfortunately, right now all this incident does is remind me of all the damage those creatures have done to everyone in this community. They have to be destroyed." Robert turned and faced Mary. "There may be a whole mine full of them out there, just waiting to attack others. And here I am standing around again."

Mary sat and thought a while before she spoke. "I always thought it was a wolverine."

"No, it wasn't. Michaela and Kristofer both told me it had wings. They called it a giant four-legged demon bat. Kristofer got a good look at it before he smashed its head in with a rock. The creatures are almost twice the size they were. The kids were afraid of saying anything. People would think they're crackpots." Turning to look out the window, Robert added, "I thank God for it getting Sarah the help she needed. If she didn't go to that party, cancer would have sent her to her mother's side by now. However, if it wasn't for Kristofer, that creature could have killed her right there in the mine. I don't know what to do."

"Be grateful that Kristofer killed it. He proved that they can be killed." Mary placed her finger under his chin and turned his head towards her. "Just do what is best for Sarah."

"Mary, I had to promise Dr. Scott that Sarah would never see the scars. That was one of the conditions I had to agree to before she was allowed to come home."

"It wouldn't hurt to get another doctor's opinion. There are a lot of doctors out there."

"Those paper that I signed grants them total control over Sarah until they sign off a medical release form. They are, in effect, her legal guardian, not me. They can even come here any time they want, take her away and put her in a padded cell until she's eighteen. I wish that I'd taken the time to read the forms before I signed them."

"She had just rejected a bone marrow transplant and her cancer was getting worse. You had no choice."

Robert took another swig of whiskey. "All I know is that an infection caused by those creatures is what's eating away at her body right now, not cancer."

Mary tried to take the bottle away from him. Robert quickly pulled it out of her reach. "It's only an infection. The doctors can cure that too."

"How? It takes time to develop a cure. Look at how much time and money has gone into fighting AIDS. That's just an infection too." Robert grabbed his hair as he looked at Mary. "After we first arrived, I overheard a couple guards talking. They couldn't even find the creature that Kristofer killed. They don't even know what they are up against."

"The kids told me that they also found nothing when they went back into the mine to retrieve all the gear they had left behind. They heard some guards searching inside the tunnels, so they got out as quick as they could."

"That's right. Think about it. What animal carries off their dead? What are they, cannibals?" Robert looked down at his hands spread out in front of him. "If so much as one other person is hurt in that mine, it will be all my fault. I've been standing around helpless for too long. That mine should've been blown up years ago."

Grabbing the whiskey bottle, Robert went into the living room and sat down in the chair next to the phone. As soon as Michaela saw him, she ran over and gave him a hug. "It's okay, Dad. We're a family, remember? We made it through Mom, and we'll make it through this too."

"Michaela, the doctor has been showing me photos of Sarah's scars all along. Both the one on her neck and the ones on her back are spreading and getting worse. They are more than just scars. The doctors' research may have saved her life, but they haven't been able to control the infection. The poison those gremlins had infected her with is slowly killing her. I can't stand by and do nothing. Not again. I'm getting sick from doing nothing."

"I thought they told you that they weren't going to worry about the infection until after the cancer was totally gone."

"Look at her. Do you see any signs of cancer? Yet the infection is spreading."

"Maybe they just haven't started to treat it yet. If they are not worried about it, maybe there's a reason why."

"Maybe, maybe not."

While Michaela fixed supper, Robert phoned around to the neighbours, taking a swig from his bottle between each call. With each one he got louder, and by his fourth, Michaela had no problem hearing everything he said. "All we need is some dynamite. . . . Who cares about who owns the property? . . . Well they should be looking after the creatures themselves. They're a public health hazard . . . We have to look out for ourselves. We also have to consider the public. There are a lot of hunters and tourists walking around in the bush, you should know that . . . That's right, we have to look out for ourselves and protect that tourist dollar."

Sarah wrapped her pillow around both of her ears. Her father's loud ravings had no problem penetrating the wall separating the living room from hers. Every word sliced through her like death's sickle. They hacked away at every ounce of hope she had for a normal future. Her fear of cancer had been replaced by the ugly, growing, strange infection hidden under the bandages.

Michaela gave her father his supper and reached over for his bottle. "You've had enough. Sarah has probably heard every word you've been telling your friends."

Robert discharged a deep breath. "You're right. Drinking has never helped solve any of my problems before. But you have to admit, it sure helps me dredge up some courage."

Michaela walked back into the kitchen with what was left of the bottle of whiskey. "That it does."

That night, as Michaela coaxed Sarah into drinking some warm chocolate milk, she uttered. "I thought I looked better than ever before. Why did he look at me like I was a monster? Is it that bad?"

Turning out the lights, Michaela laid down next to her, "You have to remember that it was just Zeb. Everyone knows he's not all there. You shouldn't worry. We're not going to let anything happen to you. Now, try to get some sleep."

Before going to work, Robert called the facility to tell them what happened. He was a bit surprised that Doctor Scott picked up the phone. "There was a problem with one of the bandages."

Doctor Scott ripped into Robert, "You mean to tell me that this happened yesterday and you are just calling me now. Those bandages can never come off. We've custom made them just for her. Without the special medication on them, the infection could rapidly multiply out of control. That is why I made it one of the key conditions for Sarah to go home."

Getting off the phone, he issued Michaela some quick instructions. "Michaela, after work I have to take Sarah in to see Dr. Scott. Apparently her bandages were specially made just to control the infection. Can you get her ready for when I get home?"

Michaela handed her father his lunch bucket. "Sure."

Robert rushed out the door with his coat only half on. "I've got to go. See you tonight."

Michaela had gone to school and Mary was on her second cup of coffee by the time Sarah woke up. Standing in Sarah's bedroom doorway, Mary saw that she was still wearing the same clothes from the day before. "If you don't feel like working today, it's all right."

Sarah carried her blanket into the living room and curled up on the couch. "Maybe later." With a yawn, she added, "I'm just tired. I didn't get much sleep."

Mary turned on the TV and threw in movie after movie of the Douglas' limited selection. Sarah had seen them all a dozen times. The pair cuddled up on the couch and stayed there all day long. Seeing the school bus stopping, Mary got up and met Michaela at the door. "She's doing fine. I let her bum around all day and it seemed to do her some good."

Michaela walked into the living room and Sarah forced a smile. "We had a movie party today and it was fun. How was school?"

"About the same as usual." Michaela hid her puffy, blood stained hand behind her. "Dad told me that you are taking a ride when he gets home. I think that we still have one of mom's old spring coats. Remember the one that has collars that can flip up. It'll cover those bandages." Michaela smiled, "You'll look like a secret agent in it."

Sarah grumbled as she followed Michaela into her dad's bedroom. "I'm still too short to fit into Mom's stuff."

As Michaela reached for the black coat, Sarah noticed her scraped knuckles. "How did that happen?"

Jolting her hand back, Michaela stopped breathing for a couple seconds. "Volleyball. I hit the volleyball wrong."

"I thought that you had finished that a few months ago."

"The teacher let us pick what we wanted today as a treat. The class picked volleyball." Handing Sarah a black trench coat, she quickly added, "Go and try it on."

The coat fit nicely over her bandaged shoulders and came down to her ankles. Seeing the belt resting against her hips, Sarah pulled it out of the loops and shoved it into its side pocket. "This is like having a portable blanket." Seizing the front of the coat, she wrapped it around herself in both directions.

Sarah saw her father come into the driveway. Forgetting everything, she ran out the door to meet him, crying out, "Dad, I'm getting big enough to wear Mom's stuff. See?" Spreading out her mom's coat wide as wide as she could, she let the wind make it flutter a while before she wrapped it around her tightly. "I know it's a little big yet, but I'll grow into it."

Sarah paid no attention to the vehicles going down the road until one rolled into the driveway. Mr. Ferguson got out and walked over to Robert's truck. Out of everyone's hearing range, he whispered, "I went over to the old mine today to figure out what we would need to seal it. The place has armed guards at the entrance and fresh 'No Trespassing' signs are posted everywhere. There's more interest in that mine than you thought. No one uses armed guards unless something really serious is going on."

"Did they see you?"

"No, I stopped before the last bend in the road in front of the mine and walked in."

Robert tightened his grip on the steering wheel. "That's good. I was told its new owners were trying to reopen it. Maybe they are having problems with the gremlins. Now I'm glad I made a few extra phone calls yesterday. Hopefully I'll be getting an answer back soon on who actually owns the property. I was told it could take a day or two."

"Well, I gotta get going. We are late for supper as is." As Mr. Ferguson got back into his truck, Zeb stuck his head out of the passengers' window. Sarah froze.

"With that coat on you look like a giant bat. Maybe that's what you're going to turn into, The Bat Queen."

Chapter Six

Questions

Robert watched as Mr. Ferguson yanked Zeb back into the truck, whacking his head against the door frame. "Sarah, don't pay any attention to him. I'll be having a serious talk to Zeb's father about his son's atrocious behaviour."

The quiet drive to the facility was unnerving. Sarah handed her dad a sandwich that Michaela had packed for them. Unwrapping her sandwich, she picked away at the thick chunk of meat until it was gone. Her father watched her and smiled. Barbecue sauce was oozing out of the side of his mouth. She casually searched around the truck for a tissue or a rag to offer him. She stopped looking when she noticed her dad pushing the dark red sauce into his mouth with his finger. Catching her glance, he commented, "Michaela really knows how to make a great moose meat sandwich. Sarah, aren't you glad to be home? How could you stand that hospital food for so long? That must have been monotonous."

Her dad's forced smile confirmed that he wanted to talk about anything but what was really on his mind. Sarah didn't want to talk about it either. "The facility's food wasn't that bad. We even got some venison once. A native working with the guards butchered a deer that jumped over the animal fence and straight into a high voltage one. That was the best meal I had there. They did try hard to make me happy, but it really does feel great to be home."

As they turned off the highway, they could see men constructing a high chain link fence through the swamp. When they finally got to the gate, Sarah looked around. It was the first time she had good look at the outside of the research facility. The only signs it had warned of the high voltage electric fence, gave entry instructions and said 'no trespassing'. The facility had no name or anything to identify it. Using a noisy, gas powered cement mixer, a team of guards were busy constructing a third chain link fence around the perimeter. The spiral roll of barbed wire mounted on top of it told her that it wasn't designed for wildlife. The entire area around the building was paved over, including a roadway outside of the fence.

The three-story cement building had lines of narrow, barred, horizontal slits cut into it for windows. Workers were still installing the finishing touches to the manned dome-shaped turrets jutting out from all four corners of the roof. With cameras and antennas pointing in various directions, security was everywhere. Both the double main doors and solid receiving gates were made of steel. Three brightly coloured metal loops extended out from each doorway leading inside. Sarah turned to her father. "I thought the equipment inside was expensive, but this place is a fortress. How can Dr. Scott afford all this?"

"According to Duncan, he has investors with deep pockets."

Without seeing anyone, the gate started to open as a voice came over the speaker. "Mr. Douglas, you are cleared to enter. Please park in spot number eight, just right of the gate, then walk along the yellow path to the entranceway. Thank you."

As Robert put the truck into gear, three guards in shielded helmets exited the facility. By the time he drove through the fenced-off tunnel encircled with cameras and scanners and got parked, a guard was approaching the truck holding a thick wand with a key pad attached to the handle. Before they were allowed to get out, he had waved the wand over the entire exterior surface of the truck. Getting out, another guard walked beside them and escorted them through the loops while the third guard waited close by with an assault rifle over his shoulder. "Mr. Douglas, you're probably used to this by now. How's Little Sister doing?"

Robert couldn't see through the polarised visor and didn't even need to look at his name tag to know who it was. The shoulder flashings showing his clearance level, plus his size was enough. With a forced smile, he replied, "We had a problem with her bandages."

They waited as Duncan punched the security code into the control panel and for the heavy steel door to open. Entering a small closed off corridor, they stopped and waited as the outside door closed. Four cameras protected behind thick, glass shields were placed in the top corners. Sarah soberly waved into each of them as Duncan unarmed the locked corridor's interior door.

After taking off his helmet, Duncan ordered the accompanying guard to escort them to examination room 'C'. Dr. Scott met them halfway there and immediately dismissed the guard. "So, how's our prize patient doing?"

"Confused."

"What are you confused about?"

"Not knowing what is happening to me, I guess. Some kids are scared of me. They think I'm turning into a monster."

Opening the examining room's door Dr. Scott gestured Sarah in. "Sarah, don't worry about what other's think. A few months ago you were chair-bound and dying from cancer. Now you can walk and even run if you want. It's hard for people to accept strange and drastic changes, that's all. Now slip into a gown and knock on the door when you are done."

Sitting on the chair next to the door, Sarah pulled off her moccasins. She could overhear her dad talking in the hall. "I think the infection is getting worse. Some people even thought she was a relative of my neighbour. She's not even white, she's native. Sarah's skin tone and facial structure have transformed her into someone that nobody can recognize. Her protruding jaw bone alone is enough to make people question who she is. She doesn't look like any member of mine or her mother's family."

"Don't worry about it. We are monitoring her progress very closely. However, the experimental method we are using to eradicate her cancer apparently has some side effects. When Sarah first arrived, our priorities were to control the damage the creature had done, stabilize her cancer in order to keep her alive and then go back and fix any complication that had occurred. There were some complications that we didn't count on. We believe that they were probably caused by her body's rapid growth spurt, along with all the hormones released by the developmental stage she is in."

Robert leaned against the wall and said nothing.

Doctor Scott paced back and forth a couple times in front of him before continuing. "Cancer victims are not usually as youthful as Sarah. The substance we used was designed to repair the body at a cellular level. With the amount of cancerous cells Sarah had, it was that or just easing her suffering until it killed her."

Trying hard to keep his composure, the doctor further added, "We believe all the hormones running throughout her youthful maturing body simply confused the substance's concept of normality. Unfortunately, some small changes could become permanent, but not harmful to her health in any way. The good news is that the vast majority of changes should revert back to what they should be after we cleanse her system." The doctor watched Robert lean against the wall and scrunch up his face. Wanting to ease his mood, he added, "We both know that she would've been in the grave long before now without the treatment. Her last doctor gave her 'til Christmas. Now, it's spring."

Robert looked at Doctor Scott, "It has been half a year. Most cancer treatments are over by now."

The doctor stared at him. "This isn't chemotherapy. At the stage she was at, that wasn't even an option."

Sarah opened the door and blurted out. "So, I'll never look like Mom?"

They both looked straight at her as she finished tying her gown. Her father turned away to cover his emotions as Dr. Scott walked toward her. "No, you won't. But I can assure you that you will have a long, full life to live."

"But I'm not going to look like a bat, am I?"

"Where did you ever get that notion?"

"That's what people are thinking. I'm not going to turn into something like the creature that attacked me, am I? They're not like werewolves or vampires are they? I'm not stupid. I know that some of their blood had to have gotten into my system."

The doctor reached out and held Sarah's hands, "No. I can assure you that you will always be Sarah Douglas." He had a hard time not to chuckle. "There is a slight possibility that you may not resemble your parents when you get older, but you're not going to turn into one of those creatures, that is for sure. I would never allow that to happen."

The long, full examination Doctor Scott put Sarah through was much more thorough than normal. A full body CAT scan was done to get a three-dimensional view of every part of her body. Added to that, over a dozen vials of blood were collected along with various tissue samples from almost every part of her body. The worst of which was running a sample extractor down her throat to get a sample of her stomach lining. By the time the doctor was finished dressing her scars, Sarah was starting to nod off.

Doctor Scott sat down beside Robert in the lounge. "Once we are confident that all the cancer has been totally eradicated, we will finally be able to tackle and deal with the infection. We are almost at that point now. It is just a matter of a little more time. We've started some preliminary steps already, like the bandages."

"So this isn't just a remission? The cancer may be completely gone, for good?"

The doctor put his hand on Robert's shoulder. "Yes, and when we are sure, then we can concentrate on the infection. Remember what I had told you before, one step at a time. We can't judge how the treatment is going if too many factors are confusing the test results. I want her to leave this facility healthier than either one of us."

Robert butted in, "But what about the infection?"

"You'll just have to tolerate these changes she's going through a little longer. They may even get a lot worse before they start to improve. But remember, cancer first, then the infection. We have to keep our priorities straight."

Robert wasn't sure what to think. Were Sarah's transformations caused from the treatments or the infection? Does the doctor have a cure, or not?

Duncan carried Sarah to the truck and strapped her in. "Take good care of Little Sister for us. A lot of us have grown quite fond of her."

On the way home, Sarah fell fast asleep. Curiosity had gotten the better of Robert as he turned onto the roadway leading to the mine. Stopping at the last bend, he left his door ajar while he crept through the muddy forest towards the entrance. Mounds of melting snow mixed with dead twigs and thin layers of crystallised ice made it hard to be absolutely quiet. He was thankful of the small sheets of snow falling off of the spruce trees for masking his movements. As one of the guards came in sight, he froze solid. His helmet and uniform were identical to the ones used at the facility. Robert thought to himself, *Where do you get your money from, Dr. Scott? There's not an ounce of gold leaving that mine.* He counted five guards outside. Seeing lights coming out of the mine shaft, he knew that something was going on inside. He had no way of knowing how many more were in there. Climbing back into the truck, he looked over at Sarah and whispered, "Doc, what is it between you and them creatures?"

Pulling into their driveway, Robert turned to Sarah. "Sarah, wake up, we're home."

Sarah slowly opened her eyes as her dad rocked her back and forth. "What, what are you talking about?"

"Sarah, we're home. Do you want me to carry you into the house?"

"No, I'm okay. I'll walk." Sarah got out of the truck and yawned. Shaking her head, all of her senses woke up. It was dark outside, but she could hear and smell things like she never had before. "Dad, can I sit outside for a while before I go to bed? That little nap woke me up a bit."

"Sure, if you want to." He smiled at her, "Do you want some company?"

"No, I just want to enjoy being outside. That's all."

Her dad walked past her wearing a funny grin. "I'll come back out in a bit to make sure you don't fall asleep out here."

Sarah sat on the steps and listened to the truck's motor crackle as it cooled down. From out of the forest, she heard strange vivid cries, grunts and moans from various creatures. All forms of life, death and renewal were echoing from the bush. Everything around her seemed alive. As she deeply breathed in the night air, her mouth started to water and her stomach turn. She hadn't eaten much all day and there was something in the night air that made her hungry.

Going into the house, she opened the refrigerator. She could almost taste everything she touched before it got close to her nose. The leftover roast moose was the only thing in the refrigerator that really interested her. Taking it over to the kitchen table, she sat down and pulled off pieces of meat and shoved them into her mouth.

"You should've eaten more of the sandwich that Michaela made for you." Standing in the doorway, her father caught her with a full mouth. "I was just about to go out and get you."

After she finished swallowing, she replied, "The bread and sauce just never appealed to me, but this meat is great. Dad, I think I've been cooped up inside too long. Outside I smelled and heard things that I can't remember experiencing before tonight." Looking down at the meat, she had to ask, "Dad, will you still love me if I become a deformed monster?"

Robert walked over to her. "Of course I will." Wrapping his arms around her, he added, "You'll always be my beautiful baby girl."

Sarah rested her head on his arm. "I can feel myself changing. The scars are not going away. I can feel them growing."

Robert felt a lump in his throat. After taking a cleansing breath, he swallowed it down and answered, "Nonsense, the doctor told me that you're getting better."

Sarah turned in her chair and hugged her father's waist. "But, my skin gets really itchy just before it starts to spread. I don't know if the doctor can stop it. I can feel it spreading and not just where I was attacked. I feel it in every part of my body. It's like the creature is growing inside me and slowly taking over my body."

Tears ran down his face as he tried to console her. "That's just the anti-cancer agents you are feeling. Soon the doctors will be flushing that stuff out of you and returning you to normal."

Chapter Seven

Growth

Dr. Scott stared at the CAT-scanned image of Sarah's brain. "I've never seen anything like it." Glancing at a couple of earlier scans, he added, "Her entire brain is restructuring itself."

Dr. Roger Hamilton walked up behind him. Shaking his head and feeling dumfounded, he told him, "The shock pads we built into the bandages should be shorting out the chips. Instead, the number of cells are actually increasing. The cells should've been dying off by now."

"They could be evolving somehow." After thinking for a few seconds, Doctor Scott added, "Or, maybe we are treating the wrong area. If the cells are content with the infected sites, they may be concentrating their attack on other parts of her body. We could be just wasting our time trying to treat reprogrammed stem cells."

"But how can the cells still be multiplying? We had eliminated the nutrients that the cells need to reproduce from her diet before she even left here."

"Her body is probably reabsorbing the nutrients in her liver, but that isn't our main concern." Dr. Scott clinched his fingers and tapped his thumbs together. "The cells are confused. They don't know what they should be doing. That's evident from the number of mutations."

"But none of the data on the chips changed?"

"They are being selective about what codes to use, and which strains of chromosomes and genetic toggles it's flipping off and on." Doctor Scott walked around with his hands behind his neck. "We designed the cells to survive. They don't want to kill off their host. The chips are choosing the DNA strains that they believe will give the host the best chance of survival."

Roger sat in his chair with his head tilted back. "How, by trial and error?"

"Sort of. Sarah had talked about having pains and tingles in different places throughout her body. I've been jotting them down in my notes. I've been finding minute changes in those locations. Some go away and some flourish. It is like they send out a few field workers before they decide what they want. Unless we can make the cells accept Sarah's DNA as normal, all of the changes could become permanent."

"So as far as Sarah is concerned, we may have already failed."

"No, we just got a better subject to work with. We need to get a full MRI done on her the next time she comes in. I have to know how her brain is functioning. They must've constructed some kind of nerve centre from which they can evaluate the changes they have made." He turned to Dr. Hamilton, "What's left of that creature's brain? The one the guards shot."

"It was partially crushed on one side, but we preserved everything that remained." The doctor turned around and left the room.

Doctor Scott studied Sarah's latest CAT scan with a magnifying glass and compared it to one of the creatures that he had on file. Doctor Scott turned to Roger as he re-entered the room with the creature's brain. "The corpus callosum of both of them are very similar and the cerebellum of both are unusually oversized." Dr. Scott pointed at a small, dark red oval shape just in front of Sarah's cerebellum. "This is strange. I have never seen a growth like this before. Does the creature have anything similar?"

While examining the brain, Doctor Hamilton twisted the right side of his face. "There's something here too. We must have previously dismissed it thinking it was a blood clot, or maybe a tumour. No brain that I know of has an appendage there."

Doctor Scott took a minute and scribbled down a list on a piece of paper. "You're not paid to assume, I pay you to think and research." Slamming his hand down on the counter with the piece of paper in it, Dr. Scott added, "I want you to re-examine the creature and compare it to all of Sarah Douglas' deformities that I've put on this list. I also want another series of DNA tests done on the samples taken from Sarah and compare them to the creature's. I need to confirm that no mistakes were made. If they were, I want to know what they were. I also want to know just how rapidly her body is actually changing. Don't fail me this time. You know what happens to the credibility of those I've fired. Instead of retiring early, you may find yourself working in central Africa."

Roger followed Doctor Scott to the viral research lab to check the developments of the next batch of vaccine. The specialist, Dr. Henry Shaw, saw the doctor enter and quickly stood up. "This may be futile. There must be another way to control the cells' ability to reproduce. The last vaccine we injected into her liver caused the cells to adjust their anti-virus and destroy the vaccine at an even faster rate. Cells shouldn't be able to adjust this quickly. It is like they're at war. The need to survive has channelled all their resources into fortifying their resistance. We have to re-evaluate how we can control them. We can filter out the cells from her blood, but not the rest of her."

Doctor Scott had stood back and listened to the doctor's frustration. As the doctor stood there, he raised his hands in the air. "We can't get the cells to even survive in test animals, yet we can't control them in Sarah. Right now she is the best and only way we have to preserve our cells. We lucked out with Terry and lightning doesn't often strike twice."

Roger butted in. "Do the two of them have anything in common?"

"You mean, besides dying?" It didn't take Doctor Scott long to think of something else they had in common. "I know. Neither one of them had any immune system left."

"Maybe that is it. Their bodies had thrown in the towel and left a power vacuum that the cells exploited. Their bodies weren't capable of fighting them off.   By the time they were, the cells were well established.   Remember that in both cases, we were pumping large amounts of nutrients into them to promote the cells' reproduction."

"That doesn't explain the bats."

Roger smiled, "Maybe the colony was infected with rabies. That would've knocked their immune system for a loop."

"Still, until we can successfully keep the cells alive, Sarah is our only source. Remember that even the very first batch of cells that managed to self-reproduce was a fluke. So far, we've never been able to create another one." Dr. Scott started to pace the floor. After shaking his head, he turned to Roger and continued. "We must offset the balance of power inside her. We need to give her body a chance to fight back." Looking a Roger, he grinned. "What we need is a filter of some kind that acts like an artificial liver. Something that absorbs the nutrients the cells need to reproduce."

Roger folded his hands behind his head and stared at the ceiling. He nodded his head. "We could do that." A couple seconds later, he added, "I'd need a lot of help."   Looking at Doctor Shaw, he said, "Henry, I may need your help."

"Fine."

Behind his back, Doctor Scott tightly gripped his hands together. "There may be one more complication. Remember the growth we found in Sarah's brain?   I'm sure that is what is adjusting and reprogramming the cells' behaviour. Most of the blood going into the brain has to pass through it. We may have to remove it."

"Brain surgery, that's much too risky. We could lose our patient along with the cells." Roger thought a while longer. "Are you finding any luck at reproducing the cells that we had collected from her?"

"No, and it's getting worse. I hoped that they would've shown us some results before they died off. Even with our best efforts, they were all dead within hours. We are missing something. We had better success before the cells started to mutate. Now, every sample we take is like dealing with a new life-form."

Doctor Hamilton turned to Doctor Scott, "It has almost been half of a year since the attack. Why the explosion of activity all of a sudden?"

"It takes time to build up an army. Until now, the cells were like snipers. Now they are finally becoming a unified attack force with a seasoned general leading the way." Doctor Scott placed his hand on the confused doctor's shoulder. "They were just waiting for the right time. A good general doesn't squander his resources."

Returning to his office, Dr. Scott pulled out a bottle of whiskey and filled his coffee cup half full. Taking a gulp, he leaned back in his chair and closed his eyes. After a deep breath, he opened his eyes and found Duncan standing in front of him. Surprised, he dropped his cup. Jumping out of his chair he blurted, "Now what do you want?"

"Sir, one of our cameras caught Robert Douglas walking around outside of the mine. He knows my men. He is also on the list of suspects that we believe had poisoned the mine. This could complicate everything."

Chapter Eight

The colony

The next morning Sarah eagerly devoured several pieces of back bacon and two poached eggs. Out of habit she took a bite of her toast. It tasted revolting. To her it was like eating ground up wood. With her finger she pulled it out of her mouth and placed it at the side of her plate. She bent over and sniffed the hash browns. They had been fried in the bacon fat and the meaty flavour made them tolerable.

After breakfast, Mary came over to watch her. Throughout the day, she could see Sarah's depressed demeanor slowly worsen. Sarah refused to do anything. She avoided the windows and insisted that all the shades remain down. She didn't want anyone to see her. She spent the day wandering around the house being tormented by the constant itching of her scars and the strange feelings that were being produced in other parts of her body. In her mind, the itching was no longer a sign of healing. It was a creature growing inside of her, gnawing away at her body, trying to get out. The feeling of its constant presence consumed her thoughts.

Curiously, she used the Internet to investigate various bats and the other creatures that dwell in the mines and caves of Northern Ontario. Nothing she could find was even close. The creature she envisioned resembled a huge, dark, whisker-less cat-like animal with huge, folding bat-like wings sprouting from its back. Bats only have two legs, plus their wings. Only mythical dragons, gargoyles, demons and fictional creatures were designed that way. *I wonder what creatures had started all the myths?*

Discouraged, Sarah curled up with her blanket on the couch. Even in her sleep, the creature haunted her dreams. She dreamt that she was in her wheelchair beside the picnic tables, at the side of The Depot. Zeb and his friends suddenly appeared and started to tease her by chanting, "Bat Queen, Bat Queen," over and over. One by one, they reached into the oil drum that they used for garbage and started to throw crunched up paper and leftover food at her. She wheeled her chair to face them and screamed, "Stop it!" They wouldn't stop. As she continued to scream at them, her skin started to peel away and her clothes ripped apart. Her body transformed into the monster that attacked her. Jumping into the, air she unfolded her wings in front of Zeb. She laughed as he stumbled backwards and fell into a deep puddle of mud. Instead of tormenting her any further, he was terrified. Soaring high in the air, she spotted her dad, Michaela and Mary all standing in the middle of an open meadow. As her shadow fell over them, she could see their terrified faces. Confused about why they would be scared of her, she yelled to them, "It's me Sarah." Suddenly her dad raised the barrel of his rifle.

Sarah almost jumped off of couch shivering. Sweat glued a few of her eyelashes to her eyes and caused them to water. With the blanket wrapped around her, she went to the bathroom to wash her face. Turning the water on, she stared into the mirror thinking, "Will everyone turn against me?" Splashing her face, the bandages that were already soaked with sweat began to peel back. Looking around for Mary, Sarah closed and locked the bathroom door. She wasn't scared anymore. She spent almost all her life being afraid. She had been terrified of everything, the teasing, the adverse reactions to the cancer treatments, dying and mostly being a burden to the people that loved her. *If I'm becoming a freak, I'll just leave and look after myself and never come back. Everyone would be better off without me. I've already put them through enough.*

Peeling back the bandage on her right cheek, all she saw was a thin blanket of soft silky hair on top of darkened skin. There was no scar. *So I'm a little hairy, I can learn how to shave. There are plenty of treatments for getting rid of hair and lots of flesh-tone makeup out there.* Sarah stared at the mirror some more. After a couple deep breaths she decided, *Now for the bad one.* The bandage that covered her right ear had always bothered her the most. It was quite tender, along with being itchy. Holding her breath, she tore it off. Her enlarged ear lobes had attached themselves to the side of her head. The top of her ear was folded over the rest and held in place with some tape. Carefully removing the tape, a huge dark brown ear unravelled to over twice its normal size. Gasping, she held her hands over her mouth. After taking a deep breath, she lowered her arms and stared into the mirror. 'Bonk, bonk, bonk.' The knock on the bathroom door made her jump.

"Are you all right in there?"

"I'm fine. I'll be done in a minute." Sarah watched the door knob and was relieved that Mary didn't attempt to open it. Quickly she taped her ear and bandages back on the best she could. Covering her head in her blanket, she unlocked the door and curled back up on the couch. "Mary, I'm out now, you can use the bathroom if you want."

Sarah heard the bathroom door click shut. Getting up quickly, she quietly went into her dad's room and wiggled opened one of her mom's stuffed dresser drawers. Fingering through her clothes, she found the heavy dark blue pullover sweater with a hood that she was looking for.

Giving out a sigh, she finished tying the hood's drawstrings at the sound of the toilet flushing.

"Sarah, where did you go?"

Strolling out of her dad's room, Sarah forced a smile. "I thought I would be warmer in one of Mom's old sweaters."

"Did something happen to your bandages? You left the tape out." Pulling out the right side of Sarah's hood, Mary saw the extra strips of tape on the specialized gauze.

"They started coming loose, so I put more tape on them. I don't want to go to the facility for every little thing."

Mary knew it was a lie. She crossed her arms and breathed out a heavy sigh. For the rest of the afternoon, Sarah pretended to be cold and kept the sweater on. It was hard for her to convince her dad not to rush her back to the facility. She stuck to her story and added, "I just felt a little cold and I'm afraid of getting sick." For eight years he had been terrified of her getting any kind of infection. She could see the agony and worry it caused in his face. Lying to her dad about what she had done was tough. It was both wrong and cruel, but she felt that she had to do it.

Spending the evening trying to avoid both her dad and Michaela, Sarah went to bed early. Instead of going to the bathroom to relieve herself, she ignored the slight pressure and had a glass of water instead. Leaving her mom's sweater on, she put on her pajama bottoms and curled up in bed.

The clock read eleven-thirty when the pressure from her full bladder forced her to wake up. Putting her ear to her door, she listened for any sounds. Michaela was starting a new job in the morning and had gone to bed early. Her father was normally asleep before ten. After relieving the pressure, she got dressed. Sarah quietly stuffed as much food as she could carry into her dad's camping backpack. Afterwards she went to the storage closet between the kitchen and bathroom and packed a couple blankets, matches, camping supplies, hatchet, hunting knife and anything else she thought she could use. With barely a creak, she left the house in her mom's long black coat and a pair of Michaela's gloves.

Sarah had never gone very far into the bush. At first she was too young, then the risk of her getting an infection made it too dangerous, then she was stuck in a wheelchair. She was surrounded by bush all her life but never knew what it was like to wander freely inside it, except from the books she read and the TV.

The Gremlin Mine was the only shelter she knew how to find. She had nothing left to fear from the creatures. Deep inside, she felt that she was one of them. The mine was big enough that even if anyone looked for her, she could simply hide in one of the crevices that cut into its walls. After four hours of walking along the road and crouching behind shrubs as vehicles went by, she made it to the side road that led to the old mine. Once away from the main road, she sat down in the middle of the road, untied her hood and pulled off her bandages. As she handled them, for the first time she could feel the pulsating shock that they were giving out. With both hands, she ripped them apart. Throughout the bandages were wires connected to a series of flat batteries and a tiny computer card.

Running her fingers across the soft velvety fur growing on her cheek, Sarah's hand rose to her enlarged right ear. Sitting there, she listened to all the unusual sounds that surrounded her. She was amazed that she could smell the ferns growing just off the side of the road a little further down. She knew that she made the right decision. "It was one thing to look after a child that was sick, another to harbor and protect a freakish monster."

Moaning as she got up, she bent over and rubbed her aching legs. A little over an hour and a half later, she saw the dim lights glowing from the mine. All she wanted to do was relax and get some more sleep. As a guard walked out, Sarah knew her instantly. "So this is Laurie's punishment for letting me duck into the elevator. But guarding an old mine? That's silly."

She took off the bright red backpack and coat. Putting the pack back on first, she concealed it by draping the coat over it. Creeping closer, Sarah grew more curious. The mine, the creature, her changes and now the guards. *Am I a patient, or a research animal?* She thought for a moment longer. *Well, if I get caught, the worst that could happen to me is that I'll get sent back to the facility.*

Spotting all the other guards huddling around a small camp stove, she followed Laurie as she went back into the mine. Staying just out of her lantern's beam, Sarah navigated her way in. She stepped only when Laurie stepped to avoid her footsteps from being heard in the echoing tunnel. It was like the games she played at the facility. Her antics had caused the guards to constantly look over their shoulders to make sure she never slipped away from them.

By the time Laurie reached the cavern, Sarah's shorter legs left her still deep within the tunnel. Then she heard some talking echoing behind her. She got on her hands and knees and felt her way along the side of the tunnel.

In the distance she saw several lights approaching her. With noise coming from both directions, she scrambled to the opening leading into the cavern. Three people in white coveralls were assembled close to the middle under a series of lights shining down on several tables of papers and various objects. She waited for the guards in the cavern to look away. The echoing noise behind her grew loud enough to cover her movement. Scooting along the cavern walls, she easily disappeared into the shadows.

Crawling behind the abandoned mining equipment that had been shoved against the wall, Sarah tied up her hood and used her coat as a blanket. Her long, busy night caught up to her as she crouched there and nodded off to sleep. Inside the mine she had no idea what time it was when two men walked by her talking. When she heard the words "Little Sister," her enlarged right ear perked up and twisted beneath her hood.

"The night shift found more skeletons like the creature that infected her. They were buried under piles of rocks. If it wasn't for the rocks looking out of place, they would never have found them. They must have been young, because the creature we carried out of here before was much larger."

"Where did they find the bodies?"

"They were in the shaft next to the one that the doctor told us to search last week. I bet you that guy isn't telling us a quarter of what he knows. His instincts are too good to be plain guesswork."

"I know. He doesn't tell anyone his secrets and I bet you there are tons of them."

Sarah got up and followed them. With her coat covering her backpack, they led her through a long maze of tunnels. Between their constant yakking and shuffling their feet, they made it almost too easy for her to conceal her movements. It was only when another pair of guards met up with them that she became scared. She knew that they were probably heading to the main cavern and would have to pass her. Quickly, she scooted back and hid in a crossing tunnel. The four stood there yakking away, swapping some stories and wild speculations. *When are they going to start moving?*

As she stood there listening to their gossip, a strange scent overwhelmed her. It came from further down the tunnel she had slipped into. Knowing the men outside couldn't hear her, she felt her way down the side tunnel. Approaching a fork, she heard high pitched clicking sounds. Sarah felt strange. She wasn't frightened, but was comforted by the sounds and a strange odour. Driven purely by her senses, she felt her way along the walls of the pitch dark tunnels until the odour encircled her. Seeming to come from nowhere, she ran her hands up and down the walls. She felt a wide crevice next to the bottom edge of the side of the tunnel. Laying down, she put her ear to the opening. The sounds were even louder.

Taking off her backpack, she looked for her flashlight. She couldn't find it. Instead, she took out a book of matches and a candle from one of the side pockets. After lighting the candle, she shoved the matches into her pocket and bent down to look inside the crevice. She couldn't see how far it went. It was too deep. Holding the candle ahead of her in one hand and dragging her backpack with the other, she began crawling inside the shallow crevice using her knees and elbows like a lizard. There was no headroom to spare, but lots of space at her side to swing her backpack forward. The clicking sound grew stronger. She stopped and looked around. The candle flickered in front of her. The tip of the flame was pointing straight at her. Fresh air was being drawn in from somewhere ahead.

Twitching her nose from all the dust, she sneezed. The clicking noise stopped. The crevice became silent. Twisting around, she smelled the air in every direction. It was worse than the boys' gym lockers. Again, the dust filled up her nose and she had to sneeze. The bombardment of echoing high-pitched clicking startled her. She twisted about and tried to turn around. As she slid her hips over a fallen beam, the lower half of her body slipped into a hole. With her backpack wrapped around one arm, she grabbed the wooden beam. Her legs flailed about, trying to find something to latch onto. There was nothing. As pieces of rotten wood crumbled in her hands, she slid deeper into the hole. The strap of her backpack got caught on a large splinter of wood. Sarah could feel her legs suspended in air. Her weight was more than the wood could handle. Plummeting downward, she landed on her side in a small cavern.

Unharmed, she stood up. She lit another candle from the side pocket of the backpack. She slowly stood up as she shaded the flame until it grew and engulfed the wick. Fear started to overcome her as she looked around. A stack of cleaned bones of various types and sizes were piled off to one side. Shocked, her hands jerked. Hot wax spilled and burned her fingers. She dropped the candle. It went out before it hit the ground.

Spotting the glowing ember at the end of the wick, she picked up the candle and relit it as fast as her fumbling hand could strike the match. Dark shadows were all around her. As they crept towards her, the flickering candle light was enough to illuminate the huge, round, cat-like eyes, elongated face and bright, glistening teeth of the creature leading the advancing horde.

Chapter Nine

Discovery

Sarah looked around the cavern as about three dozen creatures inched their way towards her. As they got closer, their heads started to rock from side to side. Moving the candle from one hand to the other in order see if there was any place she could retreat to, Sarah noticed the creatures' heads move with the flickering light. It was the candle that they were fascinated by, not her. Sticking it into the ground, she slowly stepped backwards. She held her breath as a few creatures slowly crept around her to get closer to the flickering candle.

Even as they surrounded it, fleeting flickers of light made thier way through. Sarah studied her surroundings the best she could. The cavern was a dead end. There were only two ways out: the hole in the ceiling and the tunnel that was blocked by the creatures. She slowly took a step towards the nearest wall. The air flowing through the tunnel behind the creatures meant there had to be another opening somewhere down it. These creatures couldn't survive without another exit. Sarah rubbed against one of them as she took another step. It looked up at her with its head twisted to one side. After briefly smelling her leg, it sauntered away. Sarah's breathing started to return to normal. *They're not interested in her, at least not yet.*

Sarah's eyes were getting accustomed to the dim light. Even by a single candle shaded by winged creatures, she could see that the cavern was man made. Not knowing how long the candle would last, she took the time to survey the creatures' lair. The crevice that she had crawled along was actually part of a collapsed tunnel. The support columns had been eaten away by the guano piled next to them. The strong, wide cross beams had dropped onto piles of rubble and shored up the narrow crack. The hole she had fallen into was just a short shaft leading down into an old, hand-forged series of tunnels. 'V' shaped pick marks dotted the walls instead of the smoother, long chiselled groves on the walls of the newer mine tunnels. *This pace was dug out well before Dad's time, maybe even Grandpa's.*

Sarah suddenly got a chill. "Nobody will ever find me here." The words coming out of Sarah's mouth felt strange. She had run away so no one could find her. Her mind raced. *Maybe I should have just committed myself to medical research and had Doctor Scott do whatever he wanted with me. Outside of being his prisoner, he never treated me that bad.*

As a curious creature waved his hand directly over the wick, the candle was extinguished. Sarah heard the creature roar in pain. Others joined in on what sounded like a schoolyard tussle. Growls and groans echoed about the cavern. Not knowing where to go, or even what to do, Sarah sat down inside of a small depression in the wall. She opened her backpack and started to rummage through it. Finally finding her flashlight mixed in between cans of food, she put it into her coat pocket. Unsheathing her father's hunting knife, she gripped it tightly in one hand. With the straps of the backpack wrapped around her other arm, she held it in front of her like a shield. She felt that the backpack would at least give her a modest wall of protection from the creatures.

Every once and a while, one or two would venture over to her, take a sniff and then scoot away. Sarah felt that she had become some kind of curiosity, an amusement for them. It wasn't until later that she had a clue why. Within an hour Sarah could hear a lot of hustling coming from somewhere down the tunnel. As the ruckus got more and more angry, she took out her flashlight and shone it on the commotion. They were like a pack of hyenas in a wild feeding frenzy on the remains of a deer's carcass. They all stared into the light and screamed in pain. The sudden burst of bright light was too much for their dilated pupils. Sarah knew what she had done and turned off the light. She didn't want to get them angry. Shortly afterwards, the snarling frenzy started calming down. It was over very quickly and everything got quiet.

Taking a risk, Sarah turned on her flashlight and shone it above their heads. All that was left of the deer were a few small chunks of hide. Sarah looked closer at the scattered bones and noticed maggots squirming around on the dirt. *The creatures didn't kill it. They are scavengers. Is that why they are leaving me alone? They want me to die first.*

The creatures were all curled up with full stomachs. One of them woke as Sarah stood up. She took one step towards the tunnel and it filled the cavern with a high piercing scream. All the creatures were instantly awake. Sarah took another step and they all gathered in front of her hissing. Three took to the air. They formed a circle and swooped down at her face as they passed her. Sarah blocked the first one with her backpack and slashed at the second with the knife. It caught it by surprise. Blood ran down the length of its wing. It landed on all fours and immediately turned and snarled at her. Two more creatures leaped into the air and landed on her backpack. With a firm grasp on it, they took swipes at Sarah's face with their claws. She stepped backwards against the wall and held her backpack as far away from her as she could. As the creatures started to climb over the top of the backpack, she smashed it against the wall. Suddenly, the two creatures jumped off and sat in front of her snarling. Sarah sat down and the snarls got quieter and quieter. *They don't want me to leave. They are not going to let me out of here.*

******

"Mary, I'm running late. I know it's Saturday, but I can't refuse the overtime, I need the money. Sarah is still in bed. Just let her sleep if that is what she wants to do." Robert turned to Michaela. "I love you and I'll see you later. I gotta go."

A cloud of dust followed Robert as he left the driveway. Michaela stood beside Mary and watched him race down the road. "I'll go up and check on Sarah before Kristofer picks me up for work. I still have a few more minutes."

Mary walked over to the counter and opened the bread. "I'll make your lunch for you so you won't have to race out of here like your father."

Michaela knocked on Sarah's door. "Sarah, are you awake?" Peeking in, she saw Sarah's empty bed. Walking from room to room, she called her name. In the kitchen, Mary had barely buttered the bread before being startled by Michaela's scream. "She not here!"

Mary ran to the hallway leading to the bedrooms. "She has to be here. Did you check the bathroom? I know she sometimes likes to go into your mother's closet. Did you check there?"

Michaela yelled back, "Yes, yes, I checked everywhere."

Mary put her hands on top of her head. "Maybe she snuck into the living room? She likes to curl up on the sofa."

Michaela ran passed Mary. "I'll double check."

Mary followed her as fast as she could. "Is she there?"

"NO!"

"I'll check outside. You check the basement and the rest of the house."

Kristofer pulled into the driveway to pick up Michaela for work. Mary stood in front of the house and waved him away. "Not today. Not today."

"She can't call off. I just got her the job. I realise it is only part time, but it could led into full time hours come summer."

"Sarah's disappeared and we have to find her."

Kristofer got out of the van and ran over to her. "What do you mean, disappeared?"

"She wasn't in her bed this morning. We've searched everywhere for her." Mary frantically waved her arms. "She's not here."

Michaela ran out the door and flung her arms around Kristofer, crying. "She's gone."

"People don't disappear right out of their own homes. Someone must have seen something."

Michaela cried on Kristofer's shoulder. "She's been kidnapped?"

Mary spoke up. "I'm calling the police." Before anyone could speak, she turned and marched to the door.

Within twenty minutes a cruiser pulled into the Douglas driveway. Two officers got out and walked over to the trio sitting on the front steps. The front of Kristofer's coat was soaked in Michaela's tears as she clung her arms around him. Mary sat up straight as the officers inquired, "So what's wrong here? We got a call that someone is missing. Is that right?"

Mary stood up. "Yes, Sarah Douglas is missing. She was taken right out of her bed."

"Have you searched everywhere that she normally likes to go?"

"Of course we have! Do you think that I would have called you if we didn't? Do you take us for fools?"

The poor officer stepped back from the wild Mary. "Of course not. I just have to ask."

The other officer spoke in a low voice. "We'll need more details. Was she having any problems lately? Could she have simply run away?"

Michaela brushed back a stream of tears and spoke up. "The only one that could have taken her is Doctor Scott. He runs a secret research facility on the old logging road just south of Devil's Claw Ridge."

The two officers looked at each other. "What research facility? There isn't anything like that around here."

"Oh yes there is! And ever since the party fiasco in the old Bear Den Mine, they are the ones that have been treating her. Doctor Scott is the only person that seems to have any reason to take her."

"And what reason would that be?"

"I don't know, but something is going on there."

A rolling cloud of dust rose from the road as Sarah's frightened father sped into the driveway and jumped out. "Where's Sarah? What happened to her?"

The young constable walked over to him. "We just arrived, but we will find her. We're going to need to search the surrounding area first. Maybe she wandered off in order to be by herself for a while. She could have gotten lost. Sometimes a person can get disoriented after taking only a few steps into the woods. It's easily done."

Robert scratched his head. Looking at the forest surrounding them, he answered, "Sarah doesn't know the woods at all. If she went in there, she could easily get lost. But she's a smart girl. I can't see going in there."

Within two hours, the police had organized dozens of volunteers into long search lines combing the area. Fanned out along the road in both directions, two lines headed south, and another two headed north. They examined every piece of debris, broken twig, and anything that could signify a trail. Michaela and Kristofer helped in the search. Michaela's jeans and sleeves were ripped and soaked by the dense swampy underbrush growing in the ditch along the roadway. Kristofer yelled at her, "Get out of there. She won't go in that thick stuff."

"How do you know?" Michaela worked her way around a small tree. "She could've fallen and slid under some thickets." While pulling her foot out of some mud, she added. "Someone's got to check it out."

Kristofer ploughed his way through the brush towards her. "You're not dressed for it. You should be on the road in case they find something."

"You sound like that stupid cop. I have to do something more than just wait around watching everyone else do all the work. She's my sister."

A man ran down the road towards Michaela's line. He bent over to catch his breath and said, "We need Michaela Douglas. We may have found something."

Michaela peered through the brush. "I'm Michaela. What did you find?"

"Footprints. We need to know if they are Sarah's. We need someone who can identify the prints."

"Find Mary Powless. She made the moccasins that Sarah was wearing."

Michaela and Kristofer anxiously waited as the police rushed Mary to the discovery. Everyone crowded around the road above the find as the police led Mary to a long, thin section of grass that was peeled off the side of the ditch. They were too wide and flat to be from a hoofed animal. There were no signs of any claws or toes to indicate a bear, or any other kind of forest creature big enough to cause the deep, wide skid marks. At the bottom of the ditch, the branches on the underside of the brush were broken inward. Someone had rolled underneath them. Two officers stood a few metres away from the brush. As Mary approached, one of them yelled, "Down here. We found some really clear footprints in some soft mud."

Kristofer helped Mary down the side of the steep ditch. Once down, they worked their way towards the officers. "Are these Sarah's footprints?"

Mary took a quick look at them, "Yes, they're Sarah's"

He looked at Mary. Puzzled by her quick response, he asked, "How can you be so sure?"

"I see those prints everywhere I go." Mary stepped back and pointed at the mud. "See, they are almost the same as mine. The rubber I sewed onto the bottom of Sarah's moccasins came from the same lawnmower tire as mine. Unless someone else had made moccasins that size from the same lawnmower, these tracks have to be Sarah's."

Michaela caught up to them as they tracked Sarah's footprints back onto the road. One officer turned to the other, "She's running away. She probably saw a car and didn't want to get caught."

In the quiet air their voices travelled to Michaela. Her reply was swift. "Not Sarah. She had no reason to run away from us."

The officer turned to her. "It happens."

Further down the road, the same thing. Sarah slid into the ditch and hid, only to climb back up onto the road again. After reporting the finding, the two officers looked at Michaela and then at each other, not saying a word. She knew what they were thinking and repeated, "Sarah had no reason to run away."

Mary got between Michaela and Kristofer and gave her a hug. "We'll find her. With all that has happened to her lately, she could be trying to run away from herself. She's confused and scared."

"I know." Michaela started crying on Mary's shoulder. "But she was finally getting better. What went wrong?"

******

Detective Samuel Arnold got off of the phone and sat down with Robert at the kitchen table. His eyes saw Robert's gaze at the bottle of Seagram's 83 whiskey on the shelf above the microwave. "It won't help. We need all the help you can give us right now."

"If we killed all those creatures like we should've, none of this would have happened."

"We? Were you one of the men that poisoned the mine?"

Robert stood up and looked straight at him. "We, this whole community, this whole region. Everyone who lived near or worked in that mine was terrified of them. They killed a few of my friends inside of that mine." Robert took a deep breath and sat back down. "I wish that I could take credit for poisoning the mine, but I can't. I was at the doctor's with Sarah in Sioux Lookout when it happened and I can prove it."

"The device had a timer on it."

"It did? That's news to me."

"It was mentioned several times in the local newspaper."

Robert looked at the officer and spread his fingers over the table. Looking at them, he replied, "I guess I never read those particular articles."

Detective Arnold knew his prodding was going nowhere and changed the subject. "So what do those creatures have to do with Sarah's disappearance?"

"Everything. Remember the party that went on in the mine last fall?"

"Yeah, so?"

"Sarah was there and one of the creatures attacked her. Since then, she's never been the same. At first, the doctors that the new mine owners assigned to help her cured her cancer. Then the infection that those creatures had injected into her started to spread. The doctors tried to tell me that it was just a side effect of the treatments, but I don't buy it. Cancer was one thing, doctors are coming up with new ways to fight cancer all the time, but the venom those creatures had poisoned her with is another thing altogether. Nobody is spending any money on curing that. Those doctors can't help her. She's smart. She probably figured that out."

After jotting down what Robert had told him, the detective tapped his pen on his pad. He paced the kitchen floor a few times before turning to Robert. "You said that the doctors had rid your daughter of cancer? What kind?"

"Leukemia. She had been chair-bound for years. She had gone through three sessions of chemotherapy and a failed bone marrow transplant before the attack. The doctors at the facility had got her out of her wheelchair and walking within a matter of months. It was like a miracle. I've tried to read everything I could lay my hands on about all the cancer research going on. There were no treatments in any journal, book or magazine that came close to what they were doing."

The detective tapped his pen some more. "I've a niece with leukemia. Where is this facility and what is the name of the doctor in charge of it? I'm very curious about this miracle cure of his."

"The facility is off of the old logging road south of the Bear Den Mine and the doctor's name is Scott. I'm sorry, I can't remember his first name."

"I've hunted on that road before. It's been a few years, but I can't remember seeing anything that resembles a medical building. In fact, I don't remember seeing any buildings at all."

"It's back in there quite a long ways. It doesn't have any signs or anything like that. It's privately owned and they are very protective about their research. There is a huge amount of big money involved. They even have their own professionally trained security guards and an electrified fence. I guess they don't want anyone messing around with their research." Robert stared at the detective. "Would you?"

"Maybe not. Especially if they actually have a cure for cancer." Detective Arnold folded his arms behind him and clasped his hands together. "Maybe, just maybe." Stopping in mid-thought, he turned and reached for the door. "Mr. Douglas, I think I know where your daughter is."

"Where?"

"The only place that gave her hope."

Chapter Ten

The Wall

It had been over twelve hours since Sarah had eaten and her stomach was starting to growl. In total darkness, she could only feel her way through her backpack. Pulling out a can of sardines, she started to quietly peel back the lid. She could feel one of the creatures breathe against the back of her hand. Pulling the can tightly against her breast, she finished opening it. The creature climbed onto her backpack. Sarah felt its warm breath against her face as she drew the can close to her mouth. Its hand tried to gently pull Sarah's hands away from the can. Its fingers were soft. She resisted and the creature tried a little harder. This time, she could feel the tips of its sharp claws.

Sarah scooped almost half the can into her mouth with her fingers. Then she quickly put her hand over the open can. As she chewed, she could feel the creature licking the escaping juices off of her chin. The creature's tongue was rough and at the same time very gentle. Sarah slowly placed the can on the floor. The creature quickly grabbed it. As it finished eating the remainder of the sardines, Sarah could hear more creatures waking up. A sudden low snarl erupted from the creature next to her. The others backed away. Shortly after, Sarah could feel the warmth of the creature as it snuggled up next to her.

******

Detective Arnold rolled his jeep to a stop outside of the research facility. Duncan walked over to the shut gate. The detective slowly got out of his vehicle and approached it. Standing a few steps behind the gate, Duncan said, "Good morning officer. How can I help you?"

"I'd like to talk to whoever is in charge."

"For what purpose?"

"We have a missing child and believe that she might have come here. Apparently she was a former patient."

"She?" Duncan twitched the side of his mouth. "I'm sure that you are mistaken."

Detective Arnold reached out his arm and almost grabbed the gate. The large 'Electrified Fence' sign caught his eye. In a fury, he slapped his arms to his side. "I want to see whoever is in charge of this research facility right now!" Grabbing his notepad from his side pocket, he read out, "A Doctor Scott, I was told that he is in charge here."

Duncan smiled. "Sorry, no one is allowed in here without proper clearance."

Detective Arnold stared at the smug, disfigured guard. "We'll see."

As the detective got into his jeep, Duncan grinned. "Come back any time."

Doctor Scott watched the surveillance monitor as the jeep sped away. He immediately went to his office. "Did you hear? Little Sister has run away. There is only one place around here that she could have gone. It should be easy for us to find her in the mine. As a runaway she'll be an ideal subject."

"Maybe, maybe not." The doctor picked up the phone. "First, I'll call in the lawyers. I will not stand by and watch a bunch of baboons fumbling through my research, nor this facility."

It took Detective Arnold four hours to return with a search warrant in his hand. A big, black limousine was parked crossways tightly in front of the gate. The detective started to walk towards the limo. Four police cruisers pulled up behind him and a dozen officers got out. The back door of the limo opened and two well-dressed ladies and a tall, thin gentleman got out. Karen Simpson walked over to the detective and asked, "Can I assist you?"

Karen's light pink, tight fitting suit caught the detective off guard. As she pushed her long blonde hair off of her shoulders, she asked him again, "Can I assist you?"

The detective stuck out his hand. "I have a court order to search this facility for a missing child."

Karen smiled as she took it from his hand. "Well, I've been retained by the owner to handle all his legal matters. My team will have to evaluate this document before I can allow you to go anywhere near it."

"What's to evaluate? The judge has given us the right to search this facility and I demand that you stand aside or be arrested for obstructing an officer in the line of duty."

As Karen approached the two other lawyers, she turned her head and smiled back at the detective. The tall lawyer ran his finger down every page of the warrant. He handed it back to Karen and smiled as he slowly shook his head. The other lawyer did the same and pulled out a document from a folder in her briefcase. After retrieving both documents, Karen returned to the detective, shaking her head and smiling. "This document of yours is invalid. If you even try to carry this out, I'll personally see to it that you, every officer that participates in it and the judge who issued it goes to jail for a very long time."

Detective Arnold rolled his head and peeked back at his men. "This is a court order. It's valid! Stand aside or I'll place you all under arrest."

"If I were you, I'd read this first." Karen handed the detective a fifty-five paged document.

Detective Arnold tore it from her hand. "What's this?"

"It's a no trespass notice. This missing child isn't here and your document offers no real grounds to even suspect she is. This facility is extremely volatile in nature and has biohazards, chemicals and research equipment that are extremely secretive in nature. The scribbling on that paper of yours doesn't address any safety measures at all to prevent contamination of the research media, infection of the participants, destruction of sensitive research material and equipment, or even espionage."

"What the hell are you talking about?" The detective's face turned red. "We are just looking for a little girl. We are not interested in anything else."

Karen grinned. "And what guarantees do we have that some corporation won't be questioning you or your men afterwards? One shred of what you may think is innocent information could cost my client millions. I know that you might have an idea how much our research can be worth. You may have to multiply it and then add a few more zeroes to get anywhere close to its true value." Karen smiled at the stunned detective and kissed the paper in his hand. "Have the judge contact my office and maybe we can work something out."

The pink lipstick was all the judge needed to see when Detective Arnold handed him Karen's document. It was her trademark. It was like telling him that he could kiss his job good-bye. "You fool. Did you do any research at all into that facility before you asked me for a search warrant? Karen Simpson doesn't handle anything that won't get her into the papers. She's like a venomous cobra, beautiful and deadly. She'll turn this missing child case into a political nightmare. If this case is taking her away from her five-star penthouse, someone is paying her team at least five or maybe even six figures a day."

The detective took a step back. "It's a medical facility. They have labs, examination rooms, patient quarters, a cafeteria, bathrooms. What were they to investigate? We're not a bunch of apes wanting to tear the place apart."

"You might as well be. If this document is right, I wouldn't go near this place without a spacesuit on and a spike in my hand in case I see anything that I'm not supposed too. I may have to use it to gouge out my eyes." The judge looked up at the confused, pale detective. "I'm just glad that you didn't press it. We're going to need an entire team of independent consultants to help verify that Sarah Douglas isn't in there. Have you any idea how much that's going to cost?"

"It's the only place she could be."

The Judge sat in his chair staring at the papers. "For now, I'd advise you to take a back seat. They know that we will eventually find a way to search the place. If Sarah Douglas is in there, we must be very careful and diplomatic about how we confirm it."

"So I'm supposed to proceed in the investigation as if she isn't there?"

"That's what I'd do. Try to eliminate every other possible scenario first."

Soberly, Detective Arnold drove back to the facility and talked to the officer he had left posted outside of the gate. "Has anyone been in or out of here?"

"No one. The lawyers packed up and drove off right after you did."

"I want every vehicle searched going in or out of that facility. I don't trust anything or anyone that has this many secrets." The detective returned to his vehicle mumbling, "I may not be able to go in, but out here I'm still the boss."

The officer looked at the rough road leading into the facility and then at the helicopter inside of the fence. "We can't stop them."

Shortly after the detective turned onto the road, he noticed the side road leading to the old mine. Cut into the swamp, the winding road had decayed over years of neglect. *That's where it all started.* As he passed the road he noticed that someone had begun removing the fallen trees and filling some of the larger pot-holes with gravel. Pulling over, he got out and walked back to the road. In the dirt covering the crumbling pavement he noticed the wide parallel tracks of ATVs and rugged off-road vehicles. After briefly gazing at Devil's Claw Ridge, he got back into his jeep, turned it around and made his way down the side road.

Pulling up to the open gate in front of the mine, he had a nicer greeting. Laurie casually walked over to his jeep and the detective rolled down his window and made a very sedate inquiry. "We are searching for a missing child and you probably already know that I would have a hard time getting a search warrant. How would I go about searching the mine? She is just a scared young kid."

"Sarah Douglas, we know all about her. We have started our own search for her. A lot of us grew quite fond of her when she was a patient at the facility. I wish that I could be in there right now searching with the others." Laurie placed both of her hands on the hood of the car. "How many people would be involved?"

"I could limit it to half a dozen if I was forced to, but I would like as many as I could. There are a lot of tunnels in there. The more eyes and ears, the better."

"I'll talk to Duncan. He's the one in charge of security here. He'll give you a call. I should warn you, don't let his good looks fool you. He will be in charge and he won't relinquish any of his power to anyone."

"I got that feeling when I first met him, but it would be nice to find Sarah and get her home as soon as possible." Detective Arnold studied the wall of the cliff that protected the mine. "Is there any other way in or out of this mine?"

Laurie looked back at the mine. "Not that I'm aware of. A few air vents, that's all. Nothing bigger than a bat or maybe a small cat could crawl through those narrow cracks. Even the escape tunnels haven't been touched since the mine closed down. Their locks have so much rust on them, you would have to take a torch to them to cut them open."

"Thank you." Looking up at the darkening sky, he added, "We'll see what we can work out tomorrow."

As the Detective began to roll up his window, Laurie said, "One thing you should keep in mind: don't try to throw your weight around. That'll only piss Duncan off. If you try to play any games with him, he'll take that badge away from you and have that uniform stripped right off your back before your shift is over. You don't know the resources that he can muster with a simple phone call. He takes his job very seriously."

"I'm getting a good idea of what he's capable of."

As the jeep rolled out of view, Duncan walked out of the mine towards Laurie. "He wants to search the mine, doesn't he?"

"Yep."

"Then we're going to have to hurry. The lawyers won't be able to hold them off indefinitely this time."

Chapter Eleven

The Mine

One of the guards returned to the cavern and approached Duncan as he stood over a table studying a map of the mine. "We found some footprints in the south-west tunnel. They match both the size and tread pattern that the guard helping in the search party had photographed."

"Show me exactly which tunnel you found them in." Duncan spread the entire map out over a long table.

The guard leaned over the table and put his finger on an upper tunnel. "Where she is isn't on this map." Sliding his finger towards the back of the mine, he added, "To me, it lookes like she squeezed through a crack and may have crawled into an old section of abandoned tunnels somewhere around here."

Duncan stood up and arched his back. "I guess we'll have to find the tunnels and put them back on the map." Turning to a pile of tubes containing maps, he told the guard, "I want you to search through these until you find the originals for that section."

Without a word, the guard sat down and sorted out the maps according to the colour of the paper. He then started unrolling the oldest and most discoloured ones first. By the time Duncan was suited up and ready to go, he had the map in hand. "Here it is. This one shows the tunnels before any heavy equipment was used. With all the cave-ins, most of the tunnels on this map no longer exist."

Duncan studied the map. "This could be where those creatures are hiding out." Getting on his phone, he called Doctor Scott. "I hope that new ammunition of yours is ready. I may've discovered where they are hiding."

Doctor Scott smiled. "Henry has been working on them. I'll check on his progress."

"While you're at it, make sure Wyatt Thompson is awake. Then tell him to get two squads trained on how to load and handle the new ammo."

The doctor put his hand behind his head. "What if there isn't enough ammo ready?"

"We are running out of time. We have to take control of the situation before that cop starts pestering us. If one of those creatures makes an appearance while the cops are searching the mine, it will be too late."

Doctor Scott took a deep breath. "Don't worry. I'll look after everything at this end. You just get everything secured at yours."

"If Henry doesn't have enough bullets in time, tell Thompson to load three clips of ammo per member at the highest ratio he can. Tell him to take some extra fully live mags with him, just in case. We don't know how these creatures are going to react."

With one hand on top of his head, the doctor looked up and closed his eyes. After taking another deep breath, he asked, "Where do you want me to send him when they're finished?"

"I'll get in contact with George Silver and instruct him where to look. When he has located the opening, I'll get him to show Thompson."

"Does Thompson know what he is supposed to do when he gets there?"

Duncan could hear the panic in every strained word the doctor uttered. "Stop worrying. Just tell him to call me and I'll fill him in with the details."

"I should have told Karen to press the custody issue."

"That would be a huge gamble. I've reviewed the fine print in the document Mr. Douglas has signed. Even with custody, there are issues of access to her family that need to be addressed. That alone is reason for police involvement in the search for her."

"You're right, but when she is found, all we have to do is produce the paperwork and she's ours. With her running away, Mr. Douglas won't have any grounds to contest it."

Sarah's small footprints were easy to distinguish from the larger, deep tread of the guards, technicians and medical staff that had been searching through the mine for the creatures. Roger followed closely behind Duncan and the guard that first discovered the tracks. It didn't take Duncan long to spot the small crack that Sarah had crawled into. It was too narrow for any of them to enter. As Duncan lay on the ground, shining his flashlight into the dark crack, Roger spoke up. "We'll have to use the remote."

Within half an hour, two guards showed up pulling a huge cart. On it was the remote, a huge spool of cable and a large control panel with six monitors. Roger pulled out the ramp and within a minute the remote was rolling off the cart. With its large tracks and a couple of wheels on each side to correct it if it rolled over, the tethered remote slowly entered the collapsed tunnel. The optical cable secured to a flexible safety line slowly unrolled from the large spool.

Duncan watched Roger work. "You're smarter than most of the other doctors. What made you join Scott's team?"

"Money. The work that I'm doing for the good doctor is going to make me financially sound for the rest of my life."

"How did he find you?"

"He didn't. After his old medical facility was destroyed, I hunted him down. I knew his reputation and it didn't take much to figure out that he was working on something big, so I wiggled my way in. As a plain doctor, I was just another lab jacket that he could order around. I studied my butt off when I wasn't working. I made myself indispensable to him. Now look at me."

"So you didn't know what he was researching before you joined up?"

"It didn't matter. Great minds like his will always produce a winning team and I wanted to be a part of it."

******

Empty cans and garbage were piling up next to Sarah as she continued to share each of her meals with her new bodyguard. As she recapped her empty water bottle and placed it on the pile, she heard a creature approach from the tunnel. After a few rolling growls, it was immediately surrounded by the other members. Sarah noticed the usual chatter between the members of the colony grow louder every time any member returned. It wasn't long before more creatures seemed to be leaving then returning. As her bodyguard snuggled closer to her, she knew that something was wrong. It was trembling, but why? And why was it seeking comfort from her?

******

Thompson stood back as George studied the ground in front of the opening on the side of the ridge. Trees and shrubs had almost totally concealed it from view. If the leaves were fully out, a person would've had to crawl behind them to find it. One of the weathered wooden doors had fallen off of its hinges. The other door was twisted and missing several planks. Dressed in blue jeans and a plaid shirt, the old native tracker stood up and walked over to Thompson. "They have been coming and going in and out of this abandoned tunnel for a long time. Their tracks are everywhere."

Thompson looked down and could barely see his own footprint. "It's too dark to see anything."

"That's why Duncan called me in. Tracks are sometimes difficult to spot in this terrain. That's why no one could find them."

As George disappeared into the forest, Thompson took over. He examined the opening. "We'll need a much better line of fire." Looking at the other guards, he added, "Holler at the first hint something is moving. We don't know how they will react and I don't want to take any chances."

Before the first rays of dawn, four guards got out their chainsaws and worked as two teams, clearing all the vegetation away from the opening. The rest of the guards stood on watch with guns pointing both into the tunnel and the surrounding forest.

******

Roger had no problem navigating the remote vehicle around the fallen rocks. Even with cameras pointing in every direction, the remote rolled over the badly decayed beam and, like Sarah, it lost its footing and tumbled downward into the shaft. Duncan watched as the cable spun off of the roll. By the time Roger put on the brakes it was too late. It had hit bottom. A sharp pointed rock smashed its forward camera. Through its other cameras, they could see that the unit was wedged between a large rock and the wall. Roger redirected the wheels on the sides of the vehicle and used them to help wiggle the machine upward.

"Why don't you reel in the cable and yank it out?"

Roger answered Duncan coolly. "I don't like to take any chance of damaging the cable unless it's absolutely necessary."

The cavern was lit from eighteen lights that shone from every angle off of the remote. The bright light stung Sarah's eyes. She threw her coat over her face and hid underneath it. With all the light from the remote shining up at the ceiling, the cavern's floor was still in the shadows. The creature shut its eyes and crawled towards the remote. Even with his hand deflecting some of its glare, its bright lights burned the creature's eyes. Guided by the red globes of light that still forced their way through his defences, the creature crawled steadily towards the strange object.

As Sarah's eyes started to get adjusted to the light, she lowered the coat and looked around. All of the other creatures had run away. It was just the two of them left in the cavern.

The machine started to peek over the boulder that had trapped it. The creature pounced on top of it. As its flapping wings covered the machine's bright lights, Sarah got up and dashed into the tunnel.

"What was that?"

Roger wasn't sure which screen Duncan was watching. "What did you see?"

Duncan pointed to the monitor displaying the camera on the remote's belly. "I think it could have been Sarah. Something that looked human got up and ran away."

On the monitors, they could see tiny blood vessels running through the creature's wings. "I'll try to shake the remote free from whatever got a hold of it."

With all wheels on the remote racing and turning, the creature held on by biting into the cable. The lights started to flicker. The low electrical zap made the creature angry as it chewed. A stronger electrical jolt ran through its body. Surprised, it jumped off the machine and sank into the remaining shadows. The lights continued to flicker. Enraged, the creature picked up a large rock and threw it at the remote. It glanced off the side of the machine.

"There's something wrong. We're losing power."

"What is it?"

One by one, Roger flipped switches to see what would happen. "I'm not sure. It could be the cable."

Duncan stood over Roger's shoulder. "Can you do anything?"

"I'm trying to find the problem area and shut it down. Hopefully we can reroute some power and regain some control over the remote."

The creature heaved another rock at the machine's bright lights. It bounced off the top of it and smashed against the cable. With the sudden extra weight of the rock on top of the remote, it slid back into the gully it was trying to get out of. Roger tried to work it free. With the rock wedged against the cable, every move the machine made ground the frayed, pinched wires. Roger throw his arms in the air. "That's it, we're dead. I'm going to have to pull it in. The cable has had it."

Roger started the winch. The central steel cable tightened and slowly began to reel in the remote. The camera on its belly was still working along with the one on its right-hand side. Even with only four of the eighteen lights functioning, they could make out two shadowy images in the cavern. As the cable scraped against the rocks, the monitors went blank.

Roger watched as the battered up remote was pulled out of the tunnel towards its cart. Duncan showed little care about the robotic unit as he reviewed the images that it had retrieved, frame by frame. Roger and a guard manhandled the unit to get it lined up to the ramp. As Roger stood up and wiped the dirt off of his hands, he noticed the blood on his sleeves. He glanced over at the guard. It wasn't from either of them. He quickly examined the remote. "We have a tissue sample from whatever attacked the remote."

Duncan looked up from the monitors. "Good, the more DNA samples Doctor Scott has to work with, the better."

Duncan continued to review the images. At the point where the remote first fell into the cavern, he stopped it. Sarah and the creature were crouched together and looked straight up for a split second before shielding their eyes. *What is going on with this creature and Little Sister?* The tracks and smudges in the dirt made him wonder. The creature had been lying down right next to her. They had both stood up at the same time. "All reports of these creatures indicated that they are very vicious. Why is this creature being so friendly with Little Sister?"

Roger came over and looked at the screen. "I don't know. Maybe she pulled a thorn out of its paw. That works in fairy tales."

"This is no fairy tale. There has to be a logical explanation."

******

Sarah watched as the lights were pulled away from the cavern. Quickly she dashed back for her backpack and gear. She stuffed all of her gear back into the pack. As she felt her way down the tunnel, her companion stayed close behind her. She stopped to listen. She couldn't hear any chatter from the other creatures.

******

A guard rested his axe against a tree stump. Bending over to grab a couple freshly cut saplings away from the entranceway, the sun reflected off of the shiny axe head into the tunnel. Looking up, he could see shadowy outlines of bobbing heads deep within the tunnel. Without making any gestures at all, he stood up and walked over to Thompson. "They are in there. There must be over a half a dozen about ten metres inside. I could see their green eyes shining back at me as clear as day."

"I know. I could see them through my infrared binoculars. I've been watching them gather. There are well over a dozen of them huddled inside the mine right now." Thompson put down his binoculars and looked at the guard. "I think it's time. They are a nervous bunch and we can't afford to give them any advantage. Quietly tell the rest of your squad to put down their tools and grab your rifles. I'll meet them at my ATV."

Thompson spread out sealed bags containing specially loaded magazines across the back of his ATV. The guards next to him carefully ripped open the bags and loaded them into their rifles. "Take two more each. You'll probably need them."

As the others slowly walked away from the opening and grabbed their rifles, Thompson and three others crouched down in a line with their guns tight pressed against their shoulders. On the ground beside them lay extra sealed clips of ammo. "Everyone ready?" After receiving nods back, he announced, "Fire!"

With guns set on automatic, it didn't take long to empty a magazine into the dark tunnel. As one group reloaded, the other fired. "Stop firing."

Thompson looked through his binoculars. "We need proper scopes for these guns. We are not properly equipped for this." Outside of a few sprawling on the ground, they had all vanished. Small hot spots appeared along the walls and ceiling. "They're hiding. This is probably the first time they've ever been shot at. They don't know what's happening. They are dug into any hole or crevice that they could readily squeeze into." Walking towards the entrance he added, "We're going to have to get closer. Our fire is too central. We have to spray the walls."

Right next to the entrance, the guards lined up in two rows. They could hear the creatures moving inside. Thompson peered in. He could see the creatures trying to drag their comrades away. As more joined in to help, Thompson again sent out the order. "Fire."

This time they didn't run and hide. As the first shots were discharged, several of them jumped up into the air straight towards the guards. One was instantly shot apart as several guards concentrated their fire on it. The two creatures behind it pounced on the guards as they tried to reload. As the creatures flailed their claws in every direction and bit into anything they could, most of the guards fell back. With several guards flopping and others trying to beat the creatures away, nobody could get in a shot. Thompson pulled out his knife and jumped into the mix. He stabbed and managed to pull one of the creatures off. As it hit the ground, two guards blasted it into chunks of meat. The other creature twisted his head and leaped towards Thompson. As soon as it bit into his arm, a guard shot the creature at close range. As it started to fall, the winged, weasel-looking creature grabbed the smoking barrel. The guard yanked it free and emptied the rifle's magazine into the creature's chest. "That's one that we won't have to worry about."

A badly cut-up guard grabbed Thompson's arm. "Thanks." While Thompson and another guard pulled the injured to safety, the guards behind them emptied magazine after magazine of bullets into the tunnel.

Chapter Twelve

Family

"Duncan, none of them escaped. We killed three of them for sure and wounded anywhere up to a dozen more."

"A dozen more? How many were there?"

"A lot more than we expected."

"Was anyone injured?"

"Campbell was badly mauled when they formed a counter attack. Two more men were sliced up a bit. I had them transported to the facility." Thompson took a deep breath and thought for a moment. "It was weird, the creatures that we killed were all shot while the others were trying to retrieve their wounded."

"Martyrs? That's an interesting trait. It's almost human." Duncan looked away from the monitors and adjusted his headset. "Thompson, is the situation there under control?"

The unwavering guard wrapped a bandage around his arm as he replied. "Absolutely. There are only the two of us here right now. I don't expect the creatures are willing to face another costly fire fight. They now know what bullets can do to them." Blood from Thompson's ripped arm oozed through the bandage as he finished taping it on.

"Did you use Doctor Shaw's gelled-tipped ammo?"

Thompson bit down and swallowed before answering. "Yes, until we had to reload at the end. Some of the men didn't have the time to unwrap them. They just slapped in regular magazines instead."

"Did you have enough?"

"Yes sir, the doc made plenty. The first two magazines the men used were strictly gelled. The percussion from the casings was enough to fend them off. The walls inside the tunnel are plastered with the stuff. Even if we didn't hit them, their bodies had to have been spattered by it."

Duncan grinned as he ended the conversation with a simple, "Good."

Turning to Roger, Duncan told him, "We better get moving."

With help from the remaining guard, Duncan rolled and shoved a few large rocks into the gap. By the time they were done, Roger had secured all of the equipment on the cart. Before leaving, Duncan barked out his orders to the guard, "If you see anything trying to get out, shoot it. I'll get a crew back here to properly seal it off as fast as I can."

At the main cavern, Duncan jumped onto his ATV. Halfway down the side road, he cut through the swamp and skirted around the head of the ridge towards the road leading to the facility. The road hugged the bottom of the ridge. Instead of continuing down the road eastward to the facility, he followed the bottom claw of the ridge upwards. From there, a path took him through the swamp to the old entrance that Thompson was guarding. One look at his bloody arm was enough for Duncan. "You better get that looked at."

"All right. I was waiting to be relieved first. I couldn't leave the entrance unsupervised."

"I'm here now. Use my ATV and get one of the doctors to examine you."

With only a salute, Thompson drove off. Duncan walked over to a row of bodies. Three creatures were spread out on the ground under a birch tree. Blue jell from the bullets leaked out of a couple holes in their bodies. He turned to the guard standing next to him. "You didn't touch any fluids coming out from these creatures, did you?"

Shaking his head, he replied, "Not a chance. I'm not going near that stuff. Who knows what the doc put into that blue gunk."

"Good, you are a wise man."

It wasn't long before Roger showed up. Duncan just pointed to the bodies and Roger drove his ATV next to them. With his sampling bag in hand he knelt over the first of the three bodies. He took a long tubular device out of his bag and, in a back and forth twisting motion, pushed it into the creature's thigh. After pulling up on a small lever, he removed the device containing a sample of the creature's skin, blood, muscle and even bone fragments. "This is all the doctor should require." After placing the sampling device in a plastic bag he did the same to the other two creatures. Next, using a stick, he shifted around their bodies for a series of photographs.

Duncan watched as Roger packed up. "Remind the doctor that we'll need relief. I have a lot of work to do back at the facility."

"I will."

"Then tell him that I'll still need to hire more men. We're not manned for securing both the mine and the facility, plus deal with these creatures. We are spread much too thin. My people are working twelve hour shifts as is. We need at least another dozen bodies. Without adequate security, we could lose everything."

"You know that he's working on it. Security is almost half of his total budget already." Roger looked over at the monstrous dead bodies. "Don't forget to destroy the bodies. With that stuff inside of them we can't have anyone discovering what we have done."

******

Sarah could see daylight through the old entrance as she hid inside a crevice behind a support post. A long parade of shadows slowly moved through the tunnel. Several creatures were dragging others behind them. A few turned and hissed at her as they went by. Her eyes were getting used to the dark. Through their chatter and head movements, Sarah could tell that they had no problem seeing into her shallow hiding spot. Their snarling, curled up faces made them look even more hideous.

The procession didn't go back to the cavern. Instead it squeezed its way through a small, slanted crack on the north side of the tunnel. As they disappeared, Sarah's companion reached for her hand and looked up at her. She felt strange. What was this creature to her? She could leave if she wanted to. She could go back home or even to Fort Scott. The creatures were no longer blocking her way. As the strange creature tugged at her arm, something inside her compelled her to follow.

Dragging her pack behind her, she shimmed sideways through the narrow crack in the wall. The blasts and machinery used in mining the newer tunnels above it had split the crack along a diagonal fault line. There was barely enough room for her to squeeze through. Frightened, she took out her flashlight. She twisted off the top of it so the single LED bulb acted like a candle, shining in all directions. Sarah could see the crack getting wider ahead of her. Using the extra space in the gap, she sat down and caught her breath. There was enough room that both Sarah and the creature could spread out a bit and rest. As the echo from her own breathing began to calm her, she could make out the creatures' chatter ahead of her. She knew that they didn't have much farther to go.

This was the first time Sarah had a chance to get a good look at her companion. It looked younger than most of the others. It was more cat-like. When she was first attacked, all she saw were flashes of teeth, fur and wings. When she fell into the cavern, in the dim light all she saw was wings, teeth and ugly, snarling faces. Everything had been hazy silhouettes and shadows. Sarah tried to remember everything about them that she could. Like the gargoyles that spewed evil away from old buildings, none of them were identical. A few didn't even have wings.

Looking down at her companion curled up next to her, Sarah thought, *If this is the way it is going to be, then I'm going to have to give you a name. I just wish that I knew if you were a boy or a girl.*

After listening to the chatter coming from the others and her companion's low, muffled, almost engine-like purr, Sarah proclaimed,

"You sound a bit like my neighbour's car. I think I'm going to call you Honda."

Honda led the way through the final leg of the gap and Sarah followed. She was a bit confused. She didn't understand why she felt compelled to follow this hideous creature into their lair.

The gap opened up into another tunnel. Sticking her head inside, Sarah looked around. There were creatures of all sizes lined up against the walls. A couple of the creatures were lying down suckling babies. *This must be their nursery.* The batteries were getting low in her flashlight and the creatures were not frightened by its dim light. By holding the fading light above her head, Sarah could see that the offspring of each of them were quite different. One family had mostly long, thin tails and ears, and a couple with thick stubby tails and round ears. Looking around she saw another family of mostly wingless creatures. There was a variety of creatures with horns, tusks, body armour, various colours of fur and thicknesses, all the way down to no hair at all. From what she could count, there were well over a dozen young families in total. The more she saw, the more that she realized that the creatures were a gigantic, genetic hodgepodge.

Each family huddled together as the parade of adults and juveniles slowly walked by. Some walked over to the mothers and mates. Some were welcomed, other weren't. A few of the wounded were laid down in front of what Sarah expected were their kin. A mother crept over and began licking the wounds of one dying creature. Sarah remembered seeing different dogs and other animals do the same and had thought nothing of it.

Sarah stepped into the tunnel and started to walk past the huddled groups of creatures. Holding her hand, Honda walked down the tunnel next to her. Some families had only one young, and others had up to six. A few had none and she saw one mother hugging a long dead child. Beyond the mothers and young were mounds of rocks. As she passed a mound, a rock rolled off and a small hand flopped out. Looking down the tunnel, Sarah could see hundreds of similar mounds, some a lot larger than others. The graveyard extended as far as she could see. For every child that survived, it was obvious that several had died. Sarah looked down at Honda and then back at all the families. There was nothing that looked even close to her. Honda was unique. She was much more cat-like than any of the rest.

******

Detective Arnold knocked on the Douglas's door. Michaela answered it wearing an old housecoat. "Any news about Sarah?"

With hat in hand the detective partially bowed his head. In a quiet voice he responded, "Not yet. We're going to search the old mine later today. Doctor Scott has even offered a dozen guards to accompany us. I saw your father's truck outside. I thought that he might want to help in the search."

Robert stuck his head into the kitchen. "I thought I heard your voice."

As Robert entered, the detective stood up straight. "We've been given permission to search the mine. You know it and we could use your help."

"She's my daughter. Anything, anything I can do, I'll do. I want her back."

After supper, three guards directed the parade of vehicles and told them where to park. The old parking lot outside of the mine had been overgrown with small trees and bushes. As Detective Arnold looked around, it was evident that the guards had worked hard at clearing enough room for all the vehicles. Smiling at Robert, he commented, "They make it appear like we're actually welcome."

Doctor Scott stood beside the gate in front of the mine's entrance. "I hope this will be a very thorough and well-organized search with a great emphasis on safety. The mine is old, and parts of it are in bad need of repair. Nobody wants to see anyone get hurt."

The detective spoke up. "Most of the volunteers had worked in the mine. The police officers that are present have been well trained in all kinds of search and rescue. We'll be all right." Looking around, he could see Duncan standing in the shadows.

Each volunteer was called and paired up with a guard. Laurie walked over to Robert. "I told Duncan that I'd accompany you in the search."

"Thanks, I know how fond you were of Sarah."

******

Roger looked over the DNA results as they appeared on the computer. Most of the hard work had been done for him by a series of connected computer programs. With charts and graphs to compare each sample, it was easy for him to spot the subtle differences within each strain. Looking at one set of graphs, he saw something familiar. It was similar to the sample taken from the infected patches on Sarah. He brought up both sets of DNA results and compared them. "They are like siblings. So that is why that creature was so protective of her. It thinks they're kin."

******

Honda finally stopped in front of a large pile of rocks. It was obvious that many of them were taken away by others, mostly from one side of the mound. Other piles were still neatly stacked. Honda curled up next to the exposed, mummified section of her mother. Sarah looked down at what was once the dead creature's stomach. The skeletons of dead fetuses protruded from its dried skin. A few claws had ripped through her hide fighting to get out. Two long gashes had shown that a couple of the young had succeeded. Was it the child birth or her own offspring that killed her? Nobody may ever know. Honda put out a mournful cry as she pulled Sarah's hand down to another pile of rocks next to her mother's body.

Sarah looked down at Honda. She thought of how cat-like the creature that attacked her was. Even the paramedics thought the jaw was from a cat. She glanced at the hair that had started to creep onto her right shoulder. They were the same colour and texture as Honda's. "Two creatures clawed their way out. Now only one survives." Sarah bent down and put her hand on the back of Honda's head. "Am I replacing the creature that attacked me? Is that why I was compelled to follow you? Was that the reason I didn't escape when I had the chance?"

All of Sarah's chatter confused Honda. She crawled next to Sarah and rubbed her head against Sarah's arm. Honda's gentle purr both frightened and comforted her. She scratched the back of Honda's neck. "I guess I'm a member of two families now."

Chapter Thirteen

Search and Destroy

Detective Arnold climbed up into the passenger side of the almost flat electric, four-wheel-drive mine personnel vehicle. Duncan was in the driver's seat and two pairs of searchers were in the back facing each other. His face was hidden from their view by the wide brimmed hat. Duncan talked as he drove. "We've already searched the entire mine and found nothing."

The detective turned to him and said, "Not even where the creatures are holed up? Everyone around here knows that they are hiding somewhere in the mine."

"We believe that we've discovered where. I'll show you later."

Robert was sitting right behind Duncan and heard everything. *The creatures are still here.* He turned to Laurie and cupped his hand between his mouth and her ear. As quietly as he could, he asked, "Do you know where the creatures are roosting?"

Barely above a whisper, she answered back, "No, I've been outside on sentry duty most of the time."

Robert held his tongue and waited until they were dropped off at the start of the tunnel they were assigned to search. "We're not going to find her in here, are we?"

Laurie politely answered, "No, we've been through every inch of this mine. If she was in here, we would have found her by now."

After being dropped off, they walked along their assigned tunnel. With one on each side they checked every crevice, ledge and hole. Robert looked over at Laurie. "Are you able to find out where they think the creatures are hiding? They killed a couple of my friends and look at what happened to Sarah. I need to know that they cannot get out and hurt anyone else."

"I'll see if I can, but I can't promise you anything."

"I'd really appreciate it if you could."

The search went on as Duncan had predicted. Every tunnel and shaft on his map was stroked off in red. Detective Arnold looked at the various maps of the mine and turned to Duncan. "There has to be more to this mine than this."

Duncan returned his stare. "This is a huge, fractured ridge. It's not an enormous mountain."

"You told me that you may have found the creature's lair. Maybe Sarah is in there. Dead or alive, we have to find her."

"If she is there, she is dead. Those creatures are carnivores. If there any remains left, it'll be only fragments of bones piled in with the rest of their kills."

"So be it. Robert Douglas deserves to know."

"Fine, I'll take you there myself. Just you alone, I don't want Robert with us."

The Detective followed Duncan out of the mine and hopped on the back of his ATV. He watched Duncan discretely hide his face from the others. "You don't like people looking at you, do you?"

"You know what I look like."

"That's not the only reason, is it?"

Duncan revved up the engine to go faster. "I suppose you're going to tell me."

"I looked you up on the computer. You are supposed to be dead. There was even a funeral and your obituary was posted in the local paper."

"I was. I didn't like it, so I came back." Duncan glanced around at Detective Arnold and saw his cold reaction. "I didn't want my family to go through the agony of another funeral, so I stayed dead. This way they will remember me the way I was."

"So why does the computer still say that you are dead?"

Duncan eased off of the throttle. "Too much red tape, I guess."

Once off of roadways, it was only an additional half hour drive through the swamp to get to the old entrance. One of the guards stationed there came over to Duncan. With an inquisitive look on his face he looked at the detective and then back at Duncan. "Sir, what's up?"

"It's all right. I'm taking him into the mine to show him where the creatures were found."

Duncan checked his pistol and turned to the detective. "We think that we got them all, but you never know."

The two men walked, crawled and climbed through the old tunnel. A lot of the support beams and crossbeams were cracked, broken, shifted or rotted out. Mounds of fallen rubble dictated their path. The detective said softly, "I don't think it's very safe in here."

Duncan finished stepping over a fallen beam. "It's not. That's why they were able to hide in here for so long."

The detective looked at the pick marks on the walls. "With all the mining overhead I'm surprised that this old tunnel has survived at all. It must've been one of the very first ones to be dug out."

Ducking under an angled crossbeam, Duncan answered, "It was the first. We even had locate some old hand-drawn maps to find the entrance. The rest of the original tunnels collapsed, but this one still remains."

The detective looked around the tunnel. "If you can call it that. One good shake-up and it's good-bye to this one too."

Duncan directed the detective past the newly sealed up crack in the wall. The dirt plastered over the foam sealant used to hold the rocks and debris in place made it look like all the other crevices in the wall. After another half an hour of climbing over fallen rocks and under collapsed beams, they finally made it to the cavern. Looking around with his flashlight, Detective Arnold saw the piles of bones that the creatures had left behind. Shuffling the pile around with his foot, he found what he thought could be part of a human skull. "I've seen enough. I'm going to have to bring in a forensic team to examine the mess."

Outside, Duncan showed the detective all the bullet holes where his men opened fire on the creatures and the large pile of ash where they had burned the bodies. "The only ones that we saw leave the mine were all dead. We didn't want whatever caused them to turn into monsters to infect anyone else, so my men had orders to cremate the bodies as fast as possible."

Detective Arnold bent over and felt the ashes. "They are still warm."

Duncan smiled. "I have my men to think of."

The detective poked through the pile with a stick. "So you're telling me that as far as you know, they are all dead? So where are the skulls and thick upper leg bones?"

"Crushed under the logs that were tossed on the fire." Duncan watched the detective poke some more. After he separated out a section of bone and part of a skull cap, he added, "They did a good job getting rid of all the evidence, didn't they?"

As more police arrived, nothing that Duncan had told the detective in confidence was repeated. In fact, even the bullet holes were passed off as his men just having some fun. Even the bones were just scrapes left behind by local wild creatures.

Due to the condition of the tunnel, Detective Arnold restricted the number of officers entering the mine. Even then, they went in in shifts. After the photographers snapped some photos and demanded to get out, the forensic team came in and started to collect all the bones.

******

It had been three days since the opening had been sealed off. The creatures had taken turns at listening to the activity going on in the adjacent tunnel through small cracks left at the top of the sealed off gap. Sarah could only sit at the side of the tunnel as the young creatures started to cry from hunger. The mothers' breasts were drying up. She hadn't seen any of them eat or drink anything since she got there. Along with the hunger, several of the creatures started to develop breathing problems. At the same time, small red dots appeared all over the sick creatures' bodies. The entire colony became infected by the outbreak. At first it was just the nursing young that died. Shortly after that, some of the weakened mothers, then came the older adults. There was nothing Sarah could do but watch.

With her water gone, all Sarah had left to drink was the juice from a couple cans of mixed fruit and the liquid that the tuna was packed in. Honda sat in front of her snarling the best she could at any creature that dared to get to close. The infection that had taken over the colony had also hit her. Sarah opened a can of tuna and fed it to her. The pungent smell drew several of the other creatures towards them. Honda ate as fast as she could and then gave out the most ferocious growl she could muster. The others backed off. Two big adults stepped forward and attempted to growl back. Waving her hunting knife in front of her, Sarah stood up and yelled at them, "Get away from us."

In the stale air it took a lot for the sick creatures to do anything. One of the older adults collapsed in front of her. The other stepped back. Sarah watched as the fallen adult's chest stopped moving. Honda went over to smell his last breath. She looked back at Sarah. The colony's leader was dead. One by one, every mobile creature walked by the large dead creature in front of Sarah. Several creatures looked at her with disgruntled eyes while others snarled the best they could. She knew what they thought. It was the humans that caused it. At that moment, she knew that she was nothing more than meat to them. If anything happened to Honda, it was over.

******

"How's it working?"

Duncan gave Doctor Scott a memory card. "See for yourself. When we sealed off the crevice, the camera wasn't damaged at all. We could manipulate its angle a bit and get some good images."

The doctor inserted it into his computer and watched the monitor. "It doesn't show us a lot."

"There is no light in the tunnel, but you can still see the results of Doctor Shaw's concoction."

The monitor displayed three families. In fast motion, Doctor Scott watched as one by one, all but two of their offspring died. The two sickly youngsters that survived had crawled into the darkness, out of view of the camera. The mournful cries echoing in the tunnel told the doctor the extent of havoc his virus had wreaked on the colony. "It's working quicker then I'd hoped. See what a simple virus can do to an isolated population? In poor air and cramped quarters, it's like an incubator in there."

"Aren't you afraid that it will spread?"

"It's just Measles. Who cares if it spreads? I've thoroughly tested the strain I told Dr. Shaw to use. Thanks to Maurice Hilleman's vaccine, the general population is already immunised against it. That particular strain of measles only affects humans, primates and bats. The creatures' mixed DNA makes them susceptible to it."

"I never considered measles as deadly."

"A plague in Galen decimated the Roman army. In 1529 it killed two-thirds of the native population of Cuba. When the virus was first introduced to the natives in Honduras, it killed half its population. From there, it spread death up to Mexico and all the way down to the Incas in South America. At the speed it's travelling through the colony, the death rate for these creatures may get much higher than that. It's extremely fast acting. They will be dead long before the cells have time to counteract it. The bonus is that the few creatures that are left will be too sick to fight."

With a puzzled look on his face, Duncan quizzed the doctor, "I thought that the cells infecting Sarah had great healing powers. Look what they did to Sarah's cancer. Won't the cells just wipe out the virus?"

"Not this time. They were mainly designed to repair and replace damaged cells. When it comes to viruses, they need time to work and something to work with. The creatures have no known immunity to any disease remotely close to it. Their bodies will have to start from scratch. Plus, the strain that I picked was noted as being extremely fast and very deadly."

Duncan looked at the doctor's glowing face. "So when do we strike?"

"It needs more time to incubate and spread. Be patient. Maybe by the middle of next week. Between the lack of food and water, plus the virus, the few that will be left won't have the energy to protect themselves."

"Then why not just leave them all in there to die?"

"Because we can't take any chances. There is always the possibility that some may survive. If they do, they may also find a way to escape."

******

Michaela handed Timothy Ferguson his fourth beer and her father his fifth. "I'm getting tired. I'm going to bed." After giving her father a hug and kissing him on his temple, she left the kitchen. "I'll see you in the morning."

Robert looked over his shoulder and made sure she was gone. Leaning towards Timothy, he told him, "We both know that those creatures are still in the mine. We checked every inch of it and found nothing. You know what that means?"

"The gas didn't have any effect on them."

"No, it didn't even get to them. All the time we were working in the mine, we never came across their lair. I think I know why. I remember seeing a crack when we were working there. It was only an old crossbeam from an old tunnel held up by a couple of rocks, but it may have been big enough for them to crawl in and out of. If it is, they are probably roosting in the old abandoned tunnels. They could've easily plugged up the crack when we gassed the place."

After taking a sizable gulp of beer, Timothy inquired, "Did you see the crack when we searched the mine?"

"No, I didn't, and I looked as hard as I could for it. Even the guard that I was with helped me look for it. It had just vanished."

"You mean they hid it."

Robert could no longer keep his voice quiet. "Exactly, the doctor and his private army are protecting those creatures for some reason. I remember hearing something about them using DNA research in the cancer treatment that they gave Sarah. Maybe the creatures were part of their experiments."

Michaela could hear him from her room at the far end of the hall. *Not again, Dad. Look what happened last time. Can't you leave things alone?'* She knew that there was nothing she could do to stop him. Putting a pillow over her head, she curled under her covers and tried to get to sleep.

Robert turned to the hallway. "I guess we should keep it down."

Early the next morning someone was knocking at their door. Hung over and dressed only in his underwear with a blanket around him, Robert answered the door. Laurie stood in the doorway. "I think I know where they are."

Leaning against the door, he replied, "In the old tunnels on the far side?"

"How did you know?"

"I worked in that mine for years." Robert gestured for her to come in. "Someone had deliberately sealed up the gap that leads into the old section. That was the crack along the floor that I was looking for."

"I found that out for myself. They also have armed guards posted at the old entrance. The creatures must have torn off the old gates and used it as an exit. From the rumours that I've heard, they shot up the place and killed a lot of the creatures. None of the creatures made it out alive. Rumour also has it that between Duncan and the doctor, they are going to eradicate them."

Robert smiled as he thought, *and I'll make sure that they don't miss any of them.* As Laurie turned to go back to her vehicle, Robert yelled, "Thanks, it's nice to know that I've a friend I can trust."

Something inside of Laurie caused her to quiver. *What am I doing?*

Chapter Fourteen

The Will to Survive

Outside of the old entrance, two guards looked up as dark blue clouds rolled in. Behind the clouds, only the outline of the morning sun was visible. Soon afterwards, the clouds quickly opened up and released a heavy downpour of rain. The guards steadfastly stayed at their posts until they couldn't see their own hands in front of them. Unfortunately, two pairs of eyes could still see them.

Under the shelter of a tall cedar, a large lion-like creature with a coarse mane watched the men retreat to the safety of their trailer. Beside him, a slightly smaller creature that looked more like a winged pit bull eagerly waited.

Amidst the cold downpour, the lion-like creature crawled out and prowled around the trailer and the entrance to the mine. Flinging his head straight up and down in the air, it signalled its companion that it was safe. With his strong legs and wide stance, the dog-like creature had no problem dragging the caribou carcass over the slippery mud and into the mine. Once inside, the lion-like creature dragged branches over the tracks and let the rain wash away any residual trace.

The pair dragged the carcass in front of where the crack had been. The scent of man was all over the dried plaster. The strong-willed dog-like creature growled at the wall and started to dig. It didn't take long before its huge front paws started to bleed. Once they broke through the hard outer layer, they found that the globs of plaster in the middle were still slightly green and poorly adhered to both the walls and the dusty rocks the guards had thrown into the gap. The powerful canine excavated the crack while the larger creature removed the debris. As the gap narrowed and the rocks and plaster more firmly wedged in place, the dog-like creature had trouble digging the plaster away from the rocks and walls.

Trading places, the lion-like creature picked up a rock and smashed the plaster until it broke apart. His hands were more nimble, which made picking up the debris and clearing the gap much faster. The small cavern in the middle of the gap had been filled with foam. The pair simply slashed through it. Flexing their wings, the light chunks of foam were blown out of the gap. On the far side of the small cavern, they came upon a thick steel plate. They could hear members of their colony on the other side. They both cried out as loudly as they could.

"What was that?"

Thompson put down his coffee cup and went to the window. Another crack of thunder vibrated through the sky. "Probably some fallen branches rubbing against something. The woods can make some strange sounds in a storm."

The steel plate was firmly wedged between the rock and dried concrete. Suddenly the steel started to ring out. One by one several large members of the colony squeezed into the gap and hammered their side of the steel plate with rocks. Inside the tunnel, the other members of the colony could hear the results. It didn't take long before the steel plate vibrated at a higher pitch and rang out steadily louder and louder. Using a fallen beam as a battering ram, one creature with a striped head like a badger held the swinging beam on target while others pushed it back and forth. At the end of the beam, a pair of creatures rammed it against the steel plate. After a couple dozen blows, the lion-like creature gave a rattling growl. The ramming stopped and the creatures removed all the pieces of the crumbling cement that they could. With a short cry, the lion-like creature signalled for the ramming to continue. It took only another three attempts before the top of the steel wall started to sway. Between the two creatures on one side and the huge badger-like creature on the other rocking the steel plate wildly back and forth, the plate started to work free. Leaning it into the crack, the three worked together, twisting the steel plate onto its side and pulling it inside the nursery. As the heavy steel plate slid over the reinforced cable leading to the camera, the crushed wires inside of it started to spark. Wiggling the heavy, steel plate inside of the tunnel, the camera was crushed and half buried in the ground.

Drawn by the smell of meat, one by one several of the creatures crawled through the newly reopened gap. After tearing chunks of meat off of the caribou carcass, many of them hauled what they could back through the gap. It was the first food they had eaten for days. The returning hunters watched as the sick members of the colony paraded out. As the powerful digger licked his paws, the mane of the large lion-like creature puffed out as he gave a roar that echoed out of the mine.

"Now don't try to tell me that was thunder."

The faces of both guards were glued to the windows. Thompson tried to calm his partner down. "It was probably just a wet pissed off cougar."

******

Oblivious of what was going on at the other end of the tunnel, Sarah followed a small trickle of water that was flowing along the wall. Honda slowly followed her, having trouble with each shaky step she took. Sarah knew that the water was coming from some kind of crack or fault line. *It may even lead to another way out.* She soon found its source. Droplets of water were leaking out of the wall. She felt the cool water. It didn't seem cold enough to be rainwater. Three larger holes had a steady stream flowing out of them. Putting out her hand to collect some, she could see tiny specks of algae. "It's coming from some kind of reservoir or underground basin. With the rain, it must be over flowing." Sarah looked around and found a dry, splintered chunk of an old beam. After peeling off a large sliver from it, she pounded it into the largest hole with a rock. Water still flowed around the wood and dripped out. She did the same to the other two holes.

Having water to lap up made Honda feel better. It didn't matter what colour it was. With Honda resting by her side, Sarah felt a small degree of security while she waited. Mostly, she felt that just getting away from the other members of the colony made her feel more relaxed. Honda rested her head on Sarah's lap. With each breath, she could hear Honda fighting for air. Wetting Honda's head and chest, Sarah tried to bring down her temperature.

The first piece of wood had fallen out and the water started to flow even faster. Sarah quickly got up and hammered a larger piece of dry wood into the crack. The water had pushed out the other two swollen, water soaked splinters. Sarah worked as fast as she could to keep plugging up the newly formed holes. The combination of the water pressure and wooden wedges had quickly formed a crack between two of the holes. The water started gushing out and Sarah could no long keep plugging it. Putting her hand against the wall, she could feel the rushing water causing a small section of the wall to vibrate. Another crack led up to the third and biggest hole. Sarah stood back and watched the crack widen as a third crack appeared, joining the three original holes. Suddenly the vibrating section of the wall crumbled and a river spewed straight out like a fire hose, sweeping her down the tunnel.

Sarah grabbed Honda by her hind leg as she fought the swift current. With her other hand, she grabbed one of the remaining support beams and held on. The pressure of the sudden surge of water was too much for the old beam and it gave way. The crossbeam it was holding up collapsed along with part of the ceiling. The sudden dam it created weakened the flow.

Sarah helped Honda up. After getting her safely on top of a large boulder, Sarah walked towards the hole. The water was still pouring out at a steady rate, but only from the bottom portion of the hole. Standing in knee-deep water, she peered into the hole. She could see reflections of a bolt of lightning glisten off of the rushing water. After rolling boulders and piling rocks under the hole, she climbed on top of them and pull herself inside the newly created opening. Using every part of her body, she fought the rushing current and searched for an exit. Looking up, another bolt of lightning showed her the way.

As the beam twisted and the dam gave way, a tidal wave of fast moving water rushed down the tunnel towards the nursery taking everything it could with it. By the time it got to the end, dozens of sick creatures were flailing around in pools of mud, while others lapped up the filthy water like it was fine vintage wine. Once the diminished flow of water reached the crack, it worked its way through it and into the adjacent tunnel. The water exiting the gap, formed a tiny stream that slowly seeped out of the mine.

The rain started to ease up and a guard looked out the window at the mine. "Look at that. There is even water flowing out of the mine."

Thompson got up from his chair and went to the window. "You mean into, don't you?"

"No, out of."

"Maybe the rain was funnelled through an old air shaft. Not to worry, they are all barred up solid. Nothing bigger than a bat can get out of them." Thompson looked through his infrared binoculars. He couldn't see anything. "We're safe but I better phone it in anyway. You never know what those guys consider important."

After he got off the phone, his partner asked, "Well, what did they say?"

As he put on his raincoat, Thompson replied, "Just what I said, almost word for word." Opening up the door, he added, "But I'm still going to check it out anyway."

"In an hour our relief will be here. How about checking then?"

"And have them think that we are scared of a waterlogged cat?"

"Fine, we're out of coffee anyhow. I'll come with you. You know that nobody is supposed to go near that entrance without armed backup."

As Thompson waited for his partner to come out, two large round eyes watched their every move. With their rifles slung over their shoulders, each of the men carried a flashlight in one hand and a pistol in the other. They no sooner got to the entrance than their lights reflected back a giant pair of green eyes. The first guard froze as Thompson quickly fired. The shot was wild. Both guards backed up and emptied their pistols into the dark tunnel. It took them only seconds to reload magazines into their pistols. A half second too late. The large lion-like beast swiped one of his front claws across the neck of one guard as it jumped sideways at the pair. The creature's back claws dug deep into Thompson's chest. A section of the first guard's neck was torn open. Blood from the guard was spurting over the creature's chest as it looked behind him at Thompson. Despite air from his lungs gurgling out of his chest, Thompson finished loading his pistol. The beast flipped around and bit his powerful jaws into Thompson's neck. As the pair stopped twitching, the blood drenched creature gave out a wild echoing roar.

Like a pack of dogs, the other creatures slowly came out of the mine. Two more pairs of confused hunters walked out of the woods. Sniffing the dead bodies, they didn't know what to do. Their new leader showed them. Unlike their old leader, he wasn't afraid of man. After shredding off a pant leg with his claws, he bit into Thompson's thigh and tore off most of his calf. By the time he walked away, a feeding frenzy had torn the guards apart. Within seconds, chunks of meat were being taken away to be eaten at leisure by the larger males.

While the guts of some members of the colony were puffed out, others were still starving. The weaker females and what was left of their young slowly filtered out of the nursery. By that time the males had finished with the caribou, all that was left were bones and small pieces of hid. Crawling out of the mine, they found that the males and yearlings had almost done the same to the guards. Even an elk that another pair of hunters had dragged in wasn't enough for the entire colony. The starving sick creatures cried out. Their hunger pangs forced them to chew away at the scraps and break apart bones to get to the marrow.

The new leader walked through the colony like a king and sniffed each member and every member sniffed him out of respect. He searched through them all. Giving out a mournful growl, he turned and walked to the edge of the woods. Over a half dozen of the strongest creatures joined him. With a long rattling roar he turned and walked away. His followers trailed him, leaving the sick behind.

Sarah had watched the bloody feast from the top of the ridge. The gnashing of teeth dictated who ate as the creatures fought for scraps under a gyrating canopy of flapping wings. These creatures were natural killers. Looking around, she noticed that the guards had cleared away the forest to give themselves an unobstructed view of the entrance. The mine was no longer safe for the creatures to hide in. If the colony is forced to move, that could mean the creatures would be in contact with more humans. Sarah stared at what was left of the two guards. The large lion-like creature that had taken over the colony was not intimidated by man. Sarah knew that any contact at all could get very messy.

As she watched a family of long, thin, hairless, dragon-like creatures chew the rib bones of one of the guards, she felt that she could easily be next. Within the colony, Sarah knew that she was on the bottom of the food chain. Even if Honda was healthy, she couldn't stand up to the other members if they got hungry enough.

Sarah wiggled back down the washed-out animal hole. The large water reservoir that had formed at the bottom was big enough that she could stretch and limber up her sore body, before crawling back into the tunnel. After tossing in a coil of rope, Sarah used both arms to carefully place Honda into the hole. Using the gentle flowing water to help lubricate and keep Honda's wings from getting caught up, Sarah pushed her in front of her. Once inside the reservoir, she tied the rope to Honda and looped the other end of it around her shoulder. Pulling Honda behind her, she gingerly climbed up the steep animal hole to the top of the ridge.

Feeling Honda's forehead, Sarah knew that the cool water was helping bring down her fever. Below her, Sarah could see the blood-drenched creatures returning to the tunnel. After folding Honda's wings over her body like a blanket, Sarah slipped into the hole and back into the tunnel. Grabbing her backpack, she could hear a few creatures approach. The unusual allure of fresh air and water was drawing them closer. Stepping on the pile of rocks, she stuffed her bag in first and then climbed into the hole.

It didn't take long before the creatures discovered the opening. Sarah scurried up the hole, pushing her pack in front of her. As she climbed out, she could hear some chatter coming from the reservoir underneath her. Out of fear, she rolled a large rock over the opening of the downward-sloping hole and wedged it in place using several smaller ones. "That should hold them for a while."

Chapter Fifteen

Retaliation

Duncan woke up feeling a strange numbness over his entire body. It was a feeling he had felt several times before. Each time, something had gone fatally wrong. Laurie knocked at the door. The hairs on the back of his neck were still twitching as he said, "Come in."

"We received a strange message. A flow of water was coming out of the mine. That was an hour ago. We haven't had any contact with the two guards since then."

Duncan got out of bed and hopped onto his computer chair. After switching his monitor over to the camera they had installed in the mine, he found out it was dead. "Something must have severed the link during the night."

Laurie looked at Duncan's scarred back and shoulders. The ridges of the scars made his skin look more like an alligator's than human. "Their relief is ready to depart and I thought that we should send some backup just in case."

Duncan placed the fingers on each hand together as his arms rested on his desk. "Very smart move. Excluding the ones currently on sentry duty, I want all available personnel to assemble in the garage. Hopefully it's nothing and they will be able to go back off duty within the hour. At the very least, it'll be a good training exercise."

Two dozen armed guards assembled in the garage and mounted their 4X4 ATV personnel carriers. As they approached the entrance like a well-rehearsed SWAT team, the first group jumped off their ATVs with their assault rifles and ran for cover. In sets of threes, one team advanced and covered the next team as they advanced. Methodically, the guards slowly made their way towards the mine from every direction. The wind picked up and something floated past a guard kneeling next to the trailer. He looked down. It was the front section of a uniform. Even through the blood stain he could make out the name 'Thompson'.

The guard's left arm flew into the air and Duncan made his way over to him. "What's up?"

"It's Thompson." The guard pointed to the soiled piece of uniform. "The creatures have escaped and I think that they have declared war."

Duncan looked around. "We don't know how many are left inside and how many are roaming around outside the mine. Some of them could be in the forest watching us right now."

The confused guard responded, "I thought they were all sick and most of them were dying?"

"The ones trapped inside are. There must have been some roaming around outside. Either that or they have another exit."

Duncan set up an armed ring around the entrance with every third weapon pointed into the surrounding trees. Slowly he led a small four-man unit towards the entrance. In two pairs, one on each side, they advanced, ducked, covered and protected their partner while the other pair advanced. In this leapfrogging motion, with flashlights attached to their rifles, one from each pair made it inside the tunnel. Out of the darkness, a fast horned creature flew out as a guard tried to dash forward. Its mace-like tail struck the side of the guard's head. With guards on opposite sides of the tunnel, the creature was too fast for them to get off a clean shot. Behind them, a flurry of gunfire erupted outside of the mine. Duncan turned and yelled, "Did you get it?"

A guard yelled back, "We managed to hit it a few times but it still zoomed right past us."

Duncan looked at his unit. "We're doing this all wrong. They don't have guns to fire back at us. Form a line so they can't get between us."

The flattened guard got up and rolled his head from side to side as he shouldered his rifle. "My neck will be sore in the morning." With one hand on the back of his neck, he pulled out his pistol and lined up with the other three. They worked their way down the tunnel until they got to a fallen crossbeam.

As they crouched behind the beam, Duncan got on his headset. "Send in the next team." They waited as four more guards rushed in. "Use this as a firing post."

Duncan looked behind him and saw the guard rubbing his neck. The side of his head was covered in blood. "You might as well go back and sit this one out." The injured guard rested against the wall before working his way back. In the dim light it was hard to distinguish one man from another. Duncan simply tapped the guard next to him. "You, come with us."

Laurie piped up. "Yes, sir."

They slowly proceeded forward down the middle of the tunnel. As two knelt down with rifles ready, the other two advanced no further than the ends of their rifles. They felt no need to hurry. Moving slowly and methodically, they checked every crack and crevice before they advanced any further. Twenty minutes passed before they got to the unsealed crack. Fragments of bone from the caribou were still scattered in front of it. "Let's go back. I've seen enough."

Duncan threw down a flare. As the bright red flare lit up the tunnel behind them, they moved back. "That should blind them and give us a chance to get out."

The flare was quickly extinguished in a cloud of dust. The rustling sounds of a flurry of movement echoed down the tunnel behind them as they retreated. Duncan lit a green flare to indicate that they were coming out. He didn't want a nervous finger to fire at any of them. Outside, they all ran to the tree line. Laurie sat opposite the same tree as Duncan. "You know what happened, don't you?"

"It was obvious. There were some creatures out hunting food when we sealed the rest in. The men were too rushed and we did a fast, sloppy job." Duncan put his head between his knees. "It's all my fault. We should have used cement instead of mortar mix to seal the crack. I wasn't counting on any of them digging it out from the outside."

"Not only that, but the flow of water was coming out of the crack. That much water could mean that there could be still another way out."

Duncan looked around the tree and into Laurie's eyes, "This really could mean an all-out war. We attacked and threatened their home and killed off several of their offspring and mates. I don't know what their family bond is like, but I know that if that happened to any of us, we'd be out for blood."

"Look around you. They have never attacked and consumed humans before, have they?" Duncan looked over the bloody clearing. "We may have pushed them too far."

Laurie saw a glimmer of sorrow in Duncan's eyes. "They are vicious monsters. They are not even supposed to exist."

"But they do."

Laurie thought for a moment. "As far as not attacking humans, wasn't there partial remains of a human skull amongst the bones in the cavern." Duncan quickly studied Laurie's frightened face. "Don't worry, it was too small to be Little Sister's."

Laurie stretched out her arm and gripped Duncan's shoulder, "Have you found any trace of her?"

"We got a glimpse of her in the cavern. She was with one of the creatures. I don't know why, but I think that she may be running with the pack."

******

Sarah had managed to carry Honda down the side of the ridge and into the woods. Her fever started to return. The entire body of the sick creature was burning. Sarah laid her down in the wet mud with her wings spread out. Almost immediately the fresh mud cooled off the blood flowing through Honda's wings and slowly started to drop her temperature. Her breathing was in small gasps. As Honda's eyes opened, Sarah started to cry. If it wasn't for this creature, she knew that she could have been butchered by the others. Now it was her turn. Sarah knew that she had to look after her.

Looking up in the air, she shook her head. The doctor would kill, dissect, and place Honda's organs in jars. She couldn't take her back home. Looking down into a pool of water, she saw herself. She hadn't seen her reflection since she had run away. In the short time that she was gone, the infection had rapidly spread throughout her body. The growth of fur had spread up her neck and onto her face. She stripped off her hoodie and almost cut herself with the sharp nails at the ends of her hairy fingers. A thick mat of hair was creeping over half of her body, the same colour and texture as Honda's. "Maybe those bandages were keeping the infection from spreading." The ripples in the water started to settle and she saw her face. She was no longer Sarah. The face that stared back at her wasn't human. A strange creature with large round eyes, big pointed ears and an extraordinarily long, wide nose. "How can I go home looking like this, looking like the creatures that Dad has hated all these years? What can I do?" Looking upwards into the sky, she whimpered, "What should I do?"

******

George walked over to the fallen tree that Duncan and Laurie were sitting on. "I found some tracks."

Duncan immediately stood up. "How many?"

"It's hard to tell. They are doing a good job of masking their trail. Could be three, four or maybe even up to a dozen."

"What are they doing?"

"It looks like they are hunting. The tracks are spread out like they are pushing animals towards a trap. They are herding their prey like a pack of wolves."

Duncan had known George for only a couple years. In that time he had found the prints of every reporter and nosey busybody that came near the facility. He paid him like any other guard but had allowed him to wear whatever he wanted and the freedom to do his job. From his long black scraggly hair with small pieces of leaves and twigs stuck in it, to the soft waterproof moccasins on his feet, he was at home in the woods. He was hired to patrol the outside perimeter of the facility and that is what he did. Even going inside the fence was too confining for him.

Duncan thought for a while. "Where were the tracks heading?"

"East, towards the Provincial Park."

"As long as it's away from here." Duncan handed George a radio. "Take this and keep an eye on them."

George handed Duncan back the headset. "I'll take the walkie but not the headpiece. It's too distracting. I won't be able to feel my way around with that thing attached to my ear."

Turning to Laurie, Duncan said, "We have them divided up. The healthy ones are probably gathering food for the sick ones left in the mine. We have to exploit this opportunity the best we can."

"How?"

"First, we seal off the tunnel so the virus and hunger can start killing off the ones inside. Second, we gas any that are left. I'm not going to risk anyone else's life if I don't have to."

"What about the ones out here?"

"They had all come in contact with the virus and should be feeling its effect soon. For now, let them hunt. As long as they leave us alone, we can use the time to eradicate the rest of them. Then we'll become the hunters and they'll be the prey."

At first, the guards cut down trees and began to construct a crude wooden barricade in front of the mine. Large plates of steel, generators and welders were loaded onto trailers and hauled to the site by ATVs. Duncan directed his men as they constructed a steel gateway. The design was simple: a solid steel barrier mounted on a wide footing so it wouldn't sink into the ground, with a small steel door in the middle. It was secured in place by two giant 45-degree supporting brackets going down its entire height and extending out until it was flush with the ground. Two additional smaller brackets were welded next to the two bottom corners. Next came the concrete. By nightfall every crack between the steel and rock face was sealed and a pad of thick cement was poured. "Nothing is going to get through that."

George softly whispered into the radio, "Duncan, they are coming back."

Even with the volume turned down low George had pulled his thick, insulated shirt over his head to further muffle Duncan's reply. "How much time do we have?"

"At the pace they are travelling, you have two or three hours. They are dragging a lot of meat behind them."

"That was fast. It took days for them to return last time." Duncan thought for a second before adding, "Did you manage to get an accurate count of them?"

"Eight."

"Are they healthy?"

"All but two. The sick ones are lagging behind. I won't be able to trail both groups."

"Then try to follow the healthy ones. They're going to be the most dangerous."

"I'll try. The problem will be masking my own trail from the two sickies behind them."

"Do your best and don't let them find you."

All of Duncan's men were exhausted from a long day of hard work. The thick steel door on the gateway was tack welded shut and the cement was already hard enough to walk on. Duncan got up and walked around the camp. His men had no protection from an attack. The night's darkness would only further benefit the creatures in a fight. "Let's pack it in. We're not ready of a face them yet. We'll pick our own time to fight those beasts and it'll be under our terms."

By the time the hunting party had returned, the guards had packed up and left. From the tree line the new king examined the newly constructed barrier. Leaving their kill behind, a dog-like creature and a lizard-like creature approached the entrance. The cement felt strange under their feet. Picking up a boulder, the dog-like creature dropped it on the cement. It bounced and rolled off of the pad. The large lion-like creature had watched the fine dust puff up as it hit. Going over to the pad, he looked at the few flakes of cement that had been chipped off. He picked up the boulder and heaved it into the air. As it smashed against the cement, a small crater formed. The large creature waved his arms and two creatures scaled the ridge. One by one they rolled large boulders onto the cement pad. After each impact, the others below dug away at the craters they had made. By the time they got down to the grid-work of rebar, the cement was still green. Grabbing a hold of the rebar, several creatures pulled and bent it until they had a big enough area to work in. Two dog-like creatures dug into the looser green cement and under the steel gateway. Inside the mine, others pulled apart the wooden structure and helped dig a trench.

A muffled voice came over Duncan's radio. "They're getting in."

"How?"

"The concrete wasn't set enough. They pounded through it with rocks and then dug a hole under the steel."

"So the gateway is still in place." Duncan grinned, "Don't worry, today was just a start. Tomorrow is another day."

Laurie looked at Duncan. "We'll be more prepared tomorrow."

"Yes, and we're wearing them down. All today cost us was a little cement. Remember that they are infected. Any stress we can inflict upon them will only help the virus spread."

Chapter Sixteen

Death

Before dawn, a lone creature watched as a small parade of his comrades re-entered the woods. A sharp horn protruded from its nose and two more from its forehead. Its large eyes and protective plate at the back of its skull gave it an owl-like appearance. From high on a ledge under an outcrop, the creature watched everything that went on. In the shadows, his coarse, streaked grey and black hair made him blend into the rocks. His front right leg was covered in dried blood. Blood was oozing out of the long scab on his shoulder. Lying on the ledge, the low angle of the first rays of sunlight warmed his throbbing body.

From halfway up a tall pine, George covered his head with his coat before reporting. "A large group of the creatures has left the tunnel."

Duncan rolled out of bed and grabbed his radio. "How many?"

"Eighteen, twenty, maybe more. They were bunched up and it's still too dark to get an accurate count."

"Stay put and keep an eye on the entrance until we arrive."

Looking down, the solitary creature had no problem spotting the lookout. Its leg was too sore to move, and even breathing was painful. Turning slightly to the north, he could make out Sarah kneeling in the swamp. She was feeding Honda her last tin of canned meat. It was some sort of fish. The lingering smell of it had drifted up. Both George and the creature could smell its strong odour.

George covered his head again. "Duncan, I think Sarah is outside. I can't see her but I can smell tuna. She must have opened a tin. No hunter or woodsman would carry that stuff. It's a sure giveaway."

"Thanks, that's great news."

Duncan was all smiles as he bumped into Laurie in the garage. "George has told me that Sarah is safe and is outside the mine. You don't have to worry about her anymore. Now we can finally gas inside. After that, we can hunt down and exterminate the rest of the creatures."

Within half an hour Duncan had arrived with a fleet of ATVs carrying armed guards and supplies. The concrete pad was stained in blood. To get the large elk into the mine, the hunters had to tear it into smaller pieces. A few pieces of fur and a hoof were all that was left.

Using the hole the creatures had dug, the guards rolled several canisters under the steel gateway and into the mine. After that, they quickly filled the hole with rocks. The bent up rebar was easily straightened and wired back in place before more concrete was poured. As the patch of cement dried, Duncan oversaw the fortifications. By nine a.m. the men had already started constructing a series of bunkers and a barbed wire perimeter fence. Each of the dirt bunkers had a thick bagged wall and only one gap at the rear to allow the guards to enter. The bags in the wall were filled with dirt and rocks to prevent the creatures from digging into them. A woven steel roof was designed to prevent the creatures from flying into them or dropping objects on top of the guards stationed inside.

A pair of agile guards checked and filled every crack around the door and steel structure with expandable foam and chalking. After testing the cement, they built a large bunker between the two large 45-degree brackets of the steel barrier.

After looking around, Duncan decided it was time. He walked over to his ATV and took a box out of his pack. He opened its front and set the timer. "Everyone get ready. No one knows how those creatures are going to react."

Inside the mine, the gas silently spewed out of the canisters and filled the tunnel with poisonous fumes. Slowly the heavy yellow cloud worked its way through the crack and into the nursery. The cracks around the hole that Sarah crawled out of sucked the air upward like a chimney and made matters worse.

Seeing the gas slowly rolling in, the shocked sick creatures scrambled to stay ahead of it. Several of the sick males picked up the steel plate and leaned it against the opening. Several more helped by throwing mud and rocks into the cracks. The males that breathed in the most gas started to choke. Within minutes they were lying on the ground not able to breathe. Death was quick. The same fate had happened to several of the females that helped pack the mud into the leaking holes.

Retreating farther into the tunnel, the creatures carried and pulled the sick along with them. There was no way out of the old tunnel, the far end had been sealed up from a mine collapse. The only chance they had was through the small hole that Sarah had created. Only a handful had the strength to crawl into it. Of the ones that could, none of them had the strength to push out the rocks that Sarah had jammed in.

The lion-like creature stood up on his hind legs and looked around. Many of the other members of the hunting party had also stopped. They all knew that something was wrong. Suddenly, they turned around and most of them took to the sky and flew just above the tree tops. Others broke into a feverish race through the forest back to the mine. The creatures' quick turnaround caught George off guard. He dove and sank into a swamp as they rushed by. With only the top of his head above water, George waited for them to pass. With the plant life clinging to his hair, only his eyes were visible. He patiently waited until even the slower, sick creatures had walked past him.

Crawling out of the mud, George was surprised to see one still lingering far behind. As the sick creature tried to gather the energy to continue, George drew his hunting knife and charged at him. Before the sick creature could turn to face him, George had plunged his knife deep into its back. The sick beast was too weak to put up a fight. Twisting the knife as he pulled it out, both blood and air gurgled out with it. With another quick jerk, he slit the sick beast's throat. Its blood gushed all over him. "That'll put you out of your misery."

A long lizard-like creature soared past the entrance too quickly for anyone to get a shot. The second looked like a monkey and was met with a volley of gunfire. The element of surprise had vanished. As a dragon-like beast approached, it was shot out of the air. Rolling to the ground, its lifeless body bounced several times before colliding into in front of Laurie's bunker. Its long neck and head were tossed over its side. Several other creatures rushed the perimeter. The barbed wire hidden behind the brush caught them by surprise. As they tried to get untangled, the guards riddled the trapped creatures with bullets. A couple creatures jumped up into the trees and leaped over the fence. The creatures dashed into the closest bunker. Once inside, the guards fired at will in every direction. Shocked by the speed of the attack, the three guards had barely enough time to turned and face the creatures before they were torn apart. Within seconds, one of the creatures ran out of the back door and was met with a barrage of gunfire.

On the other side of the fence, a pluming cloud of dirt rose up and covered the encircled guards. The trapped lizard-like beast crawled out of one bunker and slithered into the next. The cloud of dirt, dust and debris continued. Taking advantage of the dust-storm, the beast once again wiggled out of a silenced bunker and slithered its way into another.

Laurie's bunker butted up to the ridge. Everyone was focussed on the fence line. As the creature wrapped its claws around the first man's neck, blood sprayed the side of Laurie's face. The creature was almost hidden behind the gasping man. Only the top of the creature's head was visible. Laurie turned her rifle and shot through the guard's dying body. The guard behind her joined in. Both had emptied their magazines and quickly changed them. There wasn't any movement. Laurie attached her bayonet and with it rolled over the guard's body. Under it she found the limp body of the creature half covered in dirt . As she shot it, it came to life. The bullet ricocheted off of its tough scales and into the dirt. The small cloud of dirt it created was enough for the creature to vanish. Both guards retreated to the far end of the bunker. "It's probably hiding under Steve's body. It knows it's safe there. We couldn't shoot through both sides of Steve's body armour."

The guard squeezed next to Laurie added, "Plus, the creature has its own."

As her partner sprayed the bunker with bullets, Laurie stole a quick glance at the fence line. Another plume of dirt had started to rise next to it. When the dust settled inside, the creature had disappeared. "Make sure that it hasn't just covered itself up with dirt."

Laurie's partner attached his bayonet to his rifle and started to methodically stab the dirt walls and floor of the bunker. Duncan's voice came over the radio. "Laurie, get your men out of there. Your position is being set up for a mass attack."

As the pair ran out of the bunker, Duncan yelled at them. "Get down!"

The lizard-like creature had leaped into the air and was heading straight for Laurie. Before the pair could hit the ground, Duncan was running towards them shooting over their heads. A bullet to the side of the creature's head twisted it over. Its softer underbelly was torn apart as Duncan emptied his magazine into it. Other guards ran out of the main bunker and joined in. They continued to fire into the dead creature's body until Laurie and her partner got to safety.

All the bunkers on the north side of the gateway had been overrun. The bunkers themselves had become obstacles and prevented the guards from seeing the bottom half of the fence. Duncan turned to Laurie. "The men are not trained for this type of an assault. These creatures don't fight like normal soldiers."

With a quarter of his men already killed, Duncan made a decision. "This plan isn't working. We have to retreat."

"Where?"

"Into the mine. The only creatures left in there are the dead and dying. I'd rather face them than this crafty horde. I wasn't expecting any kind of organized attack from a bunch of mutated animals."

Laurie turned to Duncan. "Remember George telling you that they hunted like a pack of wolves? He tried to warn you. Now they're nipping at our heels. They are just waiting for a chance to come in for the kill."

The main bunker was a huge semicircle in front of the gateway. The cement pad meant that the creatures couldn't tunnel their way in. A steel mesh covered the dirt walls and prevented them from digging through. Most of the twenty-one men that remained huddled together along the wall. Duncan paced back and forth keeping an eye on the gaps being created in the fence. The creatures were stacking wood and rocks to crush it. They had turned the fence into a giant ramp. Turning around, he watched a guard grind away the welds, "Hurry up, they are getting ready for an attack."

"I'm going as fast as I can. There's only one generator in here and it can only handle one grinder. The rest were all sent back."

A dust storm started to rise behind the bunkers. At the same time boulders started to rain down on top of them. The posts holding up the thick steel mesh started to bend from the impact of the heavy boulders. The right side of the roof buckled and drooped against the wall. Duncan looked back at the door. The last weld was being ground off. "Everyone put on your gas masks."

Chapter Seventeen

Revelations

From his perch, the lone injured onlooker watched as his comrades surrounded the men. Below him, a half dozen of the best and healthiest of his fellow creatures lay dead, killed by the apes that were trying to eradicate them. He watched their new king as he orchestrated his attack and ran back and forth along the guard's destroyed fence line. The king bellowed a loud, terrifying roar that echoed off of the side of the ridge, bringing cold shivers up the guards' spines. More boulders rolled down the cliff onto the men as they began to squeeze through the narrow doorway into the mine. The dog-like creatures got closer and closer as they dug trenches toward the men. Above them, thick clouds of dust and dirt formed, helping them mask the movements of the rest.

Through the hail of dirt and debris, even the men wearing infrared goggles couldn't get a clean shot. As another barrage of boulders fell onto the roof, the welds holding the mesh roof to the gateway started to break away creating a large gap. Another roar rang out and this time it wasn't boulders coming down. Two creatures on top of the ridge released a stack of logs. Behind them was a large truck load of loose gravel. The gravel flooded the bunker. The door leading into the mine was jammed open by the falling debris. Several men on the left side of the bunker were disarmed and buried up to their waists with battered limbs. A couple more had their necks broken and one guard was buried alive.

Sweat ran down Duncan's face as he desperately used his hands and arms to help dig and pull his legs out of the gravel. After checking his gasmask, he crawled over the debris and wiggled into the mine as the creatures rushed towards the bunker.

The reigning king crawled through the gap in the roof and tossed a boulder into the doorway. He narrowly missed Duncan's leg. The helpless men and women left outside were systematically butchered by both claws and teeth. The fact that some were still alive didn't matter to the creatures as they chewed away at their flesh.

Duncan could hear the screams coming from the men left outside. It only took a minute before their voices were silenced forever. Duncan looked around at his remaining force. He was down to fifteen, including himself. Several had lost their weapons. There were only four sets of functioning night-vision goggles. The rest were either smashed or lost in the confusion. He quickly divided the men into four groups. Two groups with four each lined up across the tunnel and waited for the creatures to enter. Laurie led another group past the gap and laid out a secondary defensive line, in case any creatures were hiding at the far end of the tunnel. Duncan tried to squeeze through the crack into the adjacent tunnel. He was too big. "Laurie, we're going to have to switch."

Laurie stripped off her belt and emptied her pockets of anything bulky. With only a pistol and her goggles, she wiggled into the crack. The steel plate leaning against the far end stopped her. After working her way out, she told Duncan, "They have sealed themselves in. They have taken the steel plate inside and piled something behind it for reinforcement."

"That means that some of them are still alive. It also means that they are in there and not out here. Let's make sure that it stays that way." Duncan handed Laurie a small pack of explosives. "Seal it."

Everyone covered their ears as the BOOM echoed through the tunnel. The vibration shook the lone sentry's shelf. His sensitive ears could hear the frightened creatures trapped inside. Dust clouds filled the nursery. The sick and dying creatures had to fight even harder for any of the remaining oxygen. The sentry crawled towards the top of the ridge. The moaning got louder. He removed the small rocks and then the boulder that Sarah had used to plug the narrow hole. He could hear their voices rattling upward. The wounded creature growled down the hole and tried to comfort them. Looking down the ridge, he could see the others gorging themselves on the guard's bodies. He could also see Sarah nursing Honda back to health.

The creature crawled down the ridge and walked around Sarah in a wide circle. As the circle got closer and closer, Sarah got more alarmed. She picked up Honda and tried to carry her away. The creature paced back and forth ahead of them. It didn't take long before Sarah realized that the creature was herding them towards the ridge. Even though it had only three good legs and one good wing, Sarah knew that she was still no match for him. With its horns always facing her, it slowly forced her up the ridge. Every time she tried to resist, the creature snarled and lunged towards her. Sarah set Honda down and tried to run away. The creature leaped in front of her. Despite a steady flow of blood dripping out of his reopened wounds, the creature was relentless. After twenty-five terrifying minutes, Sarah found herself standing next to the hole.

Sarah could hear the sick choking creatures below. She looked down at the hole and then back at the creature. "What do you want me to do?"

The creature dug a small hole with its front paw and looked at her. Sarah stood there confused. The creature put his head in the hole that he made and then out again. He studied Sarah's reaction. He repeated the movements several more times until the expression on Sarah's face changed. "You expect me to go back into the hole?"

The creature could somehow sense her understanding. He put his head into his hole and picked up a stone in his teeth. Sarah understood. "You actually want me to go back in there and get your friends out, don't you?" Sarah put her hand down the hole and pulled out a handful of dirt, and then repeated it several times. The exhausted creature finally showed signs of contentment.

Sitting next to the hole, Sarah looked over at the entrance of the mine and then at the horned beast. "That is why you forced me back up here." Sarah pointed down the ridge at the other creatures. "Why not them?"

He rolled his head at the others. Slowly he walked over to Honda and nudged her onto her feet. Standing back, he looked at Sarah. "It's because I'm nursing her back to health. You think that I can do the same to the others. You think that I'm some kind of healer, don't you?"

The creature put his head into the hole and bashed the sides of his face plates against the edges. He lay down and gave Sarah a good view of the extent of his injuries. "So you are not physically able to do it. I've underestimated those guys. You are a lot smarter than you look."

Sarah opened her backpack and retrieved a long rope. After tying one end around the trunk of a small pine tree, she threw the rest down the hole. Slowly she went in head first. With her arms in front of her, she controlled her descent into the old water reservoir. Two shadows huddled along the far end. Even in the poor light, their green eyes gave them away. After turning herself around, she peeked through the hole in the wall. Over two dozen creatures were huddled together next to it. Several saw her, but didn't have the strength to get up. She threw the rope out through the hole and used it to help her climb down.

A sick young creature lifted its head and tried to hiss at her. The effort made it collapse. Sarah went over and felt its chest. It was barely breathing and extremely hot. The youngster tried to swipe her. Its claws merely scraped a couple red lines in her arm. She grabbed its paws and tied them together as other crawled toward her.

Above her, growls from the wounded horned creature echoed out of the hole. The creatures around Sarah stopped and stood their ground. After quickly climbing back into the reservoir, she pulled the young creature inside. Immediately the young creature tried to struggle free. With two pairs of eyes staring at her, Sarah had nowhere to go but up into the hole. Even that took too long. By the time she had wiggled fully in, the claws on the young creature had ripped a dozen or more gashes in her legs.

Outside of the hole the horned creature was waiting for her. He watched as she got out and started to pull on the rope. Suddenly, Sarah fell backward and landed on her back. Someone behind her had heaved on the rope. Standing above her was the king with the rope in his teeth. When the youngster popped out, the horned creature released it from its bonds.

Honda gazed at the king as he looked the youngster over. She gave out a soft cat-like meow. The king turned and saw Honda. He ran to her and rubbed his head against hers. Sarah saw the pair and smiled. The large majestic beast could smell Sarah's scent all over Honda. He looked over at her. Blood was dripping down Sarah's legs and into her moccasins as she took a step backwards. She couldn't tell what he was thinking. Was he happy or hungry? Was she safe or should she risk diving down the hole and taking a chance with the sick creatures below? The king stood tall on his hind legs and walked over to her. She couldn't move. She stood there frozen as the beast gently rubbed its head against hers.

Sarah's entire body shook as the powerful beast walked back to the hole. With a loud growl he summoned three more creatures onto the ridge. They looked over at Sarah and hissed. The king snarled at them. The creatures looked away. Feeling a small degree of safety, she rushed over to Honda. "So that's your father."

Honda's father studied what Sarah had done to extract the youngster. He softly growled at two of the other creatures. Carefully they dragged the youngster over to Sarah. The youngster tried to squirm away. A striped, winged female creature with a face between a wolf and badger softly growled at it and Sarah noticed the soothing effect that the low rattling sounds had on the youngster. The sick young creature looked at Sarah and suddenly it wasn't scared of her anymore. Sarah couldn't understand how, but the creatures were able to talk to each other in an almost human fashion. It was much more sophisticated than the simplistic howls amongst a pack of wolves on a hunt. Even a good shepherd can control the movements of his dogs with a whistle. Sarah watched Honda as she rattled back and forth with the youngster. Sarah had thought that the rattling was just a show of rank and positioning among the colony members. Now she knew for sure that it was much more than that. They were actually talking to each other.

Sarah went over to the youngster. Its body was burning. Spreading out its wings she tried to use the gentle wind to cool the blood flowing through them. "It needs water." Not knowing what to do, she turned to the leader and repeated, "It needs water. I'll have to get it some water." Sarah pulled out two empty water bottles out of her pack. Uncapping them, she shook out the last drops out of them. "I need to get water."

Sarah slowly started to walk down the side of the ridge. The striped creature suddenly pounced in front of her. She couldn't understand its rattling growls, but it was clear that she wasn't to leave the sick youngster's side. It looked at one bottle than the other and back again. Then its head looked up at hers. Sarah knew what it wanted. Sarah put down the bottles and walked back to the sick youngster. By the time she got the nerve to look back, the creature was gone and so were the bottles.

Within a minute the same creature landed on top of the ridge next to Sarah. With a bottle in one hand, she pretended to drink it. Sarah knew that the creature must have seen her drink from the bottles while she was in the tunnel.

As Sarah wetted down the sick creature, she looked around and was shocked by how quickly the creatures found a way to mimic her actions. By working together and studying her knots, they could manipulate their claws and fingers into duplicating them. With a few vocal grunts and rattles, some creatures went down the hole while others pulled on the rope.

As soon as another creature was hauled out, it was quickly carried over to Sarah and gently laid in front of her. She spread out its wings to help cool it off. Its breathing had almost stopped. Sarah grabbed its arms and pulled them outwards and then across its chest. She repeated the movement until she saw it shake its head. It was still alive. With fresh oxygen in its lungs, its breathing slightly improved. As water was used to lower its temperature, it improved even more.

The sick creatures pulled out of mine were all placed in rows. With the aid of the protective striped female and another that resembled a flying lizard with long narrow ears, Sarah tried everything she knew in order to help them. The pair watched everything what she did, saw the results and began to mimic her actions. Two dog-like creatures did nothing but fetch water from a clear flowing stream, using guard's helmets for buckets. Even with all the time she had spent with them inside the mine, she had never thought that they were anything more than vicious animals. As she worked, she thought, *they just want to survive. If a group of starving people were trapped in a mine, how would they have behaved?*

Working closely with the two erratic female creatures wasn't easy. Not being able to communicate with each other added to the extreme pressure that Sarah was under. Putting one hand on the lizard-like female's shoulder, she pointed to her chest. "Sarah." Pointing to the creature's chest, she asked, "You."

The creature twisted its head to the side and rattled out, "Meeeoo."

Well I guess that is what I can call you. Directing your finger towards the striped female she was surprised by a quick, "Baaaeee."

After taking a couple seconds to think, the trio went back to work. With Sarah calling the two creatures, Mew and Betty and the creatures referring to her as Rah, tending to the sick creatures became less stressful. Even Mew and Betty seemed less frazzled.

******

Inside the mine, the guards nervously waited for an attack. "What's keeping them? I haven't even seen any of them go near the door."

"What's their hurry? We're the ones stuck in here with no food or water. If Duncan had thought that we'd be retreating into the mine, he would've never welded the door shut, now would he?"

"Yes, but he made sure there was a door."

The guards in the line in front of the door never heard Duncan's approach. "I made a mistake. I greatly underestimated them."

A guard turned to him. "How are we going to get out of here?"

"I wouldn't worry about that. I've already requested a crew to burrow a hole into the tunnel so we can get out. They are going over the blueprints right now to find the best location. All we have to do is wait and kill anything that tries to enter that door."

As Duncan started to leave, another guard asked him, "Do you have any more batteries? The ones in my goggles are running low."

"I'll check around and see if I can find any."

With having to keep their gas masks on at all times, it didn't matter how much food and water they had. Duncan paced in every direction as his mind raced through all of their problems. All the supplies they had were from two backpacks and what the guards had in their pockets and on their belts. Without a steady supply of batteries, they would be also blind and would be left at the creatures' mercy. Getting on the headset, he asked, "Roger, can you re-open that crack and get one of your robots to deliver us some supplies?"

"We're working on that already. It will take time before we can get anything to you. Unless we can form a counterattack, you may be stuck there for two or three days before we can get you out."

"We'll also need a method to eat and drink without taking off our masks."

"I'll see what I can think of. Maybe a small tent with a steady supply of fresh air to push the gas away. Don't worry, I'll rig something up."

Duncan thought some more. "Can't you just widen the crack enough to get us out?"

"Too unstable. The ceiling is nothing but a loose pile of rocks. Any disruption inside could send them crushing down and we could lose any chance of getting supplies to you."

"I've got two women down here. If Sarah could crawl through it, maybe they could crawl out."

"Maybe, but only if they are really small framed. I bet that even Sarah had a hard time getting through it."

"You know Laurie. She could probably fit through. The other girl isn't that much bigger."

"We'll see. Anyway, have a few of your men wait in the cavern for the supplies. They should be there in a few hours."

Duncan rearranged the men. After ordering four guards to try to get some sleep, he took Laurie aside. "Get your girlfriend and wait for Roger to deliver some supplies. Afterwards, the two of you will have a chance to climb out. The rest of us are too big to crawl through the narrow crack."

"I'm here. I can help you fight if or when the creatures attack."

"If they do attack us, we need you out there. We will need someone that is capable of leading a counterattack. Roger is good with machines and technical stuff. The doctor is no soldier at all. To him this whole thing is a giant lab experiment. I need someone with your skills and training out there."

******

From the sky over the ridge, Doctor Scott surveyed carnage. Two guards sat in the back seat with loaded assault rifles in case any creature tried to attack the helicopter. Through his binoculars the three rows of creatures lying on top of the ridge were easy to spot. The doctor pointed them out to the pilot. "I want to take a better look. I can't tell if those bodies are dead or alive."

Even as the helicopter got closer, the sick creatures didn't move. Sarah helped Honda to her feet and hid her under a short, dense spruce tree. Through his binoculars the doctor could still get a good look at Sarah's topless body. He could see the fur that covered most of her exposed skin in various degrees. The only other physical changes that he could make out were the size of Sarah's ears and shape of her nose.

"As I thought, the cells were just mustering up strength. With the skin being the biggest and least vital organ, they chose it to be the first battlefield. After all, what is a little extra body hair?"

The other creatures helping in the rescue quickly dispersed among the shrubs and small trees. The sick creatures were left in the open. Doctor Scott took a closer look. He couldn't tell if they were alive or if the blades of the helicopter were causing them to move. "I can't see any blood. Shoot a couple of them, that will tell us if they are still alive or not."

One of the back doors opened and a guard emptied a magazine of bullets along the length of one of the rows of sick creatures. Bullets struck four of them. The doctor closely watched the creatures through his binoculars as the bullets hit them. They barely moved. He could see the fresh blood exiting the bullet wounds. "They are still alive. Why are they not moving?" The doctor answered his own question. "It's the virus. They are too sick to move."

The guard behind the doctor grinned as he asked him, "Can't we just put them out of their misery?"

"You may be right. We may not get another golden opportunity like this."

With both back doors open, the helicopter circled around for another pass. The king and two dog-like creatures jumped into the air and furiously flapped their wings. After a short scoop down the ridge to pick up speed, they dashed upwards toward the helicopter. The king zoomed by the craft as it tried to hover over the bodies. The sight of him caught the pilot by surprise. He swung the helicopter around as the guards started to open fire. Their bullets went wild. One of the other creatures grabbed onto the helicopter's landing gear. The two guards in the back quickly shut the doors and held on as the sudden shift in weight and increased drag twisted the machine.   The pilot did everything he knew to correct for the constantly shifting drag caused by the creature's flapping wings. "This craft isn't designed for this!"

As the pilot twisted the helicopter about, he found the wings of the large lion-like creature blocking his view. As the third creature attached itself to the helicopter's underbelly, the pilot gave it full power. He tried to use speed to loosen the creatures' grip. At the same time, he twisted and turned the nimble craft, narrowly missing tree tops and rocky outcrops.

Watching the helicopter race away, the king roared as loud as he could. The two creatures finally release their grip and hovered in the sky as the helicopter darted away. Feeling victorious, the trio returned to the rows of sick, dead and dying.

Looking down at the rows of sick creatures, the king knew none of them were safe in or out of the mine. They needed to find a new home.

Chapter Eighteen

Starting over

As the helicopter landed, Doctor Scott stumbled and almost fell out the door. The two guards that followed him got out on a run, only stopping when they got to the doorway in front of the facility. The shaky pilot took his time and slowly walked a half dozen steps before collapsing to his knees. "That's not for me. You're going to have to get somebody else to fly you around."

The doctor bent over and helped the pilot to his feet. "Don't worry, I don't want to get that close to those creatures ever again. At least not in the wild. Your job is safe. You can just continue doing your normal flights."

Gazing at the helicopter, the pilot saw the gashes torn into the craft's aluminum skin. "I'll need to get it fixed first, else there will be a lot of questions at the airport."

Once inside, the doctor went directly to his office. Pulling out Sarah's file, he carefully reviewed it line by line. "The cells seem to be multiplying at an incredible rate, but there isn't anything physically wrong with Sarah. The DNA coding in the cells is human. Unlike the creatures' bodies, her system has no major conflict with the cells."

Doctor Scott began reviewing the camera images taken from the helicopter. With the creatures lying neatly in rows, he could easily spot the vast physical variations among them. Despite being kin, their DNA has taken different paths. "Something else is controlling the cells." He pulled out all his research and locked his door.

******

"Roger, what's happening out there? We heard some shooting."

"Nothing much. The doctor had some guards shoot at some of the creatures from a helicopter. The creatures ended up chasing them away. Those creatures are still out there and they are still in attack mode. We don't have the manpower for a counterattack."

"How much longer before we can get some supplies? We are running out of batteries for our goggles. We're down to two sets."

"Your people should be seeing the remote's lights any minute now."

Attached to the remote was a large duffle bag. As it got close to the edge of the cavern, Roger stopped it and pushed a button to release the bag. Slowly the remote circled around behind the bag and used brute force to push it over the edge. The lights on the remote gave the three pairs of waiting hands the needed light to catch it. Roger left the remote next to the edge to help illuminate the tunnel and watch what was going on through its forward camera. The guards immediately opened the bag and poured out its contents. A small tent, flashlights, batteries, ammunition, flares, compressed water containers, ration packs and refill cartridges for their gas masks littered the floor. Attached to the duffle bag was a clear sealed hose and an air line. Duncan grabbed the hose and carefully hitched it up to a container. After he pulled away both seals, water leaked out of the gap along with filling the container. Letting the water run freely, he showed another guard how to exchange containers and ordered him to fill all the jugs.

Laurie's eyes roamed around until she found what she was after. A clear bag containing rope had rolled into the shadows. She picked it up and took out the rope. Through the remote's cameras, Roger could see her. He pressed another button. A florescent red ball connected to a heavy line shot out from the front of the remote. Laurie caught the ball and tied the rope to the line. The remote slowly reeled in the rope and proceeded to back up through the collapsed tunnel.

Five minutes later Roger announced, "I have attached the rope to a winch. If you want to risk it, you can try to squeeze through. I know that I wouldn't."

"I'm not you." Looking down at her baggy cargo pants, she took out her knife and cut away anything she thought could get snagged. By the time she was finished, they were barely shorts. Wearing only her boots, T-shirt, gas mask and cut offs, Laurie tugged on the rope a few times before she tried to climb it. Getting up was the easy part. The winch did most of the hard work for her. After she pulled herself over the edge and into the tunnel, she cried out, "Stop." Roger shut off the winch. Using hands, elbows, knees and feet, she began her trek through the collapsed tunnel. The fibre optics spun into the rope helped illuminate the immediate area around it. After the darkness of the tunnel, any light at all was like daylight to her. As she crawled and pulled herself through the rock and debris, Laurie saw a pair of round green eyes reflecting back at her. In barely a whisper, she announced, "One of the creatures is hiding up here."

Both Roger and Duncan yelled, "Get out fast!"

Laurie didn't need to be told. The adrenalin pumping through her veins turned her into a lizard as she scooted through the remainder of the tunnel. In the haste, jostled rocks and sections of beams brought down loose rocks on top of her. Biting down, she endured the blows and kept going. As soon as her hands were visible, two guards grabbed an arm each and pulled her out of the crack and behind an ATV. While catching her breath, she looked at Roger and the two guards. "The creature was just lying there. We had been sitting around in that dark cavern below it. It could've attacked us at any time without us being able to see it."

Roger smiled at her. "It was probably sick and possibly dying. It most likely crawled up there to escape the gas. That stuff was heavy and most likely didn't get up that high up." Roger chuckled. "If it had, we would all be breathing it in right now."

With the water and air lines safely tucked to the side, the two guards placed a thick sheet of steel against the crack and piled concrete blocks in front of it. Laurie looked at the crudely constructed barrier. "If that creature is sick, this would do, but we can't take any chances. We'll either have to go in and kill it, or seal up the crack." Turning around to Roger, she asked, "Can we get supplies to the men trapped inside any other way?"

"Not that I know of." Roger was quick to add, "And I wouldn't go back in there to kill it. That ceiling won't stand any kind of ruckus. I'd try to suffocate it."

"What do you have in mind?"

Roger brandished a twisted smile. "I'd fill the collapsed tunnel with a steady flow of CO2 and push away any oxygen left in it. Within half an hour, the creature would be dead. Then we can continue using the tunnel to supply Duncan and the others."

Laurie studied him. "You enjoy this, don't you?"

With a confused look on his face, Roger responded, "Enjoy what, exactly?"

"You enjoy being able to outsmart anyone around you. You like being the hero that comes to everyone's rescue."

"I can't help that I'm very good at almost everything I do. That's why the doctor hired me."

******

Amidst the trees, Robert knelt behind a bush and watched the guards shuffle about in front of the mine. At times there were four in front and at other times only one. They all appeared jittery and confused. Waving only the fingers of his hand, he gestured for Timothy to come over. "Something big is going on in there. I bet they found those creatures."

"Maybe they found Sarah."

"If they did, the cops would be here. I still think that they have her locked up in that facility of theirs. They're probably running a batch of experiments on her right now. Sarah has never been anything more than a human guinea pig to them. Why else would they prevent us from searching the place?"

"Now what?"

Robert glanced at Timothy, "First, did you bring everything I asked you to?"

Timothy grinned as he replied, "Everything is stuffed in my bag. I even brought a couple extra loud surprises for you."

Robert looked at his smiling face. "I bet I know what they are."

Timothy handed Robert his flask. "Are we going to do this or what?"

After taking a large swig of whiskey, he answered. "Every man should go into battle with a good dose of Canadian courage." He handed back the flask. "It's time."

The pair walked along the side of the ridge a ways before they began to climb up its steep walls. Using a rope left behind from a previous scouting mission, they wasted no time ascending the steep grade. They were lucky that the guards had been too preoccupied to notice the narrow pathway they had created up the ridge.

The remote air exhaust port rising a metre above the ground was easy to spot. Its round mesh cap made it look like a big, rust coloured mushroom. The locks on the cap were broken and despite its weight, the two strong men easily lifted it off. They had already cut one end of most of the steel bars that sealed off the round air shaft. The underside of the other end of the cut bars had been hacked half way through, to make them easier to bend. From inside the mine, the bars looked untouched. Only two short bars, one on each side, were left intact. Together, the two men grabbed a hold of a bar and with their combined strength, bent them up and over the side.

Robert threaded rope through a pulley and then a specially designed piece of wood before tying it to one of the remaining bars on the side of the shaft. Looking down the shaft, he couldn't see anybody below them. Timothy attached the threaded pulley to the steel bar on the other side to complete the sling. After putting on a pair of thick leather gloves, Robert grabbed a hold of the two short bars and lowered himself into the shaft. With both feet resting on the wooden platform that he had threaded through the rope, Robert grabbed both sides of the looped rope. Braced against the side of the shaft, Timothy slowly released the rope and lowered Robert down into the mine. The rope easily slid around the waxed groove cut into the crescent-shaped piece of wood. Once on the bottom, Robert waited for Timothy to tie the backpacks to the end of the rope and lower them down. With Robert holding onto the rope, it was Timothy's turn. Using the sling and pulley, Robert easily lowered him down into the old tunnel.

From their packs they retrieved a couple night vision monoculars they had purchased from a local sports shop. Despite knowing exactly where to go, they needed them to guide them through the maze of dark tunnels. As they approached the collapsed tunnel, they spotted the two guards standing across from a pile of concrete blocks and a large barrel. Beside the guards, a noisy, pulsating, battery operated air pump created a small cloud of dust. Robert turned to Timothy and whispered, "I told you that I knew where they were. Now let's get ready for the light show."

They retraced their steps and sat down on an old bench. Timothy looked at the bench and shook his head, "I still can remember us eating our lunch on this bench."

"That was a long time ago." Robert dusted the bench off as Timothy pulled two sets of uniforms out of his backpack. "I still can't believe that anyone off the street can buy almost any uniform they want."

"All you need to know is where to shop."

The pair left all their stuff behind and sauntered over to the guards. "We're here to relieve you."

"We've only been here an hour. What gives?"

Robert smiled and jokingly replied, "Hey, what do I know? I'm new here."

The guard looked at their uniforms. "Where are your name tags and badges?"

"I told you, we are brand new. We haven't had time to sew them on yet."

One of the guards turned to the other and mumbled as they walked away. "Fresh fodder. I could smell the booze on them. They won't last long. I heard they're trying to form a counterattack to get the others out. Guys like that will make an excellent first wave."

The second guard whispered back, "Better them than us. I'm here for the money. I don't want to become a slab of meat for some creature's dinner table."

"You said it. I'm not going to be no hero either. That's why I've been faking this limp. My twisted ankle hasn't bothered me for over a week now."

Robert couldn't make out any of the guards' banter over the air compressor. Looking at the compressor and water barrel, he grinned at Timothy. "I wonder what they are doing in there."

"Maybe they're growing marijuana."

"Not likely."

As soon as the guards were out of sight, they quickly tossed the blocks aside and leaned the steel plate towards them. A pair of large round green eyes stared at them. The creature hissed as they slammed the steel back against the wall. "I told you that's where they were. I'll hold the plate while you go and get the stuff."

Timothy ran as fast as he could and returned with both backpacks. "What do you want?"

Robert looked over his shoulder at the thickness of the steel plate. "Forget the gas. We don't have time for it. You said you brought something special. I think we'll need it."

Timothy dropped Robert's pack. Its flap was still open and one of his gas bombs rolled out. He hastily rummaged through his pack and pulled out several sticks of dynamite. After placing an extra-long wick on one, he lit it. Robert leaned the plate forward and created a small gap between it and the wall. Timothy quickly tossed the explosive into the crack as far as he could. "I used a slow burning wick. We should have a couple minutes before it goes off." They braced the plate as fast as they could with the cement blocks before running down the tunnel.

The explosion wasn't huge. The pair barely felt it. Turning around they saw that the pile blocks had been pushed back and the steel plate was resting against the broken pieces of cement at a thirty-degree angle. Dust rolled out of the opening. The side of the large plastic water barrel was split open and water was gushing out. A short piece of flailing air line was flying in circles around the vibrating compressor. As the compressor's wires were pulled off of the battery, everything went quiet. As the dust settled, their bravery increased. Timothy walked behind Robert as they approached and looked into the gap. Using their flashlights, they saw the creature's arm protruding from a pile of fallen rocks. "This was a really bad idea. Let's get out of here before we get caught!"

******

The guards saw Laurie talking to Roger. With a simple tap on her shoulder, the one with the fake limp asked her, "What's up? We were only at our post for an hour."

"Why aren't you still there?"

"Two newbies came to relieve us."

"I didn't send anyone."

Laurie barely got the sentence out before an echoing rumble stopped her. "Let's go."

The guard forgot his limp as they all ran through the tunnels towards the entrance to the collapsed tunnel. A dust cloud hovered over the tilted steel plate. Laurie shone her flashlight around and caught a reflection. The shiny electrical tape Robert had used to fasten together his homemade gas bomb glistened back at her. One of the guards leaned over and picked it up.

As soon as Laurie saw what it was, she growled, "Robert Douglas."

The guards followed the intruder's footprints through the tunnels. Robert had hoisted Timothy three-quarters of the way up before they caught up to them. The guards grabbed the rope from him and lowered Timothy to the ground. Venting his frustration, Timothy yelled down at Robert, "So this is what I get for trying to help you."

After giving out a sigh, Robert asked, "So now what? What are you going to do to us?"

Laurie pulled out her pistol and aimed it at Robert's forehead. "I don't think you have any idea the extent of damage that you have just caused."

"I know that we killed one of those creatures you are harboring."

"Harboring! You honestly think that we are harboring those killers. You're insane." Laurie lowered her pistol and took a deep breath. "We're trying to find a way to eradicate them. Now you've just endangered the lives of lot of my friends. If I had my way, I'd put a bullet between your eyes right now."

Robert stood there dumbfounded. He stared at her and found the courage to say, "What about Sarah? I know the doctor has her. Will I ever see her again?"

"Sarah! There is no more Sarah. She died a long time ago. Why do you think we couldn't find her? All that remains of her is resting inside one of those creatures right now."

"You mean the creatures ate her?"

Out of pure vile, Laurie spat out, "They consumed her entire body, bones and all."

Timothy followed Robert to a picnic table set up in the main cavern. Between the pair, they quietly polished off the rest of the flask while waiting to find out their fate.

******

"What's going on out there?"

Roger picked up the radio. "Duncan, someone blew up the collapsed tunnel. Both the air and water lines were severed. Laurie has already nabbed the culprits. Unfortunately, now we've no way of getting any more supplies to you."

"We have enough batteries and gasmask cartridges to last about twenty hours. After that, things may get shaky. At least I'd managed to rotate the men so everyone has had a good meal and drink of water. We'll need to drink more while wearing the masks."

"I'll relay the message."

All Duncan could do is wait. At least he didn't have to worry about creatures crawling down out of the collapsed tunnel and attacking them from the rear. After changing the cartridge on his gasmask, he realised why the creatures didn't attack. *They could smell the gas. They know that if they entered this tunnel they would not only be facing our bullets, but would also be breathing in the gas.* "Roger, are you still there?"

In his normal cocky voice he replied, "What's up Duncan?"

"How long will it be before the air in this tunnel is safe to breathe?"

Roger looked at his watch. "If nobody stirs it up too much, it could take anywhere from another eighteen up to twenty-four hours. It's going to be close."

"This isn't about the gas cartridges. The creatures probably can smell or at least sense the poisonous gas. They had survived the mine being poisoned before. They're not stupid. They're waiting for the gas to go away before they attack."

"You may be right."

Duncan looked down the tunnel at the light coming in the door. "Still, the door is our best way out." Crawling over a fallen beam, he asked, "I haven't heard from George lately. We need to know what's going on out there. Have you heard from him?"

"Not a word. I know that he always leaves his set turned on vibrate so the creatures can't pick it up. We've been trying to get a hold of him but he hasn't replied."

Standing behind the line of guards watching the door, Duncan could see a shadow on the ground. None of the creatures would venture into the open. The odd one would dash passed it. Not enough time to even squeeze a trigger. A frustrated guard squeezed off a shot anyway. "If this was a military operation, there would've been a counterstrike order by now to get us out."

One of the guards looked up as Duncan replied, "We're not the military. This isn't even a war. We're not even supposed to be carrying, let alone using, these weapons here. Consider this just another conflict between two parties that can't get along."

The guard took a second to adjust his gasmask. "We are just expendable mercenaries for hire. The only thing different about this conflict is that one of the parties ain't human."

Duncan recognized his voice. Like most of the mercenaries that were hired, Rankin was a loner. "I've never considered anyone fighting under me as expendable. We're going to get out of here. Every last one of us."

Rankin thought for a brief moment. "To most of us, it's how we get out that matters."

"It sounds like you've a bit of a death wish"

"Dead, my insurance will set my kids up for life. Alive, I'm just dead to them. Either way, my life was forfeited by that judge a long time ago. At least here, the men around me and the adrenalin pumping through my veins make me feel alive. I don't have a death wish. Dying doesn't scare me, but being eaten does."

******

Michaela opened the door as her father stepped out of the passenger side of his truck. He was a mess of blubbering tears. She ran out and wrapped her arms around him. As the guard that drove him home got out and went over to the jeep that was turning around in the driveway, Michaela question her father. "What's wrong?"

"She's dead. The creatures ate her. We'll never see her again."

Michaela's arms fell to her side. "Who told you that?"

"Laurie."

Michaela stood back from her father. The dust on his clothes made her question him. "Were you in the old mine? Did you do anything while you were there that we may regret?"

"Yes and yes." Robert stood there with his head and arms hanging down. "We tried to gas the creatures. I found the crack that they were hiding in and we threw in a stick of dynamite. The guards caught me and Timothy while we were trying to escape."

"You're lucky that they didn't throw you in jail."

"How?" Robert looked into his daughter's trembling face. "What for? Killing a creature that isn't supposed to exist. A creature that they said wasn't there. A creature that I firmly believe they created."

Michaela stood back and looked at her father's face. "You were trespassing and using explosives."

Robert throw his arms in the air. "They don't want anything to do with the courts. They would have too many question to explain away. It's probably costing them a bundle as is to keep the authorities away from the mine and their so-called medical facility."

"And what about Sarah?"

"Laurie told me the creatures got to her. She has never lied to me before. Despite what happened back there, I feel that she's telling me the truth. Before, I could feel Sarah inside of me." Robert started to cry and ran over to Michaela. "Lately, I'm having a hard time feeling her. She's dead. My poor, sweet, little angel is dead."

Michaela grabbed her father by his shoulder, "They didn't show you any solid proof, did they? Until I see evidence of it, I won't believe she's dead. There is still something inside of me that knows that she can't be. She's my sister. I would know it."

Chapter Nineteen

Anew

"Detective Arnold, you have someone out here asking for you."

The receptionist politely asked Michaela to wait. Kristofer put his arm around her. "No matter what happens, you know that I'll be here for you."

The detective came out and walked over to Michaela with his hand extended, "How are you doing?"

Michaela stood up and haphazardly shook his hand. "Not so good. Dad came home today and said that Laurie, one of the guards at the mine, had told him that Sarah had been eaten by the creatures."

The detective stepped away from Michaela. With an inquisitive look on his face, he said, "I was aware that your father had gotten into some trouble at the mine this morning, but Sarah being eaten by creatures was never brought up."

"So you know what happened?"

"Sure, I was summoned there to issue no-trespassing notices to both your father and Timothy Ferguson. I even saw the damage that the blast had caused. He's lucky that they didn't press charges against him."

"So you saw the creature that he killed?"

"I saw the remains of an old imploded mine tunnel. Your father was standing right next to me. He was hopping mad and swore that there was a creature in there, but I didn't see any signs of one."

"But my father would never lie to me."

"Michaela, both your father and Mr. Ferguson had been drinking. They were both beyond legally impaired. I don't know what your father thinks he saw, but there was nothing in that tunnel. You can ask the two officers that went with me. I'll give you their names and you can ask them yourself, if you want to."

Kristofer nudged Michaela. "What about all the shooting going on?"

Detective Arnold smiled at him. "They had applied to register a gun club and training facility for their guards ages ago. That's why there are all those warning and no trespass signs all over the place back there. They have over fifty square kilometres fenced off because of it. The shooting is all contained in the middle of their property and to the best of my knowledge they haven't broken any laws."

Michaela bowed her head. "What about checking out their medical facility for Sarah?"

The detective gave out a small sigh. "We're still working on it. Right now they are employing helicopters. We can't even check everyone coming and going anymore. Even if she was in there, it doesn't mean she is now. I believe that searching the facility would be a hopeless waste of both time and money."

"And the human skull? I heard rumours that a human skull was found along with evidence that the creatures had lived in an old abandoned section of the mine."

"The skull we found ended up coming from a bear cub. As for the creatures, at this point, I don't have any solid evidence that they even exist. Duncan said he killed a few of them, but all the evidence he had left was a pile of untraceable ashes. "

Michaela sat back down. "So what now?"

"We have to begin all over again. Unfortunately, this time without any traces or clues to go on." The detective knelt down and took Michaela's hands. "I haven't given up on your sister. Michaela, please help me by keeping your father away from the mine. I had to beg the doctor not to press charges, but next time, he will."

******

In the tunnel, time went by very slowly. Through the night the men could hear the constant activity going on outside over their grumbling stomachs. As the first rays of sunlight shone through the door, their bodies started to cramp up from lack of water. As the air and soil finally started to neutralize the poison gas, the activity outside of the mine increased. Poised for an attack, all the men could do was wait and check their gas masks. A few hours went by with only the odd shadow appearing in the doorway. Then something banged on the steel door. "Duncan, are you there? It's Laurie. It's safe to come out now."

The men on the front line emerged first and then Duncan. The shadows that they were seeing were clumps of carefully woven branches designed to catch any air movement they could. Suspended from the mesh above the doorway, they swung in the breeze at the edge of the guards' vision. When the dangling wind catchers rubbed against each other, to the trapped men inside of the mine they sounded like busy creatures moving about.

Duncan walked over to Laurie. "Where are the creatures?"

"I don't know. They were moving all about the area not too long ago." Laurie took out some infrared aerial photographs taken only two hours before. "Here, take a look."

Duncan glanced at them. "Do you have any older ones?"

"Sure." Laurie pulled out a handful of photos from her backpack. "Here."

Duncan studied them. "They were masking their evacuation by increasing their activity. Now they've disappeared."

"All but the dead." Laurie pointed to a line of half a dozen mounds of rocks. "They're like us. They bury their dead. We spotted another set of fresh burial mounds on top of the ridge."

Duncan did a quick calculation. "In battle, that's still a two to one loss." Looking back at the mine, he added, "I hope the gas and virus made up for it in spades."

Duncan looked at the surrounding tree tops. "Have you seen or heard anything from George yet?"

"Sorry, not a word."

"Look around the perimeter for any sign of him. After we get something in us, I'll take Rankin's squad and search along the ridge. If he is still alive, he'll know what went on outside of the mine and where the creatures have gotten to."

Leery of using the helicopter, they set out on foot. Using infrared binoculars, Duncan combed the area. Almost a kilometre away from the mine he detected something up in a tree. George pulled his leaf covered hood away from his face. As he did, his radio fell out of his hands. Duncan motioned for Rankin to come over. "From your profile, I understand that you know how to climb trees."

"Yes, sir. In my late teens I was a tree topper."

It took Rankin only a few minutes to scale the huge pine and get to George. Radioing down to Duncan, he informed him, "It wasn't the creatures that got him. He's sick. He's covered in red dots and they ain't from any insect that I know of."

Using a rope and pulley, several of the guards helped Duncan lower George to the ground. He had a bad case of the measles. His throat was almost completely shut. George lifted his head and looked up at Duncan. His eyes were barely open. Duncan looked at him. "Did you see where they went?"

George raised his hand to his throat. Before he could reach it, his whole body went limp. "We have to get him to the doc as fast as possible."

Their ATV barrelled around the police cruiser in front of the facility and through the gate before the police officers could get out of their seats. The two screaming officers ran to the gate as it quickly closed. Covered in the dust stirred up from the ATV, they watched the garage doors shut behind it.

Doctor Scott and Doctor Shaw were waiting for him. From the over twenty varieties of measles, they had used the harshest, deadliest and fastest acting strain they could isolate. Now the only person that saw where the creatures had gone is too sick to even talk. They never counted on the rural natives not being vaccinated for measles like the general population.

Leaving George's room, Doctor Scott stopped. *The creatures are no longer confined to the mine. What is stopping them from spreading out and infecting other creatures?*

******

The king carried Sarah to the shore of a large lake. The rest of the colony was already there. In front of her was a bunch of rundown buildings. A confused Sarah entered the abandoned camp grounds and looked around. The swaybacked roofs of the two main wooden structures and the birds escaping through holes in the roofs of others told her no one had used it for a long time. Sarah followed the king as he entered the only structure that looked reasonably sound. At one time, it housed the camp's nurse's office and sleeping quarters on one side and the bunk house for the female staff on the other. The two dividing walls that separated the nurse's room had propped up the roof better than the wide-open space of the others buildings.

The worst of the sick creatures were placed in the bunks. Sarah went over to the windows and opened the ones still intact. The others she left boarded up. Over two dozen creatures were piled into the bunks.

With the way the king kept her under his careful watch, Sarah wasn't sure how he was really treating her. Honda, the king and several males made the old nurse's office theirs. Sarah was corralled into a tiny room between the office and the make-shift hospital. She was given the luxury of having her own room, an old bunk, a night stand, a shelf on the wall and pegs to hang clothes. Her walls were eaten up by two doors. One went into the office, the other into the bunk house. With creatures on both sides, she felt trapped. She couldn't leave without being watched. Was she to be kept as a slave to take care of their sick, or were they treating her with high regard? She wasn't sure. No other creature or even family had their own semi-private living space.

With torn screen windows on both doors, she could see Honda through one and the other infected and wounded creatures though the other. There were only eight double bunks in the makeshift hospital ward. Most of the mattresses had been chewed apart by rodents and insects. All that was left on the wooden slats of the beds were mainly remnants of the old mattress covers. Two large creatures were placed lengthwise in each bunk, in alternating directions. Most of the creatures were small enough that only their legs overlapped. On three of the beds, pine boughs were used to both strengthen and make them comfortable before up to four younger creatures were placed crosswise on top of them. Sarah walked through the room and thought of how fragile these fierce, grotesque creatures actually were.

Sarah knelt down in front of a ferret-like creature that was shot several times and had sections of its wings ripped apart by barb wire. With needle and some old fish line that she had found, she started to sew up the creature's wounds. As the creature's mate stood beside her, Sarah wanted to cry. The poor beast was fighting for his family that was trapped inside of the mine. Deep inside, Sarah knew that she would have done the same. At times, she had to turn her head away as the blood and smell of body fluids got to her. Several family members were standing and rubbing their heads against each other. "These creatures are no different than we are." After a deep breath, she continued sewing up the creature's wounds.

Sarah could only work so fast. Mew and Betty stood beside her and tried to help as best they could. Betty studied her every move and with great difficulty tried to copy her. Mew wasn't quite as keen to trust Sarah's strange procedures. The two were constantly rattling back and forth to each other as they tried to sew up the wings of another injured creature. Betty had no problem threading the fish line into the needle, but couldn't work the needle while holding the tough, slippery skin back together at the same time. Her fingers were too short and wide. Mew's fingers were long with sharp claws. Her claws made it easy for her to squeeze and hold the gash together, while creating small holes for the other creature to work the needle through.

Betty manipulated the needle as best she could. She could only hold the needle between her thumb and first finger. Sarah watched as the frustrated creatures worked on the injured beast.

Sarah finished sewing up the creature that she was working on. Looking around for bandages, all she could find were remnants of old clothes and bed sheets. She grabbed the hand of the young, mournful creature standing beside the next bunk and led her to the closet. She pulled out a bed sheet and started to rip it into long narrow pieces. The young puppy-faced creature looked up at Sarah and tore a strip of bedding. She knew that the creature understood what it was supposed to do. The creature's mouth went wide and its jaw sank upward into what Sarah took as a smile. Sarah returned the gesture and took a armful of pieces back to her patient and used them to bandage the poor injured beast.

Tending to broken bones was harder. All Sarah could do was try to hold the bones in place using sticks and pieces of wood. For bullets, she tried to dig what she could out. Others she had to leave in. Scared of what the other creatures might think, she didn't want to cut one of them apart to retrieve it. How would they react? Especially the poor beast's family members that watched her every move.

Sarah came to the next wounded creature. The large dog-like creature's injuries didn't look that severe. A bubbling pink froth started to come out of its mouth. Sarah barely touched him before its head fell to the side. He was dead. A wild whippet-like creature pushed her way between them. With one quick thrust of her hand, Sarah tumbled backwards to the floor.

Paralysed, Sarah didn't know what to do. The creature picked up her mate, turned around and hissed at her. Others formed a circle and quickly joined in hissing and growling at Sarah as she propped herself up with one arm and protected her face with the other. As they got closer, a roar bellowed behind them. The crowd turned as the king roared even louder. The cowering crowd dispersed and the grieving creature silently carried her dead partner outside.

Standing upright, the king walked through the bunk house and glanced at the work Sarah had done on the wounded creatures. He extended his front arm. Sarah grabbed his wide hand tightly as he helped her up. They were almost the same height, but that was all they had in common. The large ferocious lion-like creature wasn't her enemy. She looked at him without fear. He wasn't as huge as he had seemed before. He was slightly bigger than any of the rest, but still was only the size of a mountain lion. When his mane was on edge, he grew to almost twice his true size. He turned and looked over at the creatures she had sewn together, then back at her. After getting down on all fours, he rubbed his head against Sarah's side a couple times and walked away.

Sarah walked to the door and saw the king lean over and pick up a few rocks as he went over to a large group of creatures. They were burying their dead companion. A small hole was dug and the creature was carefully placed in it. The king placed the rocks that he had collected on top of the body amongst the rest. They all silently stood around the grave. The funeral was over very quickly and all that remained was a pile of rocks covering the shallow grave and the poor beast's grieving mate lying next to it.

******

Michaela and Kristofer sat at the kitchen table as Robert Douglas slept. "My dad can't hear us. He'll be out cold until tomorrow morning."

"Fine, but you know how I feel. I really liked Sarah, but I can't do anything illegal. Not just to satisfy your need to seek some sort of expedient justice. My father has already confirmed the detective's story. The police are still working on finding her."

After handing Kristofer a beer, she told him, "It's not illegal."

"Maybe, but it is dangerously close to it. After your father's latest escapade, you know that they will have it in for him. They could blame him for this little vendetta of yours."

"Maybe." Michaela sat down and drank her beer across from Kristofer. "I only want the public to question what is going on around here."

"They may consider it slander and have you arrested."

"I'll be very careful how I word everything. You'll see." Michaela looked over at the very worried Kristofer. His hands had a faint tremble in them as he drank his beer. "Will you help me?"

He smiled at her and said, "Sure, I'll help you."

The following night Kristofer crept into the Douglas's driveway. He left his door open and ran around and opened the door for Michaela. Carrying a box full of flyers, she needed his help to get in. Kristofer quietly rolled his van out of the driveway and crept a ways down the road before getting out and shutting the doors. They didn't want Michaela's father to know what they were doing.

Hearing the doors shut, Mary pulled her bedroom's window curtain to the side and gazed out as the two drove away. Her face lost some of its colour as the curtain slipped through her fingers and fell shut.

Kristofer looked over at Michaela. She saw him trying to read the flyers. "I know that Doctor Scott is responsible for those creatures and I want him to be held accountable for Sarah's death. All I want is for the truth to finally come out and for him to pay for it."

Without any light, Kristofer couldn't read them. "So what does it say?"

"Pull one out and read it." Kristofer turned on his interior light and took one of the flyers. The message was short and to the point.

'We all know that the creatures living in the Bear Den Mine do exist. Several miners are dead because of them. With a medical research facility built adjacent to the same property, we should question if there is any connection. If so, are they putting our lives at risk?' On the bottom of the flyer Michaela had drawn a map of the area showing both the mine and the medical facility's location.

"I guess that's not slanderous. All you are doing is questioning if they are involved or not."

******

At the edge of the large swamp next to the Devil's Claw, the king and a winged, wolf-like creature sliced apart a freshly killed woodland caribou. Using their claws and teeth, they sliced the carcass into quarters to make it easier to carry. Hearing the roar of an ATV, they gazed across the swamp and saw the machine approach a group of men on top of the ridge. From almost a kilometre away, the creatures watched the guards destroying their comrades' graves and taking away their bodies.

Leaving their kill, they made their way to the graves next to the old mine entrance. The stones had been rolled away and hollow pits had replaced the stolen bodies. In torturous agony, the wolf-life creature howled as loud as he could.

The men on top of the ridge froze as the creature's howls were joined by the king's echoing roars. With a dead ferret-like creature in his arms, Duncan looked over at Rankin as he tossed aside a heavy rock. "They just want to remind us that they are still here."

As all the guards fumbled with their rifles, Rankin spoke up, "This is their home. They just want to remind us that we are invading their territory."

Duncan looked down at the creature in his arms. "It could be even more than that."

Chapter Twenty

Accountability

By the next morning, flyers were everywhere. Stapled to poles, taped to doorways and stuffed into mailboxes, they littered the small communities and rural roadways. The local newspaper editor grabbed a copy that was shoved through his mail slot and tossed it into the garbage. On his way to work, he noticed the brightly coloured flyers posted under almost every traffic sign. As he sat down at his desk, one was staring him in the face. After finally reading it, he smiled. He didn't care who he got in trouble. All he saw as he read it was a story. With a car crash that put two local teenagers in the hospital, it wasn't the headline. However, it still made it to the bottom of the front page.

From Michaela's few words, the editor drew another story. The article's header read, 'Medical Institution blamed for mine deaths'. While waiting in line at the grocery store, a couple of guards saw the article. They grabbed a dozen copies and brought them back to the facility along with every flyer they came across. While unloading the groceries from the van, one of them handed a set to Duncan. "Someone has posted these flyers everywhere. They even include a map. The newspaper has turned the creatures into a front page story. The editor even dug up all the old stories about the mine gremlins and incorporated them into the article."

Duncan quickly read the article. "Doctor Scott isn't going to like this."

After reading it, the doctor threw the paper into the garbage. "We don't have enough men or helicopters to guard this place from an onslaught of reporters."

It only took a few days before the first few reporters started to flood in. At first they were there to prove the article as a giant hoax to entice tourists. The constant flow of armed guards and the fortified electric fence around the facility made them step back and wonder if there was any truth behind it. After a guard was photographed carrying an assault rifle, even the day to day operation of the facility had to change. As reporters started to trail the planes that the doctor had hired to photograph the area and question the pilots, the search for the creatures was suddenly handicapped.

Into the second week, things got worse. One by one the 'No Trespassing' signs were secretly removed so the reporters could walk onto the property and claim ignorance when accused. The guards had caught one enterprising local teenager with a stack of twenty signs in his backpack. Under questioning, he confessed that reporters were paying him ten dollars a sign to remove them.

******

Karen Simpson slammed her fist down on the judge's desk. "I don't care if you hate my guts. Right now, how you feel about me is irrelevant. This is an act of destruction of private property. These reporters are openly trespassing on my client's private property with absolutely no evidence to back any of their claims. They have even resorted to hiring locals to deface my client's property. We have them on camera, along with their written confessions. I demand that you issue a court order for them to cease these activities."

The judge looked up at her and smiled. "Or what, you'll have me disbarred?"

"I always do my homework." Smiling at the judge, she almost laughed as she continued. "I'll have you publicly humiliated first."

"How?"

Karen grinned at him. "Immediately after I first heard your name, I've had you followed and your past activities thoroughly investigated. The private detectives that I hired have dug up all kinds of crap on you. I have never met anyone yet that has any real power and has remained squeaky clean. Every last one of you abuse it. You know my reputation. I've put more cops and public officials in jail than anyone else in Canada."

"This is plain harassment. You've nothing on me."

Karen tossed a couple dozen photos down on the judge's desk. "Do the job that you are paid to do, or these will go to the local press and to every branch of the police. I also have an up to date list of which officers you have pissed off the most. I'm positive that they'll enjoy getting them."

The photos spread out in front of him were of him slapping his wife, kicking his dog and yelling at cowering restaurant waiters. They were nothing compared to the photos of a cop ripping up a ticket in front of him and others of his car parked sideways across two handicapped spots.

"With my connections, I could have you up in front of an ethics review board by next week, if not sooner." As Karen watched the judge shake his head, she added, "And I won't stop there. I've also got copies of the security video from your hotel in Spain."

Sweat bubbled up from his forehead and trickled down his face. "I was with my wife. Nothing went on there."

"Not that hotel. The other one. You know the one you went to when your wife went out shopping. I'm sure that your wife's lawyer would love to see them."

As soon as she left the judge's office, he buried his head under his arms. "The press will have a field day. That crazy bitch is insane. She won't back down for anything."

As soon as Detective Arnold walked into the red faced judge's office, he was handed some papers. "Here, I want these warrants issued."

The detective looked at them and then back at the judge. The judge had turned his chair around and didn't even want to look at him. "But I thought that you…"

The judge sharply cut him off. "Not a single word."

Detective Arnold left and drove to the line of reporters parked outside the facility. Using his loud speaker, he announced, "Everyone, I have something official to issue to you today." They all ran over to him expecting a public statement. "It's all down in writing." One by one he called out their names and he handed them each an envelope.

As soon as the first one read the contents, a wild scream bellowed out of her. "I'm being charged! This is a court summons."

The detective waved his arms and tried to control the enraged crowd. "Now listen. From now on, anyone that trespasses on the doctor's private property, interferes with anyone on the property or even litters will be arrested and charged. This circus is over. Do you understand?"

Not everyone's name was mentioned. A few small time reporters lingered about while the rest returned to their vehicles and privately spoke on their phones. Several members of a small group huddled around a minibus. They had only arrived the day before and had provided the reporters free coffees, sandwiches and donuts. They had cheerfully mingled, befriended and questioned every one of them.

One by one the small band approached the back of the minibus and pulled a T-shirt over their clothes. Then they went to the side door and pulled out a large banner, several signs and a bundle of stakes. On the side of the road leading into the facility they unravelled the banner and tied it to the trees. 'RESEARCH USING ANIMALS IS NEVER HUMANE'

Court orders or not, the reporters flooded out of their vehicles and started to photograph, video and question the animal right's activists. "What organization are you with?"

"We belong to several organizations. With this being such a remote location, we decided to pool our resources on this particular campaign."

Despite knowing that the protestors were only there as a result of their media coverage, the reporters asked them questions like, "What led you to discover this research facility." And, "How do you know they are using animals in their research?"

The answers were almost taken word for word from the newspaper articles that the reporters had written. "Copies of a flyer and newspaper clippings were anonymously mailed to us." And, "Nobody can create mutant animals without first using animals, now can they?"

Detective Arnold watched everything unfold and smiled. They were on public property and weren't interfering with anyone from the facility. The small, well-organized protest group was versed in every law pertaining to public protests and obstruction of traffic. They were all veterans and diehard professionals with political connections. Within a week, Doctor Scott was given a notice. The facility and the mine were to be inspected for animal rights violations.

Without the aerial harassment of the news helicopters, a week's notice was all the doctor required. Doctor Scott even invited Detective Arnold to join in on the search. After the lawyers were finished negotiating the terms of the search, the officials' watered down mission was simple: they could look for animals but couldn't examine any of the research material or equipment. All aspects of Doctor Scott's research outside of his care for animals was strictly off limits. The only photos or videos that they would be permitted to take would be of animals found being used for research purposes or in an inhumane fashion.

The veterinarian that led the search was no stranger to the importance of privacy in the research community. His three comrades were all trained and conducted themselves in a highly professional manner. Doctor Scott and Duncan lead the group through the entire facility. Many rooms were viewed only from the doorway and a few others only by using highly sensitive heat sensors that could even pick up heat coming from electrical wires. The only rooms that they entered were ones that had another room going off of them. Even closets and storage rooms were discretely checked. They were thorough, but respectfully kept their distance from anything that remotely looked like research material or highly specialized equipment. Once it was over, all of the participants were thoroughly searched, scanned and any images that they had taken were closely scrutinized.

As Detective Arnold left the facility, Duncan put his hand on his shoulder. "Maybe now you know how a search is supposed to be done."

The red faced detective turned to Duncan. "Being searched like a terrorist was humiliating. I'm a uniformed police officer. What you did to me in front of my men was not right either."

"The search that you went through was normal procedure. The others knew what to expect. But that wasn't what I was talking about." Duncan watched the detectives face slowly return to its normal colour. "If your guys had searched the place, it would have been turned upside down. Billions of dollars and years of research would have been placed in jeopardy by your clumsy, power hungry, circus clowns."

Detective Arnold thought for a moment before he answered. "I see your point."

They all reassembled in the main cavern of the mine. Armed with maps, they all paired up with a guard and searched through the tunnels and shafts. Driving ATV's and using heat sensors, the search went quickly. Not a single animal was found except for the well-photographed guard dogs and a few wild mice and rats. Detective Arnold nudged the veterinarian in charge, "Did you check the abandoned section on the far side of the ridge?"

The vet looked at him, puzzled. "No, there is nothing on the map indicating any tunnels back there."

"No, those tunnels won't be on them. They are too old."

The veterinarian in charge approached Duncan. "Are there any other parts of the mine left to check?"

Duncan saw Detective Arnold turn away. "There is one tunnel left of the original mine on the far side of the ridge. You are welcome to see it if you really want too, but I warn you, it'll be at your own risk and you'll have to sign some liability wavers."

"Let's do it and get it over with. That way nobody can dispute the findings."

On the far side of the ridge, the guards had set up a mock training facility. They slowly drove up to it in the midst of a half dozen men shooting at each other using paint ball guns. Over the past month, even the barb wire fence and bunkers were converted into parts of their semi-military exercises. All evidence of the battle with the creatures was either destroyed or carefully concealed.

There was nothing left for the vet to find. As they exited the mine, Duncan turned to the veterinarian and grinned. "Are you satisfied now?"

"You'll get your clean ticket. Though this was the first genetic research facility that I have ever been to that didn't use at least one kind of animal, or even insect in its testing."

Detective Arnold poked around the training area. As the others left, he walked over to Duncan. "So what happened to all of the creatures?"

Duncan smiled. "I told you before, they are all dead and destroyed beyond recognition. They no longer exist, and as far as anyone else is concerned they never did."

"Well, at least now I can tell Mr. Douglas that we didn't find Sarah in the medical facility nor the mine."

Duncan took in a deep breath. "I wish she never left the facility. It would've been better for everyone."

The detective looked at him. Even through his scars, the detective could see that he was worried about something. "What's wrong? You got your clean ticket and we are going to find Sarah somehow."

"I just wish that I knew where she was."

******

Sarah looked around the crowded makeshift hospital. The plague didn't take favourites. Even Honda's large majestic father was sharing a bed with the caring striped female. The injured took the worst toll. Despite their rapid healing, the measles had greatly weakened their immune systems. The combination was deadly. As some injured creatures fully recovered, others were carried away and buried by the sentries during the night. Not wanting the guards to unearth and take away their dead, they tried to hide the graves in the swamp.

While leaning on her father's bed, Honda glanced over at Sarah. With food supplies dwindling, none of the creatures were truly healthy. Even the once spiteful mourners were bedridden and readily accepted Sarah's help. A handful of females and youngsters that had survived the measles were trying to gather enough food for the entire colony. Hunting had been normally done by the males. With only rudimentary skills, the results were very disappointing.

******

Robert stood in front of his mail box. Flipping through the flyers and junk mail, he came upon a typed envelope. It had no return address and the red imprinted stamp from the local post office was smudged all over the corner. Shoving the rest of the mail under his arm, he began to open the letter. He had barely ripped the edge when Detective Arnold pulled into the driveway.

The detective got out of his jeep and walked over to Robert. With his hands held together in front of him, he put his head down and said, "They finally completed a full search of the medical facility."

Robert shook his head. "Why didn't you tell me? I wanted to go with you."

"You weren't invited. I was lucky that he even asked me to go."
The detective put his hand on Robert's shoulder. "Outside of a few
patients, there was nobody in there. We even searched through the
mine. I'm sorry to tell you this, but Sarah wasn't there." He raised his
head and looked at Robert as he added, "and neither were any of the
creatures."

"They could've moved her before you got there."

The detective dropped his hand and stepped back from Robert.
"Yes, they could've, but where would they put her?"

"The property that they own covers a lot of bush. They could've
hid her anywhere."

The detective looked up at him. "Yes, I guess they could've."

After the detective left, Robert sat at the kitchen table. The crushed
envelope was still in his hand. He finished opening it. From the
envelope Robert pulled out a mangled, fuzzy photo and a letter. He
could still make out Sarah's face. Her neck, large ear and part of her
cheek were covered in fur. The photo slipped from his fingers and fell
to the table. He picked up the typed letter. 'Stop or you will destroy
what's left of your daughter. Stop feeding fuel to the press while she
still has a chance.'

Chapter Twenty-One

Communication

Two weeks later, the long animal rights banners were still draped along the road in front of the facility. Despite being told that there were no animals being used inside, the activists refused to leave. The local reporter set up her camera and stood in front of it next to a couple of activists. After some pleasantries and introductions, she asked, "The government has reported that they are not using any animals inside. So why are you still using this site to stage your protest?"

"That's simple. The medical research community has to use living organisms to prove or disprove everything they do. This facility is no different. So they didn't find anything this time. That doesn't prove anything. All that means is that at this particular point in time, there are no animals in the facility. They may be hiding them, or simply not requiring them during this particular segment of their research. Regardless, if they are in there or not, it's the way that animals are used in the medical research industry that we are speaking up against."

"Why this facility?"

"Our research has found that privately run facilities have the worst track record of animal abuse. They are willing to risk almost anything to make their mark in the marketplace. When we discover a rogue, independent operation like this one, we feel that it is our duty to open it up to public scrutiny. We already know what the giants are doing. We have members working inside of them."

"So you still feel that they are using animals at this site?"

"In this facility? In some form, most definitely. They can't do DNA and what is rumoured to be stem cell research without a source of live test subjects. Since using humans is out of the question, they would need to use animals."

"What would convince you that they are not using animals inside?"

"Their permission to examine all of their research notes and data."

"Do you think that would ever happen?"

"We'll have to wait and see."

******

Laurie gently rolled the ATV to a stop as she neared the end of the mine tunnel. Over the walkie, she announced, "Lunch is ready."

The entire section of the roof between two crossbeams was lowered on four thick chains. Laurie carried the four pails and three boxes off the back of the ATV and onto the lowered platform. With a cooler in hand, she yelled, "Bring her up."

After the thick, well-insulated platform was drawn up, Laurie stepped off. "How does pork chops and scalloped potatoes sound?"

"Delicious. What's for dessert?"

In a teasing manner, Laurie rocked her head back and forth smiling. "It's a surprise."

The technician started to speak as the animals behind him began rattling the bars on their cages. "Okay, okay, you'll get fed first." Looking at Laurie, he added, "They are all spoiled rotten. If I don't feed them first, they will never let me eat in peace."

******

Sarah could hear a plane flying over the area. She ran to the window and looked out. It wasn't just one plane. Two planes were criss-crossing back and forth through the sky. A helicopter joined them. Like a bee, it darted from one spot to another, staying only long enough to get a better look at the area immediately beneath it.

Sarah could hear the frightened creatures behind her. As the planes focussed in an area to the south of them, the king made his way through the main door. He watched as the planes disappeared into the sunset. With a few low, almost gargling sounds, he put the others at ease. A couple of creatures walked over to him and rattled off their concerns. Still trying to fight off the last remnants of the measles, the king looked around as he gargled out a lengthy reply. Sarah watched as the emotions in the creatures fluctuated up and down through the king's speech. Several of the healthy members moved towards him and stood erect. The king pointed to three of them. He somehow mustered up the strength to rise into the air and fly out of sight with them at his heels. Sarah looked at the ones he didn't choose. He had picked the smaller weasel-like creatures over the more powerful dog-like ones. *Maybe he left them there to protect the others.*

Honda walked over to Sarah and sat next to her. Looking up, she smiled and rattled her throat. Sarah fell back against the wall. In the midst of Honda's rattling, she could make out "Eeetsss oookkk." It was a phrase that she had said to Honda on several occasions when they were scared. Falling to her knees, Sarah gave Honda a hug. As tears flowed from her eyes she cried, "Yes, it's okay."

Over the next two days the planes continued to comb the area. At nightfall, the king led almost all of the healthy winged members away. Each morning they returned dirty and exhausted. The few healthy ones that stayed behind kept a visual at the doors and paths leading into the camp. Even Honda took her turn on sentry duty. Sarah, along with three young females, looked after the dozen and a half sick and injured that remained.

During the day, Honda would curl up at the end of Sarah's bed. Sometimes she would wake up long enough for Sarah to try to get her to say a few more simple words. Despite being tired from her night duties, Honda could see how it pleased her.

Sarah tugged at her ear, "Ear."

Honda looked at her. "Rrahh"

"No, not rrahh, it's my ear."

"Eearr. Rrahh."

It finally dawned on Sarah that Honda was also teaching her. Almost unaware of it, Sarah had been rattling a few words back to her. They started with basic words like wings, ears, eyes, claws, sleep, dead and no. Words that even the creatures' simplistic language had something equivalent too.

As it got dark, Honda looked at Sarah. "Wwwingsss, eeeyes."

Sarah smiled back at her. "Okay. So you are a better pupil than I am."

Honda left the makeshift hospital and flew into a tree to begin another night of sentry duty. Sarah stepped outside and sat on the steps. As she breathed in the cool night air, clouds of mosquitoes hovered around her. She was too tired to swat them off. Too tired to think of getting away. Even if she could escape, where would she go? Sarah looked at the claws growing on her hands and the fur covering her arms and legs. "These don't belong to any human. I can't go anywhere looking like this."

The next morning Sarah woke to a helicopter hovering overhead. She ran over to the window and saw that Honda was no longer in the tree. Her heart started to race as a sense of panic overtook her. None of the creatures had returned. The quivering sick creatures quietly lay in their beds staring at the windows. The only protection that they had was Sarah and a few of the injured creatures that were healed enough to fight back. Even with only one good arm, any one of the creatures was capable of killing a man. That is, if they could get close enough.

The helicopter landed on the beach in front of the buildings. Through a knot hole in the door, Sarah could see Duncan help Doctor Scott out of the helicopter. Four other guards circled the craft with rifles pointed at the trees. Even with Sarah's newly acquired acute hearing, she could barely hear what they were saying over the helicopter's motor.

******

Duncan yelled above the noise. "This property covers over two thousand hectares. There is only one road leading into it and it's so overgrown that it is now impassable. This section of the lake is protected from the wind enough that we could land and even moor planes on it in bad weather. In winter, the frozen lake could supply us with almost year round access. During the spring break up and fall freezing, we could use the helicopters."

The doctor turned to Duncan, "By using our present facility as a dummy operation, our lawyers should be able to keep both the press and our competition away. I'm not even afraid of any of the government agencies. What worries me is, could this place be protected if it's attacked by those creatures? We both know what happened at the mine."

"Back there they were defending their home and colony. Here, we are not a threat to them." Duncan put his hand on the doctor's shoulder. "They didn't attack the facility, did they?"

"They may still seek revenge."

"That's a human trait. These are animals. Nevertheless, I've studied their tactics. The hard rock under this area will prevent them from digging into it and the perimeter wall that I've designed should be more than adequate. Thorn bushes and barb wire won't cut it this time."

******

Sarah watched as the two walked around the camp. Two of the guards stayed with the helicopter and the other two trailed the pair. As the intruders approached the building, Sarah started to perspire. She could hear Duncan tell one of the guards, "Those shacks will make good firewood for the men while we're setting up."

The doctor didn't reply. Instead, he bent over he brushed away some of the thin topsoil with his hand and felt the hard Canadian Shield beneath it. Turning to Duncan, he finally remarked, "We'll have to do a lot of blasting to sink a foundation into this rock."

"That's just part of the price you'll have to pay to continue your research."

One of the guards walked over to one of the camp's outhouses. Opening the door, a couple of sparrows flew out. "The place doesn't even smell."

Duncan looked over and smiled at him. "It's too old to smell. Anything left in there would have rotted away a long time ago. Besides, animals don't use outhouses. Most of them bury their faeces along with the leftovers of their kills and their dead. They don't want anyone to know where they are hiding."

Sarah could see Duncan scanning the forest. He placed his hand on the back of his neck. She knew that he could sense something. His eyes rested on several piles of rocks. "They've been here and left a few graves behind. Animals must have already robbed them. The rocks are all peeled back." After looking around some more he decided, "I think that we've stayed here long enough. Let's pack it in."

The doctor looked around at the old dilapidated buildings. "Do you think the creatures are still around here?"

"Why take the chance?"

Sarah quietly moved from window to window, trying to keep an eye on them. They didn't go near any of the buildings. The planes were circling in the sky above them. Slowly the men made their way back to the helicopter and climbed aboard. As the craft disappeared from view along with the planes, the forest came alive. The creatures had surrounded the camp. They had lain there motionless, waiting for a signal from the king to attack. The small handful of men were grossly outnumbered. They could have been easily slaughtered.

The king made his way to the hospital. Once inside, he walked past every creature in it while rattling off the same phrase. Sarah could only make out, "Sshuura… Wwoooaaa… Eeeaaa" (Wing - home - go). The rest she didn't understand. From Honda, she knew that the creature's language was extremely simplistic. There were probably only a little more than two to three dozen words in it. It was all in how they were used and put together. By the way the creatures reacted, she could tell that they were going to be moving away from the camp.

The sick and injured no longer outnumbered the healthy adults. After a meal of freshly killed caribou, the healthy members of the colony began to carry the sick and injured away one at a time. Honda handed Sarah a small chunk of liver. Sarah was so hungry that all she did was bite and swallow.

Sarah helped wrap up and prepare the injured to be transported. Honda was too small to carry anything heavy. After most of the creatures had gone, Sarah glanced over at her and saw her pick up an infant and carry it outside. Running to the door, she saw Honda lift into the air and trail after the others with the infant in her arms. Her wing tips would occasionally drip into the still, moonlit water. Not wanting to be seen, none of the creatures flew any higher than they had too as they skirted around the shoreline to the far side of the lake. Outside of the protected coves, with tall trees as a backdrop, the ripples in the water and shimmering moonlight helped hide their exodus. Even the small winged creatures pitched in by carrying away blankets, pots, and bags full of bandages and other medical supplies. Sarah was surprised to see that they were taking even kitchen supplies, a bucket of old rusty nails and hand tools with them. Anything that they felt might come in handy, they took.

It wasn't long before the camp was almost stripped clean. After returning, Honda stayed behind with Sarah as she packed. Along with her backpack, she filled old jars with needles, fish line, fish hooks, snare wire, scissors and anything else she could find laying around the camp. Roaming building to building, she searched everywhere for anything she felt that she could use. As one of the creatures started to carry off a mattress, a few pocket novels and an old camper's diary fell out of a torn seam. Mice had chewed the edges of them and the covers of two of the novels were missing along with the first few pages. Nevertheless, they were something to read. Sarah stuffed them into her pack.

Sarah barely got out of the door before Honda's father dropped out of the sky and landed in front of her. He softly rattled away in creaturese as he wrapped his arms around her, 'Wing, home, go'.

He had almost taken the exact same route back to the long ridge. He gingerly flew between the trees along the same creek beds and down the same ravines. His wide wings almost touched the dense vegetation that lined both sides of the gully. Instead of heading to the mine, he flew alongside the ridge. Flying under the trees, over the swamps and barren rock formations, they made it to the northern section of the ridge, at the start of the long, curled fingernail of the Devil's Claw. From there, he circled around a clump of trees and landed. After walking through the forest for fifteen minutes, they came to a tunnel woven through thick bush and low hanging branches. The creatures had trimmed or twisted away any branches that hindered their entrance and departure. At the end of the muddy, well-used path, Sarah saw an opening between two large boulders. The creatures had excavated their own hidden entrance into the side of the ridge. Sarah watched the others as the king walked by them. Despite having fewer members, they worked together as a strong, single unit. With the release of a few rough, stern vowels, the king redirected the tired creatures and gave them additional tasks to do.

Sarah carefully listened to his growling rattles. Out of necessity, she could tell that creaturese was quickly evolving. Sarah heard sounds she had never heard before.

******

Roger walked into Doctor Scott's office and announced, "They are getting smarter." Holding a pair of jars in front of him, he continued, "Look at these brains. They are evolving."

The doctor retrieved the jar with that day's date on it. "Those creatures come in all shapes and sizes. No two are the same. Under what basis are you making this conclusion?"

"The graves that Rankin's patrol discovered in the swamp were a gold mine." Roger put the other jar down on the doctor's desk and pulled out a pair of x-rays from his lab coat pocket. "Comparing the same area that human's use for speech to these creatures' brains, their ability to communicate with each other has tripled in the last two months. Plus, when I compared one of the bodies to the first creature we unearthed, they look almost identical. It was like they were siblings."

"How interesting. This conflict is making the cells adjust their brain patterns. Before, they had not needed to think beyond their own day to day existence. Now that they need better communication skills to survive, they quickly evolve. Our cells have given these creatures the ability to reason and think their way through their problems." Doctor Scott stood up and turned to the window. With his hands tightly gripped together behind his back, he muttered, "So they are no longer mere animals. That is going to make Duncan's job a lot harder."

"The bigger problem is that I believe the entire colony is evolving. This isn't a random occurrence. Speech only works when others can understand it. You can't tell a Korean what to do in Greek."

Doctor Scott turned his back to Roger and stared out of the window. With his head down and arms folded in front of him, he asked, "What kind of cell count are you getting in these creatures?"

"The counts are getting higher."

"That means that they are having no problems getting the nutrients they need to support their growth. Find the source of the nutrients, and we will find them."

Chapter Twenty-Two

Home

Michaela stared at the family photo. In it, a happy, smiling Sarah was seated in her wheelchair. Michaela and her father were bent over behind her with wide grins on their faces, each having one arm wrapped around the back of Sarah's neck. She then looked at the wrinkled photo in her hand. "I wish I knew where you were. We're family. No matter what you look like or have become, we're still family."

Tears started to run down her face as she turned to Kristofer. "We have to find her."

Kristofer looked up at her from the couch. Putting down his coffee, he stood up and walked over to her. With his arms wrapped around her, they both gazed at the family photo on the wall. "We just have to search even harder. The only place we haven't been able to look is the fenced off area on the far side of the ridge."

While still fixated on the photo, Michaela said, "Then we'll just have to cut through the fence and search there too."

Biting his lower lip, Kristofer rested his head against Michaela's. Slightly rocking each other back and forth, neither said another word. Both were apprehensive about their next step. If they were caught, they could be arrested for trespassing plus break and entering. Ending the uneasy silence, Michaela said, "We can use my dad's tools to get through the fence. They are down in the basement."

"He'll miss them and know what we are up too." Kristofer twisted Michaela around and put his hands on her shoulders. Facing each other, he looked into her teary eyes. "My dad has stuff that he doesn't even know he has. Unlike your dad, he hardly ever uses any of it. I'll go home and gather what we need."

"And I'll pack up some camping supplies and grub. We can tell everyone that we're on a camping trip."

"With everything that has gone on, nobody should ask too many questions. They'll just think that you needed to get away for a while."

******

Hearing some clamouring in the hallway, Doctor Scott looked up and saw Duncan walking by his office. "What happened last night? All the traffic in the hallway woke me up."

Duncan stopped and backed up in front of the doctor's doorway. "A few of the low-level radar units we had installed picked up the creatures. There was a lot of activity last night. I'm just about to go over the data recordings to see if I can find out what they are up to."

"Let me know as soon as you find out."

Duncan scrolled through the recordings over and over. Once in a while bleeps would appear and then immediately disappear. He concentrated his focus on the steady line of bleeps springing up along the waterways and valleys. Almost all the bleeps were along the same path. He quickly saw a pattern. Duncan stood up and gave a sigh before dashing out of the door. Knocking on the doctor's open door he announced, "I think we have narrowed down where the creatures are hiding."

The doctor followed Duncan back to main security room. The doctor looked around at the technicians and guards. "Should they be here right now?"

Feeling his men were being belittled, Duncan took a deep breath before slowly replying, "Maybe not." Everyone had heard the doctor. Duncan looked around the room. They were all staring at him. Without a word being said, he pointed to the door and they all proceeded to leave. Laurie gave him a questioning look. Duncan smiled and told her, "Go to the café and I'll let you know when to come back."

After shutting the door, Duncan sat at the secondary radar monitoring station. The doctor stood behind him as Duncan scrolled through the overnight records. "You can clearly see how they are using the terrain to hide." Pointing to the screen, Duncan drew a line with his finger. "Last night, instead of randomly popping out in different places, they kept to this path."

The doctor studied the screen. "So they could be hiding out at either end of it or maybe even somewhere in the middle. They could be fanning out to gather food along what they think is a safe pathway."

"I don't think so." The doctor studied Duncan's face as he followed the bleeps on the screen with his finger. "I believe they are migrating. Finding a safer hideout."

"From where to where?"

Duncan tapped the screen, "From here," then, after moving his finger, "To somewhere around here."

"Are you sure? That is the campground that we just purchased. They could have been there when we were surveying it."

"They probably were."

The doctor pointed at the two ends of the dotted path that Duncan had charted. "How do you know it's not the other way around?"

"Simple, I reviewed the recordings and found the first and last sightings. Their dotted trails point the way. The rest are back and forth traffic."

"So where are they now?"

Duncan looked at the doctor, "Somewhere on the Devil's Claw."

"That makes sense. It could also answer some questions we were having. The creatures need certain nutrients and minerals to stimulate the growth of more cells. They must be getting it from somewhere around the ridge. That's why they can't stray too far away from it."

It didn't take long before Duncan had brought every plane and helicopter at his disposal into action. During the following days, they carefully photographed every tree and rock along the entire length of the ridge. At night, Duncan and several other guards examined the footage for any signs of traffic or construction.

As Duncan flipped through layers of overlapping photos on the monitor, Roger grinned. "If we don't find them soon, the infection will run its course. Their immune systems will grow stronger and make them even harder to kill. We'll have to find another way to get rid of them."

Duncan looked at Roger. "Okay hero, I can see those wheels a turning. What are you thinking of doing this time?"

"When it's time, I'll let you know."

******

Sarah explored the series of caverns that the creatures had excavated and connected together. They had converted that section of the ridge into a giant anthill with shafts and tunnels everywhere. Using her claws, she climbed through the labyrinth. She spotted six escape routes, many of which were long, downward-sloping tunnels with piles of large rocks next to them in case it was necessary to quickly plug them up. They were all narrow and twisted so no one could see down them very far. Looking up she saw additional holes dug into the sides where creatures could hide. Mounds of heavy rocks were piled in front of each one.

The busy creatures were constantly improving their defences. With the sick and wounded rapidly recovering, Sarah found that she had more and more time to explore. The colony had finally started to accept her presence and Honda felt more at ease leaving her alone, while joining the others with the day to day chores.

Except for a trusted few, nobody was allowed to venture outside of their new home. Only after the helicopters and planes had departed at night would the king permit the hunting parties to leave. Small groups of creatures would fan out and travel on foot for at least a half hour before taking to the air in search of food. Honda peered out of a small escape tunnel. It was getting dark and she couldn't hear anything flying above them. She crawled back in and grabbed Sarah's hand. "Eeeet."

Sarah smiled and followed her out through the tunnel. With fur covering her entire body, she no longer needed clothes to shield her from the cool night air. On a belt around her waist she carried a hunting knife and a couple pouches full of supplies. Out of modesty, she draped small pieces of cloth down the front and back of the belt. The guard that the belt came off of didn't need it anymore. He also didn't need the shirt that she ripped apart and made into a loincloth.

Several of the wingless creatures had started to wear belts too. The ability to carry rope, a hand saw, hatchet and knife had come in handy. Two creatures had even taught themselves how to make the guns they had salvaged fire. Despite having a little problem reloading and aiming them, they knew their potential. Once a bullet is in the chamber, all a creature had to do is point it in the right direction and pull the trigger.

With the cool night breeze enticing her senses, it felt great being outside. Sarah soaked in the smells of the forest as they walked along. Her wide, elongated nose started to twitch. She could smell something. She looked around. Honda had picked up the same scent and crawled into a small bush. A rabbit leaped out and dashed under a nearby thick thorn bush. The pair studied the fortified bush. On her hands and knees, Sarah could barely see the rabbit's twitching nose. "You win this time."

They had walked around for a couple hours. A few more rabbits and grouse had escaped them. Hunting wasn't as easy as she thought. Looking up, she could see the king soaring over the landscape with a spotted fawn in his talons. "That's how to do it." Like a cat, Sarah easily scaled a tall pine tree. Honda simply unfolded her wings and flew up to join her. In the distance she could hear a pack of wolves on the hunt. With the fluttering of bird wings, the snapping of twigs, and the odd splash in the water, the forest was alive with living creatures. "Too bad I don't know how to catch you."

On the way back, Honda took Sarah's hand and guided her to the edge of a swamp. Kneeling beside it, she started digging in the mud. A frog jumped. Honda's fast reflexes grabbed it in mid-air. "Eeeet."

Sarah was hungry and ripped off one of the frog's legs. Even raw, it tasted delicious. Honda squeezed the frog and its entrails fell into her open mouth. After handing Sarah the rest of the frog, she combed the shore for some more. It only took them an hour to catch over a dozen of them. Sarah would ram one of her claws through their heads and kill them before tossing them into a pile. When they couldn't detect any more frogs, Sarah pulled a plastic bag out of one of the pouches on her belt. After filling it with dead frogs, she tied it to her belt. Outside of berries, for the first time in her life she had gathered and killed her own food. The fact that it was just frogs didn't matter to her as she proudly grinned at Honda.

Walking back to the cavern, Honda spotted another group of creatures. Pulling Sarah's arm, she pointed at them. Honda ran over and smelled every one of them up and down, and then all over again. They were staggered several metres apart. Sarah walked over to the lead creature and saw what he was carrying. It was a 30-06 hunting rifle. It looked familiar. The second creature was dragging a backpack and the third had a set of human legs dangling around its neck. They were still wearing the remnants of a pair of blue jeans. The body was severed at the waist. The last creature came into view carrying what was left of the upper half of the body. Something inside of Sarah had to see who it was. Despite the dog-like creature hissing at her, she went over and grabbed the man's hair. Lifting up his head, she was shocked to discover that it was one of her neighbours, Timothy Ferguson.

******

Kristofer slowly crept down the trail leading around the ridge. Without knowing that it was a trail, most people wouldn't have guessed it. Over years of use, the forging woodland creatures had carved it out of the landscape. Unlike man, they easily sidestepped the rocks, boulders and tree stumps. To the caribou, a fallen tree was little more than an inconvenience. However, to an ATV, each of these obstacles made the trail hazardous and at times slowed them to a crawl. Kristofer noticed that the trail had been used recently. Fresh tire tracks had scrapped off moss and fungus from fallen trees along with squashing ferns and grasses into the swampy mud. By the tire treads, he also knew that they were heading in the same direction that they wanted to go. Kristofer stopped and studied the tracks. Turning to Michaela, he shrugged. "As long as we stay outside of the fence, at the very least we would have someone to ask if they had seen anything. At the very worst, all they could do is ask us to leave."

They followed the tracks a couple more kilometres before they came across an overturned ATV next to the fence line. Kristofer got off his ATV and looked around. The ground was fairly flat and he couldn't see any reason why it would have flipped over. "This doesn't make sense."

Michaela walked around the overturned machine with him. "This is the same model as Mr. Ferguson's." The smell of gasoline still lingered in the air. Crouching down, she tapped on the gas tank with her knuckles. It was empty. Looking further, she made a discovery. "The fuel line is cut."

Kristofer made his own finds. "So are the brake cables and spark plug wires. It looks like something was chewing on them."

Kristofer ran his fingers over the long gashes on the seat. Four even lines were torn through the leather seat and deep into the padding. Going back to his ATV, Kristofer retrieved his axe. "I never heard about any of those creatures roaming around outside of the mine."

"I guess they have to come out to hunt. Even they have to eat."

Cautiously, Kristofer followed the faint tracks leading away from the machine. Someone had cut apart a section of fence and used two branches to hold the small gap open. After following the tracks a couple hundred metres inside of the fence, he found a campsite. The collapsed tent was ripped to shreds. A large pool of blood covering an exposed section of tent's floor. Kristofer looked around while bouncing the head of the axe in one hand and maintaining a firm grip on the handle with the other. Along the edge of the campsite, he spotted another puddle of blood. Slowly walking over to it, he picked up a small piece of small intestine.

Standing at the edge of the campsite, Michaela proclaimed, "Kris, I don't think it's safe here."

He could see the horror in Michaela's pale, twitching face. "I think you're right."

They examined every bush and clump of grass for any signs of danger as they slowly walked back to the ATV. Michaela jumped on. Kristofer was stowing his axe when the forest seemed to come alive. They both watched as crackling branches raced towards them. Kristofer jumped on the ATV and started the engine. The front end bounced off the ground as he sped away. Michaela looked back.

Robert couldn't run any further. Slumped over with his hands on his knees, he yelled out, "Stop! For God's sake, stop."

Michaela tugged on Kristofer's shoulder. "We have to go back."

Over the motor, he screamed, "Why?"

"My dad's back there."

Kristofer looked behind him and saw Robert bent over in the middle of the trail. After rolling to a stop, he asked, "What is he doing out here?"

"I don't know. I thought he was at work."

Robert caught his breath for a few seconds as the ATV slowly backed up. Getting a second wind, he ran towards it. "I don't care why you are here. Let's just get out of here."

Michaela sat on her father's lap on the back of the ATV. "What about Sarah?"

Her father stared back at her. "If she's turned into one of them, she's where she belongs."

From her vantage point high on top of a tree, Sarah heard everything. Tears rolled down her cheeks. "So my nightmare has come true. I truly can't go home."

Chapter Twenty-Three

Bad News

As Kristofer started up a steep incline, his ATV began to sputter. Rolling to the bottom of the embankment, he got off. "It's all right. I just have to put some more fuel in the tank."

The planes flying overhead had become so common that they went unnoticed. Both Robert and Michaela got off and surveyed the forest as Kristofer poured in the fuel. He still had another full can left. "We've travelled a long ways since I picked you up. We should be safe now. Tell me, what happened back there?"

"I was in a tree stand when it happened. I didn't see or hear anything until Timothy started to scream. There were four of them. They weren't anything like I remembered in the mine. I watched what they did to Timothy through my night vision binoculars. They have grown over twice the size they once were. They were like the hideous gargoyles you see on top of old gothic castles. Each one looked completely different from the next." Robert paced a bit before continuing. "Those creatures started eating Timothy's guts while he was still alive. I could hear him screaming in agony. The infrared glasses may have distorted a lot of the details, but I know what I saw. I picked up my rifle but I was too scared to shoot. After they had finished eating his insides, they chewed his body in two and carried off his remains."

"So they never saw you."

"I'm here, ain't I? If they had, I wouldn't be. I stayed up in that tree as quietly as I could. When I saw your ATV, I left everything behind and climbed down as fast as I could."

Michaela turned and hugged her father. "Sarah will never turn into one of them. She can't. She's a Douglas."

Robert's emotionless face replied, "If she does, it will no longer be Sarah Douglas."

"I don't care. She will always be my sister. I will always love her."

Hugging her even harder, he cried as he told her, "Inside, so will I."

******

"Duncan, we had some intruders."

Duncan looked at the guard as he handed him some aerial photos. "Who?"

"Locals, maybe hunters."

"You mean either reporters or poachers; hunting season hasn't started yet."

Duncan knocked on George's door. Lying there with his arms behind his head, he looked towards the door. "Come on in. Why bother even knocking? Everyone just comes in anyway."

Duncan peeked in. "So you are feeling better."

Twisting onto his side, he propped his head up with his arm. "I have to get out of here. These walls are driving me insane."

"You sound like your old self. We almost lost you." Duncan walked over to his bed. "I need you to check something out."

George practically jumped out of his bed. "Anything to get out of here!"

Within three hours George was standing in the middle of the campsite accompanied by Rankin's squad. Rankin turned to George. "Tell me, what happened here?"

George was bent over studying the mess along the edge of the camp. "It looks like the creatures butchered a man, maybe even two. There is almost nothing left to go by. From the small pieces of intestines and guts left behind, they either ate or hauled the remains away."

After photographing the site, Rankin ordered his men to clean up the place. "Nobody can find out what happened here. We have to get rid of all the evidence that we can." Stopping at the tree, he added, "This pool of blood will be hard to conceal."

"Hang some ropes over the branches above it. We'll get an elk or something and butcher it. If anyone sees it, they will think that it was poachers." Rankin called in to Duncan, "We need an elk, moose, bear, anything you can get to conceal the bloody mess those creatures left behind. This place looks like a butcher shop. We'll need to disguise it as fast as possible."

As the guards methodically removed all traces of the creatures, George wandered through the forest. With the rope ladder Robert used to climb down still dangling on the side of the tree, it wasn't hard for George to find the tree stand. He grabbed a hold of the ladder and climbed up. Robert's 270 rifle was still laying across the seat. On a small shelf was a large spray bottle of scent remover, a box of bullets and a small backpack with Robert's name on it. After collecting the stuff, he climbed back down. "Rankin, your men ain't finished yet. They have more work to do over here."

Two guards ran over to the tree stand. After seeing the name on the backpack, Rankin shouted, "Leave it alone. I've got an idea."

George gathered up Robert's flung carbon embedded coat and hat. Walking back to the campsite, he handed the garments to Rankin. "Now what?"

Pointing to the sky, Rankin barked, "I need you to butcher whatever that helicopter is flying in."

In the distance a helicopter could be seen with two animals dangling under it. As they got closer, George recognized them by the 'W' shaped scar under the eye of the large female moose. It was the cow and calf that liked to graze in the swamp beside the facility. George looked over at Rankin. His sunken expression said it all.

Rankin sternly looked at him. "We needed something, and we needed it fast."

"Then you do your own butchering." George looked at the dangling creatures. "I don't butcher innocent creatures just to have their meat spoil."

******

Robert sat at the kitchen table nursing a glass of whiskey. "What should we do?"

Kristofer sat across from him. "I think I should call my dad."

"What good are the cops? You can't count on them for anything."

Michaela stood behind Kristofer and backed him up. "We have to do something. A man has been killed. Timothy was your best friend. What about his family? We have no choice. We have to get the police involved."

By the time Kristofer's father showed up at the door, Robert was so drunk that he could barely lift his glass. Dressed in his police uniform, the confused officer questioned his son. "You called and told me to rush over here. Tell me, what's going on?"

Kristofer told his father everything that he knew. The only part he had left out was them searching for Sarah. When asked, why they were there, he answered, "Michaela needed to get away for a while, so we decided to go camping. It ended up being lucky that we came across his ATV tracks. Out of pure curiosity, we followed them to see where they went."

Kristofer helped Michaela get Robert to the couch. After covering him with a blanket, they let him sleep it off. Robert barely stirred as everyone went outside. After refuelling his ATV and spare gas can, Kristofer and Michaela led a small parade of four ATVs along the rugged trail. As they approached Mr. Ferguson's righted vehicle, he abruptly stopped. Stunned, he looked over at Michaela's shocked face, and then to his father's. "That isn't the way it looked when we left it."

Officer Dennis Poirier walked over and examined the unit. "Bring over some gas."

Another officer carried over some fuel and poured it in while Kristofer slowly walked around the ATV. The ripped leather seat had been replaced with a black vinyl one that clashed with the vehicle's camo colouration. Both the brake cables and spark plug wires had been replaced. His father turned over the motor. It started right away. "They ran out of gas."

Kristofer piped up. "I had plenty of extra fuel. If that was all it was, I would've put some in."

His father ignored him. They continued to the campsite on foot. Hung on the tree branch was the dressed moose carcass. In the middle of the site lay a dead calf with a bullet hole through the side of its head. The officer only had to look around briefly before he spotted Robert's rifle leaning against a tree. He could smell the gunpowder in the barrel. "It's been fired recently."

"Dad, this isn't how the campsite was when we saw it earlier."

"I know what you told me but I have to go by what I see. You were probably in so much of a hurry to get out of here that your eyes skipped over a few things. "

"A few things! I know what I saw and what I didn't see."

"How about you just go back to your ATV for now." Officer Poirier walked over and studied the hanging carcass. Its head had been rolled to the side. "I can't see any bullet holes." Looking down at the neck he saw some black tissue. "Wait, it was a neck shot. The bullet must have gone clean through."

Michaela watched as an officer unloaded the rifle he had found. She ran over to him. "That's my dad's gun. I would know it anywhere." Pointing to the stock, she added, "Look at the butt. I bet you that you'll find his name engraved on it."

Kristofer's father turned to her. In almost a whisper he told her, "Right now, you're not helping your father any."

"What are you talking about?"

"I see two dead moose that are shot out of season, your father's rifle and an ATV that had run out of gas." He watched Michaela's puzzled look as he added, "Everything I see here leads me to believe someone was poaching."

A furious Michaela screamed back, "What are you talking about?"

"It appears like your father was hunting out of season. If the bullet inside of that calf's head matches your father's rifle, I may have to arrest him." Looking over at the other officer as he examined the site, he added, "I might have no choice in the matter."

Kristofer piped up. "What about Mr. Ferguson?"

His father turned to him and put a hand on his shoulder. "This wouldn't be his first time and not even his second. He probably grabbed all his stuff and vamoosed out of here. There is clear evidence of several trails leading away from the campsite. He probably hid their spare cans of fuel and left Mr. Douglas to take the blame."

"And why would he do that?"

"He could've heard your ATV and thought that it was the game warden. He knows that he would be sent to jail as a repeat offender if he was arrested again."

Chapter Twenty-Four

Innocence

Peering through his binoculars, Rankin watched them bicker some more before returning to their ATVs and driving away. Turning to the guard operating a surveillance microphone, he inquired, "How much did you pick up?"

"Almost everything."

The guard played back a portion of the recording that the sensitive microphone had picked up. Rankin smiled as the word poaching was mentioned. "Duncan is going to love this. Not only are they not going to be any cops combing through here searching for anyone, but Mr. Douglas may be out of his hair as well."

A guard steered the stripped ATV as they towed it away. Without brakes they had to drag it carefully through the woods. From the forest, George watched them leave. Unseen by anyone, Sarah clung to a tall tree that towered above them all.

When the guards were a safe distance away, Sarah climbed down the tree and ran to the campsite. As quickly as she could, she hauled away the calf. "If they don't have any proof, they can't trace the bullet back to my dad."

The trail Sarah left behind was easy for George to follow. After waiting about a half hour to be safe, he traced her steps to within sight of the ridge. Sarah had abandoned the carcass and disappeared into the forest. The only thing missing was a hind leg. He could see the cut marks on the hide and muscle. "She knows how to use a knife." Glancing up and down the trail, he added, "I just wish I knew why she left the rest in the middle of a path." Creeping into the forest, he sat down and waited. He suspected that Sarah or one of the other creatures would come back for the abandoned carcass and lead him the rest of the way to their lair. A wide clear trail is much easier to follow than rummaging around looking for random clues in a hostile environment.

Inside of the cavern, Sarah placed the calf's hind leg on the ground. As the rest of the creatures in the cavern stared at the fresh meat, the king watched Sarah retrieve a buck saw from the pile of salvaged odds and ends from the campgrounds. After using the saw to hack through the leg bone, Sarah tossed the chunks of meat to females with young. With saw in hand, she looked at Honda. "Eeeaaa." Placing her fist next to her chomping teeth, she added, "Eat."

Honda gazed at the rays of bright sunlight reflecting through the tunnels. Even inside the cavern, she could still pick out the sound of the planes flying overhead. Looking back at Sarah, she started to tremble as she said, "Nooo."

As Sarah turned to leave, a dragon-like creature jumped in front of her and hissed. She tried to walk around the creature. It backed up into the tunnel and blocked her way.

The king looked over at the females eating while their young tried to breastfeed. They had barely survived the plague. The young remained in danger until their mothers could regain their health and produce milk. Turning towards two stocky dog-like beasts, he rattled away his orders. As the two creatures approached Sarah, the dragon-like creature stepped out of her way. After a sigh of relief, Sarah led the two creatures through the tunnel and into the daylight.

As the trio walked past, George held his breath and crouched under a bush. Noticing the saw hanging from Sarah's belt, he knew the creatures were going back for the butchered cow. Sarah waved the creatures past the dead calf. The first one followed, but the second stopped and looked around with its nose in the air. George pulled his carbon laced cover over him to help mask his scent. The leaf-shaped slits cut into the camo cover made him blend into the surrounding brush. The faint essence of skunkweed rubbed onto his cloths also helped to mask any residue of scent he still gave off. Sweat beaded on George's forehead as the beast finally lowered his head and ran to catch up with the others.

A pair of crows sat on top of the hanging moose carcass as they entered the camp. Sarah ran toward them with her arms waving. Swiping at them with her claws, the crows flew away cawing. The two other creatures were busy chasing away the smaller birds that were picking at the entrails. Immediately after scaring the birds away, they buried their heads in the pile of intestines, liver and organs. Sarah was content just smelling the hanging meat. Cutting up moose meat had been a family affair after every fall hunt. Even if her father didn't shoot any, it didn't matter. The gang he went hunting with would always divide up the kill. Everyone got at least a quarter of a moose. It had always been her favourite meat.

As Sarah hacked the carcass into quarters, one of the creatures handed her a hunk of liver. All the work had made her hungry and she bit off a chunk. There was something in the liver that perked her up. Both her mind and body felt energized. It didn't take long for her to scoff the entire bloody chunk down as if it was rich, chocolate cake. She looked over at the others. Getting down on all fours, she crawled over and rooted through the pile of entrails for some more. Even the green mush that was stuffed into the intestines smelled absolutely delicious to her. Within minutes, she could feel her energy level increase and her body became more relaxed. Most of the tingling aches that had been bothering her had suddenly vanished.

With a full stomach, Sarah grabbed a hind quarter of the carcass and started to drag it back. The others each grabbed a front quarter and followed her. When they got close to the abandoned calf carcass, Sarah could hear something rustling in the bushes. The sound was quite a ways off. Slowly she put down the meat and squatted. The other two did the same. As the sound got closer to where she had left the calf, she quietly scaled up the back side of a large birch tree and tried to get a better look. Peering through a narrow crotch in the tree, she could see Honda sniffing the carcass.

Honda continued on the trail, then suddenly stopped. Sarah could tell she was nervous. Honda's ears perked up as she looked around in quick jerking motions. Then she slowly sank down onto her belly and crawled into the bush. Puzzled by Honda's strange behaviour, Sarah continued to watch her as she circled the dead calf. As she widened her circle, Sarah noticed something else moving. It wasn't much, just a strange object pointing straight at Honda. The breeze was blowing the other branches in the opposite direction. The movement wasn't natural and something inside Sarah erupted. She pounced out of the tree and landed on a fallen dead branch. The breaking twigs caused a couple grouse to fly out and beat their wings. George's bullet missed. Trapped under his own blanket, Sarah jumped on top of him. Pinned down, George was helpless to defend himself. In rage, Sarah swiped her claws back and forth across the blanket a half dozen times. By the time she had realized what she was doing, she could see George's bare, torn open shoulders.

Sarah stood up, took a step back and looked at what she had done. George rolled over to face her. His hands were still firmly gripped to his rifle. "You monster." Using his legs to turn, he fought the blanket and pointed the rifle at her, "Die, demon seed, die."

Sarah kicked the barrel of the rifle aside. Almost falling on top of him, she swiped her claws across his neck. His hands reached out and grabbed her throat. Blood pulsed out of his neck and sprayed Sarah's face. As George's weakening fingers relaxed, she broke free from his grip and slowly got up. Her eyes were glued to the vile, distorted look on his face. Honda ran over and bit into his neck and shook it violently. Sarah stepped back and watched the other two creatures join in the wild, bloody frenzy. With blood dripping from her claws, she shook her head. "This can't be."

Sitting down, Sarah watched as the others began dragging the meat back to the cavern. Her strange mood confused Honda as she approached her, saying, "Eeetsss oookkk."

Sarah put her arm around her, "No, it's not okay. I just killed a man. That's not okay." She put her head down and rested it against her hand. She felt the sticky blood on her forehead. Standing up, she looked at her bloody hands. Aimlessly walking into the forest, she dropped to her knees in the middle of a marsh. She didn't care if the water was black. All she wanted to do was wash off the blood. Her legs sank into the muddy bog as she splashed the foul water all over herself. Honda stood back and watched her from shore. Staring into the sky, Sarah screamed, "What have I done to deserve this?" As she lowered her head, she faintly whispered, "God, forgive me and tell me what to do."

The roar of approaching ATVs woke Sarah from her stupor. Grabbing branches and clumps of grass, she tried pulling herself out of the mud. All she managed to do was pull the wet plants out of the muck. Her legs were stuck. Sarah saw Honda watching her from the bank of the swamp. Retrieving the rope from the pouch on her belt, Sarah tossed one end to Honda. Honda wrapped it around a tree and threw the end of the rope back to Sarah. Pulling together, Sarah's could feel her legs breaking free from the mud's suction. Once freed, she squirmed out of the swamp as the ATVs drove by.

******

Two game officers followed Officer Poirier back to the campsite inside the fence. Private property or not, they had to investigate the incident. Kristofer and Michaela trailed behind the rest. As soon as the game warden saw the camp, he realized they were too late. All of the major evidence was missing. The older game warden shook his head. "In order to charge Mr. Douglas, we need at least an animal carcass. With no witnesses or bullets to examine we have nothing."

The three men looked around the site. All that was left were two pools of blood and a few chunks of entrails left from a kill. Officer Poirier looked for rope or anything that would indicate poaching. The older warden piped up. "Forget it, there is nothing here that I can use. From what I see, some people were camping here. They could've been carrying weapons for personal protection. After all, there have been a lot of strange rumours flying around this region lately."

"What about the blood?"

Seeing his partner's frustration, the younger warden butted in. "Any half-assed lawyer could get him off." The warden pointed to the pile of entrails. "They are just going to say that after they left, some animals could've killed something and carried it off. We simply don't have enough here to even justify filing charges. You should have snapped a pile of pictures when you had a chance. Then we would have had something to work with."

"What about the gun? It had been recently fired."

The older warden put his hand on the frustrated officer's shoulder and calmly told him, "He could say that he fired it into the air to signal for help." Looking down at the pools of blood, he added, "His partner probably came back and destroyed the evidence. Don't worry. We'll get them next time."

******

Sarah raced towards the campsite. Before she could get there, she heard the ATVs' engines starting back up. "They're leaving." She changed directions and headed towards the trail. As she jump down from a rocky mound, through the dense trees she saw a glimpse of Kristofer's father leading the way. Over the tricky trail, the vehicles left plenty of room between them. The empty trailers behind the game wardens' ATVs bounced around the rough terrain and slowed them down considerably. Sarah could see Kristofer and Michaela as they trailed behind the rest.

Kristofer concentrated on navigating down the rough trail as Michaela looked around. She noticed a dark shadow running through the trees. As Kristofer drove past Sarah, Michaela saw her. Even from twenty metres away and all of her changes, from deep inside of her, Michaela knew that it was Sarah. Covered in muddy fur and with pointed ears sprouting past the top of her head, Michaela could still identify her sister.

Michaela tugged on Kristofer's arm. He looked around as she reached forward for the brake lever, while screaming, "Stop!"

"What's wrong?"

Michaela pointed to Sarah. "Look."

Kristofer jolted to a stop. His father saw the cloud of dust in his rearview mirror. Raising his arm to signal the others, he rolled to a stop. Getting off his machine, he yelled back, "What's wrong?"

Sarah disappeared behind a bush. Kristofer turned to his father and answered, "Nothing, we just wanted to stop for a while and talk."

"Out here?"

"We'll be all right. Give us an hour."

"An hour? At the pace we are going, if you are not back half an hour after we are, I will be coming back for you."

Kristofer took a quick glance at Sarah and yelled back, "Fine."

As the others drove out of sight, Sarah reappeared a few metres away from their vehicle. Michaela slid off her seat and slowly walked toward Sarah. There was nothing left of her that was fully recognizable. The dark furry creature wasn't even human. It had arms and walked upright on two legs. Maybe it was the fact that she was wearing a belt with a knife sheath and pouches. Maybe it was its facial expressions. Michaela didn't know. All she knew was that the strange gangly creature standing in front of her was her baby sister.

Sarah smiled. "Do you recognize me?"

Even Sarah's rattling voice was unrecognizable. Michaela looked her over some more before answering. "Strangely, yes."

"Nothing is going to happen to Dad, is it?"

"No, they're not going to press any charges." Michaela tried to study Sarah's expressions. It was hard. Her facial fur and enlarged, flattened nose made it difficult. "Were you responsible for removing the moose carcasses?"

"I had some help."

Michaela noticed Honda curiously peering at them from a distance. "A gremlin?"

"A friend."

The appearance of Honda rattled Kristofer. For a moment he froze. Then he slowly took a can of bear spray out of its holster on the side of the ATV's gas tank. Holding the can behind his back, he peered into the woods. Honda was gone. Suddenly he could hear something behind him. A loud purr rattled within a couple metres of his feet. He quickly turned around and blasted the spray as he went. Honda knocked the can out of his hand as her head butted him to the ground like a charging ram.

Sarah screamed, "No, Honda stop!"

On all fours, Honda pinned Kristofer to the ground as the cloud of pepper spray floated in the air above them. As the powder stung Kristofer's eyes, he cried, "I didn't provoke it. It was going to attack me. I was trying to defend myself."

Sarah ran to him. "You killed her sister."

Honda looked up at Sarah. "Eeeet."

Sarah yelled, "No," as she slid her arm between them. Kristofer crawled backwards as Sarah lifted Honda off of him by her wings. "You are very lucky that I was here. If she had found you on her own, she would've killed you."

Michaela ran to Kristofer and wrapped her arms around him. She watched as Sarah released Honda. "Is it safe now?"

"Yes, but don't put anything else in your hands. She might think it's a weapon." Sarah walked over to the frightened pair. "Blood is thick and so are sisters. You are my sister by birth, but the blood flowing throughout my body also contains that of Honda's sister. The creature that Kristofer killed at the Halloween party."

Michaela looked at her with questioning eyes. "So what, or who, do you feel you are?"

"I'll always be your sister first." Sarah held out one of her hands. "But look at me. I'm not even human anymore. Honda has accepted me, and I have no choice. I can't go home and I can't survive on my own."

"But you're not one of them. I don't care what you look like. You're not a killer. You couldn't hurt anything even if you tried."

Sarah looked down. "I'm no longer innocent."

Michaela slowly walked over to Sarah. Honda's nostrils twitched. As she stretched her hand towards Sarah, her sister grasped it tightly. Her voice trembled as she told Sarah, "I don't care what you had to do to survive out here. To me, you will always be my sweet, innocent baby sister."

Honda wiggled between them. She smelled one, then the other. Michaela looked down at her as she sniffed her leg. Slowly stepping backwards, she choked out, "I better go."

Their arms stretched as far as they could before their fingertips could no longer touch, "Michaela, it's not safe out here. If any of the other creatures find you, you will be just meat to them. I won't be able to help you."

Sarah watched Michaela and Kristofer ride away. She could tell that Honda wanted to chase after Kristofer, but she didn't. Instead she looked up at Sarah and produced a whimpering rattle in her voice. Sarah bent over to give her a hug. Honda snarled back at her like a young child that didn't get what she wanted. Sarah hugged her even tighter, "It's okay. As long as your sister's blood is flowing through my veins, part of her is still alive. Somehow, she made sure that she didn't leave you."

As the ATV drove out of sight, a tear rolled down Sarah's face. With Honda pinned to her chest, she looked down the empty trail. The pair didn't move until the sharp exhaust fumes slowly began to disappear. Sarah looked down at the squirming Honda and then up into the dark cloudy sky. More tears flowed down her face as a light rain started to come down.

With a sudden twist, Honda slipped out of Sarah's arms. With her powerful legs, she sprang into the air. Before Sarah could grab her, Honda was high above the trees. She looked briefly down at Sarah before flying down the trail between the tree tops. "Sssoooorreeee."

Sarah felt helpless. Had she given them enough time to get away? Sarah dropped to her knees and started to cry.

Chapter Twenty-Five

Guilt

Robert Douglas was three-quarters of the way through a bottle of Seagram's 83 whiskey before the phone rang. Detective Arnold said, "Ain't you going to answer it?"

Robert looked up and turned to the detective before glancing at the phone. He gingerly put his glass on the table. Not being able to feel his legs, he stretched his arm towards the annoying phone sitting on the kitchen counter. He couldn't reach it. "It's probably just a wrong number."

"You mean, you are too drunk to get up and answer it."

Robert tried to get up. His numb right foot caught around the table leg and he fell to the floor. The jolted table rocked the bottle of whiskey and tipped it over. The detective quickly grabbed his mug of coffee and saved it without spilling a drop. Over half of what remained in the oval shaped bottle spewed out as it toppled off the table onto the floor. Robert looked down at the wasted whiskey. "Are you happy now?"

Detective Arnold soberly got up from the table, went over and picked up the phone. Handing it to Robert, he said, "Here you go."

As he tried to get up, Robert watched the detective pick up the bottle and pour the rest of the whiskey into the sink. Finally he answered the phone. "Hello."

"Robert, thank goodness you're home. "I haven't heard anything from Timothy in two days."

The volume on the phone was set loud enough that the detective could hear her. Robert didn't know what to say. He sat on the floor speechless as the detective took the phone from his hand. "Mrs. Ferguson, this is Sam. We had some problems in the woods involving Timothy. I'm staying with Robert while I wait to hear back from one of my officers."

"Is Timothy all right?"

"At this point we don't know. All we know is that he is missing."

"Why wasn't I informed of this earlier?"

"At this point, I still don't know what to tell you. Robert and your husband were in the woods. Robert was found frazzled and your husband is still missing."

"Missing! Are you searching for him?"

"He may have been poaching again. I can't tell you any more until Officer Poirier and the game officer return."

Mary could hear Robert's heavily slurred words as he yelled in the background, "He wasn't poaching.   Some overgrown gremlins butchered him." Mary sat on the stool and put her head down on the counter. She could hear the detective talking. "Hello, hello, are you still there?" She couldn't answer.

The store was deserted. Zeb saw his mother crying and yanked out his ear phones. He quickly got off of his stool and walked over to her. "What's wrong?"

"It's your dad.   He was in the woods with Mr. Douglas and something went terribly wrong. The cops aren't willing to say anything to me yet. You know that when Robert's pissed off, he drinks. Well, he's drunk. It has gotta be really bad this time."

The approaching ATV sent Detective Arnold to the door. He looked back and knew Robert wasn't going anywhere. His arms were folded under his head as he slept at the kitchen table. The senior game officer jumped off his ATV and walked over to the detective, shaking his head. "We don't have enough. There's not enough evidence left to prosecute anyone for poaching. He probably was, but nobody would be able to convince a judge of it. Timothy Ferguson must've come back and destroyed all the evidence that we needed to press charges."

Detective Arnold walked over to Officer Poirier as he adjusted the trailer ramps. "What's really going on here?"

The officer hopped on the ATV and drove it over to the trailer. "I don't know. Kristofer isn't a liar. He wouldn't make up anything like this." He shut off the engine. "Did you get Robert to say anything?"

"Plenty. His mouth doesn't stop when he's drinking. Too bad that it had nothing to do with poaching and everything to do with the gremlins. He blames those creatures for everything."

"In a way that's a relief. In another, it leaves us with the problem of what do we do now."

"If Timothy's alive, he'll be hiding out there until he is sure that he is in the clear. If he is dead, from what I've been told, there may not be anything to find."

Robert Douglas raised his head and heard talking outside. He stumbled to the door. With both arms spread across the doorway to hold him steady, he looked around. Michaela wasn't there. "Where's Michaela? She should be back by now. Did something happen to her? Those creatures didn't get her, did they?"

"Calm down. She's all right. They had just stopped to take a breather, that's all."   Kristofer's father walked over to Robert. "Nothing is going to happen to Michaela as long as Kristofer is with her." Looking at his watch, he added, "They should be here any time now."

Three-quarters of an hour had gone by and they still hadn't arrived. Dennis Poirier had stayed behind with Robert as the others left. "Where could they be?" He looked over at Robert sitting at the table with a cup of black coffee cradled in his hands. "They promised me that they would be no longer than thirty minutes, an hour tops."

Robert shook his head after taking a sip of coffee. "Kids do as they want. That is why Sarah ended up being attacked by that gremlin in the first place. No one should've been allowed to enter that mine. They should've blown up the entire ridge."

Dennis turned to Robert with a puzzled look on his face. Standing in the doorway, his emotionless, stone face had crumbled. He was just a scared, worried father. Unable to reply, he turned his back to Robert and gazed through the window in the door.

Robert looked at him and said, "Did you know that was where she got infected? The doctors could cure her cancer, but not the poison that creature had infected her with."

Kristofer's father looked soberly at him. "Why were you in the woods? Were you looking for Sarah, poaching or hunting gremlins?"

Robert raised his coffee mug to him as he answered. "Hunting those creatures. I want to see every last one of those vile things thrown into a deep pit and burned to a crisp."

Dennis' stone face returned as he sat down across from Robert. "So what really happened back there?"

"I told you. I told everybody. The creatures pinned him in his tent and ripped him to shreds. He couldn't even fight back." Robert put his head on the table. "You ain't going to find him. Nobody is. He has been chewed up and shit out by now." Rocking his head back and forth, he added, "I just hope and pray that they didn't catch up to Michaela and your son. They should've never gone in there in the first place."

A vehicle pulled into the driveway and Kristofer's father rushed to the door. It was Mrs. Ferguson. She slammed the truck door and ran towards the house. She was halfway there before she realized that it wasn't Robert at the door. She immediately slowed to a walk. "Where's Robert?"

"He's inside. Come on in."

Dressed in his uniform, Dennis made Mrs. Ferguson nervous. "Dennis, what's going on? What is it that you are not telling me? You know me. We grew up together. Whatever it is, I deserve to be told the truth."

Dennis looked around. He couldn't see any signs of the kids. He glanced at his watch as he told her, "You better come inside."

Dennis held the door open as she entered. Robert looked at him. He shook his head. "There's still no sign of them yet."

Mrs. Ferguson looked at the pair. "Who are you talking about?"

Using his arms, Robert worked his way to the sink. Pouring the rest of his coffee down the drain, he answered, "Our children, that's who. They are still out there in the bush with those creatures."

"What creatures?"

Robert plopped down onto a chair and put on his right boot. "The ones that killed your husband. Michaela is still out there. I gotta go and get her before they do."

******

Sarah ran down the trail. With each bounding step she prayed that Honda hadn't caught up with them. She rounded a sharp bend and noticed that the tire tracks had changed. The tires had started to rip apart the terrain and bounce all over the trail. Sarah stopped to take a breather. Looking around, she felt strange. The sweat running down her back suddenly turned cold. Sarah shook her head and continued down the trail. It was obvious that Kristofer was scared and was desperately trying to outrun Honda. Jumping over fallen trees, Sarah ran as fast as she could. The rain had made the trail even more treacherous and slippery. Kristofer's ATV had left scrapes of paint and pieces of fibreglass on almost every other rock and tree. Sarah didn't have to run much further before she spotted the ATV. It had hopped off the trail and landed in a marsh.

Its wheels were almost entirely sunk into the soupy mud. Sarah noticed the jagged line of disturbed vegetation leading deeper into the marsh. In the distance, she could hear the constant snapping of branches and then a wild scream.

Looking around, she noticed a pair of fallen trees that almost spanned the width of the swamp. She scurried along them over the marsh. Near the end, the thin dead top branches weren't strong enough to hold her weight. After jumping between the branches into the marsh, she half waded and half crawled her way to the steep muddy bank. Jabbing her claws deep into the slippery mud, she managed to get enough to grip on to haul herself onto the shore.

All Sarah could focus on was the wild screaming and shouting that rang through the forest. Through the dense brush, she rushed to its source. In front of her was Honda flailing at a large cluster of densely packed brush with a long stick. Her body was covered in thorns. Small pieces of thorn-covered branches littered the ground around her. As Honda tried to circle the brush, the thorns punctured her feet. Screaming in pain, she tried to beat her wings to hop around it in the air. The trees were too thick. The low branches prevented her from getting airborne.

Sarah got closer. She could see the glimmering edge of a knife as it followed Honda's movements from within the brush. Sarah yelled, "Stop it! Honda, stop it!"

Honda looked around and saw Sarah coming out of the woods towards her. "Nnoooo, miiiine."

"No, friend."

Honda flailed at the thicket a few move times. Sarah picked up a long, dead branch and ran towards her. Honda turned to face her. The dead branch shattered against Honda's hardwood stick. Sarah dropped what was left of the branch and grabbed Honda's stick with one hand. Honda tried to pull it away. With both hands, Sarah tore it away from her and flung it into the woods. "No."

Stunned and confused, Honda cowered down and backed away into the forest. Sarah bent over and peered under the thicket. Feeling his ordeal was finally over, Kristofer's head collapsed onto his extended arm. Sarah reached under the thorny branches and grasped his arm. His knife slipped out of his fingers. It wasn't until after he was out and lying in the open that Sarah could see the thousands of thorns that pierced his blood drenched body. Sarah peered under the brush and looked around. "Where's Michaela?"

"Kristofer looked at her as he tried to sit up. "Safe, I hope. I knew that the creature was after me, not her. As soon as we got behind some cover, I got her to jump off."

"There are others out here. We'll have to find her." Sarah looked down at Kristofer. "You're in no condition to travel and I can't be sure if Honda won't come back. She's probably still watching us."

The few drops of blood that each thorn had expelled added up. Kristofer's skin had become very pale. The thorns had almost bled him to death. Sarah looked around. She knew that she was about seven kilometres east of the main road. Another two would get her to the store. A little further, home. Even with her long legs, it would take her over two hours, non-stop, to carry him out. It would be well after dark before she would be able to return. The hunting parties would be out by then. She had to find Michaela.

Chapter Twenty-Six

Siblings

Sarah picked up Kristofer and carried him along the edge of the trail. It had taken a half an hour to backtrack to where he had made Michaela jump off. She could hear the buzz from an aeroplane flying overhead. She stopped and looked up. Two of them circled above her. In the distance, a helicopter appeared. Sarah rested Kristofer on the ground.   On her knees she looked around the forest and yelled, "Michaela, Michaela."

******

Almost everyone Dennis and Robert called joined in on the search party for Michaela and Kristofer. Out of uniform, Kristofer's father led the way. Behind each driver was someone carrying a loaded rifle. Additional rifles for the drivers were carried in gun cases mounted to the ATVs. Mary drove as Robert cradled his rifle behind her. His finger gingerly rested on the side of the trigger with the gun's safety flicked off. Every time they slowed down, she got a whiff of the whiskey that was still on his breath.

Dennis slowed a bit and stopped as soon as he spotted Kristofer's abandoned ATV. With a chorus of clamouring bullets being injected into rifle chambers, everyone approached the half-sunken vehicle. Several of Robert's neighbours were surveying the forest with rifle butts pressed against their shoulders. "I don't see anything, do you?"

Some of them shook their heads while others said, "Nope." The rest were too focussed on what they could see through their rifle-scopes to respond.

Dennis turned and noticed the nervous crowd behind him. "Lower those weapons. There are two kids out there. They may be injured and hiding in the brush. You could accidentally shoot one of them."

The sunken ATV had travelled quite a ways into the soupy bog. Dennis looked around and saw the wandering line of disturbed vegetation and debris leading further into the swamp. He glanced over the armed men and women standing around. After selecting the three that were best dressed for the ordeal, he led them into the thick muck. Robert divided the rest into three groups. Even drunk, his mind was quick. One group of mostly women stayed behind to watch over the equipment and search the immediate area. Robert took charge over one of the other two groups circling the bog. Following his directions, the couple of younger and more agile members led the way. As they were about to enter the forest, a plane flew overhead. Robert looked up and muttered, "All that money just to keep us out.   If they had any compassion at all, they would be helping us, not trying to scare us away."

With her 30-30 lever action rifle slung over her shoulder, Mary looked around the forest and down the path. Between the rain and all the recent traffic on the path, it had become a muddy mess. It was the broken and twisted limbs on a few saplings on the side of the trail that caught her curiosity. There were no tire tracks anywhere near them. Mary crawled into the wet vegetation to investigate. Mrs. Ferguson watched her from the trail as Mary studied the foliage and ground. "Did you find something?"

"I'm not sure. It could be just an animal."

Rifle in hand, Zeb followed closely behind the pair of women as they slowly ventured down the path.

******

Duncan was the first to repel down from the helicopter onto the narrow ATV path. Laurie and Rankin followed him, along with three others. Sarah could feel a slight breeze from the helicopter's propeller blowing down the trail. She stood up and saw tips of rifle barrels and bobbing heads racing toward her. She immediately dropped to her knees. Several small mounds and fallen trees along the trail hid them from view. From behind a bush a few metres away, Michaela stood up and looked at Sarah and then down at Kristofer. "We'll be all right. They won't do anything to us." Dropping to her knees beside Sarah, she looked at Kristofer's limp body and tears poured out of her eyes.

Sarah carefully slid Kristofer's torso onto Michaela's lap. Michaela held his head in one arm and pulled a few thorns out of his face with her free hand. "He desperately needs medical help."

Slipping her body from under Kristofer's, Sarah told her, "They are his only hope."

Glancing up at Sarah, she added, "Thank you, now go while you still can."

Michaela raised her head as high as she could and yelled, "Help, we need medical help", while waving at the approaching guards. As she did, Sarah crawled away and slithered into the thick brush. With Michaela as a distraction, the guards didn't get a clear look at Sarah, let alone a shot. Within seconds the guards surrounded the pair. Laurie immediately dropped to her knees and examined Kristofer while Duncan ordered Rankin and the others to go after Sarah. Laurie looked up at Duncan. "We'll have to airlift him out of here. He won't survive a bumpy ride over the trail. We're his only chance."

Duncan glanced at the three and said, "So be it." Over his talkie he ordered the helicopter to return. After a stretcher was lowered, Duncan and Laurie carried Kristofer through the forest and into a small nearby clearing. From there, Michaela and Kristofer were loaded onto the helicopter and whisked away. Duncan turned to Laurie. "We're going to need to tell that search party that the kids that they are looking for are all right."

"I know."

"You also know that you are the best person to tell them. Robert Douglas still seems to trust you." Laurie nodded. Duncan pulled a small envelope out of his pocket and handed it to her. "Use these the best you can and convince him to back off."

******

Sitting on a high branch amidst the thick cover of the maple tree's heavy foliage, Honda watched the helicopter leave. As the leaves shifted in the wind, she could see Rankin leading his men into the forest after Sarah. She watched her nimble half-sister scale trees and leap from one to another, leaving no trail for her pursuers to follow. Angry, Honda looked away. Her real sister's fleeing killer was getting away. She pulled a couple branches aside to get a better view of the helicopter as it disappeared around the northern tip of the ridge. Her claws twisted and snapped the small branches she was hanging on to. Spreading out her wings, she glided to the ground. She knew where they were taking him.

******

Mary looked up from the strange footprints embedded in the mud beside a fallen tree. The rain hadn't had time to wash the blood off of the pale birch bark. She swiped the blood with her finger to verify how fresh it was. Very little of it had time to penetrate the bark. Unshouldering her rifle, she flicked off the safety. Behind her, she could hear Mrs. Ferguson complaining about the helicopter. "Good, those damn nuisances are leaving. I wonder what was so interesting up ahead."

Zeb answered. "Maybe they found Dad."

Slowly, Mary walked down the trail as the pair climbed over the fallen birch tree. She was fascinated by the strange footprints left in the soft earth next to the trail. The forest was abnormally quiet. Not a single bird could be heard.

Mrs. Ferguson held her son's rifle as he jumped off the fallen birch tree. As he landed on the ground, his eyes glanced down the trail. "Who's that?" Zeb grabbed his rifle and fired two bullets into the air.

Laurie stopped cold. After a couple seconds, she waved to them and continued down the trail. Rifles in hand, the three just stood there watching her. They scanned the trail to see if anyone else was following her. She was alone. By the time Laurie reached them, Robert and three others were climbing over the fallen tree. Robert saw Laurie and ran to her. "What are you doing here?"

"The planes surveying the area had seen what happened. The kids are all right. They had an accident while they were riding the ATV. The boy, Kristofer, lost a lot of blood and we had to fly him out. There was no time to be diplomatic about it. Other than losing a frightening amount of blood, he had no broken bones or anything seriously wrong with him. He was found badly cut up and covered in thorns. He must have been rolling in them. The doctors should be able to pump some blood into him and have him ready to go back home sometime during the night, morning at the latest."

Robert nervously looked at her. "And what about Michaela?"

With a faint smile Laurie told him, "She's fine. There isn't a scratch on her. She refused to leave Kristofer's side, so we let her ride in the helicopter with him."

Dennis forced his way through the crowd surrounding Laurie. "Is Kristofer all right?" Laurie repeated what she had told Robert. In delight, he bellowed, "Thank God."

As the crowd around Laurie started to spread out, she spotted Robert sitting on the fallen tree with his head on his lap. She approached him. "Robert, can we talk?"

Twisting his head upward, he looked at her. "Sure."

Laurie sat down beside him. "You are going to have to give up this quest of yours. It's getting too dangerous."

"And what about Sarah?" After looking around to make sure nobody could hear them, Robert sat up and asked, "You told me that those creatures ate her. Was that true or has she turned into one of them?"

"I'm sorry for that, but the substance that the creature had infected her with is eating away at her body. Without the Doctor Scott's help, the infection took over. She isn't Sarah anymore. Your Sarah is dead." Laurie pulled out the envelope that Duncan had given her. The first photo was one of the ones taken after the guard's first attack of the mine. It showed a lineup of dead creatures stretched out on display. "We've been hunting them down and killing them on sight. Regardless of what you think, we are trying to eradicate them."

Robert didn't say anything as Laurie handed him the rest of the photos. Several showed more dead creatures and then one showed the aftermath of the creatures' counterattack. Robert studied the gruesome photo. The remains of human body parts were scattered all over the ground. "What happened here?"

Laurie took the photo from him. Tears ran down her face as she told him, "As you already know, the creatures think of us as nothing but another source of meat. A lot of my friends have already paid the supreme price and I suspect that a lot more will before it is over." Looking over at Robert's stunned face, she added, "What do you think those planes and helicopters are doing up there? Duncan and Doctor Scott are pouring in all the resources they have to do what has to be done."

"Then why don't they just call in the authorities?"

Laurie looked at the ground for a second before answering. "They wouldn't know what to do. By the time they acknowledge what's really going on, this entire region could be a battlefield. At least now we have them confined to one area."

Robert turned away from Laurie and down at the next fuzzy picture. "This creature looks almost human."

"It should. That's your daughter. That's what Sarah has turned into."

Robert studied the photo more closely. Over her shoulder she was carrying a large object. He studied it closer. It was a man leg. His boots were still attached to it. "When was this picture taken?"

Laurie flipped over the last photo. It was a close up of Sarah from the previous picture. Tree leaves obscured most of her body. Only her face peering upward was clearly visible. There was something still familiar about the eyes. They were bigger and even shaped differently. He knew that Laurie was telling him the truth. It really was Sarah. Robert stared at the picture as Laurie finally answered his question. "After a hunt. That's blood dripping down her chin. She's just another predator now. She's on top of the food chain."

******

By the time Laurie made it back to Duncan, Rankin and the others were having a break with energy bars and water. With their free hands, they were wiping the mud off their clothes and boots using sticks and leaves. Duncan got up to meet her. "Well, how did you do?"

Handing the envelope of photos back to Duncan, she said, "All right I guess."

Duncan checked the envelope, "There's one missing?"

"I know. I told him that he could have it."

"What did you do that for?"

Laurie smiled at him. "Because it was a fake. If anyone puts it under a magnifying glass, they will be able to easily see that it was digitally altered. It's harmless to us." Her face turned serious. "But to Robert, it's the death of Sarah. The techs did a good job of matching the pants and boots in the photo to the ones his friend was wearing."

"We got lucky. The plane was over top of the campsite when Sarah was carrying away the front leg of the moose we killed. It didn't take much to turn it into a human leg."

From the bushes, Honda watched as the parade of guards made their way to the clearing. Within a minute, a helicopter appeared over the ridge and headed straight for them. She patiently waited as the craft landed and the guards climbed on board. With the helicopter's loud motor whipping the foliage about, Honda quickly crawled behind it and snuck her way forward. As it lifted off, she jumped up and grasped its landing gear. Facing downward, she spread her arms and legs into an 'X' as the craft carried her to the facility.

Sarah watched the helicopter fly overhead. Even in the faint drizzle, the strange form on its bottom was easy for her sharp eyes to recognize. "You stupid little creature, you're going to get yourself killed."

As quickly as she could, she raced through the forest after her. Sarah forgot about the planes. She didn't care if they spotted her or not. After two hours of racing through the forest, a grouse was startled and flew ahead of her. Sarah leaped into the air and batted it with her hand. She landed on the ground on her hands and one knee. It had been a while since she had eaten and the run had drained her. She had to take a break. Looking back at the dead bird, she stood up and retrieved it. After cutting open its gut with a single claw, she sucked its entrails out. The rain had finally stopped and she knew that she had to press on. While ripping the bird's breasts off and chewing them one at a time, she could feel her energy coming back.

Two guards stationed by the side of a trail were stunned as Sarah darted past them. With barely a glance, all they could do was radio ahead and give the next patrol a heads up. Sarah was lucky. She turned off the trail and waded into the swamp as she neared the facility. The ambush set by the guards was avoided by a mere fifty metres. After crossing a section of swamp, she reached a large isolated island. She remembered seeing it from her window and knew no guards would be there. Various wildlife, especially moose, had used it for sanctuary. It was almost completely dark as she climbed a large cedar tree to get a better view of the facility. She could see Honda clinging to the outside wall next to the heliport on the roof.

******

Michaela brushed back Kristofer's hair with her fingers. "Feeling any better?"

He took a couple deep breaths before opening his eyes. "I no longer feel like I'm being attacked by a swarm of porcupines. Right now, I can barely feel anything. The pain killers really work." After trying to sit up he added, "But I'm so weak. I feel like a corpse."

Michaela gave him a hug and kissed his forehead. "You're lucky Sarah found you. You almost bled to death. The doctors must've pumped at least three pints of blood, four bags of plasma and bunch of other fluids into you."

From the doorway Doctor Scott could hear every word. With a smile, he entered the room. "Don't get too used to the pain killers. Your wounds were all superficial. They will heal very quickly. However, there are probably still some needle tips hidden under your skin that had broken off. It'll take a couple weeks for your body to expel them normally. Plan on being in a lot of discomfort until they are all expelled."

Michaela helped the doctor put Kristofer into a wheelchair. As she walked down the hallway, she peered into several of the open doorways. Stacks of boxes were piled everywhere. The place was more chaotic then she remembered. Everyone seemed to be scampering around in a state of confusion. "Are you renovating the place?"

The doctor calmly replied, "No, just reorganizing."

Laurie stood at the elevator waiting for them. With only a brief exchange of smiles, Michaela rolled Kristofer in. On the roof two guards wandered around surveying the surrounding area through night-vision binoculars. One yelled, "It's coming. It's approaching from the southeast."

Within seconds, the throbbing sound of the helicopter was all that Michaela could hear. As it came in for a quick landing, Laurie noticed some movement at the edge of the wall. Dropping down, she could see Honda crawling onto the roof. Laying on her belly, she drew her revolver and took aim. The landing helicopter was in the way. Seeing Laurie's alarm, another guard dropped to his knees with his rifle butt pushed against his shoulder. The last guard rushed to Michaela and Kristofer's side. Seeing the commotion, the pilot instinctively lifted the helicopter into the air. Honda was left totally exposed. Both Laurie and the guard opened fire as Honda leaped into the air. The sky wasn't dark enough to help her escape. For a second, her silhouette was clearly visible. All the guards opened fire. With the beating helicopter pushing her downward, she fell over the edge and tumbled down the side of the facility. The grounds were immediately lit up with spot lights bouncing around the perimeter trying to find her.

Sarah watched her fall. As guards ran out of the facility, she was horrified. She didn't know why but she screeched out a loud, piercing howl. "AOOOOWW."

One of the guards yelled, "She's in the swamp."

The swamp protecting the island didn't shield it from the hail of bullets that turned tree trunks and limbs into splinters. Sarah dove into the swamp and began pulling her way to safety using her hands. The barrage stopped. Sarah knew they were listening for movement. A faint breeze was all it took to cause a small bullet riddled tree to fall. The crash incited another barrage of bullets upon the small island. By the time Sarah reached solid ground, the sounds of ATVs were rattling through the forest. As the engines stopped, she knew that the hunt was on and she was the fox.

Huddled under a dense cedar tree, she watched as the helicopter landed and almost immediately took off again. "Michaela, at least you are safe now." A large shadow grew against the side of the facility and then disappeared. "Honda, now it's your turn."

Chapter Twenty-Seven

Renewal

The shelling stopped and the forest turned unusually quiet. Every movement the guards made broadcast their position to Sarah's sensitive ears. The snapping of twigs and rustling of leaves intensified as they got closer. Across the swamp, she could see Honda crawling for safety next to a small bush. She had to do something.

"RRRRRRAAAAAAAA." Sarah's low, rumbling roar vibrated throughout the forest. As its echoes stopped, many of the guards got nervous. The direction that the echoing roar came from was obscured by the trees. With the search party spread out in the middle of the forest, Rankin wasn't sure how his men should proceed. Looking at Duncan, he asked, "Is that the same creature or are there more out here?"

"I'm not sure. Their vocal ranges have become more diversified. They have even become capable of mimicking other creatures."

Outside the facility, a guard flipped the safety off his rifle. Without even looking at him, his partner responded, "Good idea," and then took off his safety. "It's hit. I was told that a wounded animal can be a lot more dangerous than a healthy one."

The pair looked across the swamp as they walked around the perimeter. Curled up in a ball, Honda looked like an extension of the bush that she was hiding next to. As they passed her, the short female guard got out her night vision goggles and surveyed the swamp. A flicker of red was all she saw as Honda wrapped her arm around her forehead. In one motion, Honda swiped the claws of her other hand across the guard's neck. Her rifle fell to the ground and the impact set its finely adjusted trigger off. Hearing the shot, the other guard turned around as Honda jumped on him. With her teeth dug deep across the lower half of his face, the guard couldn't speak. With both fighting to breath, they started to wrestle. The guard pulled out his knife. It was too late. Honda had worked her claws under his vest and quickly jabbed them under his rib cage and into his heart.

Deep in the forest, Duncan turned and faced the facility. "There is more than one creature out here. They may be setting a trap. We're too open. Get everyone out."

Standing next to Duncan, Rankin replied, "That sounds good to me."

A pack of dogs led the way as more guards raced along the side of the facility. With Honda's need for revenge partially quenched, she slithered into the swamp. Her one wing dragged behind her with pieces of bone sticking out of it.

Still huddled under the tree, Sarah watched the guards retreat from the forest. Shortly afterwards, they regrouped next to the last place she had spotted Honda. Worried that they might find her tracks, Sarah stood up and roared. "RRRRRRAAAAAA." As soon as it ended she raced around the woods roaring some more as she went. Every chance she had she caused a commotion by snapping off branches and tossing handfuls of dirt into the swamp and sticks into the trees. As the sticks slowly fell through the branches they would draw the odd shot from the roof of the facility. Even the bullets the guards shot would create more rustling and confuse the others.

Duncan yelled, "Stop firing." Each splash caused the guards to jump with nervous jitters. Their rifles were bounced around, pointing in every direction. In contrast, Rankin calmly stood beside Duncan as the other guards put their dead comrades onto stretchers. "It's hard to tell how many there are. They are not usually this vocal, nor this obvious."

Carefully following the sounds, Duncan was slow to respond, "You're right. There are maybe only two or three. Maybe even one. We may've pulled out too soon. The bush distorts sound, but from here you can hear a definite pattern. They're trying to distract us to give their colleague a chance to escape."

"So what do you want to do?"

"It's night. Regardless of how many there are, they want to draw us into the swamp where they have the advantage. They don't need night vision goggles to see like we do. Let's pick our own fights. I don't want to lose another man on a fool's mission."

******

The following morning, Rankin and Laurie wore civies as they drove to check on Kristofer's condition and give him some more ointment. Dennis heard them pull into the driveway but didn't get up from his chair. Kristofer's mother opened the door. "I'm sorry, I'm running late. I have to get to work. Everyone is in the living room." As she hurried to her car she added, "Thank the doctors for me. Michaela told me what they did for Kristofer."

In the living room, Kristofer was lying on the long chesterfield, with Michaela sitting on its edge. Both of her hands were wrapped around one of his. Not a word was spoken until Laurie asked, "How is he doing?"

Sitting across from the young couple, Dennis glanced at Laurie and puckered his lips. Michaela radiated a reassuring smile as Kristofer answered, "Better."

The smell of medicated lotion filled the room and the closer Laurie got to Kristofer, the stronger it was. Dressed only in a pair of shorts, his entire body glistened. Michaela helped him sit up. The blanket covering the cushions was soaked in lotion and drops of blood. Laurie pushed a section of it aside and sat beside them. Rankin never entered the room. With a strange look on his face, he stood outside the doorway just inside the kitchen. Laurie didn't know what to make of it.

As Laurie started to speak, Dennis interrupted her. "What the hell do you think you are doing here? None of this would've happened if it wasn't for that doctor that you are protecting." He stepped towards the desk in the corner of the room and grabbed his service revolver. Before he could turn around, Rankin had grasped both of his elbows. Dennis tried to twist away from him. Rankin immediately threw his knee into the middle of Dennis's back. The pair dropped to the floor. "Release the gun. I won't give you another chance. If you don't, I'll break your back."

The three on the chesterfield were stunned. Laurie stood up. "He just wants to vent his anger and frustration. You don't have to cripple him."

As Rankin applied more pressure, the gun fell from Dennis's hands. "I'm a cop. You won't get away with this."

"Try me. You have no witnesses."

Dennis looked at Kristofer and Michaela. "I have them."

Rankin smiled, "No you don't. They are both in it way too deep." While picking up the gun, Rankin's knee delivered a violent blow to the side of Dennis' ribs. The crack vibrated around the room. "You had an accident trying to move your refrigerator. I think that you better take a few days off." Within seconds Rankin had emptied, dismantled and tossed the various components of Dennis's revolver all around the room.

Michaela ran to Dennis' side as the guards left. As Laurie crawled into the jeep, she asked, "How did you know that he would go for his gun?"

"I've seen myself in a mirror. I know that look. You are so frustrated and want to lash out at anyone and everyone." Rankin looked at her. "He's a cop. He needs to feel like he's in total control of everything. That's what makes him so dangerous. Once he has cooled off and realizes that he has no recourse, he'll be all right."

Seeing that Laurie's nerves were a bit jittery, Rankin pulled into The Depot. They sat at the counter sipping their second cups of coffee when Laurie looked over at the crafts that were on sale. After a deep breath, she got up and wandered over to the display. She looked at a pair of moccasins similar to the pair Sarah had worn in the facility. With a smirk on her face, she picked up the price tag and took it over to show Rankin.

Rankin looked at the price. "Buy them if you want to. You have plenty of money."

As he flicked the tag along the counter back to Laurie, it flipped over and landed face down in front of her. The price was written on the back of a business card. In bold letters in the middle of the card read 'Banting Pharmaceuticals'. Mrs. Ferguson watched her as she dashed over and examined the other price tags. Cards from three more major drug companies were amongst them. Laurie turned to Mrs. Ferguson and asked, "Where did you get all the cards from?"

"Everyone that comes here wants to leave me their cards. For some reason, the drug companies are stirring up the entire community." Mrs. Ferguson started to laugh. "They think that we know what's going on around here. What a joke that is."

Rankin pulled out a twenty-dollar bill and placed it on the counter. "I'd like to buy all of those cards off of you."

Mrs. Ferguson picked up the bill and turned to him with a stunned look on her face. "Sure, take them."

Once back in the jeep, Rankin turned to Laurie. "I told you, the doctor knows a lot more then he's telling us. His intuition is too uncanny."

******

Sarah was exhausted. She had spent the rest of the night and into the morning frantically searching the forest for any sign of Honda. It was shortly after daybreak when the guards re-entered the forest and renewed their quest. That hindered Sarah's search for Honda even more. The only good thing it did was assure her that Honda had not been found. It wasn't until the guards stopped for lunch that Sarah had a chance to actually use the daylight to her advantage. From on top of a tall pine, Sarah could see the entire swamp in front of the facility. She was sure that the tree branches were dense enough that the guards on top of the roof would have a hard time spotting her.

Without the guards thrashing about the bush and stomping through dead twigs, the forest grew quiet. While the guards ate, the rest of the forest slowly came alive. Sarah made out two exceptions. One was the area around the guard's camp and the other was a small portion of the swamp. Sarah studied the small quiet section of swamp and couldn't see anything strange. All of a sudden, what appeared to be a dead log started to move. It was Honda. Sarah quickly scampered down the tree and made her way to the swamp.

"Duncan, I spotted some movement." The guard stationed on the roof glanced from the tree over to the guard's camp. "It was about three hundred metres east of your position."

Duncan put down his coffee cup. "What did you see?"

"I caught a good heat signature of something big as it was crawling down a large tree. It was too lean and wiry to be a bear. I think it was most likely was one of those creatures."

"Did you get a good visual?"

"No, there were too many branches in the way. With all the shadows, I couldn't even tell you what colour it was."

"Where did it go?"

"I lost it in the swamp."

"At least that will give us a new starting point to go by."

Duncan looked around at his men. Everyone overheard the entire conversation. One of the guards stood up. "So, lunch is over?"

All he could do was answer, "Somewhat. You can eat along the way if you want to. However, I know I'll have both of my hands on my weapon."

Sarah got to the edge of the swamp as fast as she could. She looked over at the facility. The glare of sunlight reflecting off of a pair of binoculars made it obvious that she had been spotted.   Honda's trail was easy to follow. Within ten metres of the bank, Sarah found her lying face down under a fir tree. Sarah carefully lifted her bloody, motionless body and crumpled wings out of the mud. Sniper fire coming from the facility wasn't her worst concern. Snapping twigs and rustling branches told her that the guards weren't far away. She had no time to inspect Honda's condition any further. She had to escape and hope for the best.

Exhausted, Sarah put one foot in front of the other and kept going. Fighting through the dense forest with Honda in her arms, she left a trail behind her that any boy scout could follow. Suddenly, the forest started to move all around her. The trees themselves seemed to come alive. Behind her, she could hear a deafening barrage of bullets ringing out. She didn't have the energy to move any further. Dropping to her knees, she looked up. The king was standing in front of her. Slowly he bent over and stoked Honda's mane. Honda's eyes blinked open and then shut again. Sarah looked at the sun through the forest canopy. "It's daytime. What are you doing out?"

The king crackled his voice as he picked up Honda. He held his daughter in his arms and rocked her back and forth. Rubbing his head against hers, he began to purr.

The same two dog-like creatures that helped her before wandered out of the woods dragging long, thick ropes behind them. The sticks lashed to each of the ropes caught on the brush and debris on the forest floor. As they dragged the rope, it twisted and turned around the bushes and tree trunks. The pair made it sound like a couple dozen creatures were roaming about the woods getting ready to attack. Looking over at the king, Sarah smiled.

******

As Rankin drove up to the facility, he saw Duncan leading a long line of guards out of the forest. He stopped the jeep and Laurie jumped out. "What happened?"

One of the guards spoke up. "An ambush. They were waiting for us."

Laurie made her way to Duncan. "Any casualties?"

"None. They seemed more interested in protecting the creatures that attacked the facility last night. Spread out in the woods like that, we were too vulnerable. We had no protection."

Rankin said, "That doesn't sound right. How many were there?"

Duncan thought for a moment. "I'm not sure. They have been playing it safe lately. Maybe they just didn't have the numbers needed for a head-on fight. I'm not sure, but it's still not like them to be out in force during the day."

Laurie's eyes skimmed over the swamp next to the facility. "You'll know better when the aerial photos come in."

After parking the jeep, Rankin looked over the men congregating outside. Despite showing no signs of a fight, they looked battered. Pulling the business cards out of his pocket, he walked over to Duncan and Laurie. "Duncan, I think the doctor might be interested in these."

Duncan glanced through them. "He has been expecting as much. Our cameras have captured a couple agents sneaking around the mine. I guess they want to discredit the doctor by trying to link his research to the creatures. That's why we have to keep a lid on them. If they can't prove they exist, they have got nothing to blackmail us with."

"What if evidence of the creatures' existence did get out?"

"Since we are the only research facility for hundreds of miles, they can just use speculation and innuendos to tie us to them. They will just continue what the press started. They won't even need absolute concrete proof to drive fear into the mass public market and make the doctor's treatment nearly impossible to sell."

Rankin looked around at all the guards. They're all risking their lives for a big cash payout when everything is all over. How much money would it take to turn one of them into a traitor? "What would they need for proof the creatures exist?"

Duncan followed Rankin's eyes as he looked at the other men. "Not much. A patch of skin, a clump of hair, anything that they can use to get a creditable DNA sample. That is why no one but you two has been allowed any leave lately."

The conversation disturbed Duncan. As soon as he entered the facility, he went to Doctor Scott's office. He wasn't there. Duncan looked around and saw him exiting the men's washroom. Marching over to him, he announced, "We may have a problem. Word has it that quick, easy money can be made from outside drug companies. They are putting a lot of feelers out there to make sure that the news gets to our employees. We need to rein in the men."

"I agree. We'll have a general meeting tomorrow. I'll squash any idea that any profit could be made by turning traitor." The doctor grinned at Duncan. "Besides, they will all know about the big move one way or another. Boxes are everywhere. There has to be some talk going around the place."

The next morning everyone except for a few sentries were in the cafeteria. To make room for everyone, all the tables and chairs were removed except for one set. Nobody had to stand for long. Sipping coffee at the table in front, Doctor Scott waited until every man and woman was accounted for. After a nod from Duncan, he stood up and announced, "I'm going to make this short and to the point. This facility is under attack. Not by those creatures out there, but from the government and other drug companies. Therefore, I plan to open the doors to this facility for inspection. I can't and will not have our work linked in any way to those creatures. When you were hired, you were promised a great deal of financial compensation for your loyal service. That will not change." The doctor looked around the room. A few smirks and hidden faces told him what he wanted to know. He glanced over at Duncan and nodded. After a deep breath, he continued. "In order to combat any drug company that questions our method of research, I'll also make sure that these inspections become public. I'm planning a pre-emptive attack in the media to squash any possible link to those creatures."

Doctor Scott looked around the room and smiled as a few faces in the confused crowd turned slightly pale. "I personally assure you that there's no way that your financial future is at risk. After all, that's also my financial future, plus my legacy."

In the crowd a guard raised his hand. The doctor acknowledged it, "Yes, you have a question."

"Yes, how can you be sure that the inspectors won't find anything?"

With a wide grin the doctor answered him. "Simple, we clean house. You've all seen the boxes. You've all seen the staff scrutinising every paper and computer file. You must all know by now that we are dividing our research into smaller, more manageable units. What you may not know is that some of the more sensitive components of our research will no longer be at this facility. We are on the move."

Another guard spoke. "What about those creatures? How will you explain them? Something created them."

The doctor shrugged his shoulders, "Explain what? As far as I'm concerned, there had been rumours about those creatures long before this facility was constructed. They have nothing to do with us."

"So why are we risking our lives hunting them?"

Duncan walked over to the table and answered the frustrated guard. "Because I tell you to. They have declared war on us and I've never backed down from a fight. That is why I hired you pack of mercenaries in the first place. If I wanted ordinary guards, I could've hired them off of the street and paid them minimum wage. So, if any one of you mongrels doesn't know how to follow orders, I'll teach you."

Doctor Scott looked at Duncan's angry, red face. In a calm voice he said, "Let me add to that. All threats to this facility, no matter where they come from, must be neutralized without any remorse. I hope that everyone here understands that that means any threat, no matter how big or how little it is. Is that clear enough for everyone?"

A guard turned to his outspoken, red-bearded comrade. "I wouldn't piss him off if I were you. You know Duncan's reputation. You must've heard the story about him hunting down a traitor in Afghanistan that deliberately gave him wrong information. His body was never found, just a pool of blood. That was just one reason why the Afghans put a price on his head. If you think he looks bad on the outside, you haven't seen what he's capable of. He's much worse inside."

"That was just a rumour. I don't believe he would do anything like that."

"Look at him. What kind of man can survive that kind of torture? He's not all human. He doesn't accept human flaws and frailty." The guard looked straight at Duncan. "Remember, the doctor said any threat coming from any source. If Duncan thinks that you could be a threat, he'll find you, and you will be neutralized. When you signed up, you should've read between the lines. Until this is all over, he is both God and Satan."

******

Duncan and Dr. Scott flew over the old summer camp. All the buildings were torn down and the foundation of the doctor's new research facility was being poured. The doctor looked at Duncan and inquired, "So, who do you have to man it?"

Duncan responded, "Everyone knows our present staff. I've had to enlist another team to oversee it. I don't want anyone from our present facility to know where this one is, at least not yet. The best way to keep a secret is not to tell anyone. What they don't know can't hurt us."

The doctor smiled at Duncan. "I know how busy you are, so I also hired a few extra men myself."

Duncan was speechless for a while before he could respond. "Who are they?"

"You may know some of them. Unfortunately, they are not here yet."

After they landed, the pair inspected both the new structure and the men. From preforming trellises for the roof to mixing cement, Duncan didn't hear a word of dissent from any of them. "These men will follow orders, no matter what I tell them to do."

Another helicopter hauling a sling of building supplies under it approached the camp. The doctor watched it come in and lower its load. "After we get this place set up, those inspectors will be able to go over that facility with a magnifying glass. I'll guarantee that they won't find a single drop of incriminating DNA to test. As long as those creatures leave us alone, I'll have the freedom to finish my research the way it should be done."

Chapter Twenty-Eight

Healing

Honda's father watched Sarah as she adjusted the splints around the broken bones in Honda's wings. She rewrapped the well-organized bundles of smooth, straight sticks around each broken bone. The pieces of wood were securely lashed in place using fish line inserted into tiny holes pierced through the wing's membrane. With small diameter sticks in the centre to round out the surface, and larger ones for strength on the outside, the bones were tightly set the best Sarah could manage.

The awkward setup made it hard for Honda to get around. To make it easier, Sarah wrapped long strips of a torn blanket around Honda's chest and wings. At least Honda could walk around without further injuring them. Her other injuries included a bullet wound through her right leg and several gashes where bullets grazed her skin. One bullet cut a long tear in her right ear. After Sarah had sewn it back together, the top of her right ear was twisted to the side.

When she was finished tending Honda's wounds, Sarah helped her walk to the entrance and they both took a brief look outside. Through the branches that protected the tunnel, they could see two aeroplanes and hear what could be a couple more. "They are everywhere. They must have hired more mercenaries or at least more planes." Looking down at Honda she added, "Your attack on their compound must've scared them. They're out for blood."

The planes could be heard during the day and throughout the night. The hunting parties no longer had the nights to themselves. Two days later, Sarah woke up to a loud explosion that shook every rock in the ridge. The creatures all ran to the escape tunnels and halted at the entrances. They weren't the target. They could see flames bellowing upwards and turning a large section of the forest from a moonless night into midday. A black plume hovered over the flames. The sharp smell of fuel lingered in the air. The creatures sank back into the shadows. Within a half an hour, a water bomber dropped a load of foamy liquid over the flames. Within an hour the fire was completely extinguished.

Everyone looked around at each other. Who was missing? There were two hunting parties out that night, and neither had returned. Sarah looked into each of the creature's faces. Despite their strange facial structures, they all showed signs of fear. They were trapped. Honda wrapped her arms around Sarah legs. Sarah could feel her frightened quivers as she sank her head against her stomach. Petting the back of

Honda's head, Sarah chanted, "It's going to be all right. It's going to be all right."

Honda wouldn't let go. As Sarah crouched down and sat on the ground, Honda reattached herself to her neck. They could hear the helicopters flying around outside. The rest of the creatures hid behind mounds of rocks piled in front of the crevices dug into the walls of the cavern. Huddled together in their family groups, the mothers and young were afraid to make a sound. Morning came with no sign of either hunting party. A few brave creatures guarded the entrance tunnels as the rest hid in the shadows. Sitting off to the side of the main cavern, Sarah and Honda watched the different entrances for any sign of danger.

******

"Well, what's the verdict? How many did we get?"

Duncan looked at Doctor Scott as he rubbed his hands together in anticipation. "We are not sure. They had spotted two parties with four creatures in each, verging on each other's position when they dropped the device. So far, we have only found a couple charred skeletons in the debris."

"Just two?"

Duncan took off his soot-covered beret and placed it on the picnic table that the doctor was using as a desk. "The place was a mess. More could be trapped in the swamp or under fallen trees. Regardless, that is eight adult males that are either dead or near dead. That's most of their fighting force. The heat alone would've burnt their lungs out. We were finding animal carcasses over a kilometre away from the fire. They couldn't have gotten far."

The doctor looked at the workers boarding up the sides of his newly framed facility. "As least they are confined and unable to interfere with our construction."

******

With one arm around Honda, Sarah searched through the pile of stuff that was brought back to the cavern for anything they could use. One backpack seemed heavier than the rest and she pulled it out of the pile. Bending over, she placed the bag closer to the hand that was still wrapped around Honda. With Velcro helping to secure each buckle, it was impossible to open it with one hand. "This guy is tough to open. No wonder they just left it in the pile."

Honda loosened her grip slightly and Sarah used both hands to open the bag. On the inside flap was a mesh pouch containing a family photo. Groping around inside, she found a light stick. She quickly broke the insides of it and shook it until it glowed. The red light made it easier for her to see, but the colour made everything appear strange. It was a family photo. Two parents and three children were all lined up in front of a gorgeous bed of flowers. The picture was old and faded, but Sarah could easily pick out George. Despite being only a child in the photo, his face was burnt into her brain. Next to him stood a much taller woman in her late teens wearing a beautiful pair of beaded moccasins. She studied the face more closely. It was Mary. The man she had killed was her younger brother. Sarah pulled out some papers that had been tucked behind the photograph. It was an unmailed letter. Sarah opened it.

'Dear Mary

I hope that someday I'll have the strength to mail this letter to you. Dorothy died early last year from cancer. Neither one of us had any children and I never did marry. You are all the family that I have left.

I don't know how you feel about me. I am quite ashamed of how the family treated you after you married a white man. I was saddened to hear about your husband's death. I hope that the hides that I left you have helped. When the job that I'm on is finished, I hope that we can get together.

Your little brother, George.'

The letter was short. Tears ran down Sarah's face as she put it back in the pouch. After a couple of deep breaths she continued to search through the bag. In a pocket along the side, Sarah felt something hard. Holding the light stick in her mouth, she pulled out a plastic case. Inside the custom-made waterproof case was a camo coloured berretta pistol, extra clips, a silencer and several lines of bullets all inserted into foam rubber so they wouldn't rattle or be damaged. Sarah grabbed the bottom of the backpack and lifted it into the air. All of its contents spilled over the ground. Slowly running the light over the pile, her tears quickly dried up. A Ghurkha knife that was specially designed to slit throats rested on top of it. Mixed amongst his gear were bottles of poisons, snare wire, a first aid kit, a folding saw, a pair of funny looking binoculars and a strange container. Everything lead her to one conclusion. He was not just a hunter. He was a trained killer.

Sarah opened up the strange container. Tightly packed in foam were narrow pieces that looked like metal rods sharpened at both ends with a wide ring in the centre. One end of the rods looked like it was split into sections and held together by a thick rubber band. The other was wider with dirt residue clinging to it. With them was a nylon block with a deep cone drilled into one side. Sarah placed the block over the clean end of the rod and pressed the pair into the ground. As she did, the top of it slid into the bottom. After she heard a 'click', Sarah carefully removed the block. Standing back, she took a long piece of wood and laid it on the protruding rod. As soon as the weight of the wood touched it, a loud pop echoed in the cavern as the steel spike shot upwards and razor sharp splines mushroomed up and over the end. The force split the end of the stick in two. Sarah went over and picked up the strange rod. It was an antipersonnel device. It could go through a person's boot and the razor sharp splines made it almost impossible to remove without power tools. Wound one man, and it takes a couple more to care for him. Then you could have a group of stationary targets to pick off. At the very least, you would slow down your pursuers.

Several curious faces peered from behind mounds of rocks and out of the shadows as Sarah searched further. At the bottom of the container were three small pouches. One carried extra rubber bands and small springs, another had blank .22 calibre shells and the third contained extra splines. The devices were obviously meant to be reused.

Sarah thought of George and his letter for a moment. *A device like that could also render a large animal lame. That would make it easier for someone to hunt down a weak, injured animal. Once it has bled enough, he could easily finish it off by slitting its throat.* She then looked at the pistol. The pistol wasn't designed for killing big game. It was for killing at short range without being spotted. Taking it out of its case, Sarah ran her fingers over it. The safety was easy to spot. She flipped the switch back and forth. All that she knew about pistols was from the movies and cop shows on TV. She slid the top back and saw there were no bullets in it. Fumbling around some more, she found the clip release. An empty clip popped out. She didn't really know what she was doing, but she was scared. She loaded all the clips and inserted one of them into the pistol. Searching through the pile on the ground, she found its holster. Sarah took off her belt and fed it through the loop in the holster. With a loaded pistol on her hip she felt a little safer.

After gathering up George's kit, Sarah picked up the pack and started to build a rock barricade to hide behind. The wall was only two stones high when she could hear activity coming from one of the side entrances. Dropping the light, she placed the backpack on top of it to douse it. Laying behind the rocks, Sarah drew the pistol and carefully aimed at the opening of the tunnel. *Where's the sentry? I know that one of the creatures was watching that tunnel.* Even in the faint light that was radiating down the meandering tunnel, Sarah could see shadows moving about. One upright shadow clung to the side of the tunnel before stepping into the cavern. Sarah pulled the trigger. 'Click'. She had forgot to load the chamber. Her mind raced as she fumbled with the gun. Looking up she could see the profile of the shadow leaning against the wall change shape. The shape was unmistakable, it was the king.

A brief moment of confusion was followed by a burst of excitement as she jumped up and ran to him. His chest and face were untouched. His ears and wings, however, were badly scorched. Honda narrowly beat her to him. She squeezed between them and gave her father a big hug. Sarah watched the king's lips curl up in pain as Honda's claws broke through the membrane of his charred wings. As the king stood there and endured Honda's painful embrace, Sarah softly tugged on Honda's shoulders. The king tried to talk but nothing came out. Slowly, Honda released her grip and looked up at her father's twisted face. Black pieces of his wing clung to her hands. Low rattling words vibrated from Honda's throat. The rattling continued like a chant, as her father sunk to the ground and closed his eyes.

A chorus of groans echoed down the tunnel as two more burnt creatures crawled out of it. Inside the cavern, all of the creatures started climbing down from their perches and ran to their aid. A call came from within the tunnel. A half dozen creatures ran to the tunnel to help. Within a minute two almost wingless dog-like creatures were dragged into the cavern on top of clusters of branches. Fanned out sections of scorched bones and cooked muscles stuck out of their backs instead of wings. A group of females lingered by the tunnel. As they waited, a couple ran over to the king. Sarah couldn't hear what he told her, but it wasn't good. Both females fell to her knees and beat the ground with their fists. Shortly afterwards, the rest of the creatures did the same.

******

Rankin approached Duncan's office at the old facility. The door was open and he found Duncan studying the aerial footage taken after the fire. From behind his back Rankin revealed a disc. "Sir, you may want to look at this."

With barely a glance, Duncan grabbed the disc and inserted it into his computer. It was more footage of the fire. "Where did this come from?"

"The helicopter that was confirming that the fire was out."

The playback from the infrared camera started as the helicopter took off. "Speed things up for me. Where should I be looking?"

Rankin stood behind him looking at the screen. "About fourteen minutes, forty seconds in." Duncan slid the time bar with his mouse. "You passed it." Duncan pressed rewind until Rankin pointed to the screen, "There. See that yellow circle?"

Duncan looked closely at the circle surrounded by a black ring. "I see it, but what is it?"

Rankin put it on slow play. "I believe that the creatures all huddled together in the swamp. A couple took turns splashing water on the rest to cool them off. Their watered down wings are acting like wet blankets to shield them from the fire. The dome that they had formed may have trapped enough air for them to survive." Rankin stopped the video. On the screen, two creatures were looking up at the helicopter. "These things are smart. We may not find any more bodies out there."

Duncan wasted no time. Within an hour, he was standing in the centre of a green ring surrounded by a wide trench of thick, black, muddy water. A section of the trench was half filled in as the creatures had clawed their way to a hasty retreat. Small pieces of brittle bone and charred flesh littered the area. The creatures had made very little attempt to conceal their quick escape. As Duncan started to follow their trail, he discovered that the water bombers had washed most of it away. Duncan picked up a bone with a section of membrane twice the size of his hand. Looking at it he muttered, "They may be alive, but they're no threat to us. Not right now."

"Do you want to go after them? There may be still enough clues to track them."

"They may be injured and weak, but a wounded animal can be much more dangerous. They'll be red eyed, crazed, adrenaline pumped monsters, out for revenge. We're not prepared right now to go up against a horde of creatures that don't care if they live or die." An angry Duncan turned to Rankin and told him, "Take two men and trail them as far as you can. Under no condition should you get close enough to them that they can see or hear you. Remember, right now they are running on pure adrenaline. I don't think you want to become part of their menu."

Rankin could see the frustration in Duncan as he clinched his teeth. Putting a hand on Duncan's shoulder, he told him, "Don't worry. I'll make sure everyone comes back in one piece."

With an extended arm, Duncan signalled to the helicopter hovering well above them to pick him up. "Even if you get enough to narrow down the search area, that would be a great plus."

"I hope I can do better than that."

******

The surviving creatures were carefully laid down on their stomachs in the centre of the cavern. The females huddled around them, afraid to touch their fragile wings and tails. Betty and Mew walked over to Sarah. Betty grabbed her hand and led her over to the burnt hunters. Sarah didn't know what to do. A young creature picked a muddy leaf off of one of the warrior's back. She could see the burnt skin starting to peel off with it. Sarah grabbed the youngster's arm and held it still. The creature hissed at her and stuck her claws into Sarah's arm with its other hand. Betty grabbed the youngster and forced it to release her grip.

Everyone was afraid to do anything to help their charred friends. The two worried creatures looked at Sarah and bobbed their heads. Sarah looked at the dried mud and debris that covered the backs of the creatures. The dried debris was all that held a lot of the burnt tissue in place. She suddenly knew what had to be done.

She took Betty's arm and led her over to the pile of stuff that they had collected. From a first aid kit, Sarah pulled out a pair of latex gloves. With a needle she poked holes in the fingertips. With Betty's help, she filled the glove with water and lightly drizzled it over the poor creatures' burnt flesh. The crowd of creatures surrounding her all watched as the painful rattling of the severely injured creatures quieted down. It was working.

Within half an hour all the water they had stored was used up. Sarah looked at Honda. "We need more water." Looking around, she saw Mew directing others towards the exit carrying all the containers they could find. Everyone there knew what had to be done. One of the wingless dog-like creatures that had survived the fire got up and blocked their way. He looked at the crowd and held up three fingers. Everyone stood still as he looked over the eager group. With the king lying down in agony, he was taking charge. His wings were charred to the bone, but he was still the oldest and strongest warrior left.

Within ten minutes Mew and another creature he had chosen returned with water and went back for more. The third, carrying large jugs took a while longer. Sarah placed several layers of socks over the spout of the water containers and filtered out as much debris as she could. The water was cloudy but could still flow gently out of the holes in the latex gloves. The king pushed himself onto his hands and knees and looked around. As the water supply increased, the creatures were beginning to leave a muddy trail behind them. Sharply the king rattled orders to the crowd. They had been so concerned about the burnt creatures that they stopped thinking. The handful of males that were left quickly ran to the exit. Honda looked at her father. Crawling to him, she nudged her head against his and softly purred.

Sarah watched Honda stand up and start towards the exit. The bullet wound in her leg was healing faster than she expected. Looking around, Sarah felt that the limited help that she could offer the injured creatures was being squeezed out by females. She was no longer needed. Tossing George's backpack onto her back, she caught up with Honda before she exited the tunnel. It was worse than she thought. The path the creatures used was entrenched in mud. Looking up, the tall green cedars and pines were still protecting it from the air. Two healthy warriors stayed behind to guard the tunnel. They were battle hardened and willing to fight to the death to defend the infants, pregnant females, injured and their king.

The king had taught his warriors well. Even injured, they knew what to do and did it. The others quickly followed their lead. Using branches, they raked dead pine needles over the muddy trail. After the trail was covered, they gently beat it with pine bough to give it a natural, unkept appearance. All it needed was a little time for the needles on top to dry. It would be enough to fool the average tracker and over time, anyone. Working from the cavern outwards, the crew of women, youngsters and a handful of injured warriors made their way towards the creek leading into the deforested swamp. Sarah picked up a bough and fluffed the pine needles that Honda tossed on the muddy path. The sky began to open up in front of them as they approached the scorched, lifeless swamp.

With only a dozen metres to go, the entire crew quietly lowered themselves to the ground. They had almost reached the fire zone. The overhead protection that the remaining trees gave them was gone. Any further movement they made could be easily spotted from the sky or up to a kilometre away across the swamp. Protected by rocks and thick, half-dead brush, a creature pointed at three figures working their way through the swamp. Thickened by soot, ash, debris and entangled burnt-off branches, it took them almost a minute to take four hard-fought steps through the swamp. The men were no immediate threat to them. Zigzagging about, they weren't even heading in their direction. The wingless creature and Sarah had both figured out that they were taking the path of least resistance. It was the same path the scorched warriors must have taken. The men were carefully tracking their footsteps. The footsteps that would eventually lead them to the cavern.

The wingless creature snuck away from the rest. An injured warrior with both an arm and a wing bandaged up followed him along with two females and three youngsters. Sarah grabbed Honda's shoulder as she lunged forward to volunteer. Honda desperately wanted to go with them. In a stern voice, Sarah sharply said, "No."

Honda looked at her and rattled off a low growl of disapproval. "Uurraaatatatatatat."

The group worked around the swamp towards where the mercenaries were heading. Sarah knew that if something went wrong, the creatures would be giving the guards a fresh, second trail to follow. Both muddy trails would lead them straight to the cavern. "They are wrong. Any attack from that direction would lead them to the cavern. We can't move the sick and injured. They could be all slaughtered." Looking down, she knew that Honda didn't understand. Sarah reached down and took out the pistol. The huge grin of Honda's face told Sarah that she finally understood that she wasn't going to be left out of the fight. That was enough to make Honda purr. She followed Sarah around the swamp in the opposite direction of the others. Three females and five youngsters followed them. Not knowing where they were needed the most, a few females, a handful of young and a couple injured warriors stayed behind and waited.

A slender lizard-like creature raced ahead of Sarah and Honda. Another dog-like female followed close behind her. The swamp turned from entangled roots and burnt brush into a thick pool of mud. The lizard-like creature looked back at the rest before she crawled into the swamp and slithered on the surface like a snake towards the trio. Her robust companion waited on shore. By the time Sarah had caught up to them, the creature had wiggled a third of the way across to swamp.

Suddenly Sarah noticed that the trio had stopped. They were all crouched down beside a fallen tree. She reached into her bag and pulled out the binoculars. At first she couldn't see anything. Then she looked at the dials and buttons along the sides. The binoculars were digital. She turned them on. Everything was hazy. She looked them over again. Switching the setting from night to normal made it better. Despite knowing where to look, the trio had vanished. She looked at the binoculars again. This time she switched them to daytime/infrared. She could make out a small orange dot bobbing along the fallen tree. Sarah thought for a moment. *All I have to do is wound one of them. The others will be compelled to leave to get him to safety. That will give everyone plenty of time to hide the tracks.'*

Sarah rifled through the backpack and retrieved the gun case. She screwed the silencer unto the pistol and placed a bullet into the chamber. Carefully she took aim. She fired. Nothing. The unique whistle of the passing bullet caused one of the men to look around.

Sarah's second shot splashed the water a couple metres to the right of him. She moved behind a tree and steadied the pistol in a notch. With both hands on the pistol she took a deep breath and fired. The bullet smacked into a branch of the fallen tree, only a half metre away from the man she was aiming at.

Ten metres away from where her target had been, a man popped out of the water and swept the entire forest around her with bullets. As he disappeared beneath the muddy surface, another man popped up ten metres closer to her. Like the first man, he aimlessly emptied a clip of bullets and then disappeared. Two bullets hit the tree that Sarah was hiding behind. She didn't move. Instead she tried to predict where the next man would pop up. When he did, she fired. This time the bullet hit the young man's unprotected shoulder.

Watching his colleague get shot, for a brief moment Rankin stood still. A moment was all the slithering creature needed. Lunging out of the water, she dug one set of claws into Rankin's face and her other set into his back. Her claws tore across his face and clung to his body armour. Before she could get a good grip, Rankin flipped her into the water. All at once, almost every winged youngster took to the air.

As Rankin attempted to raise his rifle, the wiry creature grabbed the barrel and pointed it away from her. The wounded guard rested his rifle against his hip as he fired at the rapidly approaching creatures, using only one arm. Rankin looked around for his other colleague. He finally popped out of the muddy water fifteen metres in front of Sarah. As soon as he saw her, his raised his rifle. Sarah fired first. His rifle blasted away as he jerked backwards. Honda and two other creatures bounded towards him. Sarah had only hit the body armour on his chest. As he regained his composure and attempted to get up, Sarah stepped away from the tree and quickly emptied the clip. He lowered his rifle and just stood there with blood trickling down the side of his face. Sarah couldn't take her eyes off of him. A couple seconds seemed like an hour. Every detail about him was burnt into her brain. He was tall, young and very handsome, barely twenty years old. Seconds ago, he had his entire life ahead of him. Now it was over. Honda was almost upon him when his body finally collapsed and folded up like a stringless marionette into the swamp.

As creatures piled on top of his dead friend, the wounded man bit down and endured the pain as he riddled the waterline above his friend with bullets. Each bullet leaving the rifle jolted the sharp, shattered bones in his shoulder. The winged creatures quickly darkened the sky above him. Rankin felt helpless. Between the thick bog, the creature clinging to his rifle and the blood blurring his vision, all he could do was pull the trigger and hope for the best. The gunfire drew the attention of even more creatures. Feasting creatures with blood, intestines and other pieces of human flesh adhered to their faces looked up and searched for the new threat. Quickly, the entire horde raced towards the two remaining guards. Sarah was left starring into the eyes of the dead man as his head bobbed above the surface facing her.

The burning heat from the rifle barrel helped Rankin shake off the obstinate creature. She disappeared before he could get off another shot. He looked around. They were coming at him from every direction from both the air and water. His wounded comrade was suddenly pulled under the shallow water. Rankin tried to take aim. The blood in his eyes blurred his vision. The soupy mud around his comrade started to boil. Debris and mud slashed in every direction as if the creatures had turned themselves into crocodiles. Rankin fired into the turbulent quagmire, yelling, "He's dead already. Isn't killing him enough for you?"

Instead of reloading his rifle, Rankin flung it against the remaining trunk of a burnt tree. Taking a deep breath, he sank into the mud. Using old roots, plant life and large pieces of debris, he clawed his way along the bottom. Suddenly his leg was stuck. Then he could feel a creature's sharp teeth bite into his calf. Drawing his knife, he lunged it down his side. The tip of the blade hit something. Springing to the surface, he tried to breathe through his clenched teeth. The same relentless creature surfaced beside him, bleeding from the back of her head. Curling his knees into his chest, he smashed both of his feet against the creature and dove into the black, soupy swamp in the opposite direction.

Not knowing where Rankin would reappear, a few creatures circled the sky above the swamp. Sarah watched as several young creatures swooped down and helped the others tear apart the young man that she had killed. It was only after one of the young creatures bit into the side of his face that Sarah was forced to turn away. Glancing back, she saw that his entire cheek and nose had been chewed off. Honda saw Sarah staring at her as she approached. Handing her a generous chunk of liver, Honda smiled. "Eeeeeet."

Sarah looked down at the pistol. Standing up, she tried to throw it into the swamp. She couldn't. It wouldn't leave her hand. Flopping back down, she placed it on the ground in front of her. Honda dropped the meat next to it. "Eeeeeeet."

"I can't."

The wingless creature dragged the other man to the far shore. His fate was almost the same. The only difference was that the wingless creature limited the carnage. He wanted to insure that there would be some meat left to take back to the cavern for the others. Only one creature was left circling overhead. They knew Rankin was there but couldn't spot him. They knew that he was bleeding, but couldn't tell whose blood was whose. So they waited.

Chapter Twenty-Nine

Youth

"Has Rankin reported in yet?"

Duncan looked at Laurie and understood her concern. "No, not yet." Standing up, he walked around his desk and stood in front of her in the doorway. "I will be leading a couple squads into the swamp to find him."

"Or what is left of him."

Duncan bobbed his head. "Even that could be useful to us."

Laurie took a step back. "What?"

Duncan reached for her hand. She withdrew it and tucked it behind her back. "All I'm saying is that the aerial images are finally coming in. If Rankin and his men drew the creatures out of their hiding place, the planes may have picked them up. The fire probably took out their main fighting force. If the others did mount an attack, they may not be as skilled. They may even get careless and lead us right to their lair." Before Duncan could finish, a guard approached him and passed him an envelope. "Here are the latest images."

After dismissing the courier, Duncan retreated to his computer with Laurie trailing behind him. She looked over his shoulder as he plugged in the surveillance data. With the time and grid location inserted on the screen, Duncan skipped over the first twenty minutes and fast forwarded some more. He knew what he wanted to see. He reversed it slightly to just before it started to fly over the scorched forest. The plane needed to take four flybys to record the entire swamp. He carefully watched each of them. Small, red blotches had formed a semi-circle around the swamp. In the middle were three small dots. Laurie said, "They are under attack!"

"This data is almost a half hour old by now." Duncan picked up the phone. "I want another plane in the air immediately. I want him to film areas C5 to C7, down to E6 and E8." After a brief pause, he added, "That's correct. I need the entire area between those coordinates covered. Then I want you to repeat scanning it for as long as his fuel can hold out." Duncan faced the ceiling before continuing. "I'm paying you to do what I want, not to question why. Just do it."

After Duncan put down the phone, Laurie questioned him. "I'm curious, why are you using outside planes for surveillance?"

"They're cheap and our resources are spread a little thin right now. I would rather use it more effectively. Besides, at the height that they fly, they can't even see what they are filming. They just push a button to start recording and another to stop. What they don't know can't hurt us."

Laurie stretched her arms and placed both of her hands on Duncan's desk between him and the monitor. "By effectively, you mean use your manpower to go and get those men out of there, right?"

Duncan looked at her. "Yes, something like that."

"You never worried about money before, why now?"

"Unfortunately, right now death payouts have destroyed my budget. As huge as they may be, the doctor's pockets aren't bottomless." He couldn't say a word to anyone about the new facility being built and a second security team. Not even to Laurie. He simply pushed her arms aside and continued searching through the images on the screen. Stopping at one, he broke his silence. "This is where we must go. The group that is huddled together was probably their starting point. The others more than likely branched off around the swamp from there." Grabbing a map, he marked various locations around the swamp with lines, circles and X's. "Now I know where we should start looking."

******

As he woke up from a semi-comatose state, the king's burnt ears twitched. Even over the grunts and groans of the others, he could hear something. He reached up and grabbed the creature drizzling water over his back. In a low rattling voice he made his wishes clear. The attendant held his arm as he made it to his feet. With the aid of a second creature, they walked him to the exit. They had to wait before entering the tunnel. Two young females were dragging in a dead caribou. Its legs and belly were badly scorched from running through the fire. The fire had made gathering meat easy. All the creatures had to do was smell the air for cooked flesh. The king looked back at the stack of animal carcasses that the females had already dragged in. They had no idea what chaos they were creating. The king growled at them as he limped by. 'Enough, meat, trail, men, see.'

Still supported by the two female creatures, the king peered outside. The high-pitched drone from an aeroplane's engine filtered its way through the forest canopy. He looked around and saw trails leading to the cavern from every direction.   The two healthy males were doing what they could to cover them, but the soft soil made it impossible. Shallow, plowed trenches and wide broken swaths of branches made the trails so obvious that anyone could follow them. Just to touch a brittle branch was enough to snap it off and create a trail. The sky began to grow dark. Rain was coming. That would only make matters worse.

Another pair of youngsters approached the entrance hauling a moose calf behind them. The king knew that they just wanted to help.

Despite this, he growled as loud as his damaged lungs could muster. "Nnnnaaa." The youngsters dropped to the ground and looked at him. The king looked up at the sky. The others stared with him and then into the sky. They could all hear the plane flying overhead. Then he looked up and down the various paths the misguided creatures had made. He didn't have to say any more.

******

Honda could hear the ATVs approaching the swamp. The creatures were doing the best they could to disguise all the trails, but they were far from being done. In no more than two seconds after they heard the engines, most of the creatures had vanished. It took a bit longer for the solo flying creature that was still searching for Rankin. As fast as it could, it dove out of the sky and ran under a bush.

It wasn't fast enough. The small parade of vehicles had broken out of the forest and into the burnt out opening. Duncan halted the small column. "Did you see it?"

The guard sitting next to him answered, "How could I miss it? I know it was a lot smaller than the other creatures that we had encountered, but it's hard to mistake it for anything else."

Two four-man swamp buggies pulled up from the rear. Sealed shells with rows of four large, finned wheels on each side enabled them to easily crawl over the twisted debris and paddle their way through the muddy water. Duncan nodded as Laurie's buggy drove by. "You know where you are heading?"

"As well as you." Laurie smiled. "Remember, I was there when you marked it on the map."

Controlling the buggy like an old tank meant Josh, a red-head, muscular giant, could steer it with his feet and holding his rifle at the same time. The sky was growing darker. Rain clouds had started to block out the sun. Laurie knew that in a downpour, the creatures would hold the advantage. She gently reached over and nudged the throttle a tad faster. With rifles pointed in every direction, the two, slow-moving vehicles made their way to the same fallen tree where Rankin and his men had last been sighted. Duncan stayed behind as the other ATVs formed two columns and proceeded to manoeuver their way around both sides of the swamp.

After removing a tarp off the back of his ATV, Duncan and his driver checked over a miniature helicopter. On each of the four corners of the machine were round guards that protected the propellers. Duncan quickly went through a checklist and confirmed its camera was working before he lifted it into the air. In a little over a minute, it was hovering over the buggies.

******

The deep, rumbling hum from the two buggies echoed over the open swamp. Under the water, it vibrated and hurt Rankin's ears. Lodged within the submerged branches of the tree, he took a deep breath through the barrel of his disassembled rifle. He dropped the barrel and pulled himself out of the maze of branches. With no air left, he popped out of the muddy water like a cork. With thick muddy vegetation draping down from Rankin's waving arms, one of the guards fired. Nerves caused another anxious guard to fire. Laurie immediately stood up and screamed, "Stop, it's one of ours."

With the aerial camera catching everything, Duncan smiled. "They found one of them." He watched as Rankin fell back into the water and fought to get up again. "I just hope they didn't kill him in the process." The ATVs had only made it a quarter of the way around the swamp. They were too far away to help. As the buggies worked their way towards Rankin, Duncan used the mini aircraft to monitor the surrounding area. On the screen he could pick up moving bushes and tree branches on the side of the swamp closest to Rankin's position. Strange movements in the water drew his attention towards a pile of logs and debris. A large splash revealed that it was just a beaver. Duncan refocused his attention towards the shoreline. The vegetation had changed. Entire bushes had vanished. He flew the aircraft in closer.

As the aircraft approached, Sarah looked at Honda. Her bandaged wing was entangled in a thorn bush. As she tried to escape, she twisted her broken wing backwards. The men in the buggies were busy pulling Rankin out of the water. The guards on the buggy weren't the problem. The closer the miniature craft got to Sarah, the more she panicked. Sarah pulled out the pistol and fired at it. She had taken the silencer off to carry it in the holster. Without it, the blast echoed above all of the motors.

Through the monitor, Duncan watched Sarah take aim and fire. The bullet hit its mark and the camera went dead along with one of the motors. Duncan pulled the lever to elevate the aircraft. Looking up, he could see that it was still airborne. "Laurie, I'm flying blind. You're on your own."

"We're all right. I haven't noticed very much activity along the shore."

"They're there. Get out as fast as you can."

As Laurie ordered Josh to turn and head back, the two guards in the back of the buggy tugged at Rankin's vest and laid him across their laps. The hollow point bullets they were issued were designed for big game. Two had hit his chest. One was straight on. The vest caused it to mushroom and its outer casing to shatter before a few fragments could make it through to his flesh. The other hit him sideways as he was falling and tore a gash across the front of his vest. One of the guards cut the vest off while the other got out the bandages. After pouring disinfectant over Rankin's chest, face and leg, they quickly strapped on some field dressing bandages.

With rain on the way, Duncan wanted his men to retreat as quickly as they safely could. The buggies were slow, but by keeping to the middle of the open swamp, at least they should see any approaching danger. The ATVs along the shore held their positions in case they were needed. Sprinkles of rain started to come down. It wasn't very hard, but enough to blur Duncan's view of the miniature aircraft. He blinked the rain drops away and then blinked again. There were over half a dozen objects in the sky. He knew that the bright red smudge high above them was the hired aeroplane taking photos of the swamp. Another object was his machine. He knew what the rest were. At least six creatures were airborne. Four were beside his machine and two others were flying high above the rest.

Duncan wasted no time. "Everyone, the creatures are in the air above you. Fire at will."

The rain started to pour and acted like a screen. Random shots peppered the sky above the swamp. With each flap of their wings, the wind turbulence caused the miniature aircraft to bounce around the sky. It was impossible for Duncan to keep it steady as two creatures flew in front of it. Out of sight, the craft became even more uncontrollable. As it bobbed around, a young creature flew too close to it. The craft bounced up and one of its propellers collided with the tip of the creature's left wing. Both the craft and the creature plummeted into the swamp.

As the buggies got closer, Duncan called in the ATVs. Every time Duncan blinked away the rain drops, he saw even more creatures in the sky. The guards fired at will. The closer the creatures got, the better targets the guards had to aim at. Within a second, two creatures faltered and glided roughly downward. The others fell back and circled the swamp at a safer distance. Duncan peered at them through his binoculars. "They aren't the same creatures that we fought before. These are much, much smaller. They ain't warriors. They don't know what they are doing." Duncan turned to the men around him. "Get out the shotguns. I want the sky peppered with lead. It shouldn't take much to scare them away."

High above the swamp, the hired pilot could see red and white flashes on the ground ahead of him. To his right lightning tore up the sky. Over the radio he called in, "It's starting to get rough out here. I think I got enough footage for them to go over. It's time for me to head back."

Out of pure curiosity, the pilot circled around and dropped his altitude enough that he could see what he was filming. What he had thought were large birds had turned into flying creatures. Wanting to get away, he looked up and started to pull the steering wheel towards him. The next second, he saw a young creature hovering in front of his plane. The pilot avoided a collision by swerving the plane to the left. A second creature approaching him was sucked into the right propeller. Pieces of wings, body parts and propeller splattered the cockpit. As the unbalanced propeller continued to fall apart, a piece shattered the side windshield and decapitated the copilot. The pilot's right arm was broken as the copilot's head ricocheted off of it and plowed into the instrument panel. With a broken arm, he couldn't regain control of the plane as it started to spiral downwards. With his knee, he knocked his co-pilot's head away from the instrument panel like a soccer ball. He was finally able to regain some control.

A large piece of the creature's wing was caught on the nose of the plane. As the plane bounced around, the flapping tissue broke free and flopped against the left wing. The suction of the air intake pulled it into the left motor. The plane suddenly looped to the left and plummeted towards the ground.

All firing ceased as the guards watched the plane twist in the air and disappear on the far side of the ridge with barely a sound. The creatures only saw the pieces of their comrade raining down. Most of the creatures that were still in the air retreated to safety. As the thunder and lightning got closer, they hid and waited with the others. Through the trees, the king watched as a lone young female hovered in the sky. Slowly she began flying around in wide circles. Like the other young, it was her first taste of battle and the violent death and sorrow that accompanies it.

"We need that recorder. It'll contain pictures of us with those creatures. We aren't ready yet. No one can link them to us." Duncan took out his compass and noted the direction of the crash. Taking out his map, he drew a line across it. Turning to the guard next to him, he pointed. "We're here. The plane crashed somewhere along this line."

Looking over his shoulder, he added, "That tree on top of the ridge intersects our position. Take the rest of your squad and go up there. Take a reading on your GPS. If I'm right, from there we should be able to easily plot our way to the crash site."

Amidst a torrent of rain, Laurie's buggy made it ashore. With visibility of only a few metres, Duncan felt the squad he had sent out would be shielded from the creatures.

The guards quickly tied a stretcher on the back of an ATV and strapped Rankin onto it. Duncan watched as a squad accompanied Rankin back to the facility. Not counting the group retrieving the GPS location, Duncan had only two squads and a medic left. With one ATV and the two, slow-moving swamp buggies, they headed out in search of the wreckage.

Heavy rain magnified the lightning as its bright light filled the sky. Thunder bolts shook the rocky ground under them. The buggies were great in the swamp but were less equipped to handle the ridge's rocky terrain. Using the ATV to lead the way and plot a course, the small column crawled through the brush. Laurie looked behind her. The chewed-up trail they were leaving could be used by a blind man feeling his way around using only a stick. "We have to move faster than this."

Duncan replied on his headset, "Don't worry. We'll get reinforcements when we catch up with the squad I sent out. That will give us two more vehicles. We might be able to load them up and dump the buggies."

"Good, these tubs are filling up with water. We're swimming back here."

******

Squatting next to the tall tree Duncan had pointed to, a guard marked his position on his GPS. He could hear the others circling the rocky knoll, taking an easier path. "Duncan, we have it. I'm sending you the coordinates."

Duncan confirmed the waypoint on his GPS. Lining it up with his starting point, he figured that they were still over three kilometres away from the crash site. However, with the rugged terrain, they may need to travel six or more to get to it. Another bolt of lightning struck the ridge. This time the light didn't go away. A small blaze spread from tree to tree. Under the protection of the higher branches, the pine needles and sap fuelled the low, burning fire. Despite the downpour, the flames grew higher.

******

After finally landing, the frightened young female ran past the king and into the cavern. The cool rain soaked into the king's skin as he leaned on a staff outside of the entrance. With his eyes, ears and nose, the worried king could tell what was about to happen. Inside, others collected the clear rainwater flowing down the walls of the cavern and poured it into a giant cistern. The lightning had struck a grove of pine trees midway between the burnt swamp and the cavern. With the aid of one of the sentries, the king retreated into the cavern as the smoke started to filter through the trees. Despite the rain and damp ground, it was just a matter of time before the trees would be engulfed by the growing fire. Inside, the females were still attending to the burnt and injured warriors along with their young. To keep themselves occupied, some of the pregnant and nursing females would cut the meat they had collected into strips. They hung them over sticks to dry into jerky. As the invading smoke swirled through the cavern, the king, propped up by a large dog-like female, reluctantly rattled off his orders.

******

On top of the ridge, one ATV was leaving as the remaining two guards climbed onto the other one. The driver looked around as he started the motor. The rain had slowed enough that he could make out the swamp. He saw a small band of creatures making their way below him. Turning to the trail, he applied the gas. As the machine surged forward, something splashed against the side of his face. He glanced back at his partner. Blood was pouring out of his mouth. The driver turned his head to face him. The wingless dog-like creature had speared a large stick through the narrow gap on the side of his partner's vest. The broken off branches at the end of the stick acted like barbs, anchoring it to the insides of his ribs. As the driver twisted the accelerator, the stick was ripped out of the creature's arms. His partner's body had turned into a rag doll as it flopped off of the vehicle and rolled on the ground. Turning his head towards the path, a set of claws reached out from a bush and swiped across his face, cutting through one of his eyes. The ATV veered head on into a boulder. The driver pulled out his pistol. With only the use of his left eye, his shots went wild as the one-armed creature leaped on top of him and bit into his throat.

After hearing the shots, the second driver rolled his ATV to a stop. The guard sitting in the rear looked back and saw a section of his comrade's ripped throat dangling from the creature's mouth. He screamed to the driver, "They're dead. Gun it or we're goners too."

A cloud of mud flew everywhere as they sped around boulders and fallen trees. Coming to a clearing, the driver yelled back, "Hold on."

Swooping out of the sky in front of him, three creatures narrowly missed the driver. It didn't matter. They stopped him from noticing the edge of a shallow ravine. The front bumper of the ATV plowed into the far bank. The driver rolled head first over the handle bars and onto his back on the other side of the ravine. Lying flat on his back, he pulled out his pistol and rolled over. The creatures were gone. Getting up, he looked around for his partner. At the bottom of the ravine, two young creatures were tearing at the back of his vest with their claws. Bones protruded from his crooked neck. As the driver raised his pistol, Mew swooped down and landed on his shoulders. The impact knocked him to his knees. As she clawed open his neck, he repeatedly squeezed the trigger and fired off his entire clip into the ground.

******

"That's close." Duncan halted the small column and quietly ordered everyone to get out. "Grab your weapons and all the ammo that you can carry."

The two squads leapfrogged forward. As one took on firing positions, the other advanced. Duncan and the medic trailed behind as the rear guard, watching for anything popping up behind them. The wingless creature watched them approach from the edge of the clearing. In a loud echoing voice, he rattled off a warning. "Rrratatatat."

Mew and the two youngsters lifted their heads. Bullets whizzed by them. Sinking back down, they crawled along the ravine.

The guards charged forward. After jumping into the ravine, two of them ran after the young warriors. Behind them Duncan screamed, "Halt. Let them go."

One of the guards looked back at him. "Why? They murdered Peter and look what they did to Randy."

Duncan looked at the dead guard lying at his feet. "Randy's dead. Right now, I need you alive. The creatures have eaten enough human flesh for today."

With a line of guards in firing position, the two men retreated. The ravine was a giant depression that zigzagged across the top of the ridge. Like most gullies, some places were deeper and wider than others. With rocks jutting out and crevices everywhere, the creatures had plenty of hiding places to choose from. The two guards had stopped just before turning into a sharp bend. They were lucky. The one-armed creature, Mew and another female were waiting to pounce on anyone that entered the narrow corridor. The three adults cried out a chorus of howls, growls and roars as the two youngsters hid behind them. The two men looked back. A cold shiver ran up their spines. "That was too close."

Suddenly all the creatures on the ridge cried out at once. Closing ranks, the guards squeezed into a wide section of the ravine. Laurie stood up and pulled out her binoculars. Brush and leaves were moving in the forest all around the clearing. "Duncan, we're grossly outnumbered."

Duncan looked around. He could hear a large group of creatures at the end of the ravine. In addition to them, he could pick out a few more in the woods ahead of him and a couple more on the far side. "There are no more than a dozen out there. We're all right. They won't attack as long as they think we're ready for them. Sarah is the only creature that can use a gun, and we left her in the swamp. These are not the same well-organized creatures that attacked us before; they are young and inexperienced. The only way they can win is to spread us out and try to ambush us two or three on one."

One of the guards crawled into the ravine and examined the ATV. Climbing on, he started it up. "I can't smell any leaks. This machine is fine." Putting it into reverse, he wiggled it back and forth until he got it sideways. Then he drove it along the side of the ravine and up over the bank.

Duncan informed him, "It doesn't matter. We are leaving it. We are better off on foot."

The rain finally stopped. Despite the downpour, the dried wood didn't soak in enough to prevent the fire from spreading along the ridge. All it did was slow it down. The smoke from the fire crept over the clearing. The forest around them grew quiet. "I think we are going to stay here tonight. Fire can't spread on rocks and this ravine will make a perfect dugout shelter."

Laurie responded, "What about the machines? They could be burnt to a crisp. We need them to get back."

Duncan looked at her. "And how many lives are you willing to risk for them?"

******

Betty stayed behind with Sarah to help her look after the injured. The rest had made their way to the ridge. Even Honda, with her sore leg and bandaged wing, had joined the blood-thirsty war party. The gentle wind was enough to fan the flames, but not enough to blow them out. It was almost perfect for drying the dead tree branches and deadfall before the fire reached them. Unfortunately for the creatures on the other side of the swamp, it was in the wrong direction. The high ridge funnelled the flames along its side, forcing the creatures and any other wildlife in its wake to trek up and over the ridge. Even for those who could fly, the high-licking flames and severe heat made it impossible. Going back to the cavern was no longer an option either. It was blocked by the flames that were finishing the job the last fire had started. As the fire looped around the end of the swamp, Sarah's small group became completely cut off from the others.

Looking over the side of the ridge, all Honda could see were flames and clouds of thick, black smoke. The loud, deafening roar of the crackling fire and falling trees filled the air. The larger and hotter the fire grew, the faster it spread. She knew what they had to do. With the flames pushing them onwards, the guards were a mere roadblock to be eliminated. As they worked their way towards the eastern end of the ravine, the wingless warrior crawled over to them. Pointing to the men in the ravine, he rattled off some brief instructions. Honda simply nodded. Putting their fear aside, the youngsters followed her lead. They slowly made their way down the ravine. A lizard-like youngster led the way. Honda followed close behind him. The skittish young creature felt every rock and twig as it wiggled its way along the ravine. It froze. A row of sharp metal objects laid in front of him. As he tried to walk around them, Honda grabbed his shoulder and pulled him back. Picking up a large flat rock, she tossed it on top of one of them. The blast shot the spike upwards and cracked the rock into three pieces. Behind Honda, the wingless creature jumped back. It took him a second to realize what had occurred. Immediately afterwards, he set off an alarm. "Rrratatatat."

******

"We got one."

Duncan turned to the guard. Before he could speak, another blast erupted from the other side of the ravine. "I just pray that those mines can either scare them off or maim enough of them that they are no longer a threat."

******

The young dog-like creature next to Honda immediately started to toss rocks ahead of them as they slowly moved forward. The blasts threw stone chips everywhere. With each lopping toss, they ducked behind a thick log that they rolled ahead of them. Any mines that the rocks missed, the weight of the heavy log would set off. Just to be extra safe, the cautious creatures would only step on the rocks as they slowly crept forward.

The boney-winged warrior looked at Honda. He had followed her father's orders for one reason. He had always looked out for their best interests and never took unnecessary risks. The king's cunning mind had taught him how to fight. Now he saw the same qualities in his daughter. The warrior put a hand on Honda's shoulder and in a low sincere voice rattled off his respect and trust. "Mmorut, Mmatat." He knew that he was no longer needed at this end of the ravine. It was the western end that needed his support. The raging fire prevented the guards from escaping along the eastern side. All Honda's small force needed to do was to scare the men enough to stop them from trying. Nodding his head, the wingless warrior turned and scooted his way around to the far side to help block the guards' escape. If there was to be a battle, he knew, that's where it would be.

As the sun started to fall and the spikes became less noticeable, the three creatures cautiously worked their way down the ravine. Two youngsters nudged the log forwards as Honda picked up a rock and flung it down the ravine. It hit a boulder, bounced up and rolled along the side of the ravine for about five metres. Inside the dark crevice, all three creatures noticed the small red LED light flash on. The series of rapid explosions that followed totally collapsed both sides of the ravine. The force of the explosions blew Honda and the log back two metres and the other two winged youngsters four. Both banks of the ravine were reduced to rubble. Honda looked up. Almost five metres of the ravine had been levelled.

Amazingly, they were all unharmed. The log had blocked most of the flying debris. The guards had rigged the blast so the shrapnel would blow across the ravine to kill anything crawling down it. Honda stood up and shook her head. The small quake the explosion created hadn't stopped the others. Blasts from the odd detonated spike could still be heard from the far side of the ravine. In a shrill voice, she bellowed out a warning to the others. "Nnaaarrr, Nnaaarrr."

Honda didn't hear a reply. She knew her warning was being drowned out by the blasts and the roaring fire or ignored. After repeating her call, and still no reply, she turning to a dog-like youngster. "Eeeaaa, Nnaaarrr." The creature quickly turned and ran down the ravine.

The rocky ground shook as the rapid series of explosions rolled clouds of debris over the ridge. It was too late. Two young creatures were blown apart and buried under the rubble. The force of the blast filled the wings of two more like parachutes and flung them over the banks. With only minor injuries to their wings, they scurried back into the ravine before the dust cleared and the guards could see them.

******

A scared guard looked at his partner for reassurance. "That's the other end. They are not giving up. They are coming at us from both sides."

"Shut up. Just keep an eye out for anything that moves. At least we don't have to worry about them tunnelling through this rock."

Duncan approached the two guards. "Take it easy. Those blasts have sealed off the ravine from both directions. They will have to climb over the rocks and into the open to get to us. Their numbers must be dwindling by now. If we are lucky, they may not even have enough left to risk a frontal attack."

Laurie crept up behind him. "Remember the bunkers. A single creature killed over half a dozen men. In another hour it will be dark. They will have the advantage."

Duncan tried to brush off Laurie's fears. "That creature was a seasoned killer. These ones are young novices."

Laurie snapped back, "You are forgetting that they are young zealots. The Hitler youth were just boys, yet they fought to the death. With each encounter these creatures are getting more confident. They live for the moment. They don't see any future without victory. Young zealots don't understand battlefield discretion, just revenge and victory."

Duncan smiled at her. "But they don't have our guns and training. This could be the battle we've been waiting for."

Chapter Thirty

The Gauntlet

Using a pair of long needle-nosed fishing pliers, Sarah extracted the last bullet out of a young dragon-like creature. Along with crash landing and breaking almost every bone in his wings, the young creature had been shot four times. By the time Sarah finished sewing up and bandaging the wounds, the rapidly expanding fire had almost completely encircled her small group. Betty put her large bloody hand on Sarah's arm. Looking at her face, Sarah knew that she was relying on her to find a way out.

After quickly assessing their situation, Sarah could see only two options. They could travel east through the unburnt gap of trees and hope that they could keep ahead of the flames, or go west into the swamp. After looking down at the injured creatures, their choices were narrowed to one. The mucky heart of the burnt swamp was their only chance. The pair of fallen trees that the guards had hidden behind was their nearest safe haven.

By twisting, weaving and tying together the limbs of two cut branches, they made a simple stretcher. After placing the badly injured dragon-like creatures on it, they waded through the muddy bog. At times, Betty had lost her footing and sank up to her neck, but she always managed to hold up her end of the stretcher. Once they finally reached the fallen trees, they found that the half submerged tree trunks were close enough that they could rest the stretcher between them. After draping her backpack on a thick branch protruding out of the water, Sarah tied George's folding saw to her belt and waded ashore to start constructing another stretcher. Betty stayed behind and broke off branches from the fallen trees. She then placed the branches between the poles of the stretcher to help reinforce it and keep the injured creature out of the water. By the time Sarah had finished the second stretcher, Betty was ashore, ready to help her lift the young injured lizard-like creature onto it. The last young, dog-like creature only had shoulder and wing injuries. Walking behind them through the mucky swamp, he used his good hand to hold onto Sarah's belt.

Next to the fallen trees, walking was easier. The water was shallow and the gooey mud that cover the bottom of most of the swamp had been replaced by rocks and gravel. The mist coming off the cool water helped fight off the smoke and gruelling heat of the fire. Overhead, the roar of a low flying plane was heard over the loud crackling fire. Despite being in the open, they were safely protected by a giant plume of black smoke. Sarah looked up. The dark, ominous smoke blocked the plane from view.

******

A small group of creatures, including a couple injured warriors that had helped conceal the pathways, had found themselves trapped by the flames. With injured legs and limbs, neither of the warriors could travel very fast. With the aid of their female mates and a few of their young, the two families climbed up the side of the ridge to escape the fire. Cautiously they crept into the east end of the ravine for protection from the flames. Seeing Honda peering around a bend, they felt relieved.

Shortly after they entered the ravine, the dog-like youngster returned. With him came news. The other creatures were planning to flush the guards out of the ravine and into the open. Eager to fight, the two females and youngsters rattled off their good-byes to the two warriors. Afterwards, led by the dog-like youngster, they crawled out of the ravine and circled the clearing in an attempt to join the fight. Honda wanted to join them. Looking down the ravine, she knew she couldn't. There were only her, the young lizard-like creature and the two slow-moving warriors left to protect her end of the ravine.

Working together, the four remaining creatures constructed a wall of rocks and mud at the end of the ravine to help deflect the suffocating smoke away from them. It worked. Black smoke from burning pine tar travelled up the ridge and blew across the clearing. Now all they had to worry about was being able to get enough clean air to breathe.

Only a dozen metres separated the guards from the creatures. Out of curiosity, Honda held a rock over her head. A bullet ricocheted off of it and knocked it out of her hands. Two more bullets whisked by even after she ducked for cover. The other creatures watched her and knew that they were trapped.

******

A guard peered over the edge of the ravine. "They're in no hurry. They are probably just waiting until it is completely dark and we are totally blind."

Laurie turned to the scared guard. "You may be right."

With less than a metre of hazy visibility under the dark cloud of smoke, the guard spotted some movement. Four figures ran out of the forest towards them. Swirls of smoke followed them. In three second bursts, the guards swept the clearing with bullets. Between each burst, Duncan searched for movement. In the swirling smoke, even after the creatures fell to the ground, he wasn't totally sure what was happening. "Stop, save your ammunition."

A couple guards ignored Duncan's order and continued to stir up the smoke with another barrage of bullets. The other guards wrestled their weapons from them. With glaring eyes, one guard stared in disbelief as Laurie took away his rifle. Duncan looked away from the scared twenty-year-old boy and searched the clearing for any signs of life. The fire made the digital thermal imaging setting on his binoculars almost useless. He put them back into their case. Only ten metres in front of them, the bleating cry of a dying deer could be heard. "They are trying to find ways to make us use up our supplies. Everyone, check your ammo. It will be night soon and it's going to be a long one." Facing Laurie, he added, "Give him back his rifle. Any bullets he has left, he'll have to use wisely. No one is to give him any."

The guard stood up to protest. Two others grabbed his shoulders and sat him back down. One of the strong-armed guards spoke up. "I'm keeping all my ammo."

Laurie switched the guard's rifle to single fire and snapped off the switch with the blade of her knife. Handing him back his rifle, she blurted out, "Here, use what you have left wisely." Turning to the other guard that ignored Duncan's order, she added, "And miss, you better act accordingly or I'll do the same to yours."

The guard lowered her head and closed her eyes. Clicking her weapon to semi, she looked up. "Yes, sir. I promise it won't happen again."

Duncan crouched beside Laurie. "They are scared. Only a fool wouldn't be. They're not as good as I'd like them to be, but if we can hold them together, their training should take over."

Night took away almost all of their light. Even the flames became just red smudges along a narrow gap between the ground and the thick cloud of smoke. The guards could only see a few metres in front of them. Even then, it was just a narrow gap above the ground. A dark brown shape dashed towards them and leaped over the ravine. Three more creatures appeared in front of them. In a flash, they quickly bounded over the ravine with their long tails draping behind them. It happened so quickly that none of the guards could get off a shot.

Duncan fell against the side of the ravine. "We're lucky that they were just wolves. We can't stay here. The creatures now know that we're blind. Gather up your stuff. We're leaving."

******

The creatures released a group of caribou. Using their wings like a fence, they pointed them towards the guard's position and let the frightened beasts go. The one-armed and wingless warriors climbed on top of the last two caribou to leave and the others ran behind them. The sure-footed beasts leapt over the ravine and race toward the grove of trees on the far side. The creatures behind them pounced into the empty ravine. In a split second, a red light caught a female's eye before two explosions flung jagged pieces of shrapnel into three of the creatures. The female creature was blown apart by the full fury of one explosion, while the other two were caught by fragments of the other. Unfortunately, that was enough to shatter one's skull and leave the other with half a wing, a severed arm and chunks of shrapnel stuck along her entire side.

Several creatures glared into the ravine while others jumped in to help. There wasn't much that they could do but cry for help. "Mmurr, Mmurr, Mmurr." The two mounted warriors jumped off and began running back towards the ravine.

Gun fire rang out along the edge of the clearing. The guards' escape had been compromised. The two dismounted warriors stopped and turned towards the gun shots. Despite all the smoke, a faint human scent was picked up by the wingless warrior. They were still close. The one-armed warrior glared at him and smiled.

Honda crawled out of the ravine along with the others. As she and the small lizard-like youngster made their way towards the gunshots, the lame warriors held on to each other and limped along the edge of the ravine.

******

"Ssuurratatatat, Ssuurratatatat," echoed above the loud crackling of the spreading fire.

Along the edge of the tree line, two guards tried to see through the dark haze while the third tried to adjust the setting of his rifle with the pliers on his multi-tool. "Did we get any of them?"

"I don't know. I heard the bullets 'thug' into something."

A caribou tried to get to its feet. The female guard squeezed off a single shot and the beast collapsed. "Stop firing, you fool. They are pushing animals ahead of them to locate our position."

"Let's get out of here. Duncan must have finished setting the traps by now." With their backpacks already on, they turned around and started to stand up. Out of the brush, the wingless warrior leaped on the guard on the right while two females jumped on the one on the left. Still on his knees, the twenty-year old guard in the middle faced the one-armed creature. He tried to pick up his rifle but the creature was standing on its barrel. With noses almost touching, the guard went for his knife. At the same time, the creature's claws almost severed the guard's head as they sliced across the side of his neck and along its front. With a bloodthirst, the creature dug his teeth amidst the fountain of blood pouring out of the guard's neck and snapped it. The dead guard's knife gently rolled out of his limp hand.

By the time Honda got there, the three guards had been torn apart. The humans had been forced onto their turf. On the western side of the ridge, away from the raging fire, the creatures all knew that they had very little time to regroup. Of the over two dozen creatures that left the cavern, only half were still capable of carrying on the fight.

******

Mew and another female tended to the badly injured creature while the two injured warriors worked together to drag a deer carcass back to the ravine. As they got there, a young creature crawled out of the western side of the ravine. Her hand was impaled by one of the clawed metal spikes. After only a brief glance at her, the two females continued their work. Using a hunk of deer hide, the pair attempted to cap off the blood pouring out of what was left of the creature's severed arm. It took them a half dozen tries before they got it tight enough to stop the bleeding. Afterwards they leaned back and rested against the walls of the ravine.

The thick smoke was starting to thin out. One of the lame warriors stood up and looked along the top of the long, crescent shaped ridge. Beneath the smoke in the night sky he could see three visible sections on top of the ridge glowing from burning vegetation. He knew they couldn't stay. In the open, after the smoke dispersed, they could become easy prey. The young injured creature helped the other lame warrior rip apart the deer carcass with his good set of claws. After taking a few bites of the liver, the injured creature ripped off two large chunks with his teeth and handed them to the females.

Using one hand to eat with, Mew reached over and grabbed the hand of the injured youngster with the other. She looked at the strange metal device sticking through it. Between the thick centre ring and the sharp claws, it couldn't be simply pulled out. After looking around, she put down the liver. Leading the creature over to a split boulder, she placed his hand sideways inside of it. Two splines rested on one side of the boulder while the other two stuck up in the air. With a heavy flat sided rock, she hammered the splined end of the spike. One claw that was resting on the boulder snapped off and the other cracked. The two splines that the rock struck only flexed a little and sprang back into place. The injured creature bit down as Mew twisted the spike to reposition the claws. 'Wack', the cracked spline snapped off. Blood poured out of the creature's hand as the spike was rotated around some more. After several more strikes, the last claw was broken off. A few jagged pieces of the claws still extended out of the spike. Mew did her best to pound away the sharp edges, but the spring inside of the spike kept pushing the sharp fragments back out. With the other female securing the youngster's hand, the remaining pieces of the splines forced Mew to take great care while extracting the spike.

As soon as the spike was finally out, Mew grabbed the bleeding hand. After studying the wound, she rattled off some direction to the other female. While waiting for her to return, she found two flat stones and placed one on each side of the injured hand to cover up the hole. The other female came back with a long section of the deer's intestine which Mew used to wrap around the youngster's hand. Their crude contraption provided enough pressure to stop most of the bleeding, while allowing blood to continue flowing to the rest of his hand.

Despite his crumpled wings, one of his legs encased in a wooden splint and a broken arm in a sling, the oldest warrior took over. They needed a place to hide that was safe from the smothering fire and they needed it quickly. He only knew of one such place.

With the guts and head removed from the deer carcass, they all worked together and placed the badly injured creature inside of the deer's empty cavity. With the two females holding on to the deer's front legs, and the other lame warrior and injured youngster the rear legs, they carried and dragged the badly injured creature out of the ravine. With no other options available, the battered group of creatures hobbled and worked their way towards the western side of the ridge.

******

Laurie gazed down the trail. "They should've been here by now. What's keeping them?"

Duncan snapped back, "They're dead. We have to press on."

Laurie looked at Duncan. "How do you know?"

"Easy, they would have been here by now." After standing up, he turned around and added, "That was the last of the explosives. If this doesn't work, we'll have to slug it out."

Laurie switched on the explosive's sensor, got up and followed Duncan down the trail. "We don't have that far to go. We should be able to make it to the plane."

Josh, piped up. "We also have to get back."

Duncan checked his GPS. "If we repel over the outcrop ahead of us, it'll only be about another kilometre."

"That will mean splitting into two teams, one above and the other below. Both would be vulnerable. We must maintain our numbers or we won't have a chance."

"I agree, but that means we'll have to travel over an additional three kilometres to get to the crash site." Duncan led them along the narrow path down the side of the ridge with Laurie following behind guarding the rear.

Despite the green leaves on the bushes, the choking smoke rolling over the ridge reminded them that the fire was still a threat. The odd glowing ember fluttered down from the sky. It was only the damp ground that kept the fire at bay. The odd puff of smoke erupted in the tall grass around them. The guards knew that it was just a matter of time before the drying heat would create the right conditions for the fire to spread over the ridge.

Looking up, Duncan heard the roar of a plane. He couldn't see it. A long white cloud formed in the sky. It was a water bomber. Duncan checked his GPS. "We have a long way to go. As soon as that plane strips away the smoke, the pilot is going to spot the crash site and call it in. We have to get to that plane first."

******

With a back drop of dark clouds, four creatures lifted into the night sky unnoticed. Their large wings seemed to melt into the ominous clouds drifting over the ridge. The other creatures in the hunting party had spread out and were slowly creeping over the rough terrain. The gut-turning smell of humans lingered in the air all around them. To the inexperienced females, the smells were slightly confusing. They didn't have the same expertise that the warriors and some of the young males had. Honda was different. With no mother to coddle her, her father encouraged her to hunt. The trick to hunting was to follow the scent without being seen, figure out where they were heading and carefully set an ambush. The wingless creature followed the tracks. It wasn't long before a pungent smell overwhelmed him. "Nnaaarrr, Nnaaarrr."

With that cry, all the creatures stopped in their tracks. The wingless warrior circled the hideous smell several times before picking up a rock and rolling it down the pathway. 'Ka boom'. The explosion made all the creatures jump back. The pungent scent of the chemicals filled the air. It was a smell that they all should have easily recognized from the ravine.

From a small pouch strapped around the wingless warrior's neck, Honda could smell a similar odour. Mixed in with the ATV's exhaust fumes and the guard's blood, was the smell of metal and explosives. Honda helped him take the bag off. All the young gathered around them as she pulled an unarmed spike from her pouch. Under the top flap of the pouch were illustrated directions on how to use them. After a single glance, Honda recalled Sarah setting off the spike in the mine.

A creature dove down and landed among the gathering. Quickly running over to the wingless warrior, she drew a map in the mud. The humans weren't that far ahead and they were keeping to a well-used animal trail. Both creatures smiled as they looked over at the rest. Every creature with healthy wings took to the air. The wingless warrior led Honda and the two other youths with damaged wings over a rocky cliff. Using their claws, they clung to the small fractures in the solid rock and worked their way almost straight down the side of the steep cliff. A creature fell. Luckily, his one healthy wing was enough to lower the impact as he landed in a tree. The warrior looked down. Both of the creature's wings were mangled, but he was all right. As they reached the bottom, the wayward creature was out of the tree and waiting for them. Both of his wings were tattered, but he was still eager to fight. Honda rested as two winged creatures landed and walked over to the wingless warrior. She couldn't hear them, but the warrior's smiling face meant the news was good. They were ahead of the humans. With a battle cry, "Wwaaaooowa," they all got up and ran through the forest like a pack of wolves.

******

Duncan stopped. "Did you hear that?"

"Hear what?"

Duncan turned to the guard behind him. "Our trap didn't work and I think the creatures have found us. Tell everyone down the line to be prepared for an attack."

As the word reached Laurie at the end, she quickly switched her safety off. Each second seemed like an hour. Every movement was in slow motion as they made their way off a rocky downgrade to the muddy soil below. They could see the trees moving around them. Clumping together, the guards moved slowly towards a large mound of rocks. 'Bang.' A guard cried in pain as a spike pierced his foot.

Duncan yelled, "No one move." Knowing that their position had already been compromised, he took out his flashlight and looked around. He could easily spot the tips of a half dozen spikes buried in the ground around them. The wounded guard reached for one of his comrades as the creatures charged. As the guard tried to turn towards the approaching creatures, the wounded man's grip threw him off balance. Spinning around, the guard fell backwards onto a spike. It missed the bottom of his backpack and its claws exploded inside his lower gut. Several guards ran behind a mound of rocks next to the side of the ridge. The attack was over as fast as it appeared. The two wounded guards were left in the open. As the guard with the spike in his foot tried to crawl to safety, the others urged him on.

It happened so quickly that only a dozen shots were fired. Laurie ran out and grabbed the wounded guard's hand. As she pulled him closer, Josh put down his rifle and helped her drag him behind the mound. Suddenly rocks started pouring down the side of the ridge. Just like the entrance of the mine, it was a trap. Disoriented they were forced to leave the wounded man behind and run into the forest. Looking back, Laurie saw a rock fall from the sky and smash into the medic's shoulder. The blow buckled him to his knees. His back was broken. Knowing that he couldn't make it, with one arm, he waved them on. "Save yourselves. Leave me, I'm already dead."

Laurie whispered, "I thought these creatures liked to fight. This is nothing but guerrilla warfare. They are using our injured as bait."

Duncan grabbed her hand and pulled her under a tree, while telling her, "It's just a more cunning way of fighting. A much smarter way." The remaining guards ran along the side of the ridge with a few of the creatures in pursuit. Laurie stopped and sprayed the forest behind them with bullets. Duncan spotted a small crevice and led them all into it. Quickly turning around, he found no targets to shoot at. They had vanished into the night. Turning to Laurie, Duncan finally finished his answer. "They want to fight, but I don't think that they have the numbers left to face our guns. Those aren't warriors out there. They're probably all that is left of their colony that are still able to fight." Checking his GPS, he found that he was only about half a kilometre away from where he believed the plane crashed. "We're so close."

Laurie looked at Josh and the other remaining guard. Josh had lost his rifle and the other had lost his helmet and pack. "So what do you propose we do now?"

Not taking his eyes off the surrounding forest, Duncan quietly answered, "Pray, for one thing, and double check your gear for another."

Chapter Thirty-One

Division

Sarah looked up as two more water bombers dropped their loads. She could feel the droplets rain down on her. As the fire around her started to die down, the dark cloud of smoke started to disappear. They were in the open. Even during the night they were vulnerable. The path the warriors had taken was their best way out of the swamp. Sarah and Betty grabbed a stretcher and proceeded down the long, twisted path. The mucky trek was exhausting. It took them several hours to get both stretchers onto firm ground. The trees beside the ridge were barren, but enough were toppled over to give them some cover if they need it.

Despite the fire raising the temperature of the water in the swamp, it was not enough to stop Sarah from shivering and rob all the warmth out of her legs. The warm ash covered ground was a blessing as they all lay on it to rest. With embers glowing off the fallen tree trunk they were lying under, Sarah warmed up quickly. The youngster with the injured arm and wing was curled up in a ball shivering. Sarah pulled him over to her and wrapped an arm around him. Within minutes he was sleeping. It didn't take long before Sarah joined him.

The whimpers from the injured creatures woke her. It was still dark out. As Sarah went to the moaning youngster, she looked around. Betty got to the frightened creature first. Sarah stood there peering into the sky. To the east, red glowing flames lit up the sky. To the west, mostly darkness, with the odd small patch of flames along the side of the ridge. To the south, dots of twinkling embers at the far end of the swamp. To the north, was a barren rocky ridge stripped of all life. All of the cover that protected the front of the cavern had been turned to ash, but she had no choice. She had to get the injured creatures back there.

Betty cuddled the badly injured youngster. As it stopped moaning, Sarah tried to tell her that she was going for help. In the mud she drew a line with a circle on the side. In the circle she placed a dozen stones. On the other side of the line, away from the circle, she placed five more stones. After pointing to herself, she picked up one of them and dragged it towards the large pile of stones. Then she picked up several stones and motioned them towards the four. Then grabbed the four and returned all of them to the circle so all of the stones were on the other side of the line. Sarah looked at Betty's face as it bounced from the stones then up to Sarah's. She understood.

******

Laurie peered into the dark forest. "What's keeping them? They must know where we are."

"They know. They're just trying to figure out a way to kill us without any of them getting hurt. Haven't you noticed that they never do a frontal attack? They like to hit us when we're moving and not ready to repel an attack." Duncan lifted his rifle. "If they knew how to use these, we would be dead already."

Laurie could hear rocks being moved. Without moving from her position, she asked, "So what do you think they are up to?"

"Preparing more ambushes for when we try to leave. That is, after they feast on our dead comrades. Those rocks you hear are the ones that they threw on top of them. They are rolling them away to get at the bodies."

Another guard piped up. "What's stopping them from doing that to us right now?"

"Time. They believe that they have it and we don't. Why should they risk a single life when they don't have to?"

Between the moving rocks and crackling forest, they were all twitching, bundles of nerves – except for Duncan. They had about seven metres of fairly open terrain in front of them. Suddenly twigs and small branches started to rain down on them. The nervous guard fired a few shots into the trees. Nothing, just a few broken branches falling from them. Some more twigs, branches and chunks of dry wood rained down. This time Duncan placed his arm in front of the sights of the guard's rifle. The young scared replacement was only hired a few days before. Duncan remembered interviewing Danny. "They're trying to get us to waste our ammo. As you probably figured out, they are not mere animals we're after. They're very intelligent creatures."

Through his binoculars Duncan tried to get some heat signals. There was nothing but bobbing waves in the distance, not enough to target. More debris rained down. He looked around. It wasn't falling on them. The creatures were laying a southern path of tinder along the ridge as far as he could see. At the end, a small fire had already been started. "They are planning on burning us out."

"So what are our choices?"

Duncan looked over at Laurie. "We have only one. We have to run for it."

"Where?"

"The plane. It must've created a small clearing when it crashed. It may have more supplies in it."

As they crawled out, they could hear the creatures screaming, 'Wwaaaoooowa, Wwaaaoooowa', over and over. The same cry started coming from every direction. In a low voice, Duncan told them, "Now stay in formation or we'll all die."

He faced forward and Laurie faced the rear. Josh and Danny covered the sides. Under the cover of night, the creatures were just shadows. Racing through trees and over rough terrain made the binoculars useless. Rocks fell out of the trees and huge piles of branches were hauled in front of their path. "They are trying to corral us into a trap."

In front of them Duncan spotted several fallen trees that created a narrow funnel-like gap that would force them to separate and go through one at a time. Retracing their steps, they went back and around the trap. As they escaped, several flying creatures swooped down and dropped heavy rocks on top of them. One hit Laurie's arm and knock her rifle to the ground. Josh picked it up and handed her his pistol. "It has a full clip."

Laurie tried to grab her rifle. She couldn't move her arm. Looking at Josh's pistol, she answered, "Thanks, but I have my own."

"Your arm's broken. How are you going to reload it? Use it as a spare."

Laurie looked at her arm. The upper portion of it was twisted and a section of bone poked out of its side. With adrenaline overwhelming her body, she barely felt any pain. Placing her hand under her belt, she tried to hold her injured arm as straight as she could in front of her. Duncan glanced back. "We have to keep moving."

Shadows dashed through the trees. The odd shot was all they could get out. Danny cried, "We are not hitting anything."

"We aren't supposed to. All we can do is make sure that they keep their distance." Duncan glanced at his GPS. "We're almost there." Travelling south-west, they ran into a small bog. "We'll have to go around it."

"The plane is right in front of us. I can see it." Laurie looked at Duncan. "It didn't create a clearing. It crashed into a swamp."

Duncan moved some branches aside and looked at the plane. It must have rolled when it crashed. One wing was torn off and the other was curled up. "At least it is upright." They could hear, 'Wwaaaoooowa, Wwaaaoooowa,' echoing through the forest close behind them.

Rushing into the swamp, they sank past their waists in mud. Keeping to the same tight formation, they worked their way towards the plane. Within minutes, the fringe of the swamp was buzzing with activity. With smoke moving in and deep darkness, each movement along the shore was little more than a hazy blur. Bushes and branches were moving in every direction. They all took turns shooting single rounds towards the shore. Both above and under the waterline lay rotting trees and dead branches. Every couple of metres they had to stop and help each other get through the tangled mess. Duncan was the first to grab the plane's rudder. With her broken arm, Laurie worked her way towards the wing. One of the guards helped her crawl on top of it. As she turned to face him, she saw a branch sticking out of the water move sideways. "They're in the water!" Getting to her knees, she fired into the water behind Danny.

Duncan ran down the length of the plane as Josh climbed onto the tail fin. With her pistol in her good hand, Laurie couldn't help Danny as he tried to get out of the bog. Duncan looked around and saw that Josh was already standing on the fuselage, rifle in hand. "Cover me," was all he said before jumping into the swamp. Duncan heaved Danny out of the muck and onto the wing of the plane. Flipping around, the grateful guard reached out his arm. Duncan wasn't there. Bubbles popped over the surface, but nothing else. Duncan leaped out of the water and dug his knife sideways into the aluminum skin on the side of the plane. Clinging to his knife with both hands, his feet still dangled in the water. "Shoot it."

Both Laurie and Josh fired into the muddy bog. The water foamed up and then died down. After slinging his rifle over his shoulder, Josh helped Duncan pull himself up. The creature had shredded both arms and the front of his shirt along with ripping his leg open. Laurie saw the large gash in his leg. "We have to stop the bleeding." Turning to Danny next to her, she added, "We have to get him inside." The side window was smashed. After clearing away the sharp glass, Danny got in and helped pull Duncan through it. Both the dead pilot and decapitated copilot were strapped to their seats. After crawling inside, Duncan twisted his torso between the pilot and the instrument panel. Danny helped Duncan manoeuver around the pilot and between the two front seats. After he got onto the floor of the cargo bay, Duncan finally released his tight jaws and gave out a silent sigh of relief.

Between the dark clouds, the slim outline of the moon rested above them. Putting down her night-vision binoculars, Laurie looked up. Seeing only a small glimmer of a new moon, she yelled, "Is this night ever going to end?"

******

The sound of Laurie's shrieking voice echoed across the swamp and down the ridge. The small group of wounded creatures looked back and smiled. The last place that the guards would look for them was the first place that they were found. All that protected the entrance to the mine were the heavy, locked steel gates. There wasn't a guard anywhere in sight. With broken limbs, they carefully worked their way down the side of the ridge behind the steel gates. Each step was carefully chosen and tested before any weight was put on it. Mew helped the best she could, but on such a narrow path, a guiding hand was the best she could offer.

Entering the tunnel, they started to walk past the 'Welcome' sign. The tired old warrior rested his good hand against the wall for balance. His claws scraped the wall as he limped down the tunnel. Flakes of florescent paint floated to the ground behind him.

******

Working her way along the ridge, Sarah made it to the tunnel. Midway down the tunnel she discovered that it had caved in. Looking around for another entrance, she raced back and forth down the ridge. Suddenly she remembered that there were escape holes in some of the dug outs near the top of the cavern. Standing away from the ridge, all she could see were shadows and outcrops. She didn't have a clue where the openings were.

With no choice, she backtracked her way to the others. Her mud drawing was still there. After leading Betty to it, she gathered up some mud and piled it on the line in front of the circle. She shrugged her shoulders in confusion.

Something caught Sarah's eye. Two bright lights beamed down from the sky further down the ridge. They were too slow and erratic to be planes. They had to be helicopters. Panic ran through her as Betty grabbed her hand and squeezed it.

Each grabbed an end of the stretcher and carried it to the sealed off tunnel. Betty looked up at the side of the ridge. With a couple flaps of her wings, she hovered next to what appeared to be a solid rock face. Grabbing onto the rock, she pulled herself into a long crack and disappeared. Sarah waited with her eyes glued to the crack. After a few minutes, she heard a branch break behind her. Looking around, she saw three female creatures. A ferret-like female that looked like she was nursing, grabbed the injured youngster and carried him off. Sarah led the other two back to the remaining injured youngsters. After seeing the great pain the badly injured youngster on the stretcher was in, a pit bull-like creature turned and hissed at Sarah. A pregnant, teary-eyed dragon-like female lifted the badly injured youngster off of the stretcher and carried him into the air. With milk leaking out of her, the large pit bull looking female that remained glared at Sarah before snatching up the last youngster and whisking him away into the darkness.

Walking back to the sealed off entrance, she found that she was alone. They had abandoned her. Under a pile of deadfall, she stared at the pile of rocks and mud. Betty crept out of the forest and sat beside her. After drawing a line in the mud, she added a circle. Pointing to Sarah, she placed an 'X' on top of the circle with her other hand.

After all this time, what was she? Sarah was a creature with a human past. Neither group could accept her. It was easier for the female creatures to accept the death and injuries of the warriors, but not their precious young. All of the nursing that Sarah had offered, and all of the care she had given them, was for nothing. In their eyes, she was still only a human, a mere naked animal.

Betty stayed with Sarah as she shivered, not from the cold, but out of confusion. She was left with nowhere to go. The loyal creature wrapped her arms around her. She too was caught in the middle. Sarah had taught her so much. Without Sarah, many of her friends would have died. The female placed her hand over Sarah's heart and softly rattled, "Mmorut, Mmatat."

Sarah understood what Betty was telling her, but to the rest of the creatures she would be nothing more than a human mongrel living off of their scraps. Looking south, she saw the search lights disappear over the ridge. The only light left came from the soft glowing fire in the distance. As the light wind changed direction, the devoured landscape offered very little fuel to keep the fire going. Even as the smoke slowly dissipated, the stars failed to shine.

Sarah opened her pack and gazed at the picture on the flap. She couldn't really see it, but knew what it was. Swinging the pack onto her shoulder, she started to walk away. The loyal companion followed her at a distance.

******

Roger turned around and looked at the men climbing aboard the helicopter. Most had put down their hammers and trowels only a moment before picking up their rifles. Dirt, sawdust and plaster covered their hands and clothes. Despite their appearance, the way they thoroughly checked their kit bags, belts and weapons showed Roger that they were true professionals. As they lifted off, he looked out of the open cargo door and saw the disappointment in the faces of the eager men left behind as they formed a semi-circle around the helicopter.

From another helicopter on route to the crash site, Doctor Scott asked, "How long will it be before you can catch up to us?"

The pilot got on the radio and answered, "Give us ten minutes." As a new fire flared up, a cloud of black smoke formed in front of them. "You better make that at least fifteen. We're running into some smoke. We're going to have to make a detour."

The pilot decided to go around the Devil's Claw. All of the helicopter's lights were shining brightly as they veered to the north and circled around the fingernail to the western side of the ridge. As they approached the claw's first knuckle, Roger looked through the open cargo door as they flew by the old burnt facility. The collapsed roof and position made it easy for him to spot it from the air. The forest had already reclaimed almost all of it. As the bright spot lights flowed over the forest, a bright glare reflected back at them from the forest a little south of the ruins.

Getting up, Roger tapped the pilot on the shoulder, "Turn around. I want to find out what that was."

"I'll have to ask the doctor."

"Give me the phone. I'll talk to him."

The doctor was on the phone almost immediately. "What's the hold up?"

"We spotted something in the woods outside of the old ruins. Unless people have been visiting it lately, it maybe what we've been looking for."

Doctor Scott looked at the men in his helicopter. They were all focussed and ready for action. After glancing through the window at the other helicopter flying beside them, he answered, "We'll be all right for a while. Do what you have to do, but catch up to us as soon as you can."

******

Laurie could see the spotlights searching the ridge. Through her binoculars, even in the hazy smoke-filled sky, the distinct shape of guns protruding out of the open cargo bays told her who they were. They weren't civilians. They were there to rescue them. 'Bang', a shot came from the shoreline. It was wild and came nowhere near them. Half a minute later, another 'Bang'. Duncan hollered up, "They're just trying to figure out how to use them. They don't have a clue. Besides, their fingers don't function like ours do."

'Bang', the shot nicked the tail of the plane. "Still, they are getting better." Laurie squeezed off a few shots close to where the gun flashes came from. 'Click', her last shot didn't fire. "Has anyone got any more shells for this?"

Josh passed her a clip. "This is my last one."

"In that case, you should get out here and take over."

With his head still out of the window, Josh answered, "With what? Neither one of us has a full rifle clip." Climbing out, he sat on top of the plane. From his pocket he pulled out a flare.

In the dark, Laurie wasn't sure what it was. "You can't shoot that up into the air. Some civilian may see it and report our position."

"Relax, it's only a road flare. The only people that will see it are in those helicopters."

The thought of getting out of there warmed Laurie. She smiled at Josh as he crawled on top of the fuselage and stuck the lit flare into it. With a wide grin, she commented, "I can't wait to crawl into my nice warm bunk and curl up."

Standing up, he replied, "You mean after you get your arm looked after."

"They can work on it while I'm sleeping. Just tell them to give me plenty of sedatives."

"Will do." Another 'Bang' rang out. Josh grabbed his side as he collapsed and slid off of the fuselage. As he hit the water, he stretched his arm towards the wing. Laurie dropped her pistol and grabbed his hand. Danny rolled out of the cabin window. Josh's hip was shattered by the bullet. The men in the first helicopter tore apart the shoreline with machine gun fire.

The second helicopter quickly dropped a rope ladder. The pair locked Josh's arms around the last three rungs. Laurie grabbed his face and turned it toward her, "Can you hold on?"

"I have no choice. Tell them to haul me up."

Blood poured out of him as he was lifted into the air. By the time they pulled him inside, it was too late. The bullet had nicked his femoral artery. They had to pry his fingers off of the rung. Doctor Scott looked at the dead guard. "At least you'll get a proper funeral and won't become creature food."

Two men were lowered with the ladder onto the crashed plane. Before they released it, Laurie grabbed it with her good hand and stepped on the bottom rung. As she was hauled up, the two men started to extract Duncan from the plane. Pointing over at a metal box the size of a microwave oven, Duncan yelled, "I'm not leaving without that." After one of the men turned to grab it, Duncan added, "That is what my men had died for."

"We know. We were told to retrieve it along with the plane's black box. The doctor doesn't want anyone to find out what they were doing."

Duncan got a closer look at him. He was one of the new recruits hired for the new site. "Are you getting an idea of what you are in for?"

"Sir, you hired me. Nobody with your reputation hires mercenaries as guards and adds danger pay to their regular salary without a good reason. You can't hide from your past. We didn't need to hear your name to know who you were. Your scars did your introduction for you. I was serving in Afghanistan when the first stories started to leak out about you. To some of us, you are a living legend; to others, a myth."

"A myth that most people can't look in the face."

******

It took Sarah an hour to find the chewed-up ATV trail. As she walked along the path, she could hear the footsteps of Betty following her at a distance. Outside her house, Sarah hid behind overhanging cedar branches and overgrown grass while she looked around. The wheels of her father's truck were sunken into the mud. It hadn't been driven for a long time. As the sun came up, Sarah found herself sitting on a fallen tree trunk facing Mary's house. The kitchen light came on. Shortly after, the smell of coffee filled the air.

With her coffee cup in hand, Mary stepped out onto the porch and sat down on the old wicker chair as she normally had done. Beside the chair she spotted a rock. Under it was an envelope. Under that was an old photograph.

Mary picked up the objects. It only took a glance at the photo before she burst into tears. Michaela saw her crying through the kitchen window. Running out of her house, she went to her side. Mary looked at Michaela and showed her the picture. "This could only mean one thing. He's dead."

******

Above the roar of the helicopter's motor, the co-pilot yelled, "Dr. Scott, you have a message."

Dr. Scott turned away from Duncan as the co-pilot handed him the phone. "What is it?"

"Sir, the cameras we set up outside the Douglas' place are relaying pictures of Sarah. It appears like she's alone. How do you want to proceed?"

"We'll be landing in ten minutes. I want every available man suited up and ready to go."

"Is that all?"

"No, I also want two extra vehicles ready to go. I have a third 'copter bringing in some more reinforcements."

Chapter Thirty-Two

Secrets

Michaela coaxed her pale, trembling neighbour to her feet. The unopened letter and photo of her family were still clutched in Mary's hand. After wrapping Mary's arm around her neck, Michaela walked her across the double driveway to her back door. All Michaela could do was serve her a coffee and make sure that she knew she wasn't alone. Sitting at the kitchen table, Mary stared at the letter. As she slowly regained her composure, she opened it. The handwriting alone brought more tears flowing down her face. "I somehow knew he was the one that was leaving me the hides. They were too well done to be from anyone around here. They were treated in the same fashion that my father had taught us when we were kids."

Robert crawled out of bed and peered into the kitchen. His week old beard and messy hair only added to his dazed appearance as he yawned. "What's wrong?"

With both of her hands gently massaging Mary's shoulders, Michaela answered, "Mary just found out that her brother George is dead."

Robert scratched his head and, after another yawn, he closed his eyes and shook his head. "How did it happen?"

"We don't know." Michaela looked at the envelope. "But I can tell you that's a blood stain on the envelope."

Robert looked at the envelope laying on the table. The letter itself wasn't stained, just the envelope and a smudge on a corner of the photo. Robert picked up the envelope and bought it up to the light. As the rising sun beamed through the kitchen window, he could see something glitter. "I know what killed him. That's not ordinary blood. I've seen it before."

Sarah had her ear pressed against the outside kitchen wall. Even through the siding, drywall and insulation, she could hear every word. Looking down at her hands, she could still see dry patches of blood. *Some must've dripped off when I was searching through his pack for his first aid kit.*

From behind her came, "Rrratatatat." Sarah turned and saw Zeb running towards her with his shotgun pointed start at her. The wild cry echoing from the forest caught him off guard. As he looked over his shoulder expecting to see more creatures, Sarah quickly slipped away. He spotted her running across the backyard towards the forest. As she leapt over the fence, he squeezed off a shot. The deer shot he was using tore into her side and ripped off a small piece of her skin. With her hand covering her wound, she twisted as she landed on the far side of the fence but she kept on running. Zeb raced after her. By the time he reached the fence, Robert was running full tilt behind him, rifle in hand.

******

As the doctor jumped off the helicopter, a guard greeted him with the bad news. "A couple locals saw Sarah and chased her into the woods."

"I bet you that one of them was Robert."

The guard grinned. "Yes sir. And the other one was Zeb Ferguson."

"I should have guessed." After seeing the vehicles lined up, ready to go, he turned around and yelled, "Come on everyone, I want those machines loaded and out of here, pronto. We can't let those two idiots destroy everything."

A set of spotlights broadcast the arrival of the third helicopter. As the men departed, Roger passed a small, battered, drab case to Doctor Stern.

Doctor Scott noticed the shiny plastic zipper and quickly came over and snatched it from him. After looking it over, he told the other two doctors, "It's no wonder we couldn't find anything. It was probably buried. The sprouting vegetation pushed it out of the ground. At least now we know that it didn't leak out."

Roger spoke up. "I found it wedged between two trees. I checked it out. There wasn't any metal to be detected. That's why we couldn't find it."

Doctor Scott walked over to Duncan's stretcher and announced, "Roger found the missing data."

"That's great, now get me bandaged up. You need someone to lead this crew. We still need to get Sarah back."

"You're not going this time. I'm giving this job to someone else. I believe that you may know him."

Duncan looked around and saw MacNeil jump out of the other helicopter. With a grin on his face, the tall red-haired man ran over and gave Duncan a hug. "Colonel, I never thought that I'd see the day that I'd be taking your place."

"You still haven't. This is just a mop up mission." Duncan looked at the other men jumping out of the helicopter. "Have you seen the others?"

"After I told them that I finally found you, the whole squad is coming. Right now, DeGroot and Ratlin are doing something for the Brits and the Yanks are presently in dire need of Drake's unique talents.

You trained us well. The brass are willing to pay top dollar to acquire the skills you taught us." MacNeil smiled as he looked down at Duncan's leg, "I thought all that scar tissue would be like wearing a suit of armour. I didn't think anything could penetrate that alligator hide of yours."

With a stone face, Duncan peered into his eyes. MacNeil grew rigid and slowly stood at attention. Duncan finally spoke. "The doctor briefed you, didn't he?"

"Yes sir. He did."

"Then you know that these creatures are part human. They may fight like animals but they think like us. Don't take them lightly. I just lost three fully armed squads and a medic. Don't underestimate them. So far we have lost at least two men for every one of them we've kill."

Laurie heard only the odd word as she watched the pair from a few steps away. As MacNeil led the convoy out of the facility, she walked over to Duncan. "Who was that? And why did he call you Colonel?"

Duncan watched the last vehicle leave while he answered. "Because the last time he worked with me, I was his commanding officer. I think that answers both questions."

"So you're a real colonel. Tell me, how many of the other rumours about you are true?" She looked for a response but got only a cold stare. "So, what are you doing here?"

"The doctor needed my help."

Roger walked over to the couple as they finished talking. "Did I interrupt something?" Laurie glanced at him and returned a blank stare at Duncan. Neither said a word. Roger placed his hand on Laurie's good shoulder and broke the silence. "So Laurie, how about we get that arm x-rayed?"

******

The trail of blood that Sarah left behind made it easy for Robert to track her through the woods. Almost every fallen tree and rocky outcrop she had climbed over or rubbed against was marked by her blood. Zeb squatted next to him as he studied her erratic movements. Noticing a rock with a tiny drop of her blood on it, Zeb swiped his finger across it while asking, "Where is she going?"

Robert stood up and looked around before answering. "I don't know. I don't think she had an escape plan. She has been yanking us in every direction on the map."

Hiding under a low hanging pine tree, Sarah bandaged up her side. Weakened from lack of blood, she slipped off the backpack and covered it with needles. Without the burden of the extra weight, she worked her way along a rock-covered knoll, trying to conceal her trail and gain some distance. It didn't work. Even over bare rocks, her blood-drenched fur left the odd droplet behind. That was all Robert needed. Even though he was still intoxicated from the night before, he noticed every speck of blood, smeared piece of moss and overturned leaf that Sarah left behind.

A small rock slipped. Sarah cringed as it tumbled down the side, smacking against some others as it went. It wasn't that loud, but enough to echo in the still morning air. Both of her pursuers smiled. Instead of following her tracks, they ran directly towards the sound. In front of them, they could see Sarah's head disappear over the far side of a rocky knoll. Robert's head was pounding from the whiskey he drank the night before as they split up to circle the small hill. Zeb raced around it as Robert squeezed his eyes together, trying to shake away his hangover.

Sarah could hear Zeb scrambling through the woods as fast as he could. Slinking under a spruce bough, she hid as he sprinted past her. As Robert slowly rounded the large knoll, he heard a ruckus. Not knowing which one it was, he raised his rifle to his shoulder and took aim. The grunting huffs spewing from Zeb's lungs announced his approach. Robert had barely enough time to lower his rifle before Zeb yelled, "Did you see it?"

Robert looked around, "No, stay perfectly quiet. Let's see if you scared the creature out of hiding."

As they looked around, it was hard to hear anything over Zeb's panting. Their heads jerked from sound to sound. The odd bird broke out in song. The odd rustling of leaves from a squirrel or chipmunk. Nothing distinctive. Nothing big enough to be the creature that they were pursuing. As Zeb's breathing returned to normal, they backtracked along his path. Moving only one step at a time, Robert felt that he constantly had to look behind him to make sure he hadn't missed anything.

Sarah could hear their faint footsteps approach. She had lost a lot of blood and knew that she was too weak to outrun them. As they stepped over the low-hanging bough that she was hiding under, she held her breath. Robert looked ahead of him. Zeb's tracks had destroyed almost all the signs Sarah had made. Between two of Zeb's footprints, Robert spotted a smudged clump of moss. "She got this far. We must have missed something." Quickly looking around, he put his hand on Zeb's shoulder. Zeb froze. Three metres behind him, Robert saw the tip of Sarah's ear poking out of the tree bough. He sank to his knees and shouldered his rifle. As he took aim, he hesitated. Lowering his weapon, he closed his eyes and shook his head. Zeb slowly turned around. From the angle that he was standing, he could see her wide eyes peering through the branches.

For a brief period, Sarah could only watch as her father raised his rifle back to his shoulder. Shaking herself out of her trace, she slithered deeper under the dense shrubbery. The subtle movement caught Zeb's eye. He barely took time to aim before he fired. Robert followed the faint, almost undetectable movement of branches and trembling leaves. Zeb fired a couple more times. Each time pushing Sarah further into the thickets. Using her hands, elbows, knees and toes, she scooted through the low hanging brush on her belly like a lizard. Step by step, they kept the sounds of Sarah's movements in their sights. They pushed her along with the odd well-placed shot, trying to flush her out like a wild animal.

Robert knew that she was heading for the dense shrubbery butting up to a small bog. There was only a narrow open gap between the two. Robert crouched and took aim at the narrow opening. This time he wasn't going to hesitate. As soon as Sarah stuck her head out, he squeezed the trigger. At the same time, MacNeil's heavy boot flashed in front of him and his rifle barrel was knocked upward sending the bullet into the air. Robert turned and saw two men in camo gear pointing their rifles at Zeb's head. "What's going on? I thought you wanted to exterminate those creatures?"

Sarah could hear every word as she slipped into the muddy water. The picture the doctor had shown MacNeil was nothing like seeing the real thing. Looking back at Robert, he replied, "Your daughter is a different matter. The doctor has found a use for her."

Tears ran down Roberts face as he replied, "How can that creature be my daughter? It wasn't human. That creature can't be Sarah. There is no way that's my daughter."

MacNeil smiled. "Then as far as you are concerned, it no longer matters what happens to her." The whiskey on Robert's breath was heavy enough to tell MacNeil that he was still drunk. "Go home and sober up. From now on, to you and the rest of the world, Sarah no longer exists. The doctor will send you a cheque in the mail. She'll soon be none of your concern. She'll be his."

A white faced Robert looked at him stunned. Zeb ran over and helped him up. "I think it's time for us to leave. Let them have her."

"No, they can't take Sarah away from me, just the creature that she has turned into." Robert slowly got to his feet and the pair walked away. After every other step, they glanced back. Within seconds, a dozen men had surrounded the small bog. "Those aren't the same guards." Under his breath, he muttered to himself, "The doctor must have hired professionals this time."

Sarah had nowhere to go. She knew that it was just a matter of time before she'd either be captured or killed. With the cold water robbing her of what little energy she had left, she stood up with her one arm spread out and the other tight against her side. Every weapon on shore was pointed at her. Her bandage was soaked in blood and a red stream drizzled down her side.

A few of the old guards watched her claws. They knew what they were capable of. Standing back, they let the new ones tie her hands behind her back. Sarah recognized a couple of them. In a low rattling voice she asked one of them, "What are you afraid of?"

Still pointing his rifle at her, the guard answered, "You."

Sarah fell to her knees and keeled over from exhaustion. Two men grabbed her feet and tied them together. She had lost too much blood to resist. With almost all the attention on Sarah, Betty crept closer. A long heavy pole was stuck through the gap between Sarah's arms and legs and two men lifted her into the air. With her head tilted to the side, she saw a pair of large green eyes peering at her from under a bush.

The parade of men started to walk away, carrying her like a trophy in an old safari movie. At a safe distance, Betty followed them. The men at the front and rear of the column were constantly looking around with their weapons at the ready. The newer recruits in the middle were a little less anxious. The two men carrying Sarah had their weapons slung around their necks. MacNeil and two other men went ahead to scout for any signs of danger.

Walking along a narrow path on the side of a gully, the main group of men approached a small, vertical mound of rocks that almost reached up to the men's shoulders. Hidden in a tree on the far side of the gully, Betty got into position. As they walked past, she sprang out of a tree at the armed man walking in front of the carriers. Digging her back claws into the side of his neck, she ripped out his collar bone along with part of his neck. Her front claws helped her leap over the small vertical mound. Landing behind the pile of rocks, she disappeared within the small brush.

It happened so fast that the men in front didn't see a thing, and the men behind the carriers couldn't react. The carriers quickly dropped Sarah. On their knees, they pulled out their pistols. Three men jumped on top of the mound and looked around. Two more attended their comrade as he died in their arms. "Uuraatatatatat, Uuratatatatat." Echoed through the forest. Sarah closed her eyes and smiled. *At least she didn't abandon me.* Without thinking, she rattled off a reply, "Mmurr, Mmurr, Mmurr."

******

Honda walked behind the wingless warrior as they left the burial site of the female creature killed in the swamp. On the eastern side of the ridge, the fire had almost died. It didn't matter. It had stripped away any cover that they could use to hide their movements. They had no choice but to travel through the unfamiliar forest on the western side of Devil's Claw Ridge. Except for the one-armed warrior, none of the terrain was familiar to any of them. Even the wingless warrior hadn't ventured to that side of the ridge. It had been considered too dangerous. ATV, game and hunting trails were everywhere. Any movement or track they left behind could give them away. Carefully, they worked their way along the ridge. With scouts and lookouts leading the way, the column slowly proceeded.

The wingless creature halted as the faint echo of Betty's cry reached the column. Each creature had their own unique tone. Honda instantly recognized the cry. It was the female that shadowed Sarah's every move. Her mournful cry could only mean that something had happened to Sarah. Honda looked at the wingless warrior and uttered, "Rrahh."

The warrior returned, "Eeeaaa." After looking at the two youths with Honda, he repeated, "Eeeaaa." With that, the three youngsters left. They had already proven their abilities to the wingless warrior. He knew that they could look after themselves. His only worry was what the king would think if anything happened to his daughter.

******

The hired mercenaries quickly regained a tight formation and proceeded down the trail. Betty made sure that her presence was known. She fell tree branches and blocked their trail to slow them down. At every opportunity she would zoom out of tree branches, or off of a cliff, and pelt the men with rocks in quick flybys. The only shots fired were done in despair.

Robert and Zeb crouched as they heard the shots. Robert turned to Zeb. "They're under attack. They might need our help."

Zeb sunk under a dense cedar tree. "Are you nuts? They can look after themselves." He looked around. "We have to get off of this trail."

As Zeb ran aimlessly into the woods, Robert started to chase him. Collapsing to his knees, he pleaded, "Slow down, we have to stay together."

******

After reviewing some of Doctor Brook's data, Doctor Scott got onto the phone. "I want Sarah picked up and flown back to the facility. We need her alive."

Two pilots and their crews ran to their helicopters. They were already fuelled up and the pilot of the helicopter on the roof quickly checked off his pre-flight checklist. Using crutches, Duncan made his way off the elevator as the first craft lifted off of the ground. Seeing the pilot putting down his clipboard and adjusting his visor, Duncan yelled, "You're not leaving without me."

******

MacNeil paid little concern to the human shoe tracks he had spotted leaving the trail and vanishing into the woods. They weren't his problem. As he cleared away debris off of the trail, he caught the striped creature in the corner of his eye. Dropping to the ground, he pulled out his pistol. The creature narrowly missed his head as she swooped across the trail. She was fast. His bullet ricocheted off of a rock.

Honda heard the shot and ran towards it. Her heart was pounding as she jumped over rocks and fallen trees. Her two comrades glided barely above the tree tops ahead of her.

******

"Look at that. We have a target."

The helicopter pilot looked at the spotter staring out of the open cargo door. "Where?"

"At your two o'clock."

The pilot searched the terrain below him and noticed the two youngsters flying amongst the tree tops. "I see them." The helicopter turned slightly and dropped out of the sky towards them. As they got into range, the gunner in the back noticed the flashes from gun fire on the ground. The pilot called back, "Why aren't you firing?"

"I can't. There's no clean shot. We have personnel down there and I can't see where they all are."

Duncan interrupted them. Over the radio he said, "That means we found our missing squads. Do a flyby and let them know that we're here."

The sound of the low flying helicopter sent both youngsters into the trees. With deer, caribou and other wildlife scurrying about, the helicopters' heat sensors were useless. "We have to get closer to get a clearer image."

Duncan hollered back, "No, and that's an order. I don't want to lose another aircraft. Just try to tag our men. Wildlife will be running away from them. Any heat source approaching them we can assume is hostel."

******

Honda looked up as the helicopter circled above them. Her two friends crouched beside her. As a helicopter approached, they sank into the cold swamp. They didn't understand why, but they knew that the strange flying craft couldn't see them very well if they were submerged in cold water. A burst of gunfire rattled from the craft. Shortly after, another long barrage of gunfire echoed through the forest. The second wasn't like the first. It didn't come from the helicopters, it came from the men on the ground. Despite being nowhere near the shooting, Honda was still nervous. She looked at her wrapped wings and shook her head. "Uuratatatat." She had seen how her father stood up against one of the crafts before. She felt useless without her wings.

Chapter Thirty-Three

Revelations

"They got it!"

As soon as the machine guns stopped firing, the four guards at the front of the column ran to the tree where the striped, female was hiding. Wanting to extract their own vengeance, the men opened fire as her lifeless body fell to the ground. Grabbing what was left of her wings, they dragged her out of the brush and down the path yelling, "We finally got it."

MacNeil approached the jubilant men and bent over to examine the creature. Even with three-quarters of its face shot off and its chest and wings riddled with holes, he marvelled at the ugly creature's formidable physique. Holding up what was left of Betty's head, he commented, "I wonder what castle this gargoyle came from."

Sarah's heart sank as a roar of celebration ran down the small column of men. Danny and another guard lifted Betty's body over their heads as the others paraded by. Sarah looked up and saw that most of her head was missing, along with an arm. Her chest, both sets of shoulders and her wings were pulverized by nearly a hundred bullets.

As the column approached the end, the two men lowered the bloody body and faced each other smiling. Their faces quickly turned to shock as a loop of rope tightened around their ankles. Their screams vibrated down the column as they were yanked to the ground and dragged into the woods. Danny grabbed his knife and tried to cut the rope. As he leaned forward, a branch caught him by the chin and broke his neck. The other man was lifted into the air just out of reach of the ground. In front of him, a sack full of rocks was resting on the ground at the bottom of another tree. The creatures had used tree branches like pulleys to do their work for them. Helpless, the battered guard screamed out in terror as Honda walked over to him and bit into his throat. He tried to fight back with his fists, but after delivering a couple soft punches, his arms went limp.

MacNeil and three others ran into the woods after them. By the time they reached the two strung-up men, both had their livers and hearts torn out of them. All of their kit, belts and weapons were missing. MacNeil radioed to Duncan. "Are you picking up anything?"

Duncan looked at the screen. "Only flashes that could be anything. Some of the creatures seem to know our equipment's limitations. They know how to mask themselves and avoid detection better than most soldiers."

MacNeil examined the knot in the rope that Honda had used as his men were cut down. "It's hard to believe that an animal was capable of fighting like this."

Duncan replied, "I told you, they're not mere animals and they are getting smarter every time we face them."

Carrying three dead bodies plus Sarah was tiring. By the time the column reached the small swampy meadow where they had left their vehicles, they were exhausted. With the protection of the two helicopters circling above them, some of the guards just collapsed on the dry elevated patches of long grass. Others tied their kits on the ATV racks. Tired and sore, MacNeil cranked over his engine. Nothing, it wouldn't start. Looking over the motor, he saw that most of the wires were either severed, pulled out or missing.

Another man examined his machine. "Mine looks all right." After he jumped onto it, everyone heard a 'Bang'. A spike had been stuck between the seat cushions. The razor sharp splines shot up and mushroomed open inside of him slicing through his lower intestines.

As the man cried out in pain, MacNeil bellowed, "No one move. They may have planted more of them around the place."

A woman lying on a raised mound of grassy ground slightly lifted her head. Turning to her right, a metal spike almost touched her nose. "I found one." Getting up slowly, she reached over and pulled it out of the ground. "That's one down. So how many more do you think there are?"

No one had an answer. With knives and rifle barrels, some of the guards combed the area around the vehicles for traps, while others tied the dead bodies of their comrades to ropes dangling from a hovering helicopter. The next to be lifted onboard was the badly maimed guard, followed by Sarah. After Sarah, they loaded what was left of Betty's corpse.

With her friend's tattered body lying next to her, Sarah knew that her life was over. All of her options had been taken away. Closing her teary eyes, she yelled, "Nnaaarrr, Wwaaaoooowa."

The terrified, maimed man jerked. The splines inside of his stomach ripped through his skin and bandages. One of the razor sharp edges sliced into his backbone. The overwhelming pain was incredible as it raced to his brain. Violently shaking his head, he went into shock.

The medic on board the helicopter could do nothing for him as he collapsed and died. Turning to Sarah, the medic wacked the back of his hand across her face. The gunner turned away from the door and grabbed the medic's shoulders as he tried to pull out his knife. "We have orders. The doctor needs her alive."

******

The wingless warrior looked up through the branches as the pair of helicopters departed. With both crafts protecting each other, he knew any attack against them would be too costly.

Duncan looked at the screen as red dots suddenly appeared from nowhere. "All this technology is useless. These creatures can come and go as they please." Turning to the pilot, he added, "Take us back and fly over the meadow." As soon as Duncan spotted the meadow, he knew that it was pointless. The creatures had already set the vehicles on fire. Duncan shook his head. "They're everywhere." The fire quickly spread through the small sections of tall grass. He noticed brief rings in the fire from the outward force of exploding spikes. "We'll mop it up later. Right now, let's get out of here."

MacNeil looked at him. "How have you managed to keep these gargoyles under wraps?"

"Luck, but on this side of the ridge, that's something that we can easily run out of." Duncan glanced at MacNeil and could see the rage in his face. MacNeil was not used to losing men under his command. Duncan calmly told him, "Gargoyles are made of stone. These creatures are flesh and blood. They can die like any other animal."

MacNeil looked out of the open side door. "They are stone cold killers. They come from nowhere and kill as they please."

Duncan grinned at him. "You mean like us?"

MacNeil shot him a fiery glare. "We're soldiers. There is a difference."

"Not much of one. Just consider them freedom fighters."

******

Honda and the two creatures with her hid in the forest next to the burning meadow. After setting the vehicles ablaze, the wingless warrior had wasted no time in getting the rest of the creatures safely away as fast as possible in case of a quick reprisal. Almost as fast as the grass fires flared up, they burnt out. The swampy ground didn't give them much fuel to feed on. Honda walked into the damp meadow amidst the burning vehicles and screamed, "UURATATATAT!" A bullet whipped through her ear before she heard the 'BANG'. Dropping to the ground, she turned and saw the faint puff of smoke coming from the barrel. The shooter was about a half kilometre away.

Zeb saw the creature fall to the ground and thought that he had killed it. Dropping out of a tree, he jumped onto to boulder and yelled, "That's for my dad."

Robert reached up and grabbed Zeb's belt. Pulling him to the ground, he harshly whispered, "Are you nuts? You just showed the rest of the creatures where we are."

After taking back his rifle and giving Zeb back his shotgun, Robert led the way out of the bush. It wasn't long before hydro poles started to appear between the trees and then a chimney stack. Robert looked back as Zeb stopped to take a breather. With one hand on his side, Zeb waved him on, "We've made it." Pointing ahead, he added, "The store is on the other side of that bunch of spruce trees."

Robert stopped and glanced above the shrubs at the chimney stack. "We still have to get there." Looking back at Zeb, he saw two winged youngsters drop out of the sky. "Zeb," was all he got out before the young dragon-like creature had knocked Zeb to the ground. Before he could fight back, the furry lizard-like creature bit into his throat and shook his head back and forth until his neck was broken. Turning towards the store, Robert sprinted towards the spruce trees. Honda ran in front of him. Robert almost toppled over as he abruptly stopped mid-stride. Totally exhausted, he didn't have any energy left to fight with. He dropped his rifle and slowly removed his belt stuffed with bullets. The sight of Honda's blood soaked face and wide demonic grin dropped Robert to his hands and knees. Nothing he could do could change his fate.

Honda slowly circled him before looking him straight in the eye. There was something strange about this human. With nostrils flaring, she smelled the air.

As Honda knelt in front of him, Robert felt both terrified and confused. He had expected to be killed instantly, or mauled and eaten alive like they had done to Timothy. With their faces almost touching each other he was frozen stiff. Trembling in fear, he shut his eyes as Honda ran a single, sharp claw down his forehead, along his nose, across his lips and all the way to his chin. Robert could feel the warm blood flowing into his open mouth and down his shirt. Opening his eyes, time stood still as he watched Honda point a single outstretched claw at his face in a back and forth motion, from one eye to the other. "Sssarrrraah."

Expecting the worst, Robert squeezed his eyes shut and slowly bowed his head. A minute went by and the only thing he could hear was some rustling going further and further away. Opening his eyes, he turned his head. His rifle and belt were gone. Honda had rejoined the others as they dragged Zeb's body into the woods. Before disappearing, Honda turned back at him and screamed, "Sssarrrraah, Wwooooaaa."

The sweat pouring off of his forehead made the long, deep cut on his face sting even more. Robert finally got the nerve to stand up. On the other side of the spruce trees he could hear Mrs. Ferguson yelling, "Zeb, is that you? It's all right. I forgive you. You can come back home any time you want to."

Robert looked at the trail of blood that the creatures had left behind. The gut twisting voice returned. "Zeb, come home right now, your supper is getting cold." Robert could hear the tears in her voice. He didn't have the strength to tell her what had happened. He had watched both her husband and her son die, and didn't fire off a single bullet to help them. He felt that he killed them himself. If it wasn't for him, they would both be still alive.

******

With needle and thread, Doctor Stern stitched up the gash in Sarah's side. Roger looked over his shoulder at the shaved skin next to it where the doctor extracted some buckshot. It had darkened into a reddish brown colour. "Did you know that more than ninety percent of the human DNA was inherited from previous life forms? It goes all the way back to the very first protein strands that came out of the volcanic ooze that all life had evolved from."

Doctor Stern didn't even flinch. "Anyone that studied genetics knows that. How about you just make sure her restraints are tight in case she wakes up."

As Roger checked the belts and glanced at the monitor, he continued talking. "Well did you know that when Doctor Scott did his experiments, he was still under the old belief that every strand of DNA was made up entirely of strictly human genes?"

"Sure. Remember, I was there."

Roger checked the belts lashed to Sarah's legs as he continued. "Doctor Brook had infused the entire DNA strand that Doctor Scott had given to him into the chips, both active and dormant. When your team added the enzymes that gave the cells the ability to reproduce, they had virtually unlocked all of the genes, and with it, Pandora's Box."

The doctor's hands were shaking. "You mean that even the dormant proteins are able to be switched on at will? No wonder we couldn't control them. The cells are more unstable than we thought. Poor Sarah didn't have a chance."

"I made a quick copy of the research data that I had found by the ruins before I even got back onto the helicopter. Some of the files are encrypted but most of them are still readable. I should send you a copy. It's a very interesting read. The two doctors were not as great as I thought they were. They were just lucky. The cells they used were so crude and pliable that they could only accept DNA information that was as pliable as they were. That's why all the restraints on the genes had to be removed."

"Then why can't we reproduce the results?"

"We're trying to put a Ferrari motor into a Volkswagen beetle. We have to manipulate the stem cells into accepting the new chips from a different angle. That will mean we need to experiment with completely different strains of enzymes."

"Maybe the answers are in the encrypted files. Doctor Scott has had time to read them by now." Doctor Stern finish tying his final stitch. "So are you the one that is going to talk to the doctor?"

Glancing down at Sarah, he said, "Something tells me that he already knows. Why else would he be so insistent on keeping Sarah alive?"

******

After tearing Zeb's corpse into manageable pieces to carry, the trio quickly found the path the rest of the creatures had taken and followed it to the mine. As they approached the entrance, they found the rest hidden, waiting in ambush in case anyone was following them.

After everyone shared the remains of Zeb's corpse, the wingless warrior led the way into the mine. Ahead of them, they pushed a large, round bush with long sticks. They didn't want another deadly explosion like the one in the ravine. Behind that, they swept the ground, using long branches in case the guards had planted spikes. The tunnel was clear. Entering the main cavern, they came across tire tracks and footprints going off in every direction. Honda forced her way to the front of the column. Standing next to the wingless warrior, she examined the tracks. Along a deep set of vehicle tracks were tracks made by other creatures. The round, evenly spaced marks made by a crutch told them who they were. The injured warriors had led their group into the mine.

Hiding their tracks wasn't possible without creating an unmarked pathway across the criss-crossed chaos of tire tracks and footprints. Like a grey brushstroke over a painting, all it would do is conceal their numbers. Instead, Honda had a better idea. Almost all of them knew every square metre of the mine from the floor to the ceiling. Those who couldn't fly followed the wounded warrior's path. Those who could rose into the air and gently stirred the dirt and dust into a giant cloud. Travelling down every tunnel, the fine dust was whisked into the air and gently laid back down. Both new and old tracks were filled in, leaving no clear trail for anyone to follow.

The wingless warrior could smell and hear where the others were. The elevator was left down and they could hear the terrified animals squealing in their cages.

******

After returning with a team to mop up the clearing, MacNeil noticed a small puff of dust blossom out of one of the mine's air vents. As the small mushroom cloud disappeared, he asked. "What's up there?"

The guard working next to him finished tying the sling around a burnt ATV before looking where MacNeil was pointing. "The air vents on top of the main cavern in the mine."

"Is there anything going on inside it right now?"

"No, not until lunch and that's not for a couple hours."

"Well, something is going on inside the mine. If that cloud wasn't caused by our people, something must be causing it, and that something is most likely those ugly gargoyles."

The men and women combing the meadow for spikes and traps shut off their metal detectors and stared at the ridge. They all watched as a second mushroom cloud spewed out of another air vent.

******

Laurie stood in the doorway and watched Rankin's chest slowly go up and down. Doctor Stern was sitting next to him, monitoring his breathing and setting his drips. "Will he survive?"

The doctor looked at her. "He had a lot of open wounds. Hiding under the water like he did, his heart had pumped a lot of crap into his body. He has algae, bacteria, viruses, dirt, and a host of other crap floating around inside him. Despite being young, strong and determined, I don't give him much of a chance. He's lucky he stayed alive this long. It's probably just a matter of time before his body surrenders to the onslaught."

"So we went through all of that for a dead man?"

The doctor looked at the twisted anguish in her face. Getting up from his chair, he wrapped his arms around her. "No one knew what the outcome would be. All those men went into that swamp thinking, 'What if it was me?' Your friends and comrades died trying to rescue their friends. They died nobly doing what they believed was right."

Saddened, Laurie walked down the hall. Roger was checking Duncan's leg. "How in heaven did that creature cut through this? You don't have skin. All you have is a tough body suit holding in your muscles. Your scars have turned your skin into thick leather. It's like you are wearing armour. I don't know how Doctor Stern managed to sew you up."

Duncan lay on the bed smiling and chuckled. "By the way it stung and pulled, I think he used saddle soap and darning needles."

The crude commentary cheered Laurie's mood up a notch. "So I take it that at least you're all right."

Duncan looked over at her glum face. "So you've seen Rankin?"

Laurie looked at the floor as she answered. "Yeah, he doesn't look good."

Duncan lay back in his bed. "In the battlefield, the killed to wounded ratio was quite different. There, we could get at least the bodies of our buddies out. Here, our beds are almost empty and the graveyard is full. Those creatures aren't soldiers, they're predators." Looking at Laurie, he added, "MacNeil calls them gargoyles. Merciless, stone-hearted demons." Duncan raised his hand and examined it. "Maybe he is right. These are not claws. They are tools. We're not savages. We kill only when we have to."

Roger laid his hand down on Duncan's wounded leg. "What choices do they have? To them, it's kill or be killed. They are fighting for their lives."

A shot of pain ran up Duncan's spine. As Roger lifted his hand, Laurie blurted out, "So are we!"

Duncan watched Laurie turn and walk away before answering. "I think you both could be right."

******

Mrs. Ferguson knocked on the Douglas' door. Michaela turned on the porch light and pulled back the curtain. Biting her lip, she turned the doorknob and slowly opened the door. "I suppose you'll want to talk to my dad."

Mrs. Ferguson couldn't look Michaela in the face. Instead she gazed down at her own fumbling hands. "No, I just need to know if you have seen Zeb lately. He's been missing for two days now."

"Two days?"

"Unfortunately, we had an argument. He's stubborn just like his father. He simply packed up everything and marched out."

Michaela could no longer look at her. Turning around, she put on a kettle of water. "What was the fight about?"

"The same things. Freedom, excitement, being his own boss, the gremlins, Sarah…"

Michaela quickly turned and interrupted her. "Sarah!"

Mrs. Ferguson finally looked up at her. "Yeah, ever since the unfortunate incident at the store, he could never get her out of his head."

Sitting in a dark corner of the living room, Robert absorbed every word. Carefully, he rested his hands on the arms of his chair, trying not to make a sound.

Michaela tried to change the subject. "So, where do you think he is?"

"I don't know. He could be anywhere. I asked his friends. They don't know. No one seems to know."

"What about the police?"

"To them, he's just another runaway. This isn't the first time he's run away." Mrs. Ferguson looked at the boiling kettle. "I better go. I'm sorry for coming over so late."

After she left, Michaela went into the living room. "Dad, are you ever going to tell me what happened?"

Robert looked at her. Grabbing the bottle on the table in front of him, he took another drink. Turning away, he stared straight ahead into the darkness, not saying a word.

******

It didn't matter if it was day or night when it came to the old mine. Without electricity, it was always pitch dark inside. MacNeil turned to the guard. "Where did you hide the lab animals?"

"We need to take two lefts and then a right. There is a trap door in the ceiling about halfway down that tunnel."

As they turned the corner, they saw the lowered elevator. A faint light beamed downward. In the pitch dark, any source of light was enough to light up the entire area around it. Everyone stood still. The old guard whispered, "We should be hearing the animals. They are always noisy."

MacNeil quietly replied, "Not if they are dead."

With barely a sound, MacNeil climbed one of the corner chains of the elevator and into the small cavern. "They're not here. We're too late." Walking around the small revamped cavern, he studied the cages. The ones in front had been pulled apart. As he got to the back, he found that the creatures undid the latches. After closing a cage door, he fumbled with the tricky latch. "These creatures are quick learners."

The old guard watched him. "Some of the animals were getting pretty smart. We had to install escape-proof latches to keep them caged up."

"So the doctor's research was working."

"I don't know what you mean."

Grinning ear to ear, MacNeil replied, "You don't have to."

******

From the air vent, Honda watched the men enter and leave the cavern. The sky was quiet, with no planes flying around and barely an insect making a sound. An owl hooted in the distance. Across the wide stretch of burnt swamp, its cry filled the air. As the men started their machines and began to leave, the silence was quickly broken.

A long column of creatures made their way back and forth along the ridge. On each trip they carried as much as they could manage. By morning, the entire stash of dead meat, animal food and seized supplies had been transported back to their lair.

******

Through the window in the door Roger watched Doctor Scott examining Betty. He almost looked giddy. Puzzled, Roger stepped into the operating room and approached the table. "You're feeling pretty chipper."

"I should be. These creatures have been doing all my work for me."

"What do you mean?"

The doctor looked at Roger with a smirk. "Don't take me for a fool. I know that you made at least one copy of Dr. Brook's data before you handed it over. All the mud on the zipper had been scrapped away and I know how curious you are."

Roger stepped back from the doctor. "Sure, I made a copy and tried to read it. But I still don't know what you are talking about."

The doctor chuckled. "I'm sorry, I forgot that the main files were encrypted." Smiling at the confused man, he almost laughed. "You just read the footnotes. The real advances we made were in how we manipulated the cells." Looking down at the dissected creature, he tried to regain his composure. "We could've done it in the lab, but we would've still needed long term patients to monitor. Patients that weren't compromised by drugs, diseases and life threatening infections. These creatures were perfect." Looking at Roger, he added, "This creature has proven to me that the cells are finally starting to stabilize on their own."

"How?"

"It appears that when the cells are content, they reprogram themselves in order to prevent any further change that could offset the balance."

"So how did this creature tell you that?"

"The information on all the chips that I've found in the creature had all been uniformly altered." Walking over to Roger, he patted him on his back. "We've done it. Those creatures have proven that my research can work."

Roger stood back more confused than ever. "So what have we all been doing here?"

"Preparing the groundwork for the next generation." The doctor's sinister smile made the hairs on the back of Roger's neck stand out straight. As the doctor stepped towards Roger, he added, "And with all the new information that is piling up, I truly believe that we're much closer than you think. These creatures may have jumped us ahead of schedule."

******

Honda sat next to her father and looked around. They had enough food and water to last for months. The humans didn't know where they were and the injured needed time to heal. Her father looked up at her with tears in his eyes. "Uuratatatat, Rrratatatat, Wwaaaooowa."

Thinking about Sarah's father confused Honda. Families are there for each other no matter what. Her thoughts turned to the large building from which the humans came out to hunt them. Except for a couple, the humans that lived in the small buildings next to the roads left them alone. Honda looked back at her father. "Uuratatatat, Rrratatatat, Wwaaaooowa." They had no choice. It was either them or the relentless humans hiding inside of the large fortress. Their only chance of survival was to kill them before they could hunt down and wipe out the colony.

Chapter Thirty-Four

All or Nothing

Detective Arnold rolled up to the facility. His driver stayed in the jeep while he got out and walked to the gate. Over the intercom, he announced, "I'd like to talk to Doctor Scott."

Laurie reached over and pressed the button to open the small narrow door next to the main gate. As the detective walked towards the facility, Doctor Scott came out to meet him. Stunned, the detective stopped. "This is a little strange. You coming out to meet me."

The doctor grinned. "You make it sound like I'm doing something wrong." Turning serious, the doctor added, "So what's the problem now?"

"We had some complaints. There was a lot of gunfire going on, and it wasn't inside the boundaries of your so-called gun club."

"We had some predator problems. Hunting season is still on, you know."

"Not to the animal rights activists camped along the road." The nervous detective added. "They said that they heard high caliber automatic weapons. They even said that some of the shots were fired from a helicopter."

"They're mistaken."

"They have both sound recordings and video of it."

"I would have no problem convincing the judge that they are all fake."

The sober detective lifted his head and answered. "I figured so." As he turned to walk away, he added, "I'm just the messenger."

As the doctor returned, Duncan met him inside the entrance. "Any problem?"

"Not from him, but the activists are still at it."

"Everything is on schedule. There's nothing those guys can do to us."

"I'm not worried about that mob. What concerns me are the radical fringe groups they attract. With those creatures still out there, we can't have doped-up hippies and curious outsiders wandering anywhere near the ridge. It could be a PR nightmare."

"Then we'll just have to speed things up a bit."

******

Next to the lake, the men inside of the new facility were removing the painter's tape from the walls. A constantly increasing number of recruits were camped out inside the fence. As Duncan and MacNeil landed, three of them approached the helicopter. Duncan smiled and opened his arms as they ran to him. "The squad's finally all together again."

Duncan looked at Ratlin. "When did you get here?"

"DeGroot and I arrived yesterday. Drake just showed up this morning."

For the rest of the day, Duncan flew them all around the ridge and surrounding area, showing them everything he could. That night, none of them slept a wink. Debriefing each other on the highlights of their various exploits took all night.

The next few weeks were incredibly busy. Helicopters were coming and going, from dawn to dusk. With the smell of smoke lingering everywhere around the ridge, it was almost completely void of all wildlife. The western side was hit the worst. Everything above the old mine entrance was stripped of all vegetation. With the planes reporting no new sightings of the creatures, there were more hands available to help with the move.

Sarah could hear the men scurrying around. Encased in a metal tube with a thick glass dome lid, she could see dollies full of boxes and pieces of lab equipment being rolled past her doorway. Even inside of the tube, the heavy nylon straps around her arms and legs confined her every move. Dozens of tubes pumped and drained fluids in and out of her body. To the doctors, she was just a cell factory.

******

Three weeks later.

The king walked around the cavern and watched as the injured warriors, females and youngsters flexed their sore limbs. Wounds were quickly healing and charred bones were showing signs of rejuvenation. Even the bones sticking out of the back of the seasoned pit bull-like warrior next to him were showing signs of regrowth.

Honda glided around the ceiling and practised pouncing using balls of animal hide. They had lost a lot of warriors. The remaining youngsters and veteran females had stepped up to replace some of them. They all knew that they would only have one chance. The battle ahead would be for all or nothing. Once their supplies dwindled, they would be forced to leave the cavern to search for food. They couldn't wait that long. With no cover, the humans could easily hunt them down with their flying machines and long range rifles. Without being able to replenish the numbers to protect themselves, they would be picked off one at a time until they were all dead.

******

Doctor Scott examined the gashes on Rankin's face. They made it clear that his body was fighting back. With a pair of tweezers, he picked off the small pieces of debris that Rankin's skin had expelled to the surface. Between pain medication, fever and exhaustion, his comatose body lay on the bed oblivious of the doctor's prodding.

Laurie pulled over a chair and sat across from the doctor. "Is he going to make it? Is he going to be normal again?"

The doctor finished pulling out a minute twig from the gash on his cheek. "Maybe, it depends on what you call normal. Remember Sarah? Was she normal before or after she was attacked?"

Laurie knew what had happened. Leaning over the bed, all she could see were the doctor's smiling eyes as she asked him, "So is he going to turn into another one of them?"

With only a small twitch on the side of his mouth and a one shoulder shrug, he calmly replied, "I doubt it. The cells have matured. They are more stable now. I guess with all this fighting going on, they stopped exploring the random mutations that they were constantly going through. War is funny. It destroys life, yet out of necessity it creates more scientific and medical advances than from any other time in history."

Laurie sat back in her chair. "So what's going to happen to him?"

While redressing the wound on Rankin's face, Doctor Scott answered, "He'll survive."

In the following weeks, Rankin's fever was gone and his scars started to heal. Laurie didn't know that he was being kept in a drug-induced coma. Looking in on him at least once a day, she noticed the added tubes strapped to his body. As more and more specialized equipment was brought in, she was reminded of Sarah. After comparing the equipment to the ones attached to Sarah, she knew what was happening to Rankin.

Laurie approached Duncan as he poured coffee from the urn in the cafeteria and inquired, "When we were hired, were all our rights taken away?"

"What do you mean?"

"The doctor is using Rankin as a guinea pig."

"He's different. In his case, as long as the infection is still multiplying in his body, the doctor has to control it. I haven't been just talking to Doctor Scott. I've made inquiries about his condition with the other doctors as well. Right now they are trying to reprogram the cells to prevent Rankin from turning into one of them."

"Can they do that?"

"It sure sounds like they can. Roger is as happy as a hockey player going into the third period up five zip."

Laurie stepped back confused. "Just how bad is the infection?"

"Not nearly as bad as Sarah's. After this length of time, Sarah had hair growing like crazy. Rankin has none. Sarah was showing signs of other mutations. Rankin isn't showing any at all."

******

It was three in the morning when the technician watching the monitors saw two men wearing dull black clothing quickly scale the perimeter fence and cut through the barbed wire on the top. With a push of a button, Duncan was alerted. As the men approached the marked electrified fence in the middle, they removed rubber mats and a few additional hand tools from their backpacks. The anxious technician watched as the men carefully cut away a section of electrified fence. After rolling the cut section of chain link fence to the side and clamping it in place, they laid a rubber mat across the gap and crawled through.

They had only made a few snips on the third interior fence before over a dozen of their colleagues rushed up to the exterior fence and started to help each other over. Once over, they crawled through the electric fence and waited for the final gap to be finished.

Over the radio Duncan said, "Now." The technician flicked the switch to electrify the interior fence. As the pair of men cutting the fence jerked around in agony, the floodlights focussed on the others as they tried to escape. A half dozen guards were waiting for them between the exterior fences. A half dozen more ran towards them from the trees next to the building. They were all trapped between the two electrified fences.

By the time Detective Arnold finally arrived, it was six in the morning. The only comforts that were issued to the captives were metallic survival blankets, water, a few bags of tea and a portable toilet. Most of them were nestled together, asleep on the coarse gravel. As the gate squeaked open, a couple woke up and jostled the others awake. The detective looked at Duncan. "What do you want me to do with them?"

The pair walked along the fence. "We have a problem. If we arrest them for break and entry, they will have their day in court. That will mean we'll be the centre of even more unwanted attention."

"So what do you propose we do?"

Duncan watched as the breeze blew a corner of an emergency blanket onto the electric fence and one of the men fought to get it off of him. "Arrest them and let them think they won. Then, as they go to court, we'll drop all charges.   That way their organization has committed a ton of money for legal expenses and gets nothing for it. In return, we'll get a few weeks without them pestering us."

"That would be a waste of taxpayers' money and my time."

"That's why I'm telling you this now instead of just doing it. Remember, they broke the law and arresting law breakers is what you are paid to do. Think about it, this way the prosecutors know how to handle the situation. If the judge gives you any problems, just tell him to give me a call."

******

Duncan pulled up a chair and placed a cup of coffee down on Doctor Scott's desk. "Your time frame was right on the money."

The doctor took a sip of coffee and smiled at Duncan. "Groups like that are so easy to predict. They get wind of something and they sit back and think about it for a while. Then they think about something else. Then back and forth a bit more, until their drugged up minds get worked up enough that they want to do something about something. Then they piece together a semi-plan and talk some of their stupid friends into joining them. After all that is done, they still have to put together some money to cover expenses and get up some nerve to actually do it. It all takes time. Over the years, I've discovered that the time it takes has been pretty consistent. They may think that their actions are spur of the moment, but they are extremely predictable."

"Should we be expecting more?"

"No, not for a while. They need time to digest what occurred before they can organize another attack on us. That could take over a month. By that time, it will be starting to get too cold to camp out. We have until spring."

Duncan sat back on the chair and took a large sip of coffee before replying. "That will give us plenty of time to complete the move to the new site."

Over the following weeks, everyone worked twelve hours a day, six days a week. Only a skeleton crew was left at the old building, just enough to made it look used. A couple guards put on lab coats as they strolled around the courtyard. To the outside world it appeared to be business as usual and nothing had changed.

******

Honda watched her father flex his wings in front of all the creatures gathered in the cavern. After everyone fuelled up with their last full meal, there were only of few more days of dried meat left. It was time. Any delay could mean trying to fight while being weakened by hunger. "Uuratatatat, Eeeaaa, Sshuura, Wwaaaoooowa."

The dog-like warrior flexed his rapidly growing wings. They weren't ready yet. They couldn't lift him off of the ground. The king looked at him. "Wwoooaaa. Teeesss."

It wasn't what the warrior wanted to hear. Guarding the cavern wasn't what he wanted to do. He jumped into the air and flapped his wings as hard as he could. He got off of the ground for a couple seconds but that was all. Disappointed, he walked over and stood beside the tunnel. As the king led most of the colony through the tunnel, all he could do was watch them go. His head fell as the two warriors that were previously left to guard the cavern strutted by him. Honda saw his disappointment. As she walked by the veteran warrior, she attempted to comfort him. "Mmorut, Mmatat."

His heart was lifted slightly from her words of respect. In return, he happily replied, "Eeeaaa, Sshuura, Wwaaaoooowa," and wished her good fighting.

******

The night sky was darker than usual, with only a narrow sliver glowing from the moon. Only a few brave stars poked their way through the dark cloudy sky. The lone guard on the roof of the facility sat down and poured some coffee out of her thermos. Her long shift wasn't even halfway over and her cold hands were enjoying the warmth of the hot cup. "I hope that weatherman was right and it's going to warm up tomorrow." After taking a sip, she discovered that the cream in her coffee had curdled. She spit it out and tossed the rest of the cup over the side of the building. "I knew I should've scrubbed it out. This is the second time this week."

She was still shaking her head as her radio started to squawk. "Do you see anything?"

Startled, she quickly got up and knocked over her thermos. The hot coffee splashed onto her leg. Trying to deal with the scorching pain, she clinched her eyes shut while she answered. "No, nothing. What's up?"

The technician informed her, "I just got a report that one of the helicopters caught something on their radar."

"Is this a Devil's Night prank?"

"I wish, but Halloween pranksters don't fly."

Her pain quickly disappeared and small tremors of fear took over. While scanning the surrounding area more closely, she replied, "How close are they?"

"Close enough that the pilot turned around. He said that there a couple dozen of them heading our way."

As the guard frantically looked around, she stepped on her thermos and fell flat on her back. Her binoculars flew up and smashed against the roof. Crawling to her knees, she grabbed the binoculars and checked them over. The large lens on one side was cracked, but the other side was fine.

The technician snickered as he watched her fall. "If you can stay on your feet, I advise you to keep looking." On the monitor he saw the guard get up and give him the finger. "I'm sending someone up to join you."

Standing up, she stretched her sore back while she gazed over the swamp beneath her. Through the bare trees, patches of snow reflected the limited light radiating from the few stars that pierced the dark clouds. "I still haven't seen anything. Nothing is moving out there, not even a falling leaf."

The guard heard a knock on the door. "Is everything all right for me to come out?"

"Fine, I guess. I haven't seen anything yet."

"So what's going on?" The guard's hand barely left the door handle before a creature's hand slipped around the doorway and briefly held the door open while slithering inside.

The guard looked at him as he approached her. "No one knows. No sightings for two months and now a hoard of them are out there flying around." As she was finishing her sentence, a shadow behind the guard approaching her caught her eye. "What's that?" She abruptly pushed the man aside with her arm and saw the door close. "Man, am I getting jumpy. Either the cold must be slowing the door-closer down or my mind's racing a little fast."

"Get a grip on yourself." The dazed guard shook his head and turned away. The lens on the camera above the door monitoring the roof turned red as the king swiped his claws across the guard's neck.

Another creature lunged over the side of the building and bit into the back of the female guard's neck. She reached over her head and grabbed the creature's ears with both hands. The king looked up from the dying man and saw the guard's exposed lower belly. As the guard fought the creature biting her neck, the king rammed his extended claws upwards under her vest and into her exposed lower belly. Thrusting his arm straight upwards into her chest cavity, he pierced her heart.

Through the blood drenched lens, the technician watching the monitor, saw her dauntless face as a chunk of her heart was being pulled out of her. Even through the red and pink streaks running down the screen, he felt like it was his own heart being eaten in front of him. He picked up the phone. Mesmerized, he continued to watch as other creatures joined in and feasted on her organs. Her clothes were sliced off as they worked their way towards her young, fat, juicy breasts and tender thighs. They were ripped off her body in seconds. "They're here and they are definitely not taking any prisoners."

Chapter Thirty-Five

Retaliation

Duncan put down the phone and turned to Doctor Scott. "There were only ten guards posted there, a couple squads and a pair of technicians. Now there are only eight left. They've locked the perimeter of the building up solid, but the creatures are smart. They won't be able to keep them out for long, not if the creatures really want to get in."

"So what do you propose?"

Duncan turned away as he solemnly told him, "Let them in. While they are busy trying to get through the interior walls, we attack."

"Why?"

"According to the numbers and the sizes of the creatures that are attacking, they are throwing everything they have at us. In their minds, it's us or them. Why else would they risk everything? If the trap works and we win this battle, it'll be all over. There won't be any left capable of putting up resistance."

"You may have a problem convincing the men there to let them in. They have all seen what those creatures are capable of."

"I know my men and they trust me. They know that I'd never risk a single life unless I had no choice in the matter." Duncan picked up the phone. "Get all your personnel together and get prepared to lock yourselves into ward three. It has no windows and the doors are made of thick stainless steel. That will provide you with the maximum amount of protection the building has to offer once the creatures get in."

"What do you mean once they get in?"

"Before you lock yourselves in, I want you to securely lock every interior and exterior door in the place except for the hallways. Then unlock the fire door outside ward three. It will take them a while before they figure out how to open it."

"So you're going to use us for bait?"

"There's no way that they can get into ward three. It was made to withstand any kind of attack. That is where all the sensitive research data was kept. You'll be safe until we get there in about a half an hour or less. We need to give them time to fall for the bait and congregate inside of the facility."

"So why should we risk our lives?"

"It's the best way to trap all the creatures in one place and exterminate them. A single door is easier to assault then a bunch of random holes dug into the walls that they may escape from. Plus, we have to control their movements to minimize the risk to the assault team."

"Fine, we're in." Turning to the guard behind him, the technician added, "As if we had a choice."

******

Honda watched as her father directed the creatures in their search for a way in. Two creatures clawed away at the roof, while others clawed at the walls, windows and doors. One pair even attempted to dig their way under the large garage doors. The king watched as the cameras moved around, monitoring their every move. One by one, he tore them off their mounts and threw them over the side of the building. Confident that they were no longer being watched, he scratched at the door on the roof. Inside, a creature pushed on the bar and the door slowly opened.

Lying at the bottom of the first set of stairs, another guard was brutally torn apart. The king cautiously led a half dozen creatures into the building. As they crawled over the body, a set of keys slid down the side of his belt and clanked against the steel stairs. Honda and the others continued to scratch away at the walls, doors and roof. They didn't want anyone inside to know that they had already gotten in.

******

"Come on you guys, we don't have a lot of time to waste." The technician locked the monitoring room door and started down the stairs.

The frightened guard behind him spoke up. "How will we know when it's safe?"

"When they knock on the door and tell us." The technician looked through the small group of guards around him. "Have you seen Fisher? He has the keys to the third floor."

"No, not lately." Pointing to the two guards closest to him, he said, "You two, go get him and make sure all the upper doors are locked."

As the rest split up to finish locking down the building, the two recruits ran to the stairwell at the end of the hallway. Their footsteps echoed as they raced up the stairs. At the top, one carefully turned the doorknob and cracked it open, while the other stood back with his rifle at the ready. "It's not locked. He must still be locking up." As the recruit opened the door, he announced, "Fisher, don't shoot, it's just us."

They looked down the hall. It was empty. "Check the doors."

As the pair walked down the hall, they quickly checked each door. Near the far end, light coming through a window cast a fleeting shadow through a doorway and into the hall. "He must be in there. Fisher, come on, we're on the clock. There's no time to waste."

The guard in the rear spoke up. "Something's wrong."

Turning around to face him, the guard saw a creature coming out of room behind them. He quickly raised his rifle and fired. The creature fell backwards inside the room.

The guard closest to the creature proclaimed, "You hit it. I can see blood on the floor." As he adjusted his rifle, he added, "I don't understand, I had just checked that door. It was locked."

"It must've held it shut."

The pair stood back to back not knowing what to do. "The two big questions are, how did it get in and how many are there?"

"Wrong, there is only one question. How do we get out of here? Without keys, that stairwell is the only way out."

Halfway down the hall were the stairs leading to the roof. A guard noticed the pool of blood that was spreading under the door and into the hall. "Now we know what happened to Fisher." As another door cracked open, the anxious pair ran to a cutaway in the hall and climbed behind the garbage bins. "At least here we have some protection."

******

"Did you hear that shot? The creatures must be inside the building."

The scared technician turned and proceeded to ward three. "Duncan was right about them. They were going to find a way in somehow. Ward three is still our best hope. It is built to withstand an explosion. Plus, that is the only place the others will be looking for us."

The large muscular guard with them questioned the technician. "Couldn't you just call them?"

"Don't be stupid. The communication room is the only place inside here that anyone can get a signal out."

The two technicians only carried pistols. The guard with them led the way with his bayonet attached to his rifle. They could hear clambering on the second floor. Looking up, they heard something rattling around. "It's just Frank and Leonard locking up."

******

The last two guards had almost finished locking up the second floor. All that was left was the cafeteria and kitchen. After a brief look around, one of the guards rocked and toppled one of the vending machines. Using brute force, he rolled it to its side. A mound of chocolate and granola bars were covered in glass shards. Dropping to his knees, Frank shook them off and filled his pockets. "Who knows how long we're going to be in there." The loud racket drowned out the gun shot.

On the floor at the end of the counter was a blue recycling bin half filled with empty bottles. Leonard ran over and turned the bin upside down. While filling the bin with bottles of water from the refrigerator, he agreed. "You're right, we better stock up, just in case."

With his rifle slung over his shoulder, Leonard lifted the bin, turned and faced his comrade. Above the row of vending machines, a grate attached to the ventilation system swung from its hinges. Before a word of warning could be uttered, a dark shadow quickly popped out and pounced onto the back of his unaware colleague. The claws of the young dragon-like creature wrapped around Frank's neck and quickly sliced open his throat. As his comrade collapsed onto the pile of glass and candy bars, Leonard heaved the bin at the creature. The creature leaped backwards as the bin smashed against the floor and broke apart. Water bottles flew into the air and bounced around the floor.

The creature sprang forward and slipped on one of the bottles. A single claw managed to cut into the guard's neck before the creature fell to the floor. The guard stepped back and grabbed his rifle. As the creature regained his footing, the guard blasted the creature's head and chest.

******

"They are on the second floor."

A nervous technician fumbled with the keys as he opened the door to ward three. "Finally, now everyone get in."

The other technician spoke up. "You aren't getting any argument from me."

The large guard looked around before stepping inside. "Me neither. Those creatures kill anything they come up against. The rest are probably already dead."

A minute after locking the door, they could hear something pounding at it. A technician went over and listened. "They are already outside. We just made it."

Outside of the door, the guard grabbed his bleeding neck. Unable to yell, he spoke as loud as he could. "Open the damn door!"

Through the thick door the technician could barely hear him. "I think I hear something. It sounds like words."

The guard listened over his shoulder. "I can't hear anything."

The technician thought for a second. Then, at the top of his lungs he yelled, "If you are human, knock three times, once and then twice."

Leaning against the door frame, Leonard used his rifle butt to bang out his replied. Down the hall he could see long strips of LED lights go out. As the hallway grew darker, more flickering shadows zoomed from doorway to doorway. The terrified guard could hear the door knob rattle. *If I shot at the creatures, the others may be too scared to let me in.* He held his fire. As the door opened, the guard inside was standing there with his rifle at his shoulder. A technician grabbed Leonard's shoulders and started to pull him inside. Shadows grew into creatures as the wounded guard was finally able to fire at them as he was being dragged into the lab. The other guard joined him. With both guns set on automatic, their magazines were empty before the other technician could close the door.

The technician immediately dumped out the first aid kit and grabbed a compression bandage to wrap around the guard's neck. With everyone standing over him, one by one, several small creatures squeezed out of the ventilation ducts above the fume hood fastened on the wall. The side door of the glass fronted metal box had been left open. The creatures fanned out across the room with barely a sound. With their weapons either holstered or laying on the floor, the men were caught off guard.

With each picking a victim, the creatures snuck up and pounced on their backs. Having no body armour, the two technicians were killed instantly. The large healthy guard shook back and forth while reaching back and grabbing the youngster with one hand. With the other hand he pulled out his knife. The strong guard flipped the small, young creature over his shoulder and drove his long, sharp, knife though the creature's back. As the other two creatures finished off Leonard, the large guard grabbed his rifle. With his bayonet still attached to it, he waved it from side to side in front of him. Shaking the rifle, he released the empty magazine. As the two creatures began to circle him, he grabbed for another magazine off of his belt. He barely snapped it into place before a fourth creature ran up behind him. Instinctively, he turned around. Within that split second, the other two leaped on top of him. As one bit into his neck, the other cut open his vest and sliced apart his stomach. While his muscles still twitched uncontrollably, the three ate through his torso and groin. With the guard's penis, testicles and large chunk of his bowel hanging from her mouth, one of the creatures still managed to rattle out, "Wwaaaoooowa."

The two guards on the third floor could hear the cry echo through the duct work. As the lights were slowly being ripped off of the walls and ceiling by blurry shadows, they checked their supplies. Between the pair they only had five extra clips of ammo. Not enough for them to waste bullets on random warning shots. They had to wait until the creatures got closer.

******

Duncan's helicopter flew straight to the heliport on top of the building. As the two other helicopters hovered above the heliports on the ground, the guards jumped out. Drake went over to the two half-eaten bodies. Both chest cavities were pulled apart. Outside of the long hair and the faint residue of makeup on one surviving eyebrow, he wouldn't have guessed that one of them was a woman. "So this is what we are up against?"

"That's why our clinic isn't full. These creatures are not in it to just take us out of action. They consider us a threat and want to eradicate us, just like we want to do to them."

"But not quite in the same manner."

On the ground, Laurie and two others covered the fire exit that was supposed to be left open. At the same time, Duncan and his squad looked around the perimeter from the roof. A squirrel was the largest heat signature they could find. Another squad of men got out the gas powered grinders and got them ready. The large diamond encrusted disks were designed to slice through both concrete and rebar. A generator and air compressor were fired up to fuel the jack hammers. After briefly double checking the building plans, they set to work. The wall outside of ward three was poured in three thick layers with shock absorbing mesh between them. It could take up to a couple hours to cut, hammer and chip a decent hole through them.

As the two remaining guards inside heard the jack hammers banging at the wall, they started to scream. "We're still alive. We're on the third floor. We're still alive."

The building's construction made thermal imaging impossible. However, suction cup devices placed on windows by guards on ladders enabled them to hear inside. The noise was crude and muffled. "I can pick up somebody talking. They are still alive."

"What about the creatures?"

The technician looked at Laurie. "It sounds like they're everywhere inside, but I can't tell how many."

"Take a guess."

"There are a pile of them, that's all I can tell you."

Laurie optimistically relayed the message to Duncan. "As far as we can tell, they are all trapped inside."

"Good. Now you know what to do. If any do manage to escape, I'll make sure they have nowhere to go."

Aiming her rifle at the door, Laurie answered, "Sure thing, sir. Good luck on your mission."

Duncan and his squad reboarded their helicopter. From a duffle bag, Duncan handed out body armour. Duncan had most of it specially made. Chest, neck and arm protectors were put on after the pants. Last was a long, drab grey Kevlar shirt to stop any creature from peeling off the armour, and a wire mesh helmet. The men looked at each other. MacNeil laughed. "So where are our swords? If they were more colourful, we'd look like medieval knights."

Ratlin agreed. "I guess when you're fighting demons, appearance is important."

Duncan peered up from his GPS and glanced at his men. They had just seen two torn apart, half eaten bodies, and yet they were still able to joke around. They all knew what they were facing and what they had to do. Leaning forward, he tapped the pilot on the shoulder. "About seven degrees to the left."

"Are you sure you know where you are going?"

"About eighty-five percent sure. We've been analysing every piece of data we could over the past months. From the latest data taken from the helicopter that detected the creatures, we've narrowed it down to one small area."

The ridge was pock-marked with small cracks, holes and crevices. Duncan tapped the pilot's shoulder again and pointed to the gap where the end of the Devil's finger turns into his long curved nail. "Make a small circle around. I want to see what kind of openings there are in that section below us." Looking down, all they saw was mostly bare rock with a few evergreen bushes that had survived the fire. "We have to get even lower."

Sweat started to pour off of the pilot's forehead as he skimmed the top of the bare, charred tree trunks. "Any lower and we could be dinner."

Along the frosty ground there was nothing at all. After twenty minutes a small opening under an overhanging rock looked promising. Long grey claw marks were cut into the shaded ice covered rock from the creatures climbing in and out of it. "There, that's what we're looking for."

******

The dog-like warrior could only watch as a pair of men repelled down from the helicopter. Retreating into the narrow tunnel, he waited in the pitch black shadows of the dark, cloudy, almost moonless night.

******

Duncan examined the tunnel. It was extremely narrow. "We'll have to slide down. There's no way we can take them by surprise. We'd better send a camera in first to see what we are getting into. I'd hate to have someone wedged inside like a cork."

DeGroot pulled a bag out of his backpack's side pouch. Inside was a small, free moving camera mounted between what looked like two halves of a knobby rubber ball. Attached to the camera was a strong stainless steel cable with both optical and electrical lines wrapped around it. As DeGroot controlled the manual cable winch, Duncan controlled the camera angle and wheels. Leaning against a rock in front of the pair was the small monitor that relayed what the camera was picking up. The tunnel appeared big enough for them to crawl through but had very little room to spare.

While the camera rolled down the tunnel, the dog-like warrior clung to the sides of a shallow crevice above it. After letting it pass, the creature released a large rock after it. The rock briefly rolled down the tunnel until it got caught in a small gap. A small avalanche of pebbles followed and completed the job of plugging up the tunnel.

As dust spewed out, DeGroot cried, "What happened?"

"Somehow the tunnel got plugged." The camera went blank. Duncan tried to manoeuver it around to see if it would respond. The sounds and directional map coming from the remote seemed fine. Rotating the camera backwards, he noticed a small corner of the monitor was showing an image. "It's just covered with dust."

"Yeah, but the cable is stuck. We can't move it."

Duncan flipped the remote from side to side, trying to knock off the debris covering the lens. After getting a clearer image, he said, "They rigged up a deadfall trap. The rock plugging the hole is too big to be a coincidence. This entrance is useless to us. There has to be another way in."

******

From the safety of a grove of spruce and jack pine, Honda watched the men chew apart the side of the building with their noisy machines. With only three youngsters and Mew crouched beside her, they were grossly outnumbered. The outside of the facility had changed since she was there last. The bushes along its side had been cut down and the fence around it had been fortified. Even a large portion of the swamp along the side of it had a fence running through it, plus another along its edge. Behind the fence next to the building lay a wide strip of open asphalt.

Laurie ordered the men to manoeuvre an ATV sideways, with its wheels rubbing against the fire exit. "Make sure it's tight. I don't want any of them to wiggle their way out. They have only one way in or out of the building and we need to control it."

Honda looked at the moon. There were only a few hours of night left. All they could do was wait while the last section of wall was being chopped away. Honda studied the perimeter. In the dark, the roof was still the best way to get in or out of the building, but how? A squad of heavily armed guards was stationed on top of it.

After tossing in a handful of green coloured glow sticks, Laurie shone her flashlight into the large ward three lab. At the end, close to the door, the remains of the guards were scattered across the floor. A single pair of green eyes glaring back at her was enough to cause Laurie to quickly jump back from the small opening. "We're too late. The whole place is infested. They're dead. We have to go to plan B."

The technician beside her cried, "But I heard them!"

"Even if there are a few survivors barricaded inside, it'll cost us at least two or three times that many to get them out." Laurie shook her head. "Like I said, they're all dead!"

Along the side of the building was a separate structure. Inside, along with the tools, ATVs and the other vehicles it housed, was a giant tank filled with heating oil. The underground tunnel connecting the out building to the facility was lined with power, communication, optical and oil lines. Laurie unlocked the reinforced door leading to the tunnel connecting the two buildings. After selecting the smallest guard, she handed her a small duffle bag and ordered her to climb down into the tunnel. The guard scurried through and put her ear to the door at the far end. She couldn't hear anything but some banging coming from the duct work. She tried the door. The lever wouldn't budge. With a sigh of relief, the guard yelled back, "It's locked."

Laurie immediately yelled back, "Then we are forced to use plan C. Use your knife and cut away a small section of the rubber insulation from the bottom of the door."

"How small?"

"Big enough that you could squeeze your hand into it."

It took Laurie longer to find and shut off the main valve to the tank than it did for the guard's sharp knife to slice the opening. "What now?"

"Turn off the large red ball valve above you."

The guard quickly turned the arm of the valve ninety degrees to the line. "It's off."

"Now open the bag I gave you and follow the detailed instructions inside."

Inside of the bag was a fancy looking metal gadget, a large hose, a torque wrench and a small battery powered drill. On the gadget was a semi-rolled plate attached by eight carriage bolts along with nuts and washers. Reading the instructions, the guard said out loud, "Step one, unfasten nuts and washers. Step two, wrap rubber lined back plate around pipe and refasten nuts and washers the same way as they were first attached. Note: be careful not to damage lining, especially around the valve. Step three, tighten nuts in order as illustrated below with the torque wrench included in kit. Note: don't forget to double check them in same order that they were tightened." The guard put down the instructions and set to work attaching the strange clamp and oversized valve combination.

"Step four, attach hose as shown and place the other end where you want it to go." The guard looked over at the hole she had cut out and then the hose. She noticed light reflecting off of the painted pipe and looked behind her. It was only Laurie making her way down the tunnel. "I'm only at step four."

"Good, then I'm just in time."

There was barely enough room for one person let alone two in the cramped tunnel. Laurie passed the guard a small oblong package. "Toss this through the hole before you stick the hose in."

After taking the package, the guard slipped it through the hole with the hose. "Now what?"

"I'll speed things up for you." Pointing to an extended hex shaped nut, Laurie said, "After fastening the hose to the nozzle on the side, tighten the clamp and attach the drill to the centre nut. Put the drill on high speed and don't release the trigger until you are completely done. It'll go in easy at first, then the built-in multi-stepped drill bit will start to drill and ream out a large hole in the pipe. When it gives way, you'll know you're through. Then quickly slap the drill into reverse until it stops solid. You may get a few drops of oil come out but nothing more than that. The drilling mechanism has a Teflon seal inside that should prevent any further leakage."

When the drill began to spin freely, the guard knew it was time to flip the direction of the drill. It quickly jolted her arm as it suddenly slammed tight. "There, now what?"

Looking at the guard's nervous but focussed face, she handed her a bag of putty. "With the valve shut off at both ends, the line isn't under any pressure. Stuff this around the hose to hold it in place and seal up the gap. When you are done, get out."

By the time Laurie had climbed out of the tunnel, the guard was finished. As Laurie slowly turned the valve next to the tank back on, the harsh fumes filtered into heating and cooling ducts, and made their way throughout the entire building. Creatures waiting in ambush for the guards to attack through the hole they had cut into the wall started to thrash around trying to breathe. Jumping out of the heating and air ducts to escape the fumes, they became easy targets for the guards armed with infrared scopes. In the opening, the guards smiled with delight as they broadcasted clip after clip of bullets into the wheezing creatures along with the rest of the lab. Laurie could hear the long bursts of gunfire as she watched the level in the tank rapidly drop. Looking at her watch, she ordered, "Everybody out, we have ten minutes."

Even from the swamp outside of the facility, Honda could smell the fumes. As scores of men circled the building, she felt desperate. With all of the guards staring at the building, the nimble creatures flapped their wings and hopped over the fence. Mew stayed behind. Laying together low on the ground in the dark, they resembled a dead clump of the marsh grass.

Laurie called up to the men on the roof. "Is it set?"

"Yes, sir."

"Then get down from there."

Honda watched in confusion as the men on the roof quickly tossed ropes over the side and repelled down. Soon afterwards, several helicopters appeared. Within a few minutes half of the men were aboard, and most of the rest were climbing up the ropes. The only ones left were guarding the hole in the wall. The helicopters flew a safe distance away before turning to face the building.

After checking his watch, one of the remaining guards heaved three duffle bags into the hole in the wall. After scampering back behind a blast shield, he clamped his hands over his ears and huddled with the other two guards that were left behind.

Chapter Thirty - Six

Devastation

"Duncan, we've found more tunnels leading inside."

Duncan stood up and asked, "All the way?"

Drake pulled back the bush covering the entrance and looked inside grinning. "Far enough that the rocks we tossed in changed their tone."

"How big?"

"Big enough to get a good echo all the way down."

As the two men left, the dog-like warrior crawled out of the tunnel and followed them.

******

From a window inside the building, the king watched the men leave. With the nauseous fumes getting stronger and stronger, he knew they had to get out. Quickly, the creatures checked all the exits. Looking at the floor, the king could hear the strange hissing coming from inside the hole that the guards knocked through the wall. Below him, ward three was being sealed off. The sticky, expanding foam spewing out of the duffle bags was creating a giant, gooey barrier to plug the hole.

The two guards barricaded in the hallway started to scream. "Help, help, we're still trapped inside!"

One of them stopped and turned to the other. "Forget it. We're just cannon fodder. They're not coming after us."

The men watched as the creatures tested the doors. The fire escapes on the two top floors were still unlocked. They heard the king roar, "Nnaaarrr, Uuratatatat, Sshuura, Eeeaaa, Wwoooaaa."

As the creatures ran to the exits, The guards knew something was wrong. Their fear turned into panic. Running beside the creatures, the guards raced to the closest fire door. A creature racing towards it noticed the first guard and swiped its claws across his face. The second guard jumped over his fallen comrade and continued on. At the door he totally forgot what floor he was on. Instead of reaching for the ladder, he jumped into the air like the creature in front of him. Instead of soaring into the air, he plummeted to the ground.

******

From the bushes, Mew watched the hovering helicopters. Honda turned around to see what was keeping her, but she had disappeared. Honda looked at the three youngsters and then back at where Mew had been. She had vanished.

Honda led her small group around the fence line and snuck behind the remaining guards. All of the guards' attention was focussed on a monitor viewing the hole. As the first creature flew out of the fire exit, its shadow alarmed one of the guards. Stepping away from the blast shield, he quickly opened fire on the escaping creatures. Honda leaped on the guard's back. Wrapping both of her hands around his face, she tore off most of the flesh in one crosscutting motion. As the other guards pointed their rifles toward her, the other creatures attacked. With neck guards protecting them, the creatures went after their hands and faces. As the guards flailed around on the ground, the creatures tore off their protective gear and started to eat them alive.

As more creatures poured out of the building, small explosions blew holes through the roof. The-well placed blasts created vents to funnel the large explosion that started in the furnace room and shot through the ducts, floors and weakened roof like a mortar cannon.

******

Laurie watched the debris explode into an enormous black cloud. The pilot handed her the phone. "So, how did it go?"

"Perfect, the walls directed the blast straight up like Duncan had predicted.   Nothing inside of the building could've survived that explosion including the men inside."

Doctor Scott turned and smiled at the other doctors standing with him. "They died for a just cause. I only hope that Duncan's squad is equally as successful."

As one helicopter started the trek back to pick up the remaining guards, the other two turned around to fly back to the new facility and refuel. Attached to the bottom of the tailing helicopter, Mew clung to the landing gear as it headed towards its new base.

******

After getting out the rope and equipment they needed, Duncan's squad concealed their duffel bags under a thorn bush. Small patches of snow fell through the bare branches onto the bags. The heat radiating from the bag quickly melted the snow. Drake volunteered to lead Duncan's squad down the tunnel and into the cavern. The tunnel was almost vertical. Each member tied themselves to their own line. Using their hands, legs and feet, they gingerly controlled their descent through the narrow gap and into the cavern.

With all of the men appearing almost at once, even the creatures that were posed to attack suddenly went into hiding. Their home had been invaded and there was very little they could do as the men lit the place by tossing dozens of light sticks. One landed beside a scared juvenile creature. He picked it up and threw it back.

"There, behind those rocks." Ratlin opened fire as he advanced on the young creature's position. A creature that was missing a foot and one arm leaped out of a crevice. Both Drake and DeGroot laced into him.

As the creature rolled around the ground, they could see his poor physical condition. Even the creature's wings were only half there. Drake turned to DeGroot. "Duncan told us that this was a mop up mission. I didn't think it was in an infirmary."

Duncan said, "With one well-placed slice from their claws, any one of them could kill you."

Behind them they didn't notice their ropes falling one at a time to the ground. Above them, the dog-like warrior popped his head out of the tunnel. Clinging to the ceiling, he watched the men poke the dead creature and flip him over onto his back. Slowly, the warrior crept closer and closer.

MacNeil could feel some flakes falling on his head. He looked up as the warrior dropped on top of him and wrapped its arms around his neck. The claws on his feet couldn't dig into the slippery Kevlar shirt. His front claws tore a gash across the wire mesh and ripped off his neck protector as he wrestled the strong soldier to the ground. Duncan opened fire with the end of his barrel almost touching the warrior's head. His head was only half there, and its arms were still frantically clawing at MacNeil back and shoulders.

Duncan fired a few more shots into the warrior's chest. Turning to MacNeil, he said, "You're lucky to be alive. If it wasn't for that funny gear I gave you, you'd be dead."

Drake looked at the pile of ropes lying on the ground. "The question is, how do we get back out?"

******

Even over the roar of the approaching helicopter, Honda could faintly hear the female creature scream "Wwaaaooowa, Wwaaaooowa," over and over. Honda looked over at her father as he searched for survivors and then back at the two helicopters disappearing in the distance. Racing through the trees, the brave female spurred Honda on.

As the oil was burnt away, the fire quickly died down. The mostly concrete and steel structure offered it very little additional fuel. In the distance, to the pilot in the hovering helicopter it resembled a gigantic backyard fire pit. The pilot reported in. "The walls seem to be intact. The fire looks like it's contained to the building."

Doctor Scott inquired, "Did the flames spark any fires in the surrounding forest?"

"Not that I can see from here."

"You better circle the area and make sure. I'll be held responsible if the fire gets out of control."

The concerned pilot asked, "What about the men?"

"Make sure that they are all right first. If everything appears safe, pick them up. Remember, they are more expendable then you are. If you see any creatures at all, get out of there."

Being careful not to get close enough to fan the flames, the pilot made a wide circle around the fire. Honda looked up as it got closer. She looked at the three veteran youngsters with her and then back at the flames that were still visible over the trees. As the helicopter passed overhead, they took to the sky. Two youngsters carried the remains of a small fallen tree trunk with them. Flying together, they climbed as far as they could. Honda and the other youngster zoomed ahead of the helicopter.

The startled pilot screamed. "Some of the creatures are still alive. Two of them just flew in front of me."

The doctor ordered, "Get out of there. You can't protect yourself."

The guards in the back opened up the cargo doors and looked around. As Honda and the other youngster whizzed by them, they opened fire. The pilot was forced to jolt the helicopter from side to side to avoid a collision. Slowly the pair manoeuvred the craft around. As Honda hovered in front of the craft, the two youngsters finally let go of their heavy load. It wasn't a direct hit. The tree trunk almost bounced off of the tips of propellers. The unbalanced propellers started to violently shake. "Mayday, Mayday, Mayday. We've been hit."

The doctor never left the radio. "What happened?"

"Something hit the propeller. We're going down."

"I'll send the others back for you."

The pilot guided the faltering craft down as safely as he could. The softest landing spot that he could find was the shallow swamp outside of the burning building. Yelling as loudly as he could, the pilot screamed, "Stay in the helicopter. If you try to get out before the blades stop, you'll be cut into pieces."

As one man jumped out, he yelled back, "And so will any creature trying to get me." Even landing in a deep section of swamp didn't help him. His legs plowed into the ground and shattered. The rest of the men tucked their heads between their knees and prepared for a crash landing.

The king had seen everything. With his heart pumped up with delight at his daughter's conquest, he cried, "Mmarut, Mmatat," as he led a half dozen creatures towards the swamp.

As gently as he could, the skilled pilot landed the helicopter. Its propellers broke apart the skim of ice and hoar frost that had formed over the swamp. The swamp cushioned the crash better than he hoped, but not enough for the four men in the back. The landing gear on one side hit a tree stump and jolted the craft to the side. With the side doors still open, two were thrown out of the helicopter. One quickly stood up and was instantly decapitated by the propeller. The rest of his body was flung against a bush at the edge of the propeller's reach. As one side of the helicopter started to sink into the soft mud, the other man was chewed up by the thrashing propellers. His body was hacked to pieces. The flailing propeller finally stopped as it grabbed a hold of the man's rib cage along with the upper half of his left arm.

As the grim sight was dangling in the air, the two surviving guards checked their weapons. The pilot looked back and inquired, "Do you have anything to spare?"

One of the guards handed him his pistol and two extra clips. "Do you know how to use it?"

"I'll manage."

Caught on the tree stump, the helicopter sank to a forty-five-degree angle. One guard peered out of the elevated open side door. The rustling bushes around them crackled from all the creatures moving inside. Looking over the top of the helicopter, he saw a creature dash across an open stretch of ground. While he fired a few shots at it, another closer one hopped over a log to position himself better for an attack. "They are all over the place."

The other guard joined him. With their backs tightly pressed against each other, they fired at every movement they saw or heard. The scared pilot squatted between the seats in the cockpit, trembling from fear. In front of him, he saw the surface of the water swirl from side to side. He knew that a creature was swimming towards him, under the surface. "They are attacking!"

As the guards fired a few more warning shots, one of them replied, "We know, they are all around us."

"You don't understand. They are in the water."

One of the guards poked his head inside the cockpit and confronted the pilot. "Where?"

The pilot pointed his finger at his windshield. "There."

As the guard looked out the window, behind him a creature crawled out of the water and into the sunken side door. The guard heard some water splash and turned around. At the same time, a creature grabbed his legs and yanked them into the water. The pilot shot wildly into the black muddy water before dropping his rifle and grabbing onto anything he could. The guard above him looked down. Both of his comrade's hands were clinging to a cleat designed to fasten down cargo. Swinging his rifle inside of the craft, he joined the pilot in shooting into the water.

The king quickly flew into the air and grabbed the distracted guard's helmet with his back feet. A loud crack came from his neck as it was snapped sideways. Twisting around, the king grabbed the top of the doorframe with one arm and swung inside of the helicopter. With his other front set of claws he swiped across the pilot's chest. While looking into the king's eyes, the guard standing in the water tried to grab his rifle. The king stood on it and roared at him as several more creatures funnelled into the helicopter. Pulling the screaming guard out of the water, the creatures slowly gnawed away at his body. Out of bullets, the bleeding pilot crawled backwards into the cockpit as the king turned and lunged for his throat.

In the water, a lifeless creature floated to the surface while others finished tearing the guards apart. Small floating patches of pink ice melted as the surface of the swamp took on a reddish tinge. The king looked into the sky and knew that the battle wasn't over. In the distance, the other two helicopters were mere specks, but they were rapidly growing larger and larger.

******

Mounds of rocks were piled everywhere in the cavern. Duncan and his squad systematically started checking all of them. They discovered that behind most of them were empty, crude beds. A few soft pieces of clothing and fur pelts were laid on top of moss and tree boughs. As they approached a large mound, Drake saw a small stone wiggle loose and roll down the side. DeGroot immediately circled around to the far side of it. As the others joined in, an infant ran out from behind the rocks. The sudden movement caused DeGroot to fire. MacNeil joined in. Before they realized what they all were shooting at, the tiny enfant was ripped to threads.

Drake turned back to the large mound as a large rock struck his head. As his companion dropped to the ground, Ratlin and Duncan fired on the young female. Their bullets were well placed. Her head and chest were riddled with a dozen holes. Ratlin walked over to a dog-like creature as she lay on her back. Breast milk was dripping from her chest. Duncan looked behind the mound of rocks. Two more young infants looked up and stared at him. As they hugged each other, Duncan put a bullet in each of their heads. "We can't leave any behind. No matter what, we have to kill them all."

DeGroot quickly spoke up. "We've never killed women and children."

Duncan answered him coldly. "I don't see women and children. All I see are dangerous creatures that could grow up and attack us."

Drake looked over at the dead mother. "She was only defending her family."

Ratlin patted him on his back. "You know the score. When people are at war, both sides are defending their families and their way of life. We're no different."

No one talked as other infants, mothers and cripples were systematically discovered and shot. After searching the entire cavern and finding no more creatures left alive, they started looking around for a way out. There were a number of exits. The problem was that most were extreme vertical climbs with overhanging rocks blocking them. Duncan looked one over. "This could be passable with a lot of hard work and a little squeezing." The others came over to examine the tunnel. The initial steep gap offered very little to grip. After that, a sudden bend blocked Duncan's view.

They all looked around for objects to pile together to reach the high, overhanging edge in front of the tunnel. Ratlin spotted Zed's shotgun amongst the pile of items that had been tossed along the edge of the cavern. He picked it up and tore it apart as he walked across the cavern towards Duncan. With only the gun's barrel left in his hand, Ratlin grabbed one of their fallen ropes as he walked past them. Standing next to Duncan, he tightly lashed the end of the rope midway on the barrel. "Let me show you how it is done."

Tossing the barrel into the tunnel like a spear, Ratlin held onto the end of the rope. He could feel the barrel reach the end of the rope. As it whipped his arm forward, he quickly took two steps sideways and gave the rope a tug. The highly calculated motion jammed one end of the barrel into the side of the tunnel, while the other end rested against the other side. "It works every time."

Keeping tension on the rope, Ratlin lit his headlamp and climbed hand over hand until he crawled inside of the tunnel. There wasn't much room inside. He had to take his rifle off of his shoulder and hang onto it as he made his way to the poorly anchored barrel. Using the steel butt of his knife as a hammer, he chipped out a small cavity in the rock and secured the barrel better. With a wave, Drake tightened his headlamp and grabbed the other end of the rope.

Using their hands, elbows, butt, knees and toes, they wiggled their way through the tunnel. At times it was round. At other times it was only a narrow crack. As Ratlin rounded the bend, he could see light bouncing down the tunnel. He also noticed some movement ahead of him. He had taken the clip out of his rifle to make it easier to crawl with. Reaching down, he pulled out his pistol. He could see the creature's long neck and dog-like face as she poured a pail of debris on top of him. The wire mesh on his mask caught most of it as it pinged off. He could smell the rust as he shook his head. Small fragments got into his eyes. With blurred vision and small nails sticking through the mesh, he pointed his pistol and shot an entire clip at the creature.

A gush of sticky liquid rushed down the tunnel. As the men pushed forward, the foul smelling, sticky liquid and rusty nails dug into their hands and clothing. The men had no choice but to crawl and work their way along the narrow tunnel. The old nails clung to their Kevlar garments and wiggled their way through. As Ratlin got closer to the creature, he could feel a pair of squirming objects trying to wiggle their way back to their mother's dead body. Focussing his headlamp on them, he saw that they were small, immature fetuses. As he crawled over their dead mother, he could feel more moving around inside of her. Face to face, he could hear her ribs crack as he squeezed by her. If it wasn't for the slight lubrication from her blood and other body fluids, it would've almost been impossible for him to get his broad frame around her.

As MacNeil crawled past the pair of fetuses, he pulled out his knife and stabbed them repetitively until they stopped moving. As DeGroot passed the chopped up piles of flesh, he commented, "Did you have to make sausage meat out of them?"

MacNeil grinned and answered, "Anything out of the womb is a potential threat that has to be neutralised."

Once outside, Ratlin puked out everything he had inside of him. A couple of tiny rib bones were stuck to the wire mesh on the side of DeGroot's helmet. After pulling off the slimy a piece of flesh, DeGroot threw down his helmet and joined Ratlin in empting his stomach. Drake, MacNeil and Duncan smirked and smiled at the pair as they pulled the brittle, rusty nails out of their hands, arms and legs.

Duncan scanned the sky, then looked at his watch. "Something must have gone wrong. By now I should be seeing at least one helicopter."

******

As the pair of helicopters approached, Honda led the youngsters through the woods towards them. Mew heard Honda's cries, "Wwaaaooowa, Rrrataatatat," and discretely let go of the landing gear.

She quickly flew to the ground and answered her. "Uuratatatat."

As Honda ran through the forest, Mew caught her breath. Clinging onto the cold landing gear had zapped most of her strength. Honda found her shaking her head. She looked at Honda and rattled, "Uuratatatat, Eeeaaa, Wwoooaaa, Mmmooo."

Confused, Honda followed her along the side of a creek. Afterwards, they scaled a high pine tree and Mew pointed towards the old camp. Honda knew exactly what she had seen. Their enemy had moved. *So that was why the attack on the facility was so easy.* Honda looked down at the three youngsters and then at the helicopters full of men hunting for both human and nonhuman survivors. "Wwaaaooowa."

Only a clock could tell that it was morning as the sun was forbidden to cast a shadow. As the small band of creatures raced through the forest, the temperature was constantly rising despite the dark gloomy clouds. Droplets of melting frost and snow rained down on the creatures as they dashed through the thick fog that covered the bottom three-quarters of most of the trees in the dense forest.

It was almost noon before Honda finally reached the outskirts of the camp. The high main fence surrounding it was completely finished. A secondary fence, a few metres inside of the main one, was three-quarters done. Every thick, solid, steel post was firmly cemented into a deep hole drilled into the hard bedrock. The tree line was cut back to leave a wide open field of view. Honda knew that the strange objects on the roof were for. As soon as they point at you, the men would somehow know exactly where you are. She could see that it would be impossible for them to simply fly in and attack the building during the day. However, with most of the guards gone, it was now or never. Honda looked over her small group. With only the five of them, she decided that she had to change her strategy.

Under the protection of thick fog, Honda circled the camp. It didn't take long before she caught a familiar scent. Looking at the large building, she whispered, "Sarah." Even more anger festered inside her as she led the small band of creatures into the lake.

Despite the fence going along the waterfront, the small pier was the only gap that wasn't entirely fenced in. With the thick fog concealing their movements, they quietly worked their way along the waterfront. A large double gate had been installed to allow the guards to pull boats and tenders ashore. Large electronic locks near the top and bottom secured it tight. Honda glanced at two of the youngsters and pointed to the small moving boxes on the roof of the building. As they pointed away from them, she whispered, "Eeeaaa."

As the others pulled on the gates to increase the gap under the section where the two gates met, the two tiny creatures crawled under them. Once inside, they hid under the fog until Honda signalled that it was clear. The pair dashed towards the building and scaled its walls. The lizard-like creature almost ran up them, while the dog-like creature lagged behind. The others sank back into the frigid water and waited.

******

From inside her sealed capsule, Sarah could feel Honda's presence. Slowly she rotated her head and looked around. Along the wall were cages of giant fruit bats. "Soon they won't need me anymore. You'll be the ones pumping out cells for the doctor." Thinking of Honda, she curled her long sharp nails and slowly scratched fine cuts into the nylon straps around her waists.

******

"Doctor Scott, come ASAP. We have a problem."

The doctor ran to the guard's monitoring station. "What is it?"

"The cameras, they are going dead."

"Quickly, turn the cameras towards each other and see what's going on."

After a few adjustments, their suspicious were confirmed by the glimpse of a creature's wing. "There are creatures on the roof. We're under attack."

The doctor thought for a moment as a roof alarm went off. "I've sent almost everyone out to hunt down any surviving creatures that attacked the old facility. There are only a handful of men left to protect this place."

The technician looked up at the doctor as a second alarm went off. "The creatures the cameras are picking up are much smaller than we accounted for. They've penetrated the air ducts in the roof, dug through the inside wall and opened up the fire door next to it."

The alarms woke up the sleeping guards. As they bumped into each other getting their gear, one of them looked at the alarm board as a third red light turned on. "They've got through to the research labs on the third floor."

"Where is everyone?"

The white-faced guard forced down a swallow before he answered. "I believe, we're it. After all the creatures attacked the old facility, the doctor assumed that they didn't have enough to attack this one too."

"Well, I guess he was wrong."

The doctors and technicians all huddled together. Doctor Stern looked at the siren as it blared away. "The vault, it's the only safe place in here. We can lock it from the inside."

Roger glanced at him. "You're right."

Everyone scurried around and quickly gathering what they could before filing into the main lab. In a corner of the lab was a small, heavily reinforced room. The vault wasn't meant as a safe room, it was designed to store records and DNA samples. As technicians made room by tossing out everything they could, Doctor Stern clinched his jaws and fists.

Chapter Thirty-Seven

Mayhem

Duncan could see the healthy creatures helping the injured along the edge of the swamp. Putting his binoculars down, he looked at the others. "This is what we really came for. They are beaten up and it appears that most are injured. Some of them appear to be quite bad off."

The sun broke through the clouds and the line of beat-up creatures became clearly visible without any visual aid. Behind them, they could see the rapidly approaching helicopters. Ratlin grinned. "This won't even be a fight. It's another slaughter."

Suddenly the helicopters turned around. MacNeil spoke up. "What's going on?"

Duncan dryly said, "It doesn't matter." Looking over his men he added, "We didn't need their help anyway."

******

The anxious Doctor Scott called from the communication room down to the data vault. "Is everyone safe?"

Doctor Stern answered. "We think we lost a couple technicians that were working on the third floor. Outside of that, Sarah and the animals are still confined in the lab."

"What about Rankin?"

The doctor looked at Rankin as he lay on a metal shelf designed for sample jars. "He's in here with us."

"Are the air tanks working all right?"

Doctor Stern nodded at Roger. "Roger is monitoring them as we speak." The nervous doctor asked, "How long will we be in here?"

"I've called back the helicopters. They should be back and have everything under control within a half an hour."

The guards stuck together. Moving from room to room along the hallway, they checked the bottom floor and proceeded to the second. Through the door window on top of the stairs they could see creatures searching through the rooms. The guard at the window counted them and whispered, "I only can count four of them. That makes it fairly even odds, five on four."

The guard in the rear grumbled, "That's not even. They've been averaging over two and a half kills to our one."

The guard at the window turned to him. "If you want, you can stay back and protect our rear as we go in."

******

Led by Sarah's scent, Honda was pulled towards the steel door and the end of the hall. As she tried the lever on the locked door, the guards burst out of the stairwell and blasted the hallway with gunfire. A bullet tore a gash in Honda's side as she ducked into an open door. The other creatures hid wherever they could.

Mew looked down the stairway as the last guard peered into the window to watch. Along the outside of the stairs she manoeuvred above him. A piece of mud fell off the fur of her hind leg and down the stairwell. It landed with a 'thud' and the nervous guard turned around to check the stairwell. With his back to her, Mew dropped on top of him. Digging her claws into his chin, she snapped his head backwards. She worked her other claws under his neck protector and straight into his windpipe and chest cavity. She removed her arm and he was dead before he hit the floor. Fragments of his lungs clung to her hair as she pulled out his heart through the wide opening in his neck.

The first guard tossed a flash grenade into the first room. After a quick search by two of them, they went on to the next room. They briefly covered their eyes when the ultra-bright flash went off. Mew leaped into the hall and plowed two of the men over. Before dashing into the room they had just cleared, she grabbed a hold of the helmet of one of the guards and twisted his neck. Down the hall, the other two guards swung around and opened fire. As the remaining guard tried to get up, a bullet caught him in his side. The guard who shot him stopped firing, ran over and knelt next to him.

From within the room, two young creatures dashed out and leaped on the back of the guard that was still standing. The unfortunate guard looked back as Mew pounced out of the room and, with an upward thrust, rammed her claws up through his exposed chin and into his brain. Even the smallest creature ran out from hiding and joined in on the mayhem. At close quarters, despite their body armour, the guards were helpless. They barely had time to fire a shot as their wrists, ankles, faces and necks were methodically sliced apart. Every joint and crack in their armour was an entry point for the creatures' nimble fingers and sharp claws.

From the end of the hall, holding onto her side, Honda watched the slaughter. A camera in the corner above the stairwell door also caught most of it. Doctor Scott watched the monitor while pacing back and forth across the small room. "How long before the helicopters get back?"

"Another ten minutes."

"By the time they find us, we could be dead."

******

Ratlin pulled the duffle bags out from under the torn bush and opened his. From it he pulled a large case. Within a minute he had assembled his .50 caliber sniper rifle. Lying on the ground, they took careful aim on their prospective targets. With his rifle laying on the ground beside him, Duncan watched the small parade of battered creatures through his binoculars. "Not yet, but soon they will be coming up to an opening that they will have to cross. It won't be long now."

From behind a clump of trees, the battered creatures slowly filed out. With each man taking a quarter of the line, in the same order they were lying in, they picked out the healthiest first. Duncan watched the sky as a hole in the clouds slowly worked its way toward the creatures. As it hit them, the bright sunlight beaming down stripped away the fog. Duncan quickly adjusted his rifle and called, "Mark." At that distance, the high powered bullets were through the creatures' heads before either Duncan's call or the first volley of gunshots could be heard. Caught in the open, the rapid firing of the elite marksmen didn't give any of the creatures a chance to escape.

As the injured creatures sprawled around on the ground, the king, who was guarding their rear, ran forward to witness the final volley tear through the last surviving creature as he tried to crawl away. Within seven seconds, they had killed over a dozen creatures. The king could see the puffs of rifle smoke coming from the ridge above the cavern that had been their only safe haven. There was nothing he could do.

******

Mew and two youngsters roamed the building, trying to find any humans that were left. The small lizard-like youngster stayed with Honda as she tried to find a way into the research lab. The steel door was firmly cemented to the concrete wall. Honda sniffed around the two adjoining rooms. From the exterior, a bunch of electrical conduits and plumbing ran through the walls. Scratching the mortar, she found out that it was much weaker than the reinforced cement wall.

At first she used her claws. The mortar only filed them down. Grabbing the oversized plastic drain pipe, she tugged and pulled at it. Finally a 'T' joint attached to the sink cracked and the pipe popped out. Honda thought for a moment. After running to the dead guards, she returned to the room with a hand full of bullets and several grenades. Honda dropped the bullets as far down the pipe as she could. Rattling the pipe a bit, she made sure that they were well into the lab. Bending and holding the pipe into the air, she rolled down a flash grenade. She could hear it click against the bullets. She had seen the guards pull the grenade pin before. Shaking a bit, she placed the grenade halfway into the pipe before pull out the pin. Quickly ramming a broom handle down the pipe, she heard the grenade click against the other grenade. Honda let go of the broom and ducked behind a desk.

The blast was enough to sever the pipe inside the lab and cause a couple of the bullets to go off along with the lights. Honda went back to see what damage was done. After pulling out the loose pipe. She noticed that a large section of the mortar inside the lab had been shattered. Smiling, she pulled the pin off of another grenade, rested it on the mortar in the gap and ran out of the room. After it exploded, she returned to the room. This time she found a pile of shattered mortar and chunks of concrete.

The hole was big enough that she could stick her head through it. Trapped in their cages the chaotic bats were crying out in pain. Honda could see Sarah's face though the capsule's glass cover.

Sarah watched the equipment next to her flicker and grind to a stop. The blood pumping in and out of her, along with the nourishment and air she needed, had stopped flowing.

On the floor above her, Honda could hear bullets ringing. Frantically, she tried to get to Sarah. The hole just wasn't big enough. She placed two grenades where she placed the last. Running out of the room, she didn't notice them rolling off of the wall and along the floor inside the lab. While one fell next to the wall, the other grenade rolled by a shelf of chemicals as it went off. The secondary explosion lit up the room as flames poured out of a severed pipe.

******

Laurie led the first squad into the building through the open door on the roof. Two more squads followed close behind her. Assuming everyone outside of the lab is dead, they fired without discretion. A flash grenade was immediately followed by a spray of gunfire set on automatic. Two clips went into every room before anyone even looked inside. In larger rooms they used live grenades. Laurie didn't care what the collateral cost was, as long as it wasn't another one of her men.

The communication room was next. The steel door was locked. With all of the gunfire, Doctor Scott's screams for help were unheard. In the room next to it Laurie placed a grenade between the wall and a filing cabinet. It went off and blew a small hole through the concrete wall. Laurie re-entered the room and tossed a grenade in the hole. It was quickly tossed back out. Laurie rolled out of the door to safety as it went off. Laurie grabbed another grenade. With her fingers just about to pull the pin, a waving arm stuck out of the hole. As Laurie returned the grenade to its belt, another guard grabbed the arm. Giving it a yank, the technician inside screamed, "Stop. What are you doing?"

The guard released the technician's arm. "I wanted to make sure a live human was attached to it."

Laurie looked down as Doctor Scott's face looked through the small hole. "How many are left?"

"Only the ones in the security vault inside the main lab. The creatures made short work of the squad of guards that remained behind."

"How many creatures are we dealing with?"

"Five in total, one adult female and the rest juveniles. A guard shot one of the juveniles in its side and another that is so small that you could call it a child."

Laurie put her head down as she replied. "I guess age doesn't matter. They are all dangerous."

The doctor was safe where he was, so Laurie led her squad down to the second floor. As they entered the hallway, they sprayed it with bullets. Two teams went to the first two rooms and tossed in grenades. Clinging to the ceiling above the door off of the stairwell, Mew picked her moment. As they tossed a couple grenades into the next room she swooped down the hallway. Ripping her claws across the face of one and wrist of another, she wreaked havoc on the tightly packed group of men. As she flailed her claws in every direction, the men jumped back. She lunged at one of them and got him by his chin. Laurie yelled, "Get back, everyone get back."

The creature ripped the lower jaw off one man as she lashed towards another. As the guards ran, crawled and ducked to safety, Laurie and two others opened fire on the menacing creature. Mew's body fought every bullet that ripped through it. Wild ricocheting bullets caught two guards as they ducked into a room. Even as the creatures' limbs were being torn off, they seemed to be defiantly swiping at the frightened guards. Laurie yelled, "I told you all to get back. Next time, listen. We can't fight these creatures up close."

The medic ran into the room after the two wounded men. He was too late. Two young creatures had already finished them off. With blood dripping from their claws and teeth, he stumbled backwards into the hall. A youngster grabbed a grenade off a dead guard and tossed it at him.

The medic leaped to the floor, screaming, "Grenade!"

The men scattered for safety. It didn't go off. A guard scrambled over to it and picked it up. "The pin is still attached."

Another grenade rolled out. He reached over to pick it up as the others returned. He looked for the pin as it went off. The flash blinded them as the two young creatures attacked. One sliced at the guards' faces, wrists and throats, as the other creature yanked out all the grenade pins it could. The attack lasted barely a few seconds. With the live grenades still attached to the guards' belts, the pair vanished. The guards looked at their belts. They had no time to remove the grenades before they went off. With all the men confined to the small hallway, only a few were untouched by the shrapnel. Laurie stood up. Her right arm and left leg were bleeding. As the men around her screamed, she waited, rifle in hand.

Laurie didn't have to wait long before the creatures dashed out of two different rooms. She was ready for them. Spraying bullets just above the injured men, she caught one creature along his side. Two more guards opened fire as the second creature tried to get away. A bullet ripped across his back as he almost made it into the next room. Two guards ran to the injured creature as his claws dug into the floor tiles, pulling his limp legs behind him. Standing over the helpless youngster, the two guards shot his body to pieces. By the time they stopped shooting, parts of his head, chest and arms were scattered all over the floor. In the hallway another guard propped himself against the wall and emptied a clip into the other twitching youngster.

Two guards stood over their wounded comrades while the others cleared the rest of the rooms. Tossing live grenades into every room they came to on the floor, Laurie and two other guards approached the lab door. In the last room next to the lab, a guard noticed smoke pouring out. Laurie saw the smoke and looked in the room. She noticed the hole in the wall and knew that the smoke was coming from the lab.

The lab door was locked. "We have no time to waste." Reaching into a pouch on her belt, she pulled out a small pack of plastic explosives. Slapping it on the wall, she yelled, "Everyone run for cover." Unable to find her blasting caps, she embedded a flash grenade to the explosives. Looking around to make sure the others were safe, she pulled the pin and ducked into the second room away from the lab.

The blast blew a hole through the wall and shook the door frame enough that the door twisted and tilted in.

Chapter Thirty-Eight

Closure

The blast cracked the glass on top of the capsule that Sarah was trapped in. With her hands cut free, she pushed on a large chunk of glass. Slowly it started to budge. As it crashed to the floor, she pulled the tubes out of every orifice except for her ears, along with the needles and tubes out of her arms and legs. After undoing the other straps, she used her knees to help her extend a crack in the glass and break another piece free. Finally the hole was big enough that she could crawl out and she wasted no time.

Lights from three flashlights bounced around the blown apart doorway. Laurie ran through the smoke and banged on the vault's door. "Quickly, get out. The place is on fire and there is no time to waste."

In the thick smoke from the smothering fire, no one noticed Honda and the small youngster crawl into the lab. The doctors and technicians poured out of the vault, carrying with them whatever vital data and precious samples they could. Unprotected, the coughing men were easy targets for the two creatures. A gargle and a moan were all some of them got out before dropping to the floor. As Roger turned around and collapsed in front of him, Doctor Stern screamed, "What's going on?" Roger's throat had been sliced open. As air bubbles and blood poured out of Roger's throat, the scared doctor side-stepped around him.

Laurie turned around and saw a flashlight rolling along the floor. "They're in the lab. Everyone get out as quick as you can."

******

One helicopter hovered above the building as the second filled its fuel tanks on the ground. The smoke began to spew out of the side of the building. The pilot hovering overhead radioed the pilot on the ground. "I wouldn't worry too much. It looks like the fire is confined to the far corner of the second floor."

The pilot below whipped out, "Yeah, you have nothing to worry about. You're not surrounded by fumes."

As the pilot slowly circled the building, an object suddenly appeared out of the dark clouds above the helicopters beating propellers. A large rock fell out of the sky and smashed into the fragile windmill. Without warning or room to manoeuver, the helicopter nosedived into the roof. The pilot rolled out of the open helicopter door. With two broken legs he pulled himself away from the craft as fuel leaked out of its full tanks and trickled down the stairs.

The pilot on the ground ran for cover as the king swooped down and glided over his craft. The only safe place he could find was a small shed used to store chainsaws, gas tanks and boat motors. The unattended nozzle fell out of the tank and started pumping fuel over the ground beneath the helicopter.

******

Dropping everything, Doctor Stern crawled towards the door. Staying behind, Laurie pulled out her knife. Waving it around in the dark smoke, the blade struck something solid. "Rrratatatat," rang through the lab. Sarah ran towards the cry. Laurie heard the movement behind her and continued slicing her knife through the empty air. Sarah saw the twirling smoke and quickly ducked. Scooting along the floor, she circled Laurie and got to Honda. Pulling the injured creature to the side of the room, she gave her a hug. The knife had been lucky. Honda wasn't. It had penetrated the side of her chest and pierced her heart. All she got out was, "Ssisssterrr, Mmmooo," before she died.

With tears in her eyes, Sarah gazed at Laurie. Even with all the smoke, Sarah could vaguely see Laurie as she wildly twirled around, swiping her knife in every direction.

The oxygen tank that Roger set up inside of the vault exploded. The sudden release of oxygen fuelled another burst of flames. Almost everything on the far side of the lab that was flammable was set on fire, including the lab coats and uniforms of the dead men and women. As the flames outlined Laurie's dark silhouette, the twisting smoke that hid her disappeared. Sarah jumped up and ran towards her. As her claws swiped across Laurie's chest armour, Laurie struck back and stuck her knife into the side of Sarah's chest. As she pulled it out and tried to stab her again, the small creature bit into her wrist.

For the first time, Laurie saw that it was Sarah that she had stabbed. Face to face, she froze. Even through the dark nose and fur, for a brief second, all she saw was the little girl that entered the facility. A second was long enough. Filled with adrenaline, Sarah rammed her claws into Laurie's chin. Laurie's eyeballs popped out as Sarah's hand penetrated her skull and turned her brain to mush.

Looking around, Sarah saw and heard the giant fruit bats trapped inside their cages. Coughing up blood, she fumbled her way towards them. Holding herself up the best she could, she worked her way along the row of cages. One by one, she released the terrified bats. "I guess you are all my sisters now. You certainly have enough of my blood flowing through your veins."

******

Duncan grabbed his stomach. Looking at MacNeil, he told him, "We're too late."

The other members of his squad stared at him. No one said a word as they all turned and looked at the black smoke rising from the facility.

******

After feeling the helicopter crash and shake the entire building, Doctor Scott and the communications technician got more and more scared. Finally, they felt that it was time to make a run for it. As they made it to the stairs, they could smell the leaking fuel. Not hearing any activity in the stairwell, they rushed down the stairs as fast as they could. At the exit, Doctor Scott cracked the door open and saw the pilot waving a chainsaw in the air. "Let's wait here a bit until we can find out what is going on."

Doctor Stern ran passed the wounded and dead guards as he raced towards the stairs. Behind him, a guard helped Rankin walk down the hall. Turning to the wounded on the floor, the helpful guard said, "If you can, get out. This place is already lost." As the guard spoke, Rankin reached down and grabbed a rifle off the floor. Trying to stand on his own, he discovered that even using the rifle as a crutch, he still wasn't capable of taking a single step on his own. After being confined to his bed for so long, the atrophied muscles in his legs were unable to hold his weight.

After getting Rankin through the door and into the stairwell, the guard assisting him heard screams and gun shots coming from the hallway. Setting Rankin down, he went to the door and looked through the window. The last small creature was systematically going from one man to the next, making sure they were dead. Hiding behind the dead bodies and covered in blood, the quick small creature was hard to spot. The guard placed a full clip into his rifle before he opened the door. With one hand on the trigger of his rifle, he used the other to pull two wounded guards to the stairwell, one at a time. One of the wounded guard's boots was jammed in the doorway as he re-entered the hall. As the guard grabbed a hold of another wounded guard, the small creature seized the moment and leaped into the air. The frightened, wounded guard tugged at his arm as he tried to raise his rifle. The fast creature bounced off of his head and ran through the door. Falling to the floor, the unconscious guard's finger squeezed the trigger and ran a line of bullet hole up the wall and across the ceiling.

The creature found the two wounded men in the stairwell as easy prey. Lying on the stairs next to the platform, Rankin checked over the rifle he had grabbed. There were only three bullets left in the magazine. The small creature climbed on the wounded guard closest to the stairs and bit into his neck as Rankin took careful aim at its head. 'Bang', it only took one well-placed bullet. "They may be vicious, but they can be killed like any other animal."

Doctor Scott opened the exit door and looked around. The pilot wave him back inside. "There is still a big one out here." Next to the door, the communications technician stood with two other guards. Doctor Stern stood on the stairs behind them. Crawling down the stairs, Rankin inquired, "What's wrong now?"

Doctor Stern glanced at him. "I don't know exactly, but there is a lot of fuel spilled all over the bedrock and maybe even more creatures out there."

Using mainly his hands and elbows, Rankin pulled his body towards the exit. "This place is on fire and we don't know if there are any more creatures in here. I would rather take my chances out there."

******

On her hands and knees, Sarah peered out of the doorway. With the loss of blood and a punctured lung, most of her energy had drained out of her. She had no choice. She had to find a way out. Holding her side, she pulled herself along the floor. Barely glancing at the dead bodies, she made her way to the stairwell. The scared and wounded guard saw her and pulled out his pistol. 'Click, click', quickly he scrambled for another clip. Sarah saw a rifle and rolled over to the dead guard on the far side of the hall. She grabbed his rifle. After hearing, 'Click', the guard snapped in a full clip and raised his head as high as he could in order to get a better aim. Sarah fired the dead guard's pistol and shot the guard in the forehead. Looking back at the rifle, she took out the clip. It was full. "Next time, I have to remember to make sure there's a bullet in the chamber."

Sarah pulled herself up and leaned against the wall as she walked towards the stairwell. Suddenly one of the bodies started to move. Fearing for her life, Sarah took a quick step towards it and fell on top of it claws first. With her claws trying to dig through his armour, the guard quickly shook off his headache and rolled Sarah off of him. Disoriented, he got to his knees. Something inside of Sarah snapped. Wild eyed as she stared at the guard, her pain and agony was replaced by an animalistic need to survive.

Lying on the floor, Sarah reached up and latched onto his testicles. Her claws dug through his clothing as he grabbed her hand with both of his. As he bent over and tried to extract her claws, Sarah saw a gap in his armour. Sarah pulled the knife out of his belt and thrust it under the side of his vest and into his kidneys. The guard released her hand and went for the hand with the knife. As he twisted his head to the side,

Sarah released his testicles and jabbed her claws into a gap between his neck protector and the side of jaw. "Die vile scum, die." Between the knife in his gut and blood pouring out of his neck, it didn't take long before he finally gave up the fight. With adrenaline flooding her blood vessels, Sarah forced her battered, exhausted body to keep going.

After finally getting to the stairwell, the voices below her forced her to go up. One of the large bats landed next to her. Its strange hiss and clicking noises confused her. As it flew up the stairs, she whispered, "You're welcome."

Halfway up the final set of stairs, the king sat in front of her. Flashes of bright light erupted out of the dark sky behind him and turned him into a shadow. She grabbed his arm and softly rattled, "Mmarut Mmatat," as he helped her to the roof. Once there, he looked over the edge. Men were running out of the building towards the small shed. Revving up a chainsaw, the pilot waved it in the air as the men approached the shed. A guard fell to his knees and shut off the nozzle before continuing. Along the side of the building, Rankin steadily crawled away from the helicopter and spilt fuel.

Rain started to pour down. The king looked at Sarah and then down at the men on the ground below him. A large rainbow coloured puddle surrounded them. Grabbing Sarah's limp body, he flapped his wings. As he got airborne, the helicopter pilot crawled out from behind the facility's large air conditioning unit, raised his pistol and fired.

The flash from the pistol's muzzle ignited the fumes coming off of the puddles of fuel laying on the roof. Soaked in fuel, the pilot's body was quickly engulfed in flames. Within seconds the remaining fuel in the helicopter exploded and blew his flaming body over the side of the building. The same explosion sent a giant fireball into the air. Both the king and Sarah were hurled into the rumbling clouds, and then their flaming bodies were dropped into the lake.

The burning pilot plummeted downward from the roof towards the helicopter as it was lifting off of the ground. His charred body was immediately chopped apart by the propeller. As blood and body parts were strewn around, the pilot lowered his craft away from the spilled fuel so he could inspect the damage. Pieces of the pilot's uniform floated to the ground. A flicker of red amber was all that was required to set a puddle of spilled fuel ablaze. The rain only helped the burning fuel spread from puddle to puddle along the side of the building.

The remaining guards ran out of the shed and tried to get away. They were all trapped behind the fence. Suddenly, out of the dark clouds, a bolt of lightning struck the burning building. The grounding wire directed the white hot current down the side of the building and into a pool of fuel. The explosion blew apart the shed and turned several guards into human torches. The two doctors had managed to crawl under an overturned aluminum boat and used it as a shield as they made their way to the lakefront like a headless turtle. The weakened jolt of electricity that ran through the wet ground struck them like a Taser. The sound of thunder and explosions filled the air as another bolt of lightning struck the shattered building. This time, it was large enough to ignite the spilled fuel under the tank. Seconds later, the tank exploded and the helicopter was set ablaze.

As small explosions blew the building apart, pieces of cement and steel ripped through the fence. Several larger explosions flung debris high into the air. The shrapnel was strewn all over the lake and surrounding forest. Rankin saw a large chunk of steel sticking out of the small opening it had sliced in the fence. After glancing back at the chaos, he slowly crawled towards it.

******

From the top of the ridge, Duncan and his squad could barely see the flames through the pouring rain. A small red glow above the trees in the horizon was enough to make their hearts sink. MacNeil turned to Duncan. "We lost."

Duncan put his hand on MacNeil's shoulder. "No, we are the lucky ones. We survived to fight another day."

DeGroot watched as the second lightning bolt hit the burning building. "I'm not sure if Mother Nature is fighting with us or against us."

Drake looked at him. "The old lady probably wishes none on this ever happened. What the doctor did wasn't natural. He was playing God."

It took the rest of the day to hike back to the camp. The fire had almost died out by the time they finally reached it. DeGroot pulled back a section of damaged fence and held it open while Duncan and the others crawled through.

Duncan looked around the grounds, yelling, "Is anyone here?"

Doctor Scott flipped over the ash covered boat. "We are still alive."

Drake watched the two doctors brush the soot off of their lab coats. Turning to DeGroot and Ratlin, he smirked. "Great, the generals survive while all the foot soldiers are dead."

Ratlin quickly replied, "We're not."

Drake glanced at Duncan. "But we're not just foot soldiers, are we?"

Duncan and his men did a quick search of the area around the building. Ratlin climbed up what was left of the steel stairs and glanced over the building's hollowed out centre. With nothing to obstruct his view, Ratlin could see the remains of the bat cages attached to the wall at the far end of the building. The square edged, swinging doors of a few of the badly mangled cages ran a cold shiver up his spine. "The cages had to have been opened before the explosions. I hope they were empty. Maybe they were cleaning them out when everything happened."

Outside, Duncan walked around and examined every body part, both man and creature. Picking up a singed clump of fur, he knelt and thought of Sarah. As he stroked the fur with his thumb, a strange chill came over him. Looking into the forest, he got a glimpse of something in the trees. "We're not alone. This isn't over yet."

MacNeil sighted something moving in the trees and fired a couple bullets at it. A large bat spiralled to the ground. Mistaking the bat for a creature, MacNeil clenched his teeth. "I hope that was the last of them."

From a hole in the wall, Ratlin saw the bat flop around on the ground. By the time he got out of the building, MacNeil was putting a bullet through the bat's head. Walking over to Duncan, he told him the news. "None of the bats were in their cages. They are all out there."

Looking over at the two bewildered doctors, Duncan could see their stunned faces as they sat on the cold rocky ground. They had lost virtually everything they had worked for. With the clump of fur still in his fist, Duncan glanced beyond the lake at Devil's Claw Ridge. "Don't make any travel plans. I think that we may be sticking around here for a while."

Ratlin looked at the fur. "Was it Sarah's?"

"No. It's from a wing." Duncan glanced at Ratlin. "Until I see Sarah's body, this mission isn't over."

"If her body was flung into the water. It could take weeks before it surfaces."

"If she's still alive, maybe a lot longer than that."

The End

www.ingramcontent.com/pod-product-compliance
Lightning Source LLC
Chambersburg PA
CBHW061552100726
47898CB00002B/335